The
Better
Woman

Ber Carroll was born in Blarney, County Cork, and moved to Australia in 1995. She worked as a finance director in the IT industry until the release of her first novel, *Executive Affair*. Occasionally, in search of inspiration, she dons a business suit and power shoes and returns to the world of finance. Ber lives in Sydney with her husband and two children.

If you would like to know more about Ber, you can visit her website at www.bercarroll.com

'This novel is a wonderful, full-bodied read. Ber Carroll has a clever eye for characterization and story'   Cathy Kelly

Also by Ber Carroll

Executive Affair
Just Business
High Potential

The
Better
Woman

Ber Carroll

PAN BOOKS

First published 2009 by Pan Macmillan Australia Pty Limited

First edition in the UK 2009 by Macmillan

This edition published 2010 by Pan Books
an imprint of Pan Macmillan, a division of Macmillan Publishers Limited
Pan Macmillan, 20 New Wharf Road, London N1 9RR
Basingstoke and Oxford
Associated companies throughout the world
www.panmacmillan.com

ISBN 978-0-330-46062-0

1 3 5 7 9 8 6 4 2

A CIP catalogue record for this book is available from
the British Library.

Printed and bound in the UK by CPI Mackays, Chatham ME5 8TD

This book is dedicated to my sisters, Catherine, Deirdre and Angie

Acknowledgements

This book began its life in Caroline Ross's front room, born over many hot chocolates and glasses of wine. Thank you, Caroline, for sharing your fascinating, funny anecdotes about New York, and for ensuring that I did not go thirsty while I listened!

Thank you to Bernadette Balkus for describing your life as a concert pianist and for those lovely cups of peppermint tea and glasses of wine (mmm . . . there's a worrying pattern here!).

Thank you to the awe-inspiring Victoria Havryliv for educating me on the intricate world of criminal law, and for reading over my drafts and correcting my mistakes. If I ever end up on the wrong side of the law, I know who to call!

Thank you to Catherine Hammond, Karen Penning, Trish Thorpe, Angie Glavin, Deirdre O'Mahony and Amanda Longmore for your feedback and recommendations. Thanks to Kylie Alexander and Stuart Folkard for answering all my questions on what it's like to live and work in London. Thanks to Cate Paterson at Pan Macmillan for your enthusiastic response to the first draft of this book, and for your amazing commitment since.

Thank you to Julia Stiles for your wonderful editing, to Trisha Jackson, for your excellent notes and suggestions, and to Jane Novak, Jane Hayes, Louise Bourke and everyone else at Pan Macmillan.

Thanks to the usual suspects: my agent, Brian Cook, and my husband, Rob, for many, many reasons . . .

Finally, I pause to remember my remarkable grand-aunt, Hannie Burke, who spent ninety-nine years of her life in a village not dissimilar to Carrickmore. May she rest in peace.

Sarah

Chapter 1

Cork, 1980

Sarah's breathing sounded sharp and shallow in her ears. She regulated it with deep intakes of cold air. Ignoring the burning in her lungs, she pushed herself harder, faster. Wild grass tickled her shins. Mud squelched beneath her new sneakers. Nan would not be happy.

'You've ruined them!' she would cry. 'Fifteen pounds, they were!'

Sarah would bite on her lip. There was no point in retorting that sneakers were for running and, as they lived out in the middle of the countryside, an hour's drive from Cork city, she had nowhere else to run but across the fields.

Sarah trained for at least thirty minutes every day. She wasn't training for anything in particular: Carrickmore was too small for an athletics club and her school's sports day wasn't for another six months. She ran because she loved the sensation of creating distance with her feet; because the exertion tingled every part of her body, even the inside, which often felt a little empty; because her father had been a runner too and it made her feel connected with him.

A drizzle started to fall and sprinkled Sarah's flushed face. At first she defied it and ran on. But it grew steadier. The grass became slippery, the earth even more soggy. Cold drips rolled down her forehead. Reluctantly, she turned back towards home. Nan thought that rain should be avoided at all costs: one drenching and you'd surely be struck down with the flu.

'Jesus, Mary and Joseph!' Sarah could hear her say. 'Get out of those damp clothes before you catch your death.'

It meant that Sarah would be in trouble on two counts: the state of her sneakers, and being caught in the rain.

Sarah climbed over the last gate and came out onto Whitfield Road. There was no traffic in sight and she sprinted down the centre of the unmarked road. Her grandmother's house, two storeys of white pebble-dash, stood as the finish line.

She was at full throttle when Mr O'Hara, holding a bottle of milk, came out of Nan's shop.

'Jesus, Sarah, is it the devil that's after ya?'

Sarah overshot her imaginary finish line and came to a stop outside Delaney's pub. She bent over, hands on knees, to catch her breath.

'You're a fine runner, Sarah,' said Mr O'Hara as he came alongside her. 'Just like your father, God rest his soul.'

Sarah devoured casual mentions of her mother and father like a starved child scrounging for evidence that they had actually existed. She loved her grandmother and knew she was loved in return. But it wasn't the same as having a mum and dad, being part of a family unit, being normal.

Mr O'Hara pulled his cap down further on his head. 'I know

you young ones don't feel the cold, Sarah. But this rain has a chill to it. I'd better be getting home.'

He walked briskly in the direction of his house. A sprightly old man, he'd once said to Sarah that keeping busy was the only answer he had to old age. For that reason, he had taken on the maintenance of the cemetery and the village park in his retirement.

'He's a hard worker,' Sarah had heard her grandmother comment many a time. 'The graveyard is a credit to him. You wouldn't know it from the way it was before.'

As a result of Mr O'Hara's toil and sweat, the cemetery's gravelled pathways were weed-free and the hedging along the outer wall was trimmed in a neat line. He had even planted a new bed of flowers inside the main gate.

'So I can put them on the graves of the poor souls who have no one,' he'd explained to Sarah.

Sarah saw a lot of Mr O'Hara because she was a regular visitor to the cemetery. She'd sit on the concrete kerb that outlined her father's grave and daydream about the man she couldn't remember.

'I'll make you proud of me,' she'd whisper to the mottled headstone. 'When I grow up, I'm going to be someone very, very important.'

She didn't precisely know why she wanted to make her father proud. Maybe it was a sentiment that all daughters had towards their fathers. And mothers too, perhaps. All Sarah knew was that she felt very close to him when she sat by his grave. He had grown up in Carrickmore too, run across the same fields, and lived in Nan's pebble-dash house right up until the day he got married. His spirit was still here. He was watching over her. She was sure of it.

Sarah crossed the road to her grandmother's shop. It jutted out from the front of the house like an oversized porch. Colourful promotional posters, stuck to the large panes of glass, lent a little razzamatazz to the ordinariness of the building and the village around. Carrickmore was built on a single crossroads. Nan's shop presided over one corner. Delaney's pub, with its black and maroon signage, was situated diagonally across. The church and cemetery occupied the third corner. A park, with lush green grass and a magnificent oak tree as its centrepiece, was on the fourth.

'I'm back,' called Sarah as she opened the door of the shop.

'Oh, hello, Mrs Burke.'

'You've been running again,' smiled the kindly old woman, a regular customer and a close friend of Peggy's.

'Yes, but I had to cut it short because of the rain.'

Sarah gave her feet a good wipe on the mat and didn't meet her grandmother's eyes.

'Sure, it's in the genes,' said Mrs Burke. 'Soon you'll be winning medals, just like your father, God rest him.'

Sarah saw a flicker of emotion across her grandmother's face. A tall, regal-looking woman, she wore her seventy years well. Her snowy white hair was pulled back into a neat bun and the skin on her narrow face was only lightly lined. She had sharp blue eyes and thin lips. She was proud of the fact that she didn't need glasses and her teeth were her own.

'Is that the lot?' Peggy Ryan asked her friend a little abruptly.

'Yes, I think so.' Then Mrs Burke laughed. 'Well, you're not far away should I have forgotten anything.'

With precise handwriting Peggy wrote the price of each item on a sheet of butcher's paper. She underlined the figures and, her expression intense with concentration, manually totted them up.

'That's ten pounds forty pence. Sure, the ten will do.'

'God bless you.'

Mrs Burke handed over the cash and, her cane basket full to the brim, made for the door.

'Shouldn't you wait on until the rain passes over?' asked Peggy.

'Sure, a bit of rain never did anyone any harm,' replied Mrs Burke. Then, realising the tactlessness of her words, she flashed a silent apology with her eyes and left, the door swinging shut behind her.

Sarah watched her grandmother become immediately busy with wiping down the counter. The old woman's face was devoid of emotion, her mouth a line of efficiency. But her eyes weren't as sharp as usual. Memories blurred their blueness.

The rain had in fact done a lot of harm to Peggy Ryan and her family. In 1944 her beloved husband had caught pneumonia after a bad soaking. Billy had not recovered and Peggy had been left alone to manage their small son, Tommy, and the family business. Twenty-five years later, Tommy skidded his motorbike off the Mallow Road. The coroner's report cited a severe downpour as the cause of the accident. Visibility had been poor and the road surface slippery. The only mercy was that Tommy had been killed on impact. Once again Peggy was left with a small child to rear – Sarah – and the business.

Peggy scoured the countertop until she had her memories under control. She stepped back and, still holding the cloth, put her hands on her hips.

'You'd better get out of those damp clothes before you catch your death.'

'Yes, Nan. I'll be back in a tick so you can take your break.'

Sarah exited the shop through the back door, which led directly into the kitchen of the private residence behind. She ran the tap at the sink and lowered her head to drink from its flow. Then she left her new muddied sneakers by the back door and went upstairs to change.

'Are you sure that's right, girleen?' asked Mr Glavin, one of the more cantankerous customers.

'Yes.' Sarah nodded vigorously.

'But you didn't write down the numbers,' he said, looking very suspicious.

'I can add in my head,' she told him.

'I like to see the evidence before me.'

Sarah, well trained in customer service by her grandmother, didn't argue. 'Right you are.'

She wrote down the figures on the butcher's paper and did the long addition out loud. Once complete, and her earlier total confirmed, she used scissors to cut out the sum.

'There you are, your receipt,' she said and smiled brightly as she handed it over.

He gave it a brief glance before shoving it deep in his trouser pocket. Then, without saying a word, he strutted out of the shop, clearly annoyed that he hadn't got the better of her.

Later on that night, when they were sitting down to a dinner of floury potatoes and fried lamb chops, Sarah told her grandmother about Mr Glavin.

'He's an awful sourpuss,' Peggy agreed. 'But he's the customer and you should write down the sums for him if that's what he wants.'

They started to eat. The potatoes were lovely but the chops were tough. Peggy was a good cook but sometimes the meat, which came from the butchers in the next village, was of poor quality.

'We should get a cash register,' said Sarah, pushing her half-eaten chop to the side of her plate.

'What would we want with one of those?' Peggy sniffed.

'We could give customers like Mr Glavin a nice printed receipt,' replied Sarah, having thought it through. 'We could also use it to keep record of the day's takings.'

'Those contraptions cost a fortune,' Peggy remarked. 'Money is tight enough as it is.'

'It would be well worth the investment,' was Sarah's reply.

Peggy thought that her granddaughter sounded more like an adult than a twelve-year-old schoolgirl. Sarah was too old for her age, both intellectually and physically. She was always top of her class. 'Brains to burn,' one of her teachers had said. This was no news to Peggy. Sarah's mathematical abilities had made themselves evident from a very young age. She'd been helping out behind the counter for three years now, but she'd worked out how to count money and calculate a customer's change long before that. Peggy didn't know where the girl got her brains from. Her father, bless him, was no Einstein. And her mother, well . . .

In the last few months, Sarah's face and figure had become more defined. She was tall for her age, her body lithe from all the running. Her straight chestnut hair fell below her shoulders, its colour so rich and its texture so thick that it alone could have made the most plain-faced girl look pretty. Sarah's face was by no means plain. Her hazel eyes, fringed by thick lashes, dominated its oval shape. Her nose and lips were in perfect proportion, her pale skin free of the usual teenage blemishes. She could easily pass as sixteen or seventeen.

It was her emotional maturity that Peggy worried about the most, though. Sarah took life too seriously. She was always trying to prove herself, be it at school, at running, or at the shop, as if she felt she wasn't good enough as she was. Her thoughts ran deep and she didn't always share them. She was a lot like her mother. And that frightened Peggy.

'Investment indeed,' she muttered. 'What kind of things are they teaching ye at school these days?'

After dinner Peggy, weary after a long day, retired to the front room with a cup of tea. Sarah washed up. It didn't take long. Two plates and two cups, a pot, a frying pan and some cutlery. She hung the damp tea towel from the oven door, wiped down the table and laid out her schoolbooks.

She did her maths homework first: fractions – easy. Irish next: ten sentences to read and translate. English: a poem to learn off by heart. She was reciting the lines of the poem when she heard a knock on the kitchen door: John.

'Hi.'

His anorak was slick with rain. He unzipped it and hung it off one of the hooks on the back of the door.

John was the only other twelve year old in Carrickmore and Sarah's best friend. His parents owned Delaney's, the pub across the road. Like Sarah, he went to school in Kilnock, a neighbouring village five miles away. The bus left on the dot of half past eight in the morning. The driver didn't wait for anyone.

'Single file please,' he'd order as the children jostled to be first on the bus.

The best seat was the back one and Sarah always sat there with John. Sometimes they'd talk the whole way along the narrow potholed road to Kilnock. Other days they would hardly exchange a word. It didn't matter either way. They were best friends and sometimes friends didn't feel like talking. They both understood this.

After school, John practised the piano and Sarah did her run. Then John helped out at the pub and Sarah with the shop. But John always called around after dinner. Sarah rarely went to his house. His mother wasn't very welcoming.

Tonight John was early, a sure sign that he was having trouble with his homework. This was further evidenced by the copybook he extracted from the inside pocket of his anorak.

'I can't do the fractions.' He pulled out the heavy chair at the head of the table and sat down with a despondent thump. 'Can I see your answers?'

Sarah opened her copybook at the right page and put it in front of him. His brow furrowed as he compared her answers to his.

'I've got it wrong again,' he sighed.

John struggled at school only because his head was in the clouds. He sat in class, a faraway look in his eyes, his fingers drumming the edge of the desk in a beat that only he could hear. He was going to be a professional pianist when he grew up. Sarah didn't yet know what she was going to be, other than someone very, very important.

Sarah put out her hand. 'Let me see yours.'

He obliged and she looked closely at his pencilled workings. 'Look, this is where you went wrong.'

Their heads close together, hers brown and his fair, she demonstrated how to multiply the fractions. This was their last year at school together. Next year John's parents were sending him to boarding school in Dublin. There he would have access to master classes at the Royal Irish Academy of Music and his promising talent could be nurtured into something magnificent. Mrs Delaney often said that her son was meant for great things. But that wouldn't stop Sarah from missing him terribly. The weekends would be the worst. No tennis at the park or wheelies on Whitfield Road. Just the thought of John going away was enough to make Sarah feel desperately lonely. She did her best to block it out.

Chapter 2

1984

'Nan, I have an idea.'

Peggy regarded her granddaughter somewhat warily. Sixteen years old now, Sarah was full of ideas, some of them feasible, all of them well beyond her years.

'What is it now?' Peggy asked with a sigh, for she found Sarah's bright ideas draining. Peggy was seventy-four years of age and content for things to stay just as they were.

'We should sell meat.'

Peggy blinked. '*Butchers* sell meat, child. We're not qualified –'

'We don't have to be,' argued Sarah. 'The supermarkets in the city do it – just plain things like chicken and chops, prepackaged. If we source them fresh, they'd keep for at least a week –'

'Why would people buy meat from us?' Peggy cut in. 'There's a perfectly good butchers in Kilnock.'

'Nan,' Sarah's tone was admonishing, 'you've said many a time that the butchers in Kilnock are only so-so, and that you'd buy somewhere else *if you had the choice.*'

Peggy couldn't disagree: the girl had quoted her verbatim. It always took her some time to warm to her granddaughter's ideas. It had taken nearly twelve months before she'd agreed to the cash register. She loved it now, though, pressing the buttons and letting the machine do the adding up.

'I'll think about it,' she promised. 'Now, time to close shop.'

Sarah took her cue and walked over to the door. She flipped the sign around so it read CLOSED. The sun, low in the sky, streamed in through the glass panes and outlined her profile: the soft fall of her hair, the roundness of her breasts, her long flat thighs. Peggy, watching on, felt momentarily out of her depth. The child that she had reared was totally gone, replaced by this young woman. How was she to guide her? Ensure that she made the right decisions? Make certain that she was strong enough to take life's blows? And that she knew right from wrong by today's standards? Sarah was the spitting image of her mother and that worried Peggy the most.

God help us all, I hope Sarah doesn't end up having the same problems as Kathleen, Peggy prayed, not for the first time.

John's fingers struck the keys, leaving a trail of loud, crashing chords. Sarah stood by the doorway, unnoticed. She didn't know the name of the piece, she knew very little about classical music, but she loved to watch John play. The way he hunched over the piano. The way he bobbed his fair head to herald a change in the tempo. The way his long elegant fingers scaled so quickly up and down the keys. During the school holidays he'd practise for hours and hours on end.

'You're so dedicated,' she'd say in admiration.

He'd shrug. 'If I'm serious about competing, then four hours a day is the minimum I should be doing.'

John had his sights on the RTE Musician of the Future award. He was giving himself two more years to get to the required standard.

'Nineteen eighty-six, that'll be my year to win it. Then offers will come in from all over the world.'

'What about Trinity College?' Sarah had asked. 'I thought you were going to do a Bachelor of Music there.'

'Mum's idea!' He'd thrown his eyes to heaven. 'She wants me close to home so she can keep her beady eye on me.'

John finished the piece softly, his foot pressing on the pedal to mute the sound, his head hanging as his fingers eased out the last chord.

'Bravo!' Sarah clapped and he looked around with surprise.

'I aim to please.' His face, with its summer tan, broke into a smile.

'Welcome home.'

John had spent the first few weeks of summer on a student exchange in France.

'Merci,' he replied.

'How was it?' she asked.

'Magnifique!'

Sarah came further into the room. Plush with rich red curtains and swirly patterned carpet, it was very different to her grandmother's plain front room.

'Play me something I know,' she said, standing behind him.

He immediately launched into 'Karma Chameleon'.

Laughing, Sarah clapped her hands over her ears. 'Anything but that.'

Without a second's thought he switched to 'Red Red Wine'.

'Better,' she said when he looked to her for approval.

He lolled his head, pretending to be drunk.

Sarah giggled, glad he was home and that she had her friend back.

'You make a very believable drunk,' she told him.

He grinned. 'The best thing about the trip to France was the wine. The family had it every night – kids and all – it was like water to them.'

'Really?' asked Sarah, her eyes wide.

'Yeah,' he replied. 'I got to like it. You should try some.'

The thought occurred to them both at the same time.

'Tonight?' he suggested.

She nodded. They didn't have to agree on a place. All their previous misdemeanours had been carried out in the same place: the park.

That evening, when the shop had closed, Sarah went upstairs to her bedroom. A small box-shaped room, its décor was depressingly old-fashioned. The walls were covered in floral paper and the floor in a plain green carpet. Redecorating hadn't been one of the ideas she'd managed to sell to her grandmother just yet.

Sarah surveyed the meagre contents of her wardrobe. Money was tight, the profits from the shop providing only just enough to pay the bills, with little left over to spend on clothes. She slipped on her only pair of jeans. Standing in her bra, she tried to decide between a plain white T-shirt and a fluorescent pink one.

Which would John like?

She startled at the thought.

Why would I dress to please John?

Confused, she put on the one she thought he would like the least: the bright pink. She surveyed herself in the mirror as she brushed her long, unfashionably straight hair. Several of the girls in Kilnock Secondary School had perms. Her grandmother had nearly fainted when she'd said she'd like one too.

'Are you gone mad? Your beautiful hair would be ruined with a perm.'

Sarah sighed and wished that Peggy wasn't so set in her ways. Wished that she had a mother closer to her age and able to understand things like fashion. Wished that she possessed a pair of big hoop earrings to make her outfit look a little more with it.

'I'm off to see John,' she called out as she descended the narrow stairs.

'Don't stay out too late,' her grandmother called back.

John was like family. Peggy wouldn't have been quite so casual if it had been another boy that Sarah was going to see.

Sarah crossed over the road towards the park. The freshly mowed grass stuck to her sandals. John was on the far side of the oak tree, sitting under a canopy of leaves and acorns. He wore faded jeans and a black T-shirt. His fair hair was tousled with gel and his navy-blue eyes were strangely unnerving as they smiled at her.

'Do you think your mam and dad will notice?' she asked, eyeing the bottle of red wine in his hand.

'Nah,' he replied. 'Sure, they have tons of bottles in the cellar – and if they did notice one missing, they'd only think Granda was up to his usual tricks.'

John's grandfather lived in the room over the pub, whilst the rest of the family lived in the adjacent bungalow. Granda Delaney, very fond of the bottle, often couldn't resist having so much temptation so close at hand.

Sarah kneeled down on the grass and sat back on her heels.

She glanced surreptitiously in John's direction. It wasn't only the tan, or the gel in his hair, or his new clothes. He was different. What was the word? Sophisticated? Yes, he was more sophisticated. She felt as though he was someone she didn't know all that well. Which was ridiculous!

'Do you want to uncork it?' he asked, totally unaware of her feelings.

She nodded. 'You'll have to show me how.'

He handed her the corkscrew.

'Okay, first peel off the covering . . . Now stick the screw in . . . Keep turning it . . . that's right . . . now pull.'

Sarah pulled but the cork remained stubbornly in place.

She felt his arms come around her, the heat of his body against her back, the flexing of his muscles as he pulled with all his might. The cork popped and the bottle jerked, spilling some of its contents on Sarah's jeans.

'Sorry,' he said, mopping the angry splash of red with his handkerchief.

'Did you bring glasses?' she asked, feeling very unsettled by the sensation of his hand on her thigh.

'No – we'll have to swig from the bottle.'

The wine tasted heavy and sweet. They took turns with the bottle while John recounted the finer details of his stay in France.

'There are four kids in the family – Pierre is the second oldest. They live in Brittany, in the countryside . . . a bigger village than this. Pierre's mum and dad are really cool. They play loud music . . . drive really fast . . . '

John didn't say that Pierre's parents were worlds away from his own: he didn't need to spell out the obvious. Joe and Mary Delaney were both nudging sixty. Their marriage, and John, had come late in life. Their life revolved around the pub and Mary's aspirations for her son.

Sarah drank some more wine. She felt light-headed. But happy.

'Summer holidays are boring without you around,' she told him.

'Ditto,' he replied.

'You've just been to France, you idiot. You *can't* have been bored.'

He shrugged. 'I missed you.'

He stared down at the ground and Sarah sensed a change in his mood. She wished she could see his eyes.

They were mostly silent for the next half-hour as they passed the bottle to and fro. Dusk fell steadily and everything but John lost focus for Sarah. Her feelings puzzled her. This was her friend. She had played with him, grown up with him. Why was her heart thumping like this?

'This feels different,' he said, reading her thoughts.

She nodded, not trusting herself to speak.

His hand reached through the dusk and touched her cheek.

'Can I kiss you?'

She scanned his shadowed face, the new chiselled lines to his cheekbones, the hair on his jaw that would eventually need to be shaved. Her childhood friend was gone. This was someone else: a grown-up stranger. And she wanted nothing more than to kiss him.

His lips were soft and tentative and warm. He tasted like red wine. Intoxicating. She clasped her arms around his neck and it seemed easier to lie back in the grass than to stay sitting. The heaviness of his body pressed her shoulder blades into the ground. She could feel his heart beat. She could smell the fresh grass and the citrus scent of what must have been his aftershave.

'*Sarah! Sarah!*'

The voice pushed them apart. It was Peggy, calling from the shop door.

'I have to go,' Sarah whispered, straightening her T-shirt.

John nodded.

Unsteady, she got to her feet.

'See you tomorrow,' he said.

She ran across the park and called ahead to her grandmother. 'I'm here. I'll just lock up the yard before I come in.'

Thankfully, Peggy went back inside. Sarah darted around the back and made much ado about bolting the gate.

Then she stole in through the shop and up the stairs.

'Goodnight, Nan,' she called down from the landing.

Once inside her room, she had a long look at herself in the mirror. Her hair was askew, her cheeks pink, and her jeans a mess of red wine and grass stains. Her lips were the biggest giveaway. They looked bigger than usual. Stung.

Thank God Nan didn't see me!

Sarah got ready for bed. She washed at the basin, brushed her teeth and imagined John doing the same across the road. When she finished brushing her hair, she picked up the picture frame that had pride of place on her dresser. The black and white photograph was of a bashful groom and a slip-of-a-thing bride.

'Is this how you felt when you first kissed Dad?' she asked her mother's image.

As usual, an answer wasn't forthcoming and Sarah was left to work things out on her own. She set down the frame and climbed into bed. The mattress creaked as she leaned over to turn off the lamp. She lay wide-eyed in the pitch black. Her heart was still thumping, her lips still tingling. Her first kiss. How perfectly right that it had been with John. She'd never ever forget this night. This happy confused feeling.

Chapter 3

'Well, Sarah, today's the big day,' Mrs Fahey announced in a dramatic tone. 'What time are you expecting the results to be out?'

'We're to go to the school around eleven.'

Sarah felt sick at the thought. Five years of study would soon culminate in a single sheet of paper: her Leaving Certificate results.

'Best keep busy till then,' was the older woman's recommendation. 'Now, twelve pounds fifty, did you say? Would you mind putting it in the book for me?'

'No, not at all.'

Sarah took out the red book from under the counter. Mrs Fahey's account already had eighty pounds owing. Her husband was out of work.

'He's still drawing the dole,' Mrs Fahey looked embarrassed, 'and it isn't enough to keep up with the bills. Please God, there'll be more work around after the holidays.'

She didn't sound at all convincing. Her husband, unskilled and on the wrong side of fifty, had slim chance of finding work with the record levels of unemployment in Ireland. She knew that, and so did everybody else.

After Mrs Fahey's departure, Sarah flicked through the book of debtors. The total amount owing was higher than it had ever been. Some of the balances were unrecoverable.

Peggy, using a newly acquired and much detested walking stick, hobbled in from the back.

'Another one on the book?' she asked when she saw what Sarah was reading.

'Yes.'

Peggy tutted. 'I'll have to start refusing credit, else we'll be put out of business.'

It was an idle threat. Sarah knew that her grandmother would rather shut up shop than take a hard line with her long-standing customers.

We need to make our profits bigger, Sarah thought, *so that the bad debts are easier to absorb.*

She glanced at Peggy. The old woman looked weary and irritable. It was clearly not the right time to have a discussion about profits.

Sarah arrived at the school at ten minutes to eleven. Most of her old class were already there, waiting. The confident girls looked nervous, the nonchalant girls tense. There was no getting away from the fact that this was one of the most important days of their lives.

'Sarah! Over here!'

A short girl with bouncing dark curls waved furiously. Nuala Kelly was a relative newcomer to the school, having joined at the start of sixth year. Her father worked for the Bank of Ireland and had relocated his family from Dublin to Cork as a result of a promotion. On her first day at Kilnock Secondary School, Nuala had promptly decided that Sarah Ryan was going to be her new best friend. Nuala hated physical exercise of any form and couldn't keep quiet for more than five seconds, but she wasn't at all fazed by the fact that her new friend's personality was so different to her own. For her part, Sarah was glad that Nuala had insisted on being her friend. She had other friends in her class, but they were superficial girls who were happy to talk only about themselves and didn't notice how little Sarah revealed. By contrast, Nuala demanded to know every detail of Sarah's life. She'd invited herself to see the shop. She'd chatted away to Peggy as if she'd known her all her life. And, when she'd met John on one of his school breaks, she'd immediately guessed he was something more than the boy-next-door.

'He's your boyfriend, isn't he?'

'Well . . .' Sarah had hedged.

'Oh, come on. I'm not a fool. The kitchen crackled with chemistry the minute he came in!'

Sarah was alarmed. 'Oh my God! I hope it's not that obvious. My grandmother . . .'

Nuala smiled slyly. 'Don't worry. I'm saying it was obvious to *me*, that's all. Anyway, what's with all the secrecy?'

'For a start, his mother wouldn't approve,' Sarah replied with a grimace. 'She wouldn't like to think of her son being distracted from his music studies. Least of all by me! She sees herself as a cut above everyone else in the village.'

'But you don't need to keep it from your grandmother, do you?'

'It makes things easier,' Sarah shrugged. 'Being friends means more freedom. We can go to the park and Nan doesn't watch the clock . . . doesn't worry.'

'Does she have reason to worry?' Nuala asked astutely. 'What do you get up to at the park?'

Sarah blushed. 'Kissing, that's all.'

'You've gone all red.'

'Thanks for pointing out the obvious.'

'So you only see John during school holidays?'

'Yes. And we write to each other while he's away. Every week.'

Sarah smiled at the thought of John's letters. They were almost as good as having him next to her, talking. In some ways, even better. With letters there were no silences. No inhibitions. John told her everything, about the antics of the boys at the school, how much he loved the master classes at the academy, and how much he missed holding her.

'God, you have it bad for him, don't you?' Nuala remarked.

It was true, Sarah did have it bad. She thought about him all the time, and when he was home it was as if her body was on tenterhooks, aching for his next touch. She was glad that Nuala knew: her feelings for John were too big to keep to herself any longer.

'Oh God, I'm sick with nerves!' Nuala exclaimed when Sarah came to stand next to her in the school hall. 'Would they ever put us out of our misery?'

Sarah couldn't understand Nuala's nervousness. She had categorically decided, much to her father's disappointment, that she'd had enough of studying and wouldn't be continuing on to university. Nuala planned to join the work force, earn a decent wage and enjoy herself spending it. Her Leaving Certificate results didn't have any bearing whatsoever on her plans.

The principal's secretary, a painfully thin woman with over-sized spectacles, entered the hall and a hush fell over the girls.

'Good morning.' She bestowed them with a brisk smile. 'Sister Stella has now compiled all of the results. When your name is called, please make your way *quietly* to her office. When you are finished, wait outside the school for your friends. Do not return to the hall. Your names will be called in alphabetical order. Angela Buckley is first . . .'

The longest half-hour of Sarah's life followed. Sometimes it was of benefit to have your surname towards the end of the alphabet, like when you had to read out loud in class. The bell would ring before the teacher reached you. Inevitably, they would start at *A* again the next day. Sarah dreaded reading out loud and was thankful that her surname began with *R*. Not now, though. The longer she had to wait, the more she doubted herself. There was the question in Irish that she didn't get to finish. And the trick multiple choice answers in Physics . . .

The big clock at the front of the hall edged past eleven-thirty and Sarah thought of John. He'd have his results by now. As it was impractical for him to travel to Dublin to get them in person, he'd been told to phone the boarding school at eleven-thirty. Was he pleased with how he'd done?

'Sarah Ryan,' called the secretary.

'Good luck,' whispered the few girls remaining.

With trembling knees, Sarah walked towards the principal's office. She knocked.

'Come in.'

Sister Stella was seated behind her desk, a well-worn piece of furniture that had many scratches and marks.

'Sit down, Sarah.'

Obediently, Sarah sat in the straight-backed visitor's chair.

Sister Stella smiled across at her. Then she let out a loud sneeze.

'Pardon me,' she fished a handkerchief from her pocket, 'I seem to have picked up a summer cold.'

She blew her nose three times, tucked the handkerchief away, sipped from a glass of water, and finally cleared her throat to read.

'Mathematics: A, English: B, Chemistry: A . . .'

A huge weight lifted from Sarah's shoulders as she listened to the nun reel off the A's and B's. She didn't need to convert the grades into points, anyone could tell that there was more than enough to qualify for university.

'Congratulations,' said Sister Stella at the end. 'Your marks were the best in the school this year – an excellent result for all your hard work.'

Rather suddenly, she stuck her arm across the desk. Surprised, Sarah extended her own. So fierce was the nun's grip, the life was nearly squeezed out of Sarah's hand.

'Good luck with university. It's Commerce you're doing, isn't it?'

'Yes, Sister.'

The nun nodded with approval. 'You'll be very suited to it – you have a great aptitude for mathematics, as well as good leadership qualities.'

'Thank you, Sister.'

'Most importantly, though, you're a hard worker.'

'Yes, Sister. Thank you, Sister.'

Sarah went outside with the brown envelope that carried official proof of her results. Nuala came bounding over.

'How did you get on?'

'Good,' Sarah beamed. 'Very good, actually. How about you?'

'Well, I passed. That's all I wanted – so I'm happy.'

Sarah looked across the road and saw a bus approaching.

'I'd better hop on that. I have the afternoon shift at the shop.'

'Okay. See you at the disco later on. What are you wearing?'

Sarah was already running across the road. 'I don't know.'

She'd been so worried about her results that she hadn't given more than a fleeting thought to the disco that was jointly organised by the girls' and boys' secondary schools in celebration of the Leaving Certificate results. Now Sarah was excited at the thought of going. Everyone would be there. John would finally be able to put faces to all the names.

'Oh, Sarah!' Peggy had tears of pride in her eyes. 'I knew you were worrying about nothing. And to get top of the class . . .'

'I know – I can't believe it.'

'Well, you should believe it! And you should have more confidence in yourself in the future.'

Sarah might not have been confident all along, but she was now. She suddenly couldn't wait to go to University College Cork. Her grandmother's shop had given her a taste for business, but there was so much more to learn. She would discover her niche, her career, over the next four years. It would be something to do with numbers, something that was fast-paced and exciting. In her mind's eye, she could visualise herself behind a desk, speaking authoritatively into the phone, her secretary waiting on the side. She would be very important, the boss of the secretary and ten or twenty others. She would be fair but tough.

'Did John come over while I was gone?'

Peggy shook her head. 'There's not been a word from across the road.'

'Do you mind if I pop over to see how he got on? I won't be long.'

'Take as long as you want, love.'

Delaney's pub consisted of two rooms, the bar and the lounge. Most of the patrons clustered in the bar area, sitting on backless stools and watching the horse racing on the TV set at the far end of the mahogany counter.

John, wearing a white shirt and black pants, was behind the bar. He looked up when Sarah came in. His lips twisted in a smile that looked more like a grimace. She immediately began to worry.

Sarah sat on one of the stools and watched as he angled a glass under the Guinness tap. A mixture of froth and beer oozed into the glass and he pushed back the handle when the pint glass was half full. Sarah wasn't the only one watching John's movements. Mr Glavin sat with folded arms and a critical face as the froth separated from the stout. John stacked some dirty glasses and, after a minute or so, returned to fill the rest of the glass. Finally, he set it down in front of the old man, who took a slug, a layer of froth sticking to his upper lip. He emitted a small gasp of pleasure before giving John a begrudging nod of approval.

John, having checked along the counter to see that all his customers were content, came Sarah's way.

'Well, how did the acclaimed winner of RTE Musician of the Future do in his Leaving Certificate?' she asked in an upbeat tone.

John had achieved his ambition to win the prestigious competition and, after a live performance on the *Late Late Show*, he was somewhat of a local celebrity.

'A in Music, B in French, but downhill from there – I failed Chemistry.'

All the practising for the competition had obviously taken its toll.

She made a sympathetic face. 'Well, good thing you didn't want to go to Trinity.'

'It would have been nice to at least have had the option,' he said sharply. Then he added in a softer tone, 'How did you get on?'

'Five A's and two B's.'

'Congratulations.' His voice was hollow.

'Come on, John,' she said, trying to coax him back to his usual positive self. 'You were practising for the competition – you *won* the competition, for God's sake.'

'I still feel dumb.'

'Don't!'

'It's embarrassing, not getting good enough marks for Trinity.'

'You'd no intention of ever going to Trinity! You're going to use the RTE grant to study in Paris, remember? The great Cécile Marcel invited you personally, and I'm sure she couldn't care less about your Chemistry marks!'

One of the customers cleared his throat, letting John know that his services were needed.

'Do you think your dad will drive us to the disco tonight?' Sarah asked as she stood up.

'I'm not in the mood to go – sorry.' And with that, he walked away.

Sarah felt hurt.

He's just disappointed, that's all, she told herself as she crossed the street to the shop.

In the end it was Mr Fahey who gave Sarah a lift to Kilnock.

'I've scored some bouncer work for the night,' he said, looking as proud as if he'd found himself a full-time job. 'I've never done it before, but I'm sure there's nothing to it.'

He was shorter than Sarah and of a slight build. She doubted that he had the mettle to handle a swarm of drunken teenagers. She hoped he'd be all right.

'I'll be leaving at two-thirty,' he told her as he locked the door of his car. 'Be back here by then if you want a lift home.'

Sarah headed towards the pub across the road where she knew she'd find her school friends. The air inside was thick with smoke. She blinked, her eyes watering.

'Sarah!' She felt a heavy arm sling across her shoulders. 'I heard you're the star of your school.'

She turned around to see Daniel Fox, his good-looking face distorted with the effects of alcohol.

'I did okay,' she said warily. 'How about you?'

'Failed Maths and Irish,' he replied, sounding bizarrely proud.

She nodded because he looked as if he didn't need her to commiserate.

'There's Nuala,' she said, seeing her friend. 'See ya.'

'Ah, there you go again,' he called after her. 'Snobby Sarah Ryan – too good to talk to someone like me.'

Sarah ignored him and pushed her way through the crowd.

'What were you talking to Daniel about?' Nuala whispered urgently. She'd had a crush on Daniel for months now but couldn't get him to notice her.

'He failed Maths and Irish,' Sarah replied matter-of-factly. 'I'm getting a drink. Do you want anything?'

It took ages to get served at the bar and Sarah spilt half the drinks on the way back. She stood next to Nuala. Waves of conversation and laughter rose and fell around her. The cigarette smoke cast a haze over the talking, laughing faces. She felt strangely detached. Like she didn't really belong. Like she should be somewhere else. With John. Then she became annoyed with herself. Why couldn't she have a good time without him?

The dance hall was a basketball court by day. Rotating lights, extra seating and a cocky DJ were all that was needed to convert it into quite a convincing discotheque: you just had to remember not to look at the blue and yellow lines on the floor. Alcohol was not allowed, the admission fee was five pounds, and it cost ten pence to put your coat in the cloakroom.

Nuala was determined to hang on in the pub for as long as possible, though. 'There'll be nobody on the dance floor yet,' she declared. 'Better to arrive when it's really going. Make an entrance.'

The bar staff eventually rang the bell for last orders and Nuala decided it was time to make their 'entrance'. They left the pub and walked uphill to the hall. A breeze blew against them, soft and pure after the heavy smoke in the pub. The sky was a canvas of stars. Nuala was mildly drunk, Sarah cold sober.

In the foyer of the hall, they were passed by Mr Fahey, a determined look on his face, a head of dark hair locked under his arm. Sarah said hello before dropping her eyes to see who he was removing from the premises.

'Daniel?'

Daniel, through no will of his own, disappeared outside. Nuala spun on her heel and ran after him. Sarah felt obliged to go too.

'Daniel! Are you all right?'

Freed from Mr Fahey's grip and bent over at the waist, Daniel didn't respond.

Nuala glared at the bouncer responsible for removing the one boy she had wanted to impress that night.

'You've no right to throw him out, none at all!'

Daniel started to retch and Nuala quickly changed her mind.

'God, that's disgusting,' she said, her face screwed up with distaste as she stepped out of the way. 'Let's get inside, Sarah,' she ordered, as if it had been all Sarah's idea to go rushing to Daniel's aid.

Nuala's good spirits were restored when she saw that the dance floor was full to capacity. Hands raised above her head, she danced her way through the crowd. Sarah followed. She tried her best to enjoy herself. She danced under the spinning orbs, sang along with some of the songs, and smiled on cue. But her heart wasn't in it. She didn't want any of the immature boys who asked her to dance. She wanted John.

The last set of slow dances came on. The lights dimmed. Sarah was asked to dance: once, twice, three times. Mr Fahey was leaving at two-thirty: only forty more minutes to endure. Another boy sidled up and she turned him down with a shake of her head.

'Crazy for You' sounded out over the speakers. Sarah's eyes were inexplicably drawn to the doorway. Her heart somersaulted at the sight of the tall, achingly-familiar figure standing there. John had come after all.

She was instantly scared that he wouldn't see her.

'John! John!' She pushed her way through the crowd.

Finally they found each other and she was in his arms.

'I'm sorry,' he whispered.

They became one of the circling couples on the dance floor. Sarah's body moulded to his. She rested her head on his shoulder. For the first time in the entire evening she felt like she belonged.

Sarah didn't know exactly when she made up her mind. It could have been earlier in the day when she'd heard about John's exam results and realised that Paris would take him much further away from her than boarding school ever had. Or maybe it was the sheer rush of love she'd felt when she saw him standing in the door-way of the disco. Or when he'd started to kiss her, the intensity such that it seemed imperative they find somewhere they could be alone. Somewhere along the line, she didn't know exactly when, she made the heady decision that tonight was the night.

Her hand tight in John's, they left the hall and walked across the gravelled yard to his father's car. She sat in the passenger seat while he took the wheel. She turned on the radio. Soon Kilnock's lights were behind them, and there was much more than a dark country road in front.

A little way from home, John turned the car into a wide gate-way and switched off the headlights. A half-moon provided enough light to see his face: his sensual mouth, dark eyes and the strong line of his cheekbones. Sarah was rocked by another surge of love for him. Two years of dating, kissing and touching had culminated in this moment where there was only one way forward. Very sure of her decision, she made the first move.

'Let's get into the back.'

The leather of the back seat was cool beneath her bare legs. She kissed him, softly at first, but soon she was carried away by his urgent response. She fell back on the seat, her legs straddling him as he lay on top. His kissing took on a new level of urgency as his slender fingers removed most of her clothes. The leather seat warmed, feeling much like a second skin.

Boldly, Sarah pulled down the zip of his jeans and took him in a confident grip. She heard him moan. Wet and hot under her hand, she imagined him inside her. She touched him against her cotton underwear. She wanted more. No barriers at all. She moved her underwear to one side.

'Sarah?' he asked in question. They had never gone this far before.

'Yes.'

'Are you sure?' he checked again.

She loved him even more for that.

'What about contraception?' he asked.

'It's a safe time of the month.'

She guided him inside her. It didn't hurt. In fact, it was surprisingly easy, as if she was made for him.

'I love you,' she heard him murmur.

'I love you too,' she whispered in return.

And she did. With all her heart.

When it was all over she held him tightly and tried not to think that it was only a matter of weeks before he would be leaving for Paris.

Chapter 4

Ten weeks later

Peggy turned around from the stove to greet Sarah as she came in the kitchen door. 'You look pale, girl.'

Sarah replied with the first excuse that came into her head. 'I've got a touch of the flu.'

She unwrapped her scarf and tried not to inhale the salty smell that was emanating from the pots on the stove.

'Do you have a temperature?'

'No. Just aches and pains.'

'Don't bother with the shop, then. I'll cover tonight.'

Sarah realised that she had made a tactical error. Now the old woman would be watching her like a hawk. The last thing she needed.

'I'll be fine, Nan. And you want to go to the church, don't you?'

All Souls' Day held special significance for Peggy, her husband, son and daughter-in-law all needing her prayers.

'Yes. But are you sure?'

'I'm not that bad, really.'

'Do you have much homework to do?'

Sarah had explained several times that students were given assignments, not homework. This time she let it pass without correction.

'No.'

Peggy finished at the stove and turned around with a plateful of steaming food.

'Here's your dinner. A good feed will make you feel better.'

The sight of the jacket potatoes, cabbage and ham was enough to make Sarah want to throw up. The bell sounded from the shop. A customer.

'I'll get it.'

She darted away from the kitchen, its smells, and her grand-mother's sharp eyes.

The shop was quiet; most of the villagers were at the vigil mass. Sarah opened her Economics book and tried to study. The words made no sense. How could she possibly concentrate when she had so much else on her mind?

The door opened.

'Good evening, Mrs Delaney.'

'Sarah.'

Over the years John's mother had perfected the disapproving tone she used when speaking to Sarah. She had her suspicions that the girl was more than just her son's friend. Friend or girl-friend, she used every opportunity to make it clear that Sarah didn't meet the standard. One day John would play to audiences all over the world. Beautiful women from privileged families would be wooed by his genius and charisma. It would be a travesty if he was tied down to the girl next door.

'Do you have any meat left?'

'Plenty – have a look in the fridge.'

Mrs Delaney, her lips pursed together, assessed the contents of the fridge. Her thin face, under a head of roller curls, wore a perpetual look of dissatisfaction.

'Are you sure it's fresh?'

'Like it's just off the farm,' Sarah answered airily.

With a reluctance that suggested she had no alternative, Mrs Delaney selected some chicken breast. She picked up a packet of cream biscuits on the way to the counter and Sarah entered the items on the cash register.

'Is that everything?'

Mrs Delaney nodded. Then, with calculated nonchalance, she announced, 'I believe John has found himself a nice French girlfriend.'

Sarah felt the nausea that she had been holding down all day rise in her throat.

'I got a letter from him today. Vanessa is her name.'

Sarah pressed down hard on the TOTAL button and the cash drawer came flying out.

'I'll put it on your account,' she mumbled and rose from her stool. 'Excuse me.'

Somehow she made it through the shop and into the kitchen. She hurled herself over the sink and heaved thick yellow bile over the shiny stainless steel. She wanted to die.

Peggy shuffled into Sarah's bedroom. 'Here's a cup of hot lemon for you.'

'Thanks, Nan.'

Peggy studied her granddaughter closely. Too closely.

'You look very peaky. Will I call Dr O'Mahony?'

'No,' Sarah said in as firm a voice as she could manage. 'There's nothing he can give me for the flu. I just have to sweat it out.'

'I suppose you're right,' Peggy conceded. 'Any road, let's see how you're feeling in the morning. Goodnight, love.'

'Night, Nan.'

Peggy closed the door softly behind her. Sarah, ignoring the cup of hot lemon on the bedside, propped herself up against the pillows. She hugged her arms around her knees.

'John and Vanessa,' she said, trying to make herself believe it.

'John and Vanessa,' she repeated, louder.

He had every right to see someone else, didn't he? Hadn't he said that they were too young to tie each other down, that they should use the time apart to spread their wings, see what life was about? Sarah had agreed at the time. It had sounded like a worldly approach. But she hadn't known then that in a matter of weeks he would meet a girl worthy of mentioning in a letter to his mother. And of course she'd absolutely no idea that as they hugged goodbye she was already two weeks pregnant with his baby.

'You are so stupid, Sarah Ryan. So stupid. *Stupid, stupid, stupid.*'

Yes, it had been a 'safe time of the month' when she and John had first made love. Their downfall was that they had done it again the following week, when it was not safe. After that they'd used condoms, blissfully unaware that it was already too late.

She'd played with fire. And got burned. Now, as far as she could see, she had two choices. Tell John. He would come back, robbed of his scholarship and the chance to spread his wings. Don't tell John. Wipe out the mistake. Start a new, wiser, page.

Sarah's hand touched her stomach, slightly rounded, its usual shape. The baby was nothing more than a tiny jelly bean. It wouldn't know.

Nuala was the kind of girl who thrived on a crisis.

'There's a place in town that will tell you where to go in England,' she said knowledgeably.

Sarah nodded, relieved that her friend knew what to do.

'I'll go with you to the appointment,' Nuala offered. 'In Cork, I mean – I wouldn't have the money to go to England.'

'How much will it cost?' Sarah asked, not having thought of the financial implications until now.

'About a thousand pounds – or so I've heard. Where will you get it?'

Sarah sighed raggedly. 'I suppose I'll have to tell Nan that I need extra money for tuition fees.'

Nuala shook her head slowly. 'Jesus, I never thought that someone like you would get into this situation. You're usually so sensible . . .'

'I wasn't thinking straight,' Sarah explained in a faraway voice. 'He was going away . . . and I loved him so much . . . I kind of lost my head for a while . . .'

Nuala nodded, though it was very clear that she didn't really understand.

The clinic was located in one of the side streets off the Grand Parade. Nuala looked surreptitiously over both shoulders before she pulled Sarah into the doorway.

'Okay?' she asked, giving her a last-minute chance to change her mind.

Sarah nodded and Nuala pushed the solid varnished door

inwards. A narrow hallway stretched in front of them, a glass-panelled reception on the left-hand side.

'Sarah Ryan,' Nuala announced.

A bespectacled woman with a kind face looked up from her paperwork.

'Which one of you is Sarah?' she asked.

Sarah stepped forward. 'Me.'

'We're running a little behind this morning, Sarah. Fifteen minutes or so. The waiting room is through there.' She pointed to the door at the end of the hallway. 'The doctor will call you when she's ready.'

Sarah and Nuala sat down on wooden chairs in the small rectangular waiting room. There were two other girls there, but nobody spoke or made eye contact. Sarah wondered how she could get through fifteen more minutes of waiting. How she could last until it was time to go to England. How long things would take once she got there. She desperately wanted it all to be over.

Dr Lenihan was surprisingly young. Her fair hair was tied back in a neat ponytail; she wore no make-up and looked the part in a pristine white coat.

'Well, Sarah. How can I help you?'

'I'm pregnant,' Sarah blurted in response.

Dr Lenihan rummaged in her desk and took out a plastic container.

'Let's confirm our facts before we go any further. The toilet is outside, first right.'

Sarah, feeling a faint surge of hope that it was all a false alarm, followed the doctor's directions. She had based her conclusion solely on the fact that she'd missed her last two periods. There could be another reason that she hadn't bled. What sort of reason, she didn't know, but maybe there was something.

Back in the room, the doctor tested the sample.

'Positive,' she declared before throwing the testing stick into the bin.

Sarah felt the hope drain out of her. She was pregnant. It was confirmed. Funny how she had a baby in her tummy, yet she'd never felt so empty.

'How do you feel about having a baby?' asked the doctor.

'I don't want it.'

'Does your family know?'

'No – only my friend, Nuala – she's waiting outside.'

'Nuala is welcome to come in while we talk,' the doctor suggested. 'To give you support while we go through your options. Would you like me to call her?'

Sarah shook her head. There was only one option as far as she could see and she didn't need Nuala to hear all the graphic details. 'No, thanks.'

The doctor nodded and clasped her hands on her lap. 'How about the baby's father? Does he know you're pregnant?'

Sarah examined her fingernails. 'No.'

'How do you think he'd feel about it if he knew?'

'Resentful,' she answered in a small voice. 'But he'd come back and do the right thing by me.'

'Come back from where?'

'Paris.' Sarah looked up from her hands. 'He's studying music there. Have you heard of Cécile Marcel?'

The doctor shook her head.

'She's very famous,' Sarah told her. 'She's tutoring John – this is the opportunity of a lifetime for him.'

'Don't you want to give him the chance to decide for himself?' the doctor asked gently.

Sarah almost broke down, almost cried out, *He's with Vanessa now. I'd be forcing him away from his new girlfriend as well as the scholarship.*

'No,' she said out loud, just about holding it together.

'Okay. Enough questions for now.' Dr Lenihan seemed to understand how painful it was to talk about John. 'Let me do the talking for a little while. I'm going to tell you about your first option: being a single parent. It's a big undertaking: the twenty-four-hour care of your baby, the feeding, the nurturing, the financial needs . . . Are you ready for that? Will you be able to do it alone if there is nobody to help? Will you be able to have the life you want for yourself?'

No, No, No.

'Your second option, Sarah, is adoption. You could give the child to parents who want it and would care for it. You would give the baby up after nine months of carrying it, giving birth to it . . .'

No, No, No.

The doctor paused. It was obvious that she thought adoption was the best option.

'I can't carry this baby for nine months,' Sarah stated, panic threading her voice. 'I come from a small village . . .'

'There are places you can go, nobody needs to know.'

The idea of there being options was an illusion. This doctor, with her white coat and kind eyes, was part of that illusion.

Quite suddenly, Sarah felt angry. 'You don't understand. I can't just disappear for a few months, my grandmother needs me. Adoption is just not an option.'

Time stood still.

The doctor sought Sarah's gaze.

'I'm here to support you, no matter what your decision.'

Sarah drew on the last of her strength. 'My decision is to

have an abortion. Give me the information on how to go about it – please.'

Whether it was seasickness or morning sickness, Sarah didn't know. Either way, she spent the four-hour ferry ride to Pembroke in the toilet, the heaving so violent that she wondered whether the baby would survive.

After a series of complex lies to her grandmother about why she was going to England for the weekend, the tense bus trip from Cork to Rosslare, and now this ferry ride from hell, Sarah was at the very end of her endurance. All she could think about was getting off the ferry and putting her feet on dry land. She couldn't contemplate that another long bus ride, to London, was ahead.

A middle-aged woman tried to strike up conversation at the basins.

'You're looking a little under the weather, love.'

'Why are you off to England?'

'Any friends over there to meet you?'

'Will you be staying long?'

Sarah's answers were weak, unconvincing.

The woman stuffed a leaflet into her hand. It read, *Pro Life*.

'Please don't do it,' she whispered in an imploring voice.

Sarah realised that the woman was a regular on the boat, on the watch for pale worried young women, with small talk targeted to establish the purpose of their trip, all in the hope of saving unborn babies.

'It's none of your business,' she muttered and threw the leaflet in the bin.

A girl Sarah met at the clinic, whose name she didn't know, told her that it was a nurse's full-time job to reassemble the parts of the babies to ensure they had been fully removed. Sarah couldn't get the image out of her mind. Was it true?

She was given Panadol and antibiotics on leaving the clinic and reminded that she had to go for a check-up in six weeks. The drugs didn't work. The cramps were excruciating. Were they normal? Or were they pangs of guilt?

Bus to Pembroke, rocky crossing on the ferry, bus to Cork. Almost home. How could she look Peggy in the eye? The girl in the clinic had also said that whilst the mother was given an anaesthetic, the baby wasn't given anything. Was that true? Did the baby feel itself being taken out bit by bit?

Sarah turned her head towards the bus window so that the other passengers wouldn't see her tears. Why had this feeling of horror taken so long to surface? Why hadn't it made its presence felt when she had been on the bus leaving Cork? Why hadn't she met that girl somewhere else, before it was too late for both of them?

Icy rain dashed against the window. Sarah was overcome with bleakness. Those last few weeks of summer, the happiness of being with John, the headiness of their illicit love-making, all that seemed a world away now. John was lost to her. She was lost to herself.

She cried the whole way back to Cork. For the baby. For John. For Peggy, who would be devastated if she knew the truth. For the nurse, if there was one, who had to piece the babies back together. For her mother, because if she'd been alive there might have been some other way forward.

Chapter 5

Sarah went through the motions of everyday life. She attended lectures, drank the awful coffee at the college canteen and made small talk with her classmates. At home she picked at her dinner, helped in the shop and tried, mostly in vain, to finish the day with some study. But her daily routine was an act, a farce. Inside she was dead.

Nuala was the only one who had any inkling of how bad she felt.

'You need to talk about it,' she urged.

'No,' Sarah shook her head vehemently. 'Talking makes it worse.'

At night, in her bed, she wept and wept, her knuckles pressed against her mouth, muffling the sound so it wouldn't travel to Peggy's room. She hated herself for being so stupid as to get pregnant. She hated herself for being so spineless as to have an abortion. She hated herself, period. By the time morning came around, the skin around her eyes was taut with dried tears, and her insides were hollowed out by self-hatred.

She thought a lot about her mother, particularly late at night, as she wept. Kathleen Ryan: mother at twenty, dead at twenty-three. Had she ever made a mistake of this proportion? Had she ever felt that she'd totally and irrevocably screwed up her life?

Sarah had known from a young age that her mother had died from kidney failure. She'd accepted it at face value. Mother: kidney failure. Father: motorbike accident. Was it that cut and dried?

'Why did her kidneys fail?'

Peggy, knitting by the fireside, stalled over her stitch.

'Because her health was bad,' she replied. 'She hardly ate.'

'Why? Was she anorexic?'

'Not as such. Her problems were mostly in her head. She had chronic depression and that was at the root of the eating disorder. Whenever she was black, she would lose interest in food – sometimes she wouldn't eat for days on end, she'd be as weak as a kitten.'

Sarah was gripped by fear. She had her mother's genes. Was she predisposed to depression? Was that why she couldn't hold it together now?

'On her wedding day she was so thin she looked as though she'd float away in her white dress,' Peggy continued, memories clouding her face. 'She improved when she became pregnant with you. But she was deeply depressed after the birth and she regressed again. Of course, she went from bad to worse when Tommy died. It wasn't any wonder that her kidneys failed in the end.'

Peggy had never been so frank, had never talked to Sarah in such a grown-up way.

'I worry about you, Sarah. I worry that you're like her . . .' Peggy trailed off before adding, 'But at least you eat. Thank God for that.'

Sarah was overcome by an overwhelming need to talk to her mother. She wanted to ask her what the depression felt like. To find out what, if anything, made it go away.

'Why did they have to take her body back to Donegal? Why didn't they let her be buried here in Carrickmore with Dad?'

'Well, all of her family was in Donegal . . .'

'But I was here. Didn't I count?'

'Of course you did. Maybe I should have pushed harder, but I wasn't feeling too strong myself . . . Tommy and Kathleen dead two years . . . you needing my care . . .'

Peggy, her face a sheet of sadness, took a stitch. The wool slipped off her needle and her expression changed to one of annoyance.

'Why didn't they want to take *me* back to Donegal?' Sarah persisted.

Peggy, having recovered the dropped stitch, looked up. 'That was never discussed.'

The conversation ended there but it left another layer of blackness in its wake. In short, Sarah hadn't been good enough for her mother's family in Donegal. Just as she hadn't been good enough to make her mother want to eat, to live. Just as she hadn't been good enough for John's mother or, when it came down to it, for John himself.

The occasional letter came from France. John told her he was very privileged to be tutored by someone of Cécile's calibre.

She's quite the character with her florid clothes and flappy upper arms. She calls me her 'petit penguin' – apparently I keep my arms too close to my body when I'm playing. She criticises every little mistake in her booming voice; it was daunting at the start but I'm used to it now – in fact, I'm in awe when she plays back my pieces to show me where I've gone wrong. If I could be half as good as her . . . She says I have the potential to be one of the best in the world, I just have to practise, practise, practise. So no holidays at Christmas or Easter for me; just practise. Why don't you come and visit me instead? I can speak fluent French now and I should be able to nip away from the piano for long enough to show you the city the locals love.

The underlying tone of his letters was friendship, not love. Sarah kept them in her bottom drawer but didn't pen a response, and certainly didn't intend to visit him. As far as she was concerned, it was better that they never spoke again. How could she face him? How could she hide the bleakness that was now her life? How could she hide that she still loved him, despite Vanessa, the baby, and everything else?

Sarah turned over the exam paper and her eyes skimmed the questions. They seemed manageable; she wasn't going to be punished for cramming a year's study into a few weeks. She carefully reread the first question and began to write her answer in the booklet provided.

Three hours later, the supervisor rang the hand bell.

'Pens down. Please stay seated until I give you permission to go.'

Sarah and the other students waited in the stuffy hall for a few extra minutes while their papers were collected.

'What did you think?' asked Tim Brennan as they walked outside.

Tim was in her class. He was intelligent and, unlike most of the other boys, quietly self-assured. Sarah had vaguely noticed that he was rather attractive. On first look, there was nothing too remarkable about his near-black hair and pale skin. It was his eyes, dark and brooding, that made you look again.

'It wasn't too bad,' she replied.

'I thought it was tough.'

Sarah looked at the faces of the students around her and realised that most of them, like Tim, weren't very happy.

'I really didn't think it was too bad,' she repeated sheepishly. 'But then statistics, or any kind of maths, are my strength.'

In truth, the exam had given Sarah a sense of achievement, something she hadn't felt in a long time.

When she got home that evening, she went for a run. Her legs were stiff and jerky on the tarmacadam road. She climbed a gate. The grass was softer, kinder to her legs. Adrenalin kicked in. She'd almost forgotten how good it felt: a natural high.

Economics was the next paper. Sarah was more focused. Some of the darkness had cleared from her head. She was smiling when time was called. Tim noticed.

'You actually like exams, don't you?'

'It's like an adrenalin rush,' she admitted. 'Not knowing what the questions will be, trying to decide which ones to answer, cramming it into the time allowed. I bet you think I'm weird.'

He laughed, which she assumed meant that, yes, he did think she was weird.

On the day of the last exam he asked her if she was coming for a drink with the rest of their class.

Sarah hesitated. She'd promised Peggy that she'd be home by four-thirty.

'I have to –'

He jumped in before she could finish. 'Come on, Sarah. You've kept to yourself all year. Why don't you come to the pub and get to know the people you'll be graduating with three years from now?'

Suddenly she saw herself through the eyes of her classmates: moody, remote, unfriendly.

'Okay,' she agreed and put her satchel over her shoulder. 'Lead the way.'

The Western Star, the favoured pub of UCC students, was packed to capacity. Tim, after buying two beers at the bar, pushed a path through to the beer garden and joined a group with several familiar faces. Sarah knew some of their names, but not all. Self-conscious, she drank down her beer quickly.

'Surprised to see *you* here,' one of the girls remarked.

Sarah shrugged. 'There's a first time for everything . . .'

'We were just talking about our plans for the summer,' said another, more friendly girl. 'Are you going anywhere?'

'No. I have to help my grandmother with her shop – she's getting on and she relies on me for all the heavy work.'

'Is that why you don't hang around at the college much?'

'Yeah.'

Any remaining animosity fizzled away under the hazy May sunshine. Sarah went to the bar next and, at huge expense, bought a full round of drinks.

'Making up for lost time,' she explained when she returned.

Tim eyed the wine she'd bought for herself.

'Not a beer girl?'

'I'm good for one or two. Then I switch to wine.'

'I'll have to remember that for the future,' he said, giving her a long, meaningful stare.

Sarah, with a faint blush, started to talk to the girls once more.

The friendly one, Emma, told her that she was going to spend the summer au pairing in the south of France. Sarah swallowed a large mouthful of wine. France. John. Would it ever stop hurting?

The afternoon stretched into evening.

I should call Nan to let her know where I am.

But every time she looked over at the public phone booth, there was someone using it. Finally, it was free. She slid twenty pence into the slot and waited for Peggy to answer.

'Hello.'

Sarah could hardly hear her grandmother's voice over the cacophony of music and loud voices around her.

'Hi, Nan. Sorry, I should have rung sooner. I went for a drink after the exam was over – it's been hard to drag myself away. I hope you weren't worried.'

Peggy responded but Sarah couldn't make out what she was saying.

'I'm sorry, Nan,' she repeated. 'Look, I'll be on the last bus.'

Again, Peggy's voice was an indecipherable murmur. Sarah hung up, hoping that her grandmother wasn't too angry with her.

She turned away from the booth and came face to face with Tim.

'Not calling a boyfriend, were you?' he asked with a worried frown.

She shook her head.

'Before we get really drunk, and you think I don't mean this, I want to tell you that I really like you, Sarah Ryan. Will you go out with me sometime?'

Sarah returned his gaze. His eyes were magnetic. She felt as though she could get lost in them.

'I'm complicated, Tim. Best not to get involved with me.'

'What does complicated mean?' he asked in his forthright way.

'You don't want to know.'

She did like Tim. There was something romantic about his pale skin and those dark, deep eyes. But he'd run a mile if he knew the truth about her.

Emma gave Sarah a knowing wink when they returned to the group.

She leaned forward to whisper, 'You and Tim seem to be hitting it off, at last.'

'What do you mean "at last"?'

'Well, he liked you from day one. But he thought, *we all* thought, that you had a boyfriend.'

'I *did* have a boyfriend,' Sarah admitted, her voice choking despite her best efforts.

'Sorry,' Emma looked dismayed, 'I didn't mean to upset you.'

'It's okay. It's all over. Has been for ages.'

Much later on, after promising Emma that she'd write to her in France and exchanging phone numbers with another girl, Fiona, Sarah said goodbye.

'I have to make a run for my bus,' she explained.

The street outside was thronged with students, some going home, others heading off to the many end-of-term parties that were being held in the digs close to the college.

'Sarah, hold on.'

Tim had followed her out.

'Can I walk with you?'

'Okay,' she shrugged. 'But we have to be quick.'

They set out at a brisk pace towards the heart of the city. Sarah's senses were heightened and everything around her seemed more vivid, more immediate. The night air was deliciously warm, the sky a blanket of stars, the headlights of passing cars dazzlingly bright. She was drunk. But only a little. Just enough to be able to pretend for a moment that the last nine months of her life hadn't happened.

She kept a close eye on her watch.

'I think I'm going to miss it . . .'

'You can always get a taxi,' Tim replied, already a little out of breath.

'Not to Carrickmore – it would cost a fortune. We're going to have to run . . .'

'You're joking.'

She giggled. 'No.'

He caught her hand. 'Right . . . marks, set, go!'

Laughing, they raced the rest of the way, dodging pedestrians and lampposts. When they arrived at the bus station, the Carrickmore bus was already in its bay, the engine running.

'Well, I'll see you so,' said Sarah, feeling awkward all of a sudden.

'Bye, Sarah.'

Tim lowered his head, his breath ragged. His kiss was gentle, hopeful. The bus's engine began to rev and Sarah pulled back.

'You won't change your mind about going out with me?' asked Tim.

'No.'

She got on the bus and sat on the side where she could see him. He waved as the bus pulled out of the station and she smiled the first genuine smile in a long time. At eighteen, it was perfectly normal to kiss a fellow student after a rake of alcohol. And that was all she wanted: to be normal again.

Chapter 6

Sarah worked full-time at the shop over the summer holidays. In the first few days it became blatantly obvious how much Peggy had been struggling on her own. All too often the heavy bundles of newspapers were carried in by a kind customer from where they were left on the footpath. And if something was needed from the top shelf, the customers would climb the stepladder themselves.

Peggy sighed as she shuffled to and from the milk fridge. 'It takes a while to get these old bones up and going.'

'Why don't you take the mornings off?' Sarah suggested. 'I can do them – it'll be a nice change from working evenings.'

Peggy agreed readily enough. They both knew that she wouldn't be able to resume the morning shift when the summer ended, but they could deal with that problem when they came to it.

Sarah, with a year of business education behind her, looked at the daily operation of the shop with fresh eyes and soon compiled a list of potential improvements: the fitting of modern space-saving shelving; an extension to the weekend opening hours; and, an idea that had been forming for some time, the installation of petrol pumps at the side of the premises.

She enjoyed pulling all the numbers together. She asked the customers for their opinions. Would they come in if the shop was opened for a full day on Sunday? Would they buy petrol if it was available? She created best-case and worst-case scenarios and, after a few weeks of careful research, presented her findings to Peggy.

'The petrol pumps have a dual benefit, Nan,' she explained. 'Not only would they bring in profit in their own right, but they would also attract passing trade.'

Peggy's eyes widened when she saw the numbers.

'And you say that's the worst-case scenario?' she queried.

Sarah nodded. 'You see, there's no petrol available in Kilnock, so I've made a conservative estimate that some of the residents will come here to fill up their tanks – and spend money in the shop while they're about it!'

Peggy knew a good investment when she saw one. 'The bank will take some convincing – we've never been more in the red. And I'm too old to be haggling with those big oil companies. If we're going to do this, then you need to manage it, Sarah – from start to end.'

Sarah agreed, secretly proud that she had managed to sell such a significant investment proposal to her canny grandmother, and very excited that success of the project was down to her alone.

After much to-ing and fro-ing with the bank and the planning office, the installation of the petrol pumps got underway. A monstrous digger excavated the side yard, and gleaming steel pipes were laid before the area was levelled and concreted. A canopy, costing twice as much as Sarah had budgeted, was constructed to shelter both the pumps and the customers from the elements. Glass doors were installed on the side of the shop, creating a new entrance.

'I hope it will all pay off in the end,' Peggy commented as she signed cheque after cheque.

Sarah, feeling nervous about the escalating costs, hoped so too.

The development ate up the entire summer and it was September before the pumps were ready for business.

'Are you sure your prices aren't more expensive than the city?' asked Mr Glavin, the very first customer.

'That's our guarantee.'

Sarah had understood right from the outset that the venture wouldn't work unless their prices were competitive. Nuala was a vital cog in the price-setting process. She worked in retail, across the street from one of the biggest petrol stations in the city, and phoned every day with the prices.

Sarah put up advertisements in Kilnock's supermarket, post office and school. With the cost blow-out on the construction, the neighbouring village's trade would play a vital role in the success of the venture.

The first week's takings were promising, the second week's even better. By the third week, Sarah's best-case scenario had been surpassed. She felt elated. As if her existence was finally worthwhile.

As September drew to a close, Sarah focused her energy on convincing Peggy to take on an extra pair of hands.

'I'm going back to university next week. You need help lifting things, especially in the mornings, when it's so busy.'

'But the cost –' Peggy started to object.

'We can afford it,' Sarah cut in. 'Thanks to the petrol pumps, we're not just getting by, we're making *profit*.'

'But who –'

The new doors slid open and Peggy stopped midsentence. Sarah glanced over to see who had come in. Black spots danced before her eyes.

'John Delaney,' Peggy beamed. 'Well, would you look at you – aren't you a sight for sore eyes.'

Sarah felt herself tremble.

Oh, my God. Why didn't his mother mention that he was coming home? What can I say to him?

Peggy had hobbled around the counter and was hugging John like a long-lost son. Sarah caught his eye. Then looked away. The trembling got worse, she was shaking all over.

'And how are you getting on?' she heard Peggy ask. 'You must be a concert pianist by now.'

'Not exactly,' John replied with a smile. 'Cécile is so talented that sometimes I feel as though I'll never reach her standard. But when she's not yelling at me, she says I'm doing okay.'

'Ah, go way outta that.' Peggy slapped him playfully. 'There's no place in Carrickmore for such modesty.'

They laughed, and a silence followed as they both turned Sarah's way.

'Are you busy?' John asked her.

'No,' Peggy replied on her granddaughter's behalf. 'It's only nagging me, she is. Take her away and give me some peace for an hour or so.'

Peggy and John laughed again. Sarah thought she would cry if she tried to join in. She moved away from the protection of the counter. Conscious of her cut-off shorts and uninspiring T-shirt, she wished she'd known he was back. It might have helped if she was looking her best.

The park seemed the obvious place to go. Mr O'Hara had been round with his mower that morning and the scent of freshly cut grass brought back poignant memories of the summer night when she and John had first kissed. If only she could turn back the clock. If only they had left it at kissing. How much sadness they would have saved.

She glanced at him as he walked by her side across the neat grass. His hands were stuffed deep into the pockets of his beige shorts, his head bent in thought. His white polo shirt enhanced the golden tan on his arms and highlights streaked his fair hair. She almost reached out to link his arm, like old times. The realisation that she had no right to touch him was like a douse of cold water.

He's not mine – hasn't been for a full year now.

They reached the oak tree and he leaned his back against the gnarled trunk.

'So,' he said, looking down at her. 'Why haven't you replied to my letters?'

The old John would not have been so direct. This John was much more sure of himself. His face was longer and leaner. His eyes, staring at her, had a worldliness about them. His mouth looked ready to slip into fluent French at a moment's notice.

She shrugged. 'Been busy. Study, the shop . . . you know how it is.'

His navy eyes narrowed. 'Have you met someone else? Is that it?'

She grabbed at the idea, like a drowning swimmer to a floating branch.

'Yes.'

'Someone from college?'

'Tim,' she improvised.

'Is it serious?'

'Probably no more than you and Vanessa,' she heard herself say and regretted the words as soon as they were out of her mouth. Mentioning Vanessa would entice a full confrontation. The last thing she needed.

'How do you know about Vanessa?' he asked, his smooth brow furrowing in a frown.

She shrugged again. 'Your mother.'

His mouth tightened until it was nothing more than an angry line. 'She'd no right to imply that Vanessa is my girlfriend. She knows well enough that she's one of Cécile's students – a friend.'

His denial rocked everything that Sarah had believed for the last year, and undermined all the decisions she had made as a consequence.

'*Do* you have a girlfriend?' she asked weakly.

'Nothing serious,' was his less-than-satisfactory response.

'Is that a yes?' she pressed, needing to know.

'I suppose.'

So it wasn't Vanessa, it was someone else. A change of name, but the facts were still the same: John was with another girl, there was no hope of reconciliation. Sarah realised that she was relieved. It would be terrifying to love him again.

Feeling more in control, she turned the conversation to Paris and his studies.

'Have you done any performances yet?'

'I've played at the Conservatoire de Paris twice,' he replied. 'The last time Cécile invited a critic without telling me. It was quite a risk – my career could be squashed by a bad review.'

'What did he say about you?'

John grinned. 'Don't know if I caught the guy on a good day or what, but everything he wrote was positive.'

'I'm sure you deserved it.'

Sarah was proud of him. Putting the last few years aside, when their friendship had transformed into something else, this was the boy she used to play with in the park and sit with at the back of the school bus. It was amazing to think of him performing in a city known worldwide for its role in the evolution of music, and for its brutal critics.

'I'd better go,' she said, her emotions on a slippery slope. She gave him a brisk hug.

'Sarah . . .'

She didn't meet his eyes, afraid of what would happen if she did.

'Yes?'

'I –' he faltered.

She realised that in John's mind they were breaking up now. He lived in a fairyland where you could date other girls and still keep the one back home.

'It's been over since you left last year,' she told him in a hard voice. 'This is just a formality, John.'

'But –'

'Take care of yourself, okay?'

It took everything she had to walk away from him, to cross the road and go inside the shop, leaving him standing there staring after her.

'How about Brendan Fahey?' she asked Peggy, picking up the conversation where they had left off earlier: the new shop assistant.

Peggy looked thoughtful. 'I suppose he's reliable . . .'

'And he'll be glad of the work,' Sarah added. 'I'll ring him tomorrow and ask –'

Their conversation was interrupted by the sound of a loud engine pulling up outside: the delivery truck. Sarah was instantly busied with checking the delivery and, later on, stacking the new stock onto the shelves.

Later on that night, while they watched *Coronation Street*, Peggy proved that she wasn't so easily distracted.

'He's looking well, isn't he?' she commented.

'Who?' asked Sarah, her eyes frozen on the screen.

'John, of course.'

Sarah didn't answer.

'Is the romance back on between ye?'

'There was never any romance,' Sarah said quickly.

'God love us!' There was a smile in Peggy's voice. 'You must think I'm an awful fool altogether.'

'Look, Nan, I don't want to talk about it.'

'Fair enough,' Peggy agreed in a reasonable tone. 'But I've just got one thing to say . . .'

Sarah gave a reluctant sigh. 'Go on, so.'

'This last year has been a hard one for you – I've seen how . . .' Peggy paused, searching for the right word. 'I've seen how *down* you were.' Sarah was inordinately relieved that her grandmother hadn't used the word depressed. 'And now, just when you seem to have bounced back, he's turned up. I don't want to see you getting low again. Your mother . . .'

Sarah finally took her eyes off the television. 'My mother what?'

Peggy heard the defensiveness in her granddaughter's voice and changed tack. 'John will be away for a number of years yet. Even when he's finished in Paris, who's to say he'll ever come back to live in Carrickmore. You must ask yourself if you have the mettle for a long-distance relationship.'

Sarah got to her feet and made a show of puffing the armchair's cushions into shape. 'You're barking up the wrong tree, Nan. John has a French girlfriend . . . and I'm seeing someone else too.'

As she told yet another lie about Tim, Sarah resolved that she would at least go on one date with him when the term started up.

Peggy, visibly relieved, reached out for her granddaughter's hand.

'I'm glad to hear that. I want you to be like other girls of your age: having fun, staying out late. I was happy that you didn't come straight home the day you finished your exams. I was happy that you stayed out with your friends.'

'I thought you were angry with me.' This was the first time Peggy had made mention of that day.

'Why would you think that? Young people must do what young people must do. I remember when I was nineteen like it was yesterday. Times were hard, but we knew how to have fun. We tested the boundaries like any other generation . . .'

There it was: the perfect opening. Sarah wavered; if she was ever going to tell her grandmother about the baby, it was now. She longed to get it off her chest, to cry in Peggy's arms, to be forgiven. But she couldn't – she knew it would shatter her grandmother.

'I didn't realise that you worry about me so much,' she said lightly.

'Only in some ways, love. You're a great girl, really.'

The *Coronation Street* music sounded from the TV. The show was over, as was the moment for confessions.

Chapter 7

Over the next year Sarah did everything to prove to herself, and her grandmother, that she knew how to have fun. She never turned down an invitation for a drink or a party, and the driver of the last bus came to know her by name. On the nights she missed the bus, which were frequent, she would stay at Emma's mother's house. Arms linked, she and Emma would stagger up Patrick's Hill and fall in the door of the terrace. It didn't matter how much noise they made, it would take nothing short of an earthquake to rouse Emma's mother from her valium-induced sleep.

Tim started the term with a steady girlfriend and Sarah lost the opportunity to go on a date with him. There were plenty of other boys, though, with their nondescript faces and sloppy kisses. She tried not to compare them to John but it was hard, especially when it was so hopelessly obvious that they couldn't compete either physically or intellectually.

'Are you determined to kiss every boy in UCC?' Emma asked one night.

Sarah giggled. 'I'm just trying to find one who makes the world spin.'

'You don't need a boy for that,' Emma quipped. 'Just go and get yourself another drink!'

Sarah laughed. On the inside, though, she wondered why the boys left her so cold. Had the passion she'd shared with John been for real? Would there ever be anyone who would come close to him?

The student parties began to get more adventurous as the year went on. On one occasion, when Tim's dad was away for the weekend, twenty or so of the class went to stay at the family farm. After some drunken nocturnal games in the hay barn, the rooster called the start of the next day. Fiona had the bright idea of joining the rooster on the roof of the chicken pen, which promptly collapsed under her weight. She landed on her bottom, the alarmed chickens flapping and squawking around her. The stories from that particular weekend were relayed over and over, and never failed to bring tears of laughter.

On another weekend, the university social club hired a train to Tralee. Students lurched from carriage to carriage, drinking, cheering and singing. But when the train arrived at Tralee Station, nobody wanted to get off; they were having far too much fun. The organisers and railway staff conferred and decided to allow the party to continue at the platform. A few hours later, the train departed at its scheduled time and the party, still going strong, trundled back to Cork.

Easter involved a rented house in remote Connemara and a few bottles of poteen; everything else was a blur.

Parties aside, Sarah was very focused on her studies and her career, but she was still not entirely sure what area of business she wanted to work in when she graduated. She decided to attend the milkrounds to hear what the prospective employers had to offer.

'The milkrounds are for students in their final year,' Emma pointed out. 'There's no need for us to sit through hours of boring presentations. We can relax for another couple of years.'

Sarah shrugged. 'I'm interested, that's all.'

'And I'm interested too,' said Tim, who had overheard their conversation. 'I'll go with you if you like, Sarah.'

So Sarah and Tim went to the milkrounds together. They listened to the speakers, watched the videos and pored over the information packs. They agreed that all the employers seemed to promise fulfilling and successful careers. But one stood out above the others.

'I think I want to work in banking,' said Sarah.

'Me too,' Tim concurred. 'All that money flowing in and out. Irresistible!'

It wasn't just their future careers, Sarah and Tim concurred on lots of things. Sometimes she caught herself regretting that she hadn't gone out with him when he'd asked her. But it was too late now. Louise, his girlfriend, looked like she was going to be a permanent fixture.

The end-of-year exams were staggered over two weeks of beautiful weather. The papers held a few surprises but Sarah was well prepared. The weather broke on the last day, hail pelting down, soaking them en route to the Western Star.

'To think we were out in the beer garden this time last year,' Tim commented, shaking white pebbles of hail from his dark hair.

'To sunshine and the U S of A,' toasted Emma when they had

completed the arduous task of ordering drinks from the over-crowded bar.

Sarah clinked her glass and tried to quell her envy. Emma, Fiona, Tim, and Louise were all off to New York for the summer. Tim and Louise had green cards; the others were hoping to work illegally. Sarah would have loved to go. But how could she let Peggy down? Who would cover for Mr Fahey when he took his hard-earned summer holidays? Who would catch up on all the book work that slipped Peggy's notice these days?

Not for the first time, Sarah was niggled with resentment that she was so tied to her grandmother and the shop.

I can't even take a summer off! How will I ever be able to get away to build my own career?

The answer obviously had to do with continuing to increase the profits of the shop so that one day they'd be able to afford a general manager to run the place while Sarah followed her career.

I've got two years till I graduate. Two years to build the profits. Two years to sell the idea of a manager to Nan.

Sarah searched for a challenge to make up for missing out on New York, but with the petrol pumps running well and the extended opening hours long established, she could see no obvious area of improvement for the shop.

Peggy was very apologetic about the state of the paperwork. 'I'm sorry it's in such a mess. My eyes become addled from all the numbers and I get headaches. Getting old is a very frustrating business!'

Some evenings Nuala would call around and Sarah would temporarily leave the outstanding invoices and overdue tax returns to go for a ride in her friend's new car. If the day was sunny they'd drive as far as Crosshaven and wince their way across the pebbled beach to the cold sea. If it was dull or raining, as it was more often than not, they'd go to the city. Sarah loved to walk through the wide-aisled supermarkets and study their merchandise. Nuala knew she was looking for ideas and wasn't shy to put suggestions forward.

'How about selling essential clothing like socks and under-wear?' she proposed one rainy evening as they strolled through Dunnes Stores.

'I'm not sure they'd sell in any great quantities in Carrick-more,' Sarah replied. 'No, I need something that's on the up-and-up . . .'

'Wine?'

'Delaney's pub is right across the road, remember?'

'How could I forget!'

They came to the last aisle.

'Where to next?' asked Nuala.

'Why don't we go to the Southside?' Sarah suggested. 'Where the posh people shop.'

Nuala, not a very experienced driver, grimaced at the thought of crossing the city. 'I'm not sure how to get there, but I'll give it a try. We can only get lost, right?'

Nuala had proved to be a staunch friend over the years and regularly put herself out on Sarah's account. The only thing she refused to do was socialise with Sarah's college crowd.

'I'm the only one in this entire pub who's not doing a degree,' she'd pointed out the first and only night she'd met them. 'I feel like a fish out of water. I know they're all very nice, but I'm just not comfortable here.'

As a result, Sarah usually saw Nuala on her own and they steered clear of grungy college bars. They talked about every-thing. Everything but the abortion. Even though it was never spoken of, the abortion had accelerated their friendship from the adolescent to the mature and bound them together in the way that only shared secrets can.

After a few wrong turns and a lot of swearing, Nuala parked her little Fiat on the main street of Douglas village. It was worth all the effort as Sarah found the idea she'd been looking for.

Peggy, as expected, was resistant at first.

'Videos? Who in Carrickmore would want to buy videos?'

'Not buy,' Sarah corrected. 'Hire.'

'Buy, hire, what's the difference? Don't you need a contraption to play them?'

'Yes, you do need a video player. I'd say practically every house in the area has one already.'

'Go way outta that!'

So Sarah asked the customers.

'Do you have a video player?'

'Would you be interested in hiring videos from us?'

The answer, on both accounts, was a resounding yes.

Peggy could hardly believe it.

'If everyone has one of those contraptions, then why don't we?' she asked indignantly. Then she folded her arms. 'Well, I'm not selling, or *hiring out*, something I don't understand. So you'd better buy one so I can see for myself if it's worth all the fuss.'

Despite being too frail to do anything but serve at the shop counter, Peggy was still an astute businesswoman. It made perfect sense to buy a video player!

Two weeks later Sarah's new business venture got the big thumbs-up. Peggy considered the video player the best invention since sliced pan: being able to choose exactly what you wanted to watch and then pause, fast forward or rewind as suited, not to talk about recording off the TV.

Sarah found a supplier for the video tapes and reorganised the shelving in the shop to accommodate them. She designed a poster and paid a printer to run off fifty glossy copies. Most of the posters went to Kilnock, but she also put a few in other villages further afield.

Unlike the petrol pumps, the video business was slow to take off. The tapes often got damaged or weren't returned on time. Sarah soon realised that she had to strictly enforce late fees if she was to make any profit at all.

Peggy, not too bothered with the meagre profits, became a home-based film critic. She watched each and every tape, putting a green sticker on the ones she liked. It took Sarah a while to cotton on that some of the new blockbusters weren't getting Peggy's *Recommended* sticker.

'What's wrong with *Dirty Dancing?*'

'It's not the right moral message to be giving young people,' was her grandmother's reply.

'Nan, this isn't a church youth club! It's a business,' Sarah said, exasperated. 'Where are the stickers?'

'They're *my* stickers,' Peggy stated, all high and mighty. 'It's *my* recommendation, not yours.'

'Well, I'll get my own then,' Sarah threatened. 'Red, I think, meaning *Red hot love scenes*. Recommended by *me*.'

Peggy stuck to her guns. Sarah carried out her threat. It didn't take the customers long to figure out the difference between the green and red recommendation stickers.

One cold wet October night, at the start of Sarah's third year of university, she locked up the shop and sat behind the counter to begin balancing the cash. She didn't take much notice when it was fifty pounds out and proceeded to go through the numbers again. Twenty minutes later she finished all the adding and cross checking, the fifty pounds still unaccounted for.

Did Nan give someone too much change? she wondered, but found it hard to believe.

While Peggy openly admitted to becoming muddled with detailed paperwork, she was as sharp as ever when dealing with hard cash.

Or maybe Brendan made a mistake?

Mr Fahey, whom she now called Brendan, did make the odd mistake, but Sarah found it hard to imagine a scenario where an amount as significant as fifty pounds could be overlooked.

Mulling it over, she stretched elastic bands around the wads of cash, bagged the coins and prepared the deposit slip for the following day's lodgement. She carried the cash and deposit book through to the house, and locked them away in the strong box hidden beneath the kitchen sink.

'We're out fifty pounds, Nan,' she said as she walked into the front room.

Peggy was snoozing, her chin resting on her chest. The plastic case of *The Secret of my Success* was on her lap. Michael J Fox, cocky and ambitious, grinned from the TV screen.

'Nan?' Sarah shook Peggy's shoulder. 'You can't be sleeping on the job –'

In a heart-stopping moment Sarah realised that her grandmother's body was frigid to her touch.

'Nan, Nan,' she cried and lifted Peggy's chin to see her face. Her eyes were open.

She's okay.

Then it sank in that the staring eyes had no life in them.

*

'Sorry for your loss.'

'We'll all miss her.'

'She lived a good life, God rest her soul.'

'A great loss to Carrickmore.'

'Sorry.'

Sarah acknowledged each quiet condolence with a slight nod of her head. Some of the mourners were too emotional to say anything and just squeezed her hand. This rocked her composure even more.

'I'm so sorry, Sarah.'

Sarah's face crumbled when she saw Nuala. She choked on a sob. Had she let it out, she wouldn't have been able to stop.

Don't lose it, she told herself. *Cry later. At home.*

She'd been repeating that mantra, *Cry later*, for the last three days and, somehow, she'd held on. Until she was alone. Then she'd cry and cry and cry.

'Sorry, Sarah.'

It was Tim. Followed by Emma, Fiona, and other faces from her class, some of whom she hardly knew. Cries of despair lodged in her throat, a nanosecond from coming out.

Hold on. Hold on.

The funeral moved from the church to the cemetery, the casket borne on the shoulders of old friends. Sarah walked behind. Nuala linked one arm, Tim the other. They stayed by her side as the casket was lowered into the ground.

Ashes to ashes, dust to dust . . .

It was over. Everyone blessed themselves and headed across the road to Delaney's.

'Are you coming?' asked Nuala.

'In a while.'

'We'll see you there, okay?'

Sarah was left alone, all but for Mr O'Hara who was waiting, shovel in hand, to fill the grave. She gazed down at the coffin, covered with a few clods of earth and a single red rose. The finality of it shattered her resolve not to cry.

Mr O'Hara moved forward uncertainly when he saw the gush of tears. 'Are you okay, Sarah?'

She nodded and stumbled away.

In Delaney's, the mourners would be marking the end of Peggy Ryan's life in the traditional way: raising their glasses and sharing fond memories and anecdotes. They would be waiting for Sarah to join them. But she couldn't do it. She couldn't face them. The tears she had to cry wouldn't stop now that they'd started. They were more enduring than any tradition.

Chapter 8

Sarah pounded around the track, her breath fogging the icy air. Her lungs hurt. The pain was welcome. She wanted to feel something and if physical pain was the only thing on offer, then she'd take it. Gladly.

The sleepless nights were back. The crying. The self-hatred. The helplessness. The hopelessness. Fear of the future. Of not ever being good enough. Of being alone.

When she wasn't crying, Sarah would self-analyse. She looked at herself dispassionately. She saw a girl who had been defined by those close to her. Her happiness had emanated from Peggy and John, not from within. So it wasn't any wonder that without them she was nothing.

She had to force herself out of bed every morning. Had to force herself to eat. To run. To believe that if she kept going, kept doing everyday things, she would eventually pull out of the darkness. The running did give her a sense of pleasure, much diminished than usual, but she clung to it nevertheless. She ran as often as she could, pounding round and round the track at the Mardyke, as though her life depended on it.

Head down, eyes on the red clay underfoot, Sarah hardly noticed the other runner join the track. Her legs eventually lost their strength and she veered to the grassy centre. There, she bent over, hands cupping her knees, and took deep breaths of bitter cold. The runner swished by.

She straightened, balanced herself on one leg and bent the other back.

Hold. Hold. Next leg.

Then, one foot slightly in front of the other, she pushed forward and felt the muscles in her calf loosen in response to the pressure.

The runner was coming round again: male, wearing a navy tracksuit and a peaked cap that hid his face. He was going fast, too fast for the ten thousand metres.

Maybe he's in training for the five thousand.

Sarah unzipped her gear bag and took out a towel. She buried her sweaty face in the soft cotton before draping it across her shoulders. Then she unscrewed her water bottle and gulped back half its contents. With her bag slung over her back and water bottle in hand, she made for home. As she crossed the track, the runner, about two hundred metres away, raised his hand in salute. She lifted her hand in response and continued on towards the exit.

In general, Sarah tried to run the shop as Peggy would have liked. Rule number one: the customer is always right. Rule number two: keep the shop, and consequently your reputation, spick and span. Rule number three: only buy stock you are two hundred per cent sure you can sell.

It took six weeks before she veered from Peggy's modus operandi and ordered a small sample of tasteful Christmas decorations on a strict sale-or-return basis.

'There's nothing as dead as Christmas when it's over,' Peggy had declared more times than Sarah could count. 'There you'd be, up to your eyeballs in tinsel, hanging from the rafters it'd be, and you with no chance to sell it till the following year.'

Contrary to Peggy's dire warnings of the past, Sarah's Christmas balls and tinsel sold out within days.

There you are, Nan, thirty pounds profit. What have you got to say to that?

Sarah ordered some more decorations from the supplier but, knowing there was some truth in Peggy's view, she was careful not to overdo it.

A few days later Mrs Burke, Peggy's old friend, dropped in.

'You poor love, you,' she tutted as she set down a bowl wrapped in foil on the counter. 'You must be missing her terrible. Sure, I'm lost without her myself . . . I can only imagine how you feel. She used to love my plum pudding, God rest her soul. I brought some for you.'

Sarah thanked her.

The old woman lingered on for a chat, as she often did when she dropped by. A widow in her eighties, with her children overseas, Peggy had been a big part of her life.

'The days are long,' she sighed. 'It's hard to keep myself occupied. I'm twiddling my fingers now that all my Christmas baking is done.'

'Why don't you make a few cakes for us here?' asked Sarah, thinking that they'd fly off the shelves if they went anything like the decorations.

The old lady became flustered at the thought. 'Sure, nobody would pay money for my old cakes.'

'Ah now, Mrs Burke,' Sarah smiled cajolingly, 'doesn't everybody know you're the best baker in Carrickmore?'

Mrs Burke's cakes were an enormous success and the shop had record takings in the last few days before Christmas. Sarah and Brendan were run off their feet, the shop almost sold out of perishables by the time they locked up on Christmas Eve.

'Are you sure you won't join us for dinner tomorrow?' asked Brendan yet again.

'I promised Nuala I'd spend the day with her,' Sarah replied, as if she'd not told him a dozen times before, 'but thanks anyway.'

Truth be known, part of her wanted to spend Christmas Day on her own. If she didn't care enough to get dressed or cried herself stupid, then who would be any the wiser? However, another part of her, the part that desperately didn't want to end up like her mother, welcomed the opportunity to be in the midst of Nuala's big family. Surely, she wouldn't feel depressed with so many people around her?

Nuala climbed into the single bed and pulled the covers up to her chin.

'Padraig fancies you,' she announced out of nowhere.

Sarah didn't comment as she brushed her hair. It was longer than usual; she'd been too preoccupied to get it cut.

She set down the hairbrush on the dresser and, her back modestly turned towards her friend, she slipped on her flannelette pyjamas.

'Can you move over a bit?' she asked as she squeezed into the bed they were sharing for the night.

Nuala shimmied a little to the left.

'Did you hear what I said about Padraig?' she asked.

'Yeah.' Sarah reached towards the lamp. 'Ready?'

'Okay.'

Sarah flicked the switch and waited for her eyes to adjust to the dark.

'Well, do you like him or not?' Nuala asked, exasperation in her voice.

'He's your brother!'

'I know that, you eejit,' Nuala exclaimed in frustration. 'But sure isn't every fella out there somebody's brother? I'm asking you if you fancy him – yes or no?'

Sarah gave the question due consideration. Nice enough looking and working as a trainee solicitor, Padraig was by all accounts a good catch. She tried to imagine what it would be like to kiss him. The thought left her cold.

'No.'

'Fair enough.' Nuala paused. 'Tell me the truth, Sarah. Have you fancied anyone at all since John?'

Sarah was filled with hopeless yearning. She saw John's face in her head. His eyes stared through her. To her heart. She relived the feel of his skin, the heat of his body, the meeting of minds, the closeness. If she had known how hard it would be to replicate those feelings, she would have fought harder for him, she would have told him about their baby.

'Sarah?'

'No,' she said, coming out of her reverie. 'The answer is no.' Then, in an attempt to end the day on a positive note, she added, 'Goodnight, Nuala. And thanks again for inviting me for dinner today. I had a lovely time.'

She was sincere in her gratitude. The hubbub of Nuala's family had raised her spirits no end. She didn't know why there were tears creeping stealthily down her face now. Glad that Nuala couldn't see she was crying, she turned on her side and tried to go to sleep.

He was there again. The runner. Wearing shorts rather than the usual tracksuit, his peaked cap shielding his face, his elbows moving in perfect rhythm to his long stride. Sarah crossed the track and set her bag down on the damp grass. She unzipped her jacket, gathered her hair in a ponytail and began her stretches.

She ran out slowly, a little out of shape after the short break she'd taken over Christmas. Steadily she built up speed. Out on the track everything was simple. One leg in front of the other. Breathe in, breathe out. Heat soon tingling her skin. This was therapy. She shouldn't have stopped, no matter how briefly. She needed it.

Round and round they went, countless laps, she a hundred or so metres behind him. She used him as a moving target and kept going well beyond the half-hour she'd originally planned. Just when she thought she'd have to give up first, he slowed and she caught up with him.

'Training for anything in particular?' he asked when she drew up alongside.

'No,' she puffed, glancing his way and meeting heavy-lidded brown eyes beneath the peak of his cap. 'I run to de-stress.'

'You should compete,' he advised. 'You've got good stamina.'

She shrugged. Competing meant structured training, impossible with her commitments at the shop. She flipped the question back to him.

'Do you compete?'

'Five K.'

She smiled. 'Thought so.'

She blushed as she realised that she'd admitted to thinking about him.

A lap flew by.

'Are you a student?' she asked.

'Yeah – engineering.'

'What kind?'

'Civil. How about you?'

'B Comm. Third year.'

They ran another few laps. They seemed to go quicker with him at her side.

'That's it for me,' he said.

'Okay, bye so.'

She pulled ahead.

He shouted, 'Do you have a name?'

She looked over her shoulder. 'Sarah.'

'I'm Kieran. See you next time, Sarah.'

Peggy's death left a gaping hole in the staffing and running of the shop. Sarah did her best to cover it: relieving Brendan at four every evening and working through to closing time at nine; placing the orders and organising returns; keeping up with the debtors and creditors, as well as all the usual paperwork. Not surprisingly, her studies began to suffer. One assignment was late, another scraped a bare pass. Something needed to be done.

Sarah's action was twofold: she advertised for a full-time shop assistant, and she decided to buy a car. Neither was without its problems.

The profits from the shop weren't yet high enough to pay for a manager, but they could accommodate an assistant. Sarah was looking for someone hardworking, honest and with a good customer manner. Finding the right person proved a lot harder than she expected.

'I think you're being too fussy,' Nuala declared when Sarah complained that most of the job applicants were mopey teenagers.

'No, I'm not,' Sarah replied tersely. 'I'm trusting this person with everything I have – the cash in the till, the stock on the shelves, not to mention my reputation. The wrong person could jeopardise everything.'

'How did you ever trust Brendan enough to hire him?'

'That's different – I've known him all my life.'

Similarly, Sarah was accused of being too fussy about the car. Tim was helping her on that front.

'For Christ's sake, Sarah,' he swore after an unsuccessful visit to view a Peugot for private sale. 'If perfection means that much to you, then you should get a new car rather than a second-hand one.'

He has a point, thought Sarah, her eyes glancing down to the newspaper on her lap. She'd highlighted a number of advertisements but she suspected that the cars would be the wrong colour, or have dings on the body, or high mileage.

Can I afford something new?

Finally, a mature woman from Kilnock applied for the position at the shop. Mary Malone had a warm face and an obliging manner. She possessed the down-to-earth practicality of a mother who had raised four children to become self-sufficient adults. Sarah knew straight away that she was the right person for the job.

Mary started and within days she proved to be everything Sarah had hoped for: resourceful, not afraid to make decisions, and trustworthy. She quickly became confident with the run of things and Sarah was able to reduce her work hours.

On the transport side of things, Sarah finally acknowledged that nothing but a new car would meet her high standards. Peggy had bequeathed a lump sum that was just enough to buy a zippy red Fiesta. Sarah stuck L plates on the front and rear and persuaded Tim to give her driving lessons.

Having the car saved almost two hours a day, time she'd previously wasted waiting around for buses. She put the extra hours into running and studying, the things that made her feel good. Achievement, she discovered, was the answer to depression: beating a personal best, getting top marks in an assignment, hearing words of praise from a satisfied customer. Every accomplishment, small or big, chipped away at the depression's hold.

Sarah built on her achievements until she was sleeping soundly at night. Winter became spring. As the days brightened, so did her outlook. Her confidence returned, as did the small joys that were part of everyday life. She still missed her grandmother every minute of every hour, but she knew she was going to be okay on her own. She was no longer scared of the future; she was looking forward to it.

Jodi

Chapter 9

Sydney, 1980

The beach was a twenty-minute walk from the house. Jodi spent a lot of time there. She swam far into the sea. She swam where twelve year olds shouldn't dare swim. Out where the water was deep and cleansing. Sometimes it took all her strength to swim back to shore. Sometimes she wasn't sure she could make it. Sometimes she didn't really care.

Today the waves had a sinister tug. The battle was brutal: Jodi Tyler against the sea. It was exhilarating. Hard work, but she was holding her own. Not like at home, where she was drowning.

Head down, she ploughed against the current. She turned her face to take a breath and caught sight of the lifeguards pulling the rescue boat trailer down towards the water.

Someone must be in trouble, she thought, taking a quick glance around to see who it was.

There was no one else around.

They're coming to get me.

'I was okay,' she protested as they pulled her aboard.

There were two of them: a woman with sandy hair and a sun-freckled face, and a guy, younger, with pin-up good looks.

'The hell you were,' the guy replied and the toned muscles on his upper arms bulged as he began to motor the boat back towards the shore.

Jodi stared sullenly at the horizon.

'Where are your parents?' the woman asked.

Jodi glanced at her briefly. 'At home.'

'How old are you?'

'Twelve.' She raised her chin defiantly. 'Old enough.'

The boat nudged the sand and Jodi hopped out. Her face burned when she realised that she was the talk of the beach.

'She looks to be okay.'

'Is she with anyone?'

A young child ran up to ask what it was like to ride in the rubber duckie.

Jodi ignored him, and hurried to where she'd left her beach bag. She shook the sand from her towel and rubbed herself dry.

'Hi,' she heard the female lifeguard say from behind.

She turned around. 'What do you want?'

'What's your name?'

'Jodi.'

'My name's Sue.'

'I'm going now,' Jodi warned and hoisted her bag from the sand.

'What's the rush?'

'Everyone's staring at me.'

'So what?'

'I'm getting out of here,' Jodi repeated and took a step away.

'I just want to know one thing.'

'What?'

'How would you like to compete for the surf lifesaving club?'

Jodi didn't tell her mother what had happened at the beach. She hugged the secret to herself.

Sue said I'm a really strong swimmer for my age. She said I could be a champion one day.

Jodi savoured the idea of being a champion. She visualised herself running through hot sand, diving into waves, bowing her head for medals. It made her feel strong and brave, and happy for the first time since the night Bob had come into her room.

That night had started out like any other in the long summer. The fan whirred irritatingly as it circulated hot air. Crickets hummed loudly outside the window. Jodi tossed and turned, trying to get comfortable.

Finally, her body started to feel the floaty sensation of sleep. She was suspended, on the very precipice of consciousness, when she heard the distinctive creak of her bedroom door. Her eyes flew open.

'Mum?'

The mattress sank with an extra weight. She smelled the stale odour of cigarettes and beer.

'Bob?'

Her stepfather of two years had never come into her bedroom before. Yet Jodi wasn't all that surprised that he was here now. At some level, despite her innocence, she'd known that the playful slaps on her backside, the accidental brushings against her developing breasts, and the tickling sessions that only he found funny, would end up like this.

A callused hand slid inside her nightie. Whilst her body froze, her mind went into overdrive. She pictured her mother's trusting face transforming with the devastation. Then she pictured her gran, tight-lipped. Her uncles, hot-headed. This thing that Bob was doing impacted all of them, not just her.

His hand roughly squeezed her breast. It hurt.

'Stop!' she cried.

His hand stilled. She heard him breathe in short heavy pants.

'It's only because I love you, Jodi,' he said.

'I'm going to tell my mother,' she started. 'She'll –'

He cut her off with a low menacing whisper. 'I'll kill the pair of you if you open your stupid mouth.'

Suddenly both of his hands were clasped around her neck, his thumbs pressing against the hollow at the base. For a few seconds Jodi couldn't breathe.

'I mean it,' he hissed in her ear. 'This is our secret.'

He stood up from the bed and his shadow moved along the wall. The door creaked on opening. He was gone, but not his threat; that would never go away.

Afterwards, Jodi couldn't look Bob or her mother in the eye. Scared and confused, she played the scene over and over in her head. He'd said he loved her. But he'd also threatened to kill her. Did he mean any of it? Would he kill someone he loved? Or was he lying about either the loving or the killing?

Of course her mother could tell that something was wrong.

'What is it, darl? Someone at school giving you a hard time?'

Jodi wished it were so simple. A school bully was much more straightforward than a stepfather who'd come into her bedroom and put his hand inside her nightie.

'Nothing's wrong, Mum,' she snapped every time her mother asked. Then she'd flounce to her room, playing the role of the angry teenager when she was really just a frightened child.

Bob showered attention on her mother.

'Mmm, you smell nice, Shirl,' he'd say, hugging her from behind while she was cooking or washing up.

Or, 'What's a bloke gotta do to get a kiss around here?' and nuzzle against her neck.

Shirley loved his flirting.

'Bob, I've got work to do here,' she'd protest, but she wouldn't push him away.

Her happiness showed on her face. Bob wasn't a handsome man, but Shirley was done with handsome. Good looks didn't carry a marriage very far. She'd learned that from Tony, her first husband. Tony was the kind of man women fawned over, and Shirley had had to work hard to keep him from straying. She always had her hair done nicely and was never seen without her lipstick. She hung on to him for eight exhausting years before he left her for the most predictable of reasons: another woman.

Bob's head wasn't turned by other women and they didn't pursue him. Shirley could bask in his devotion without looking over her shoulder. Her first marriage hadn't been a success but she'd got it right the second time. She'd struck gold.

'Go, Jodi! Go!'

Sue's new recruit was well out in front. She sprinted along the sand as if she'd been training for months and had a respectable lead as she hit the water. Her strokes, though not technically perfect, were strong and confident. Her lead lengthened as she approached the buoy.

'Go, Jodi! Go!'

The crowd was behind her. They knew they were watching a future champion.

It hadn't been Sue's decision to rescue Jodi that day. She'd seen her out with the surfers on other occasions and knew she was capable of making it in. However, Brett, her colleague, had got carried away at the opportunity to be a hero and Sue'd had no choice but to follow when he'd started to lug the boat trailer down to the water.

Jodi was out of the sea now, her skin glistening as she tore along the last leg of the race. The crowd, mums and dads of the other kids, cheered her on. Her own parents were noticeably absent.

In fact, Jodi tensed up whenever Sue suggested her parents might like to come along to watch.

'They aren't interested.'

'They may become interested if they could see how good you are,' Sue would point out gently.

'You don't know them.'

Sue began to get a strong feeling that something wasn't right with Jodi's home life. Her swimsuit revealed most of her young body and Sue would, without her knowing, check her over for bruises. She never found anything, though.

Jodi flew over the finish line, a smile beaming across her face. Sue gave her a high five.

'Well done. You killed it.'

A few others from the club added their congratulations. Jodi's smile widened even further.

Back at the club there was a sausage sizzle to celebrate. Jodi, freshly showered, walked into the room. Her golden hair, usually worn back in a ponytail, fell to her shoulders, shiny from its recent shampoo. Her brown almond-shaped eyes glowed. She looked astonishingly pretty. And terribly vulnerable.

'Over here, Jodi,' Sue called, letting her know in every little way she could that she was a friend.

*

The phone rang early the following morning. Two rings and it stopped. Jodi guessed her mum had picked it up.

She stretched her arms behind her head. Her body felt a bit achy after yesterday's race. She still couldn't believe she'd won. She smiled triumphantly and whispered, '*I'm the Under 13s champion.*'

Her euphoria was short-lived. Her bedroom door flung open.

'Grandma rang to say your picture's in the paper,' said her mother.

Jodi flushed guiltily. Her secret was out. She hadn't even noticed any cameras going off. She remained silent, not sure how to defend herself without knowing the full extent of what was in the newspaper.

Shirley crossed the room to sit on Jodi's bed.

'She said that you won some competition down on the beach. Why didn't you tell us about it?'

She sounded hurt and Jodi felt bad. She sat up in the bed.

'It was only a race.'

'The article said there were a few hundred spectators.'

For a moment, Jodi was back in the race and could hear the shouts of encouragement from the crowd.

'Why don't you share things with me any more, Jodi? I would have loved to have seen you race – win or not. Why wouldn't you give me that chance?'

Because Bob would come too. He'd see me in my swimsuit.

Jodi couldn't say her reasons out loud. She had to keep the secret, for both their sakes.

Shirley shook her head sadly. 'I suppose that's teenagers for you. I just didn't expect this to happen so soon. You're only twelve years old. Not officially a teenager till next year. How come you've grown up so quickly?'

She sighed resignedly and stood up.

'I'll go down to the shop and get a few copies of the paper. Maybe this will be the start of a scrapbook . . .'

The family had a party in Jodi's honour. All the aunts, uncles and cousins came over. Grandma too. Jodi was embarrassed by all the attention.

Her mother put on a buffet lunch with roast chicken, sliced ham and a large quiche from the deli where she worked. The family sat with plates on their knees and bantered boisterously while they ate.

Jodi stayed aloof. On guard. She didn't look Bob in the eye but she felt his stares. He slugged back ten bottles of beer and smoked twelve cigarettes throughout the course of the afternoon; Jodi counted from afar.

Grandma beckoned her over. She sat in the largest chair, her walking stick between her legs.

'What kind of girl doesn't tell her family that she's won a big race?' she asked, her lips pursed.

Jodi hunched her shoulders.

'What's wrong, girl? What's the cause of this strange behaviour?'

'Nothing.'

'Are you getting on okay at school?'

Jodi nodded. In truth, her grades were slightly down but she was still close to top of the class.

'Why didn't you eat any lunch?'

'I'm not hungry.'

Jodi was so apprehensive about Bob getting uncontrollably drunk that her stomach was churning.

Grandma fired another question. This time it was closer to the mark.

'And you're getting along okay with Bob?'

Jodi flinched inwardly. Although a token 'yes' would have thrown Grandma off the scent, she couldn't bring herself to speak.

'It's hard, I know,' her grandmother's wrinkled hand squeezed hers, 'seeing your mother with someone else, but you wouldn't want her to be on her own, would you?'

Jodi, still unable to utter a word, shook her head. Grandma loosened her grip. Jodi was free to go, but she stayed. She desperately wanted to tell her grandmother the truth. She was old and wise and very brave. Maybe, just maybe, she could think of a solution that didn't involve Bob killing them all.

'Bob's come –' she began.

'Jodi, come here for a photo,' called Auntie Marlene. 'Quick, while the baby's smiling.'

Jodi took the interruption as a sign that she shouldn't tell. She swallowed the truth back down. It left a bad taste in her mouth. But still she crossed the room and smiled into the camera when Auntie Marlene called, 'Cheese!'

The party went on late into the evening. Auntie Marlene, who was breastfeeding and not allowed to drink anything more than a small glass of wine, had to do three runs in her station wagon to get everyone home.

Jodi slipped away to her bedroom after a mumbled goodnight to her mother and Bob, who were still drinking out on the deck. She brushed her teeth, ran a comb through her hair and put on clean pyjamas. She hadn't worn a nightie since that night; it had been far too easy for Bob's hand to slide inside the flimsy material.

She climbed into bed and said her prayers.

'God our Father . . .'

She recited her bedtime prayer in a solemn whisper. Then it was time to pray for special intentions.

'Please, God, please let Bob break up with Mum, so I never ever have to see him again, and please let her find someone else, someone *really* nice . . .'

Jodi leaned across and switched off the bedside lamp. She lay in the dark, straining her ears to listen for sounds of Bob and her mother coming in from the deck. Bob was very drunk. Earlier on, he'd accidentally knocked a photo frame from the bookshelf and the glass shattered on the tiles. Her mother had been affectionately cross as she swept up the debris.

'Bob! You've had far too much. You'll bring the house down around us if you're not careful.'

She'd steered him back out to the deck and into a chair.

'Sit,' she'd ordered.

He'd pulled her onto his lap. 'I'm the luckiest man alive to have this woman as my wife,' he'd told the family, a big grin on his bulldog face.

Tears smarted in Jodi's eyes and she turned on her side in the bed.

Why did Mum marry Bob? Why did Dad leave her? She's much nicer than Grace.

Her father had married Grace no sooner than the ink was dry on his divorce papers and Jodi had a baby stepbrother now.

She slid one hand under her pillow and pressed it to her face to soak her tears. Her hand touched against something foreign beneath the pillow: paper. She sat up and turned the lamp back on.

It was a sheet from a lined copybook, like the ones she used for school. She unfolded it.

I'm so proud that you won the race. I love you, Golden Girl.
Bob.

Chapter 10

1984

Jodi looked at her reflection dispassionately. She'd been kissed for the first time. Did it show? Unlike most sixteen year olds, she rarely looked in the mirror.

Who are you? Who is Jodi Tyler?

She saw a round face framed by wavy blonde hair that was parted in the middle. Her skin was tanned and clear but for the shadows under her eyes. Her recently kissed lips looked the same as ever: too full at the bottom. Her school uniform, a plain white shirt and blue checked skirt, hung loosely on her body.

Yesterday, after the sausage sizzle at the surf club, Nicholas Green had told her she was 'cute'. Nicholas was the Under 18s runner-up. He had tousled hair and piercing eyes. His lips had tasted like sea salt when he'd kissed her.

'Jodi, you're going to be late. What's keeping you?' her mum called from the kitchen.

Jodi was being deliberately slow. Bob hadn't backed out his

Holden Commodore yet. She'd developed some core survival techniques over the past four years of living under the same roof as her stepfather: on weekdays she didn't leave her bedroom until he had left for work; after dinner, a meal her mother insisted they have as a family, Jodi would retire to her room to study; Saturdays and Sundays were spent training and competing at the beach. Avoiding Bob had some ancillary benefits: as a result of all the training and studying, Jodi was excelling in both sport and school.

She heard the front door slam, and a few seconds later the engine of the Commodore revved up. She stood by the window and peered through the small gap between the mesh curtain and the wall. Bob was looking over his shoulder as he reversed out of the drive. Once out on the road, he changed gear and drove off. She breathed a sigh of relief.

For breakfast, Jodi ate a large bowl of cereal. She kept a daily diet sheet to ensure she ate enough calories. Sportspeople needed to eat lots to keep up their energy levels and maintain their body weight. It had to be healthy food, though. No junk.

'What's on at school today?' her mother asked as she wiped down the counter.

'We're getting the results of last week's maths exam,' Jodi replied with a grimace.

Her mother glanced over her shoulder with a smile. 'I'm sure you have nothing to worry about.'

'It was really tough this time,' said Jodi. 'I'm not sure I got it all right – question ten was a killer.'

Her mother laughed. 'Darl, I wish I'd had half your brains when I was at school. There you are, aiming for full marks, when I would barely scratch a pass . . .'

This was the best part of the day. The kitchen was dated

but homely. Jodi had her mum all to herself. They chatted and laughed together. Bob was blocked out, in another compartment, not to be worried about for another ten hours.

Shirley took a compact from her handbag and, using the mirror, applied a dash of lipstick. She liked to look her best when she was working at the deli. Lots of the customers commented on her lovely smile. Jodi thought her mum was pretty too. She couldn't comprehend why she'd settled for Bob.

'Nearly ready to go?'

'Yes.' Jodi scraped back her chair.

I'll never settle for less than I deserve when I get married, she thought, picking up her satchel from the tiled floor. *Even if it is for the second time*.

Miss Butler, the maths teacher, stood at the front of the class, a pile of exam papers hugged to her ample breast.

'Quiet!' she ordered her pupils, who were settling into their seats. 'We have a lot to get through today. First, your results from last week . . .'

The class groaned and Jodi felt a twinge of worry.

'Katrina, you passed – only just . . .'

Katrina Stuart, looking rather pleased that she hadn't wasted any effort, sashayed up the aisle to collect her paper. Her skirt was rolled up at the waist so that the boys could admire her shapely thighs. Everybody knew, including Miss Butler, that she was much more interested in smoking cigarettes in the toilets than in mathematics.

'Jodi, an outstanding result, well done.'

Jodi stood up to take the outstretched test paper. She glanced at the mark on the top right hand corner: one hundred per cent.

'Samantha, you stumbled on question ten . . .'

Miss Butler finished distributing the papers and then, in brisk tones, began to explain methods of integration. She hadn't quite finished by the time the bell rang for morning break. Much to the disgruntlement of her pupils, she continued on for a few extra minutes.

'What have you got?' Samantha asked Jodi when Miss Butler finally gave them permission to leave.

'Cheese, crackers and an apple. You?'

'Banana bread – Mum baked it last night. I had it for breakfast too!'

Samantha didn't like sports and ate whatever she liked. Taller than Jodi, with red hair and freckles, she was starting to show the signs of her relaxed attitude to food. She and Jodi had been friends since Year Seven but their friendship was limited to school; they didn't go to each other's houses and didn't hang out at weekends. Samantha didn't know about Bob. Nobody did.

It was already oppressively hot in the school yard and most of the kids clustered under the trees to eat. Jodi's heart missed a beat when she caught sight of Nicholas Green, his friends circled around him. His blond hair glinted under a stray ray of sun that broke through the canopy of trees. Colour flooded Jodi's face as she recalled what it felt like to be kissed by him. Her lips suddenly salty, she gulped back some water from her drink bottle. The cold water regulated her blush and she risked another look his way. Her heart fell when she saw that he was talking to Katrina Stuart.

Jodi glanced at the wall clock: five minutes past six. Bob was slightly late.

Shirley wiped her brow. The dinner, roast chicken with boiled potatoes and mashed pumpkin, was ready. The kitchen was like a sauna thanks to the hot oven. But Bob loved a roast dinner.

Shirley's work day finished at four. She'd spent two hours preparing Bob's feast, with no time for even a cup of tea. It didn't stop there: after dinner she would do all the cleaning up while Bob slouched with a beer and newspaper.

'Cup of coffee, Bob?'

'Need that shirt ironed for tomorrow, Bob?'

She was perpetually at his service, so eager to please that it made Jodi want to gag.

'We're getting a real stretch from summer this year,' Shirley commented, her face flushed as she wiped her brow once again.

'Go outside, Mum,' said Jodi, becoming the adult. 'I'll get you a cold drink.'

Shirley took a look around the kitchen to ensure all was in order before leaving her post. Jodi poured two glasses of icy water from the pitcher in the fridge.

'You should do salad in the summer months,' she said when she joined her mother outside.

'Bob doesn't like salad,' Shirley replied, moving along the wooden bench so Jodi could slide in next to her. 'He's a big man, he needs a hearty dinner.'

Silence fell and ten minutes passed. Bob was unusually late.

'Must be bad traffic,' Shirley remarked, looking down at her watch.

Jodi allowed herself to drift into a fantasy where Bob had a fatal crash on his way home. Taking one of the bends on Spit Road, he veered into the next lane, his driving as sloppy as his personal hygiene. The oncoming bus, propelled by the steep incline, had no chance to stop and crushed the Commodore as if it was nothing more than a matchbox car. The police read Bob's address from his driver's licence and radioed the Dee Why station to send a car around to Lewis Street. The officers, a man and woman, took off their hats respectfully when Shirley opened the door.

The sound of an engine in the driveway brought her fantasy to an abrupt end.

'He's home.' Shirley smiled.

A few moments later Bob walked around the side of the house and up the steps to the deck. With patches of sweat on the underarms of his white shirt, a red tinge to his heavy jowls, he was horribly alive and, other than hot, well.

'Hard at work, ladies?' he asked sardonically.

Bob worked in a government department pushing paper and sitting on his fat ass while his staff did all the work. Shirley was on her feet all day serving customers, yet Bob didn't count her job as *real* work.

'You've caught us playing truant,' Shirley giggled, not hearing the sarcasm in his tone. She started to get up. 'I'll get you a cold beer.'

'No, I'll do it.' Jodi jumped to her feet, not wanting to be left alone with Bob.

The kitchen was still boiling hot. Jodi got a bottle of VB from the fridge. Unfamiliar with the bottle opener, she used too much force and the lid bounced off the counter and under the cooker. Unrecoverable.

Outside, she handed Bob his beer and addressed her mother.

'I'll put out the dinner.'

Dusk was starting to fall and Jodi lit the citronella lamp on the table. She served the food, Bob's plate piled high. They ate mostly in silence. Conversation, when it occurred, was between Bob and her mother. Bob rarely spoke to Jodi. His means of communication were the letters he periodically left under her pillow.

Last night's had read: *Have I told you how beautiful your legs are? So evenly tanned. So lean. I love all of you, but your legs are my favourite part.*

The letters were irregular. A few months would pass without any. But Jodi could never relax. The bastard knew that.

She read them and then destroyed them, tore them into a thousand tiny pieces that could never be put back together and read by her mother.

'Are you keeping our little secret?' he'd whisper in her ear every now and then. 'You'd better be.'

She'd nod, feeling more like his accomplice than his victim.

Because of the reference in last night's letter to her legs, Jodi had slipped on some track pants after school. The heavy cotton clung to her thighs in the sticky heat. She kept her eyes down as she ate, away from Bob's face. But his hands were in her direct line of vision. Those hands, with their fat, bulbous knuckles, commanded her silence. She could see them around her neck. Around her mother's neck. Squeezing. Killing. So she kept quiet about the letters, about Bob's so-called love, about everything.

It won't always be so, she promised herself. *One day I'll have a job where I can speak out. Where people will respect what I have to say. Where I'll be the boss, and not some fat bulldog man.*

Chapter 11

1986

'My baby girl going to *university* – I'm so proud of you!'

Shirley had tears in her eyes. Jodi felt emotional too. Today was her first day at the University of Sydney. It hadn't been her preferred choice; she had wanted to go to the Australian National University.

'Why go all the way to Canberra?' Shirley had protested.

'ANU is the best.'

'Nonsense – you can get just as good a degree here, and I wouldn't have to pay your rent.'

'I can get a part-time job.'

'It doesn't matter, you're still throwing good money away.'

'It's what I want to do.'

'Until you're eighteen, you'll do what *I* want you to do.' Then, seeing that her daughter was on the verge of tears, Shirley softened her tone. 'Bob says that there's alcohol – and drugs – and *all sorts of things* available at universities these days. We want to protect you from that. Give you some more time to be mature enough to say no if you're offered anything.'

So Bob was behind this, pulling strings, making sure she could never get away from him. Jodi had no choice but to play along and pretend she was reconciled to living at home. But in her head she was counting every day to her eighteenth birthday, when Shirley would hopefully give both her approval and some financial assistance towards the rent.

'Wish me luck,' she said to her mother.

Shirley kissed her cheek. 'You got the best HSC in your school, you're too smart to need luck.'

Jodi heard a door open and another slam shut. Bob was up and had gone into the bathroom.

'See you, Mum.' She rushed out the door. Now that she was the first to leave the house in the mornings, she would have to finetune her timing so she wouldn't cross paths with Bob. She couldn't cope with seeing him, especially not after last night's letter.

University! Golden Girl is all grown up. A young woman now.

She didn't want him thinking of her as a grown-up. Being a child was better, offered some level of protection.

Jodi inhaled gulps of humid air and tried to erase Bob from her thoughts. She walked towards the bus stop, only a short distance from the house. Wearing bootleg jeans and a sleeveless T-shirt, she felt both excited and nervous, grown-up and naive. Never would she have to wear a school uniform again. Sick notes, end-of-term reports and parent-teacher meetings were all part of the past. In fact, tertiary education came with unnerving freedom.

Will I make friends at university? Will they be more worldly than my school friends? Will they be able to tell that my stepfather is in love with me?

Jodi reached the bus stop to see that her bus was already there and a long line of commuters were in the process of getting on. She was the last to board and had to stand, hanging onto the overhead railing, for the entire forty-minute journey to the city. The airconditioning wasn't working and her jeans felt heavy and uncomfortable.

Getting off in Wynyard, she walked briskly to Martin Place and then up to Castlereagh Street. This time she was luckier and got a seat on the 422 bus which, according to the timetable, would take fifteen minutes to reach the campus. When she was settled into a routine, she could run this part of the commute. It wasn't the same as running on the sand, but it would keep her fitness up. Next year she wanted to compete in the Ironwoman Series. She hoped that her schedule would allow some early marks, afternoons where she could get to the beach and do some serious training.

Jodi's degree doubled Economics and Commerce, an ideal qualification for the banking career she'd already decided on. She'd always liked going to the local bank with her mother. The environment was clean and efficient, the staff polite and respectful. Transparency ruled: deposits and withdrawals were always double-checked, and sometimes the paperwork had to go to another staff member for sign-off. It seemed that nothing untoward could ever happen in a bank. She really, really liked that idea.

Jodi's goal was to end the four-year degree with first-class honours. That goal was at the forefront of her mind as she walked towards the Faculty of Economics and Business, a building of faded brown brick on the corner of City Road. Once inside, the first thing she noticed was a large poster, in bright orange, advocating Marxism. Much less noticeable were the directions for the new students: *Orientation address in auditorium downstairs.*

Jodi descended the dappled grey stairs. She paused when she reached the lower level. She spotted another inconspicuous poster and turned in the direction of its arrow.

The auditorium looked quite full. Jodi noticed some free seats towards the front. She had only just sat down when the address began.

'Good morning all! I'm Professor Phelps, the dean of the Faculty of Economics and Business.' The man who spoke into the microphone looked extraordinarily young for his exalted position. His face was classically handsome with a strong sculpted jaw. His hair, dark, thick and wavy, had not a strand of grey.

The girl sitting next to Jodi leaned over to whisper, 'Isn't he drop-dead gorgeous?'

Jodi nodded without taking her eyes off him.

'On behalf of all my colleagues, I have great pleasure in welcoming you as a student of the faculty. Founded sixty-four years ago, the faculty has an outstanding reputation for excellence in teaching, learning and research.'

'My name is Alison,' the girl whispered.

Jodi glanced her way. She saw a silver nose stud, purple hair and a friendly smile.

'I'm Jodi.'

Professor Phelps spoke in a clipped voice that suggested he had lived in the UK for some part of his life. 'The faculty is a part of an international learning community incorporating academics, students, corporate partners and governments. We equip our students educationally for a professionally rewarding and successful career in their chosen field, with many of our alumni holding senior positions in the business, professional and government communities within Australia and around the world.'

Jodi felt a wave of ambition as she listened to him speak. She was very determined that she would be one of those who went on to hold a senior position; someone Professor Phelps would not forget.

It transpired that Alison was also doing a double degree and was in many of Jodi's classes. She would flash her friendly smile and move places to sit next to Jodi. Once class was finished, they would stroll to whatever venue was next on the schedule or grab a Coke from one of the many dispensers around the campus.

Alison lived in student digs in Ultimo.

'You can stay over at my place any time you want,' she offered generously.

Shortly into the term, Jodi took her up on her offer.

'I'm going to a social event at the university tonight,' she told Shirley, a spare set of clothes packed in her satchel along with her books. 'I'm sleeping at Alison's.'

Jodi left the house feeling high at the thought of having a whole day away from Bob. She was still on a high that night as she knocked back countless shots of spirits that burned her throat and brought water to her eyes.

'You Spin Me Round' blared over the speakers. Students flocked to the dance floor. Rather than join them, Jodi went to the bar to get another drink. On the way back, a boy she recognised from Political Science asked her to dance.

'No, thanks. Two left feet.'

It wasn't a lie. She had no rhythm when it came to dancing.

'Hey, you need to slow down,' Alison advised when she returned, her drink already half gone. 'You won't last the distance if you drink too fast.'

Jodi, dismissing her advice, declared drunkenly, 'You know, Alison, I've just discovered that I *love* alcohol . . .'

'Well, that's becoming obvious.'

'And I *love* being at university . . .' Jodi continued.

'Anything you hate?' asked Alison wryly.

'Bob.'

'Who's Bob?'

'My stepfather.'

Jodi hadn't as much as mentioned Bob's name the entire six years she'd been in high school. Yet here she was, telling Alison, a girl she barely knew, that she hated him.

'He says he's in love with me,' Jodi heard herself confess. 'He wants to fuck me.'

She was appalled at what she was saying, but relieved too. Extraordinarily relieved.

Alison looked utterly shocked. '*No shit!*'

'It's true. Horribly true.'

'Does your mother know?'

'No.' Jodi shook her head so vehemently that she began to feel dizzy.

'Why haven't you told her?'

'Because he said he'd kill us both.'

Alison's horrified expression was blurring before Jodi's eyes. In fact, everything was blurring. And spinning. The words from the song reverberated in her head. She staggered on her feet.

'Jodi?' Alison's voice sounded far away. 'I think I need to get you home . . .'

Alison propelled her through the gyrating crowd. The exit was in sight when she slumped and fell to the floor.

A series of discomfiting sensations followed. Gentle slaps to her face. Hands under her armpits, dragging her along the floor. Horrible bile in her throat. Floating on the flat of her back. Pin-pricks on her arm. Then, at long last, she was left alone to sleep.

She woke with a sandpaper mouth and clanging head. Her eyes felt like they were glued shut. She forced them open. The first thing she saw was a floral curtain. It swept around her bed, ensconcing her in a cell of fabric. She was wearing a blue cotton gown, and her right hand was bandaged and attached to a drip.

I'm in hospital . . .

Shirley would be so disappointed with her, and rightly so. Moving out of home would be off the cards for years. Jodi squeezed her eyes shut, the consequences too much for her to face.

A few minutes later she heard the curtains being drawn back. Warily, not knowing what to expect, she opened her eyes again. A nurse, who looked not a lot older than her, stood by the bed.

'How are you feeling?'

'Awful.' Jodi propped herself up. 'And embarrassed.'

The nurse gave her a small smile as she checked the drip. 'You're not the first and you certainly won't be the last person we've had in here in that state. We monitor you while you sleep it off. That's all we can do.'

'What hospital is this?'

'Royal Prince Alfred.'

'Does my mother know I'm here?'

The nurse gave her a sharp look. 'Your friend told us that your parents were away on holiday.'

Jodi felt a wave of gratitude towards Alison.

'Sorry that she lied, but it's best my mother doesn't know, it really is.'

The nurse checked Jodi's pulse and pressed her fingers around her tummy. 'You seem to have survived okay. You'll have to wait until the consultant comes around before you can be discharged, though.'

'Okay.' Jodi was relieved but already thinking ahead. Her overnight bag, which contained a spare set of clothes, was at Alison's digs. 'Is there a phone I can use to call my friend?'

'If you're referring to the girl who was with you last night, she's in the visitors' room. She slept on one of the armchairs.'

'Yes – that's Alison.'

'I'll tell her to come in.'

The nurse slipped away through the crack in the floral curtains.

Jodi's overnight stay in Royal Prince Alfred Hospital was a life-changing event in more than one way. Firstly, it cemented her friendship with Alison, who had not only shielded Jodi from trouble at home but had waited faithfully in the visitors' room until the next morning.

'Thanks,' said Jodi when Alison, bleary-eyed and dishevelled, came to her bedside.

She shrugged. 'That's what friends are for.'

Jodi hung her head. 'You know what I said about Bob last night . . .'

'Yes . . .'

'Well, I don't like to talk about it – I only blurted it out because I was drunk . . .'

'No worries.' Alison squeezed her hand. 'I won't bring it up if you don't. Just one thing, though . . .'

'What?' Jodi looked up, apprehensive.

'My digs, as you know, are pretty basic, but you're welcome to stay on my spare mattress any time – seven nights a week if you want.'

Her offer turned out to be a lifeline.

When Jodi got home from the hospital, she found a letter waiting under her pillow.

I can't get you out of my head tonight – where you are, what you're doing, who you're talking to. You're too beautiful for those spotty boys – I'm the one who should teach you how to kiss, how to touch a man . . .

The letter became more and more explicit and, despite it being a torturous experience to read the full length of it, Jodi did so. Her survival instincts told her it was better to know what he was thinking than not.

I want to love you in your bed, with all your girly things around us – pink sheets, soft toys . . .

Jodi tore it up when she finished, the tiny pieces fluttering into her plastic rubbish bin. She was frightened. The letter had moved things onto another level. He had never been so graphic before, so sordid. It seemed as if he wouldn't be able to contain himself to words for much longer.

Jodi thanked God for Alison's spare mattress. From now on she would stay with her friend as much as possible. Until she was eighteen and got her own place.

Being rushed to hospital from a university social function had another consequence that Jodi didn't discover until she went to class on Monday morning. She sat down next to Alison and didn't notice the administration assistant handing a slip of paper to the lecturer.

He looked at the slip of paper and then at his students. It was too early in the year to know any of them by name.

'Can Jodi Tyler, if she's present, go straight to the dean's office, please?'

Jodi, who was busy taking her textbook from her satchel, didn't register that she was being called until Alison gave her a nudge.

'That's you, sleepyhead.'

'Oh.'

'He must have heard about Friday night,' Alison whispered.

'Oh no.' Jodi was suddenly very scared. 'Can you get expelled from university? Or does that only happen at school?'

Alison shrugged. 'I don't know.'

Her face white, Jodi walked out of the lecture theatre. She didn't know the location of the dean's office but guessed it was somewhere upstairs. She walked along the blue-carpeted corridors, which formed a square around the perimeter of the building, and checked each varnished door for his name. Eventually, after doing nearly a full circuit, she found it. The door was open.

'I'm Jodi Tyler,' she announced to the secretary who sat inside.

The secretary, casually dressed in jeans and a plunging top, looked at Jodi over the top of her glasses.

'Go along in. He's waiting for you.'

Jodi knocked carefully on the door behind the secretary's desk. She didn't want the rapping to sound too harsh or too meek. But maybe her fate was decided regardless.

'Come in,' she heard him say.

She took a deep breath and pushed the brass door handle downwards.

'Sit down,' she was instructed before she had the chance to get her bearings.

The dean sat behind a large desk that overflowed with books and paperwork. In fact, the whole room was overflowing, the shelving on the walls chock-a-block too.

The dean regarded her with a grave expression. His hands, clasped together, rested on the desk, and his grey eyes were narrowed. Jodi tried not to squirm.

'Have you recovered from Friday night?' he asked in his clipped upper-class voice.

She nodded, feeling like a schoolgirl.

'Do you have a problem with alcohol? Do you need help?'

'No.' Her voice sounded breathless. 'I don't drink much at all – I think that was the problem.'

He seemed unswayed by her denial. 'The university provides excellent counselling services.'

Jodi raised her chin. 'Thank you, but counselling isn't necessary. What happened on Friday night was something I have no intention of repeating.'

'The university expects its students to be responsible in relation to the consumption of alcohol, especially when on campus, as you were on Friday night.'

Jodi nodded, not wanting to repeat that it had been a one-off.

Professor Phelps unclasped his hands. He pushed back from his desk and, when he stood, Jodi took it as her cue to stand too.

'Your records say you're doing a double degree,' he commented, coming around the desk.

'Yes,' she confirmed.

'Commerce and Economics are a powerful combination in the employment market,' he said measuredly. 'But it's very elite – only those with the best marks get chosen.'

He opened the door for her to leave.

Jodi looked up at him and said, 'I can assure you, Professor, the next time you hear of me will be because I *have* got the best marks.'

He looked taken aback by her confidence. She was taken aback herself!

She turned to go.

'I'll watch out for those marks, Jodi Tyler,' she heard him say before his door clicked shut.

Chapter 12

Over the next few months Jodi went to extra lengths with her assignments and studied late every night. Her efforts paid off and she sailed through the exams at the end of the first semester. She daydreamed of Professor Phelps sitting in his cluttered office, smiling when he saw her results. She had something of a crush on the professor, the first crush she'd had since Nicholas Green.

Her eighteenth birthday fell in the holidays after the exams. Shirley insisted on throwing a party.

'Invite all your friends,' she said. 'Numbers don't matter!'

Jodi, knowing that soon she would be bursting her mother's bubble by moving out, allowed herself to be carried along with the party plans. She invited Alison and two other girls, Jane and Amanda, from university. She also invited a few people from the surf club, including Sue. Unfortunately, Samantha, her old friend from school, couldn't come because she worked in a bar on Saturday nights.

'I've invited your father,' Shirley announced a few days before the party.

'Are you sure that's a good idea?' Jodi asked, not wanting her mother to be on edge all night.

'We're both happy with other people now,' Shirley smiled, a little sadly. 'I think it's high time we buried the hatchet – and what better occasion than our daughter's eighteenth birthday?'

Jodi worried that the mix of guests would turn toxic. How would Alison, the only one who knew the truth, act around Bob? Did Grandma, and her aunts and uncles, still bear a grudge against her father and his second wife? And would Sue, who was healthy and fit, find her family overweight and too fond of their alcohol?

To hell with them if they don't get on, she thought as she dressed for the party.

For too long she had compartmentalised her life, keeping everybody and everything separate so that her awful secret wouldn't be found out. She was turning eighteen, becoming a young adult. It was time to stop worrying, to be bolder.

Jodi heard a car pull up outside, the first of the guests, and gave her reflection one last critical look. Her face, with its foundation, mascara and lipstick, looked like a grown-up version of what she was used to seeing. Her golden hair was twisted and teased up into a funky style. The black party dress hugged her figure. She was as ready as she'd ever be.

The first guest turned out to be her father, Tony, with his wife, Grace. They'd been married for eight years and had six-year-old Cory, but Jodi still thought of Grace as her dad's new wife. She saw her very rarely, usually only at Christmas. Tony was always on his own when he took Jodi out for a pizza or a movie over the school holidays. After a few hours he'd drop her home, his fathering complete for another few months.

Tonight Grace looked very glamorous with a pashmina around her shoulders and teeteringly high shoes. Shirley, who was wearing a new dress and had her hair styled for the occasion, seemed like a poor second cousin.

'Happy birthday, pumpkin.' Tony broke the awkwardness by giving Jodi a hug. 'There's five hundred dollars in there,' he whispered as he slipped a card into her hand. 'Spend it on something that's important to you, okay?'

'Thanks, Dad.'

Jodi noticed that he looked different.

He's dyed his hair, she realised, his previously grey temples now a glossy and fake-looking jet black. His clothes were different too: a slimline shirt and chinos. He didn't look like himself: he was trying too hard to look young.

Another awkward spell followed the hug. Then Bob trundled into the room, his face with its usual glisten of sweat.

'Evening all,' he boomed, jutting his hand out at Grace, then Tony.

Shirley, her voice wavering a little, asked, 'Champagne everyone?'

The other guests began to arrive. Grandma glared at Tony. Marlene tried to make conversation with Grace. Alison couldn't stop glancing at Bob.

Jodi moved outside with her fizzing glass of champagne. Shirley had laced fairy lights around the deck and rented two long rectangular tables, one for the alcohol and the other for food. Jodi sipped the champagne slowly, very wary of alcohol since her overnight stay in hospital.

'Hello, birthday girl.' It was Sue. With her sandy hair and

freckles, she could almost pass for one of Jodi's university friends.

'Hi, Sue.' Jodi kissed her cheek affectionately.

'Having a good time?'

Jodi's eyes rested on Grandma, who was sitting with her walking stick poised between her legs and didn't look very happy at all. Right behind her was Bob, guzzling a bottle of beer.

'Trying to,' she replied with a little more honesty than usual. 'Just worried about my Grandma whacking my dad with her stick, and my stepfather falling down drunk . . .'

Sue laughed. 'That's what parties are all about!'

Jodi laughed too. 'I'm glad you could come tonight.'

She knew it wasn't easy for Sue to get away: she had twin boys in their terrible twos and her husband was hopeless at settling them down for the night.

Jodi liked and admired her coach. Sue had a warm heart and really cared about the kids in the club. She was also a superb athlete in her own right.

'Those were good times you did earlier today,' Sue said in reference to their training session that morning.

'Need to do better if I'm to have a chance next January,' Jodi replied with a grimace.

Sue smiled. 'There's plenty of time yet.'

The Ironwoman Series was still six months away. Jodi did the heavy training at weekends, but managed to get a run or a swim in on most weekdays too. She was fitter and stronger than ever, and some days she dared to hope that she would be a real contender for the title.

The sound of breaking glass caused them both to look around.

'Clumsy oaf, I am.' Bob grinned as he picked up the shattered glass from the floor.

Jodi's mouth closed into a tight line.

Sue said nothing. She'd seen the stepfather, Bob, at some of the more important events over the years and couldn't help but notice how Jodi, even when she was high on the euphoria of a win, always covered herself up before going near him.

Sue had given Jodi as much opportunity as possible to confide in her. Yet, even though the girl had opened up somewhat since starting university, she still held her cards close to her chest. All Sue could do was to continue coaching and supporting her, and hope that whatever was going on in Jodi's home would sort itself out.

Tony and Grace, at a loose end, came over. Jodi made the appropriate introductions.

'This is Sue, my coach. Sue, this is my dad, Tony . . . and Grace.'

Grace looked piqued at not being introduced as Tony's wife.

'We'd like to enrol our little boy in the local Nippers club,' she said in her sugary voice. 'What kind of activities do you do with them at that age, Sue?'

Seeing that she wasn't needed to keep the conversation afloat, Jodi excused herself. She went over to check on her college friends.

'Who's the bloke in the blue T-shirt?' Amanda asked, looking in the direction of the crowd from the surf club.

'That's Nicholas,' Jodi replied nonchalantly, 'the star of the club. He got to the semifinals of the Australian Surf Lifesaving Championships last year.'

'Handsome *and* talented,' Amanda commented in an approving tone. 'Lucky you – training and getting sweaty alongside a hunk like him!'

Nicholas had lots of girls interested in him, but Jodi was no longer one of them. In fact, all of the boys at the club and at university seemed immature and unworldly when compared to Professor Phelps.

'Do you want me to introduce you to him?'

'No.' Amanda shook her head confidently. 'I reckon I can get him over here without your help.'

Sure enough, about ten minutes later, Nicholas came over and began to chat to Amanda. Jane went off to the bathroom, and Jodi had the chance to catch up with Alison.

'Well, what do you think of my oddball family?' she asked.

'Your grandma asked me about my nose ring – does it hurt when I blow my nose? – your mum keeps bringing me around little plates of food – I must look as if I'm starving . . .'

Jodi laughed and then quickly became serious.

'Bob's really pissed,' she whispered.

'Are you worried?'

At that moment Jodi saw that Samantha, her old friend from school, had turned up after all. She gave her a welcoming hug and introduced her around. She didn't get to answer Alison's question.

Tony and Grace were the first to leave. They kissed Jodi's cheek and promised to see her soon, even though they all knew it would be several months at least before any contact was made. The irony was that they only lived a half-hour's drive away.

Sue was next to leave. 'It was a lovely party,' she said.

Jodi smiled. It had gone better than she had expected: there had been no family brawl and Bob, somehow, was still standing up.

'I've hardly seen you all night,' Grandma complained as she shuffled to the door, leaning her weight heavily on Auntie Marlene's arm.

'I had to mingle.' Jodi kissed her soft wrinkly cheek.

Grandma eyed Jodi up and down. 'It's a lovely dress, but it doesn't leave much to the imagination.'

'She used to say the same to me,' Shirley laughed when her mother had gone, 'even when the dress was well below my knees.'

Amanda left with Nicholas, the two of them arm in arm. Jodi phoned a taxi for Jane and Alison who were heading back to the city.

'Do you want to come with us?' asked Alison.

Jodi remembered their unfinished conversation from earlier. She would have loved a carefree night on Alison's spare mattress. She looked around at the empty glasses, crumpled tins and dirty plates that seemed to have been left in every nook and cranny of the house.

She sighed. 'I'd better stay and help Mum clean up.'

'Happy?' Shirley asked as they started the big tidy-up.

'Yeah – thanks for organising it.'

Jodi collected the crockery and scraped it clean. Shirley immersed the dishes into sudsy water and began to wash up. Bob sat outside, smoking a cigar, oblivious to the work going on around him.

'I can't believe you're eighteen,' Shirley sighed when Jodi picked up a tea towel to dry. 'Seems like only yesterday I took you home from the hospital, a little pink bundle in my arms.'

'Well, I'm all grown up now,' Jodi replied pointedly. Then, before she lost her nerve, she added, 'I want to move out, Mum.'

'What's the big rush?' Shirley asked in a resigned tone.

'The commute is almost two hours a day.'

'How much will the rent cost?'

'About a hundred a week, but I've already applied for part-time work at the college library.'

She also had the five hundred dollars from her dad: enough for a bond.

Shirley's fingers squeaked as they rubbed the inside of a dirty glass. She said nothing for a while.

'I suppose you'll bring truckloads of laundry home at the weekends.'

Jodi went to sleep with a smile on her face. Her party had gone well, all things considered, and she finally had her mother's approval to move out. Her life was shifting to a new phase, one where she could relax and not have the constant worry of Bob.

She woke after a short while, her mouth dry. She wet her lips, swallowed, and tried to go back to sleep. It was no use. She swung her legs out of bed and found her way through the dark to the kitchen.

She turned the tap, filled a glass with water and gulped it back. It was deliciously cold, an instant balm to her mouth. She rinsed the glass and turned it upside down on the draining board. She was about to turn around to go back to bed when a hand, smelling of cigar smoke and spilt brandy, pressed over her mouth: Bob.

She tried to shrug him off. But she was no match for his bulk, his strength. He pulled her left arm high behind her back, the shoot of pain bringing an involuntary cry to her throat. His hand clamped harder against her lips, muting her cry. She tasted blood, its sweetness contrasting with the stale skin of his hand.

'Lovely eighteen,' he breathed in her ear. 'At long, long last.'

She realised that this was what he had been building towards, all the letters over all the years, culminating to this point, her 'coming of age'. He began to drag and pull her across the kitchen, in the direction of the back door. She could see now, as though a light had been switched on in the darkness, how deranged he was, how mad, and she was terrified because she knew what would happen if he managed to get her outside, away from her mother's earshot. She grabbed at the counter top with her right hand, her fingers clinging to the edge, her nails bending back with the pressure. Her eyes focused frantically on the knife block, almost within reach. She lurched forward, desperation making her momentarily stronger than him. Her hand made contact with one of the knives and lifted it out in a clean sweep. The tip of the blade glinted as it sliced through the dark. Bob didn't see it coming.

'Arghhhh! You bitch!'

Warm liquid spurted her face and hair: blood. She screamed and tried to wipe it away.

'You *fucking bitch.*'

He let go of her and she stumbled backwards. In the shadows she saw him pull the knife from his neck. For a moment she thought he was going to come after her with it. But he fell to his knees and it clattered to the floor.

The room was suddenly lit up. Shirley, her face shocked and grey, surveyed the scene before her: her daughter, wearing a cloak of blood; her husband, bent over on his knees, his mouth gurgling.

'Jesus Christ!' Her voice was so weak it could hardly be heard over Bob's gurgling. 'What have you done, Jodi?'

'I'm sorry, Mum . . . I'm sorry . . .'

Bob fell forward, his head hitting the floor with a thud.

Shirley's knees buckled. She held on tightly to the doorframe, the only thing keeping her upright.

'He's dying,' she whispered. 'You've killed him.'

Chapter 13

Her words jolted Jodi into action.

'Mum, hold him while I get something to stop the bleeding!'

Shirley came forward in a trance. She knelt down beside her second husband, the one with whom she'd thought she'd struck gold.

Jodi knotted two tea towels together and knelt alongside her mother.

'Let's roll him over . . .'

His body was a dead weight as the life drained out of him. He landed on his back, his eyes glassy.

'Now lift his head so I can tie this around the wound . . .'

Shirley wordlessly did as her daughter instructed.

'You stay with him.' Jodi got to her feet. 'I'll call an ambulance . . .'

She went out to the hall to make the phone call. She kept it short: her stepfather was dying; they needed to come quickly.

She called Grandma and told her she needed to come too. Then she broke down, loud gasping cries racking her body, streams of tears diluting Bob's blood, still on her face.

He was dead by the time she came back into the kitchen.

'I'm sorry, Mum . . .'

Shirley didn't respond. Tears slithered down her face as she held him.

'Mum . . .'

Jodi held her mother's shoulders and looked into her vacant eyes.

'I'm sorry, Mum . . . he was going to rape me . . .'

Shirley looked right through her.

The police arrived. Two cars, sirens flashing silently, parked outside the house. Blue-shirted officers swarmed the small kitchen.

Shirley stood shivering in her frayed baby-blue nightgown.

'I think we'll send your mum into hospital with the paramedics,' said the sergeant in charge. 'She needs to be treated for shock.'

He sounded so matter-of-fact, as if it was all normal. Then again, he had probably seen plenty of dead bodies and shocked people in his time.

Grandma arrived, her face drawn and her hand quivering on her stick. There was no sign of Auntie Marlene; Grandma must have paid for a taxi.

She blessed herself at the sight of Bob's body. Then she hobbled in the direction of Jodi and the sergeant.

'Don't say anything to him,' she commanded, lifting her stick off the ground to point at the policeman. 'Don't say a *word* until I get you a lawyer.'

'Do you know someone?' the sergeant asked.

'No,' Grandma snapped. 'But I'll ring around. And I'll get the best there is!'

She spoke with a lot of authority for a woman who knew precious little about criminal lawyers.

'We need to take your granddaughter to the station. Can you bring along a change of clothes for her?'

'I'll see to Shirley first.' Grandma began to step away but she turned back with one last warning. 'Remember, Jodi, keep your mouth shut.'

At the station, Jodi was vaguely aware of being fingerprinted and photographed. They took her bloodstained pyjamas and sealed them in a plastic bag. She showered Bob's blood from her skin and hair. Someone gave her a cup of tea loaded with sugar. Then she was told that her lawyer was on the phone.

'Jodi. I'm Prue Ledger.'

The woman had a strong, confident voice. She didn't sound at all daunted by the circumstances of her newest client.

'Have you said anything to them?' she asked.

'No.'

'Good. I'll see you in court tomorrow.'

'What for?'

'Your grandmother has requested that I make an application for bail.'

'Does that mean I can go home afterwards?' Jodi asked hopefully.

'Good God, no!' the lawyer exclaimed. 'I'm afraid no magistrate in the country would grant bail the morning after a death like this. No, tomorrow is just the local court down in Manly. A formality, really, until we get a bail hearing in the Supreme Court.'

Jodi swallowed nervously, too scared to ask how long it would take to get to the Supreme Court and what would happen her until then.

She was taken to a cell and told to get some sleep. She lay down on the thin mattress and closed her eyes. Her mind was spinning, so much so that when she opened her eyes the room seemed to be spinning too. Eyes open or closed, she couldn't stop the rotating images. Some of them were insignificant, like her father's newly dyed hair and the smile on Samantha's face as she made her surprise appearance at the party. Others were perhaps a sign of what was to come: Bob knocking the glass; Grandma commenting that her dress 'left little to the imagination'.

The most bittersweet was the chat with Shirley following the party. She'd finally been given her mother's blessing to leave home. Too late, though. Too late.

What if they lock me up for the rest of my life? What if I never run on the beach again, or finish my degree? What about Mum and Grandma? I can't end up in prison – my life would be as good as over.

There was nobody to hold her, to listen, to say it would be all right. She had to make do with wrapping her arms around herself and whispering her fears into the listening dark.

A police van transported Jodi to Manly Court the next morning. Initially she was taken to the cells but a short while later they moved her to an interview room. They sat her down in front of a window with toughened glass. A woman entered the room on the other side. She wore a short black skirt and fashionable high-heeled shoes. Once the woman was seated, and they were eye to eye, Jodi critically assessed the face of her lawyer.

Prue Ledger's eyes were sharp and knowing, set deep into her angular face. Her short gelled hair had edges and angles that suited those on her face. She looked streetwise and chic all at once.

'Did you sleep?' she asked.

'No.'

Prue Ledger stared hard as she, in return, assessed her new client. She looked past the bleary eyes and dishevelled hair. She saw a pretty girl with golden skin and hair, a beach girl who didn't belong in this court or this terrible situation.

'Your grandmother mentioned something about a birthday party last night,' she said in opening.

'My eighteenth,' Jodi replied in a voice that had been cried into hoarseness.

'She said that most of the guests left around midnight,' Prue continued. 'What happened after that?'

'I helped Mum clean up. Then I went to bed. I woke up about an hour later, thirsty. I went to the kitchen to get a glass of water. I was just about to go back to bed when Bob grabbed me from behind. I didn't set out to kill him . . .'

Prue looked at her intently. 'Did you have a sexual relationship with Bob?'

'No!' Jodi shuddered. 'He never touched me, other than once when I was twelve. But he used to mess with my head. He used to send me letters . . .'

'What kind of letters?'

'Love letters. He was in love with me, or so he said.'

'How did he give you these letters?'

'He left them under my pillow.'

Prue's mouth, with its plum-coloured lipstick, tightened in a sceptical line. 'Your mother never came across them?'

'Mum works,' Jodi told her. 'She doesn't have time to go

around cleaning up after me. I was responsible for keeping my room tidy from a young age.'

Prue nodded and her mouth relaxed. She had teenage children and tried to run her household along the same lines.

'Bob only left the letters once every few months,' Jodi went on. 'So it was even more unlikely that my mother would find them. I never knew when there'd be one waiting. I was on tenterhooks all the time . . .'

'Where are the letters? Did you keep them?'

'I tore them up. I couldn't risk my mother finding them. He said that he'd kill us . . .' Jodi bit her lip to contain an involuntary sob. 'But now all I have is my word – I've no letters to prove anything. I'm really in trouble, aren't I?'

'Yes you are.' Prue's tone contained neither sympathy nor softness. She was tough and if Jodi Tyler was going to survive this ordeal, then she needed to be tough too. 'But it's not hopeless, Jodi. I need you to stay strong.'

Through the glass she saw the young girl rally. Jodi wiped her tears away with her hands. Her shoulders squared. Her chin rose.

'Will I need to speak at the court?' she asked.

'No. You're not to say anything to anyone except me. Understood?'

'Yes.'

As Prue predicted, the bail application was turned down.

'This is a very serious and violent offence,' the magistrate declared, directing his words to Jodi. His face was grave. 'Based on the police report and the presence of a weapon, it is a strong case for the prosecution. Bail is refused.'

Grandma and Auntie Marlene were in the courtroom, both dressed in their Sunday best.

Is Mum still at hospital? Or is it that she can't bear to look at me?

Jodi asked the question with her eyes, but Grandma and Marlene stared blankly back at her, unable to interpret.

Jodi was led out of the courtroom. At the doorway, she looked back over her shoulder. Marlene was crying, Grandma comforting her.

'I'll start work on the Supreme Court application,' said Prue when they were back in the interview room.

'How long will it take?'

'At least ten days.'

A silence followed, underscored by Jodi's dread and Prue's empathy.

Then Prue answered the question that Jodi was too scared to ask. 'They'll take you to the prison in Silverwater. Initially, you'll be put in a safe cell. If you're very lucky, they'll leave you there, away from the main population, until the application is heard . . .'

Going to prison was simply unthinkable and Jodi shut off from the process as much as possible. She was given a number and a green tracksuit to wear. She half listened as a faceless woman reeled off the rules and regulations. En route to her cell, she was dimly aware of the bare floors, walls and faces. Rough voices, sounding more like those of men than women, broke through her daze.

'Got any cigarettes, darlin'?'

'Don't look so scared, pretty thing.'

Jodi's cell was square and painted in drab grey. Her bed constituted a mattress on a raised cement block with rounded edges. The wash basin was made of stainless steel, and the perspex door had a surveillance camera perched overhead. Looking around, Jodi understood what Prue had meant by the term *safe cell*: it was a place where they put people who were at risk of killing themselves.

A day passed. A day where she wasn't tired enough to sleep. A day with too much time to think.

'Can I get a book to read?' she asked the officer who delivered her meals.

'No. Not allowed.'

'Why?'

'Because you might self-harm.'

'What harm could I do with a book?'

'You'd be surprised.'

'What am I supposed to do in here? I'm going crazy.'

'You can watch TV.'

The TV was outside the door and could only be watched through the perspex. The screen was fuzzy, the volume blaring, the channel unalterable.

Prue was her one and only visitor. She stalked into the inter-view room in a short skirt, a folder tucked under her arm. In her abrupt manner, she asked how Jodi had slept. She made a brief complaint about having been kept waiting at security. Then she talked about the bail application.

'Your grandmother has put her house up as security. I received the deeds yesterday and filed them with the court.'

Tears pricked Jodi's eyes at the mention of her grandmother. She longed to be with her family, to feel their touch, to hear their voices, to witness their everyday habits, like her mother putting on her lipstick and Grandma shuffling after her walk-ing stick.

'Will Mum be at the hearing?'

'I don't think so,' Prue replied. 'She's not doing too well, your mother. She's still very shocked.'

'Does she hate me?'

'I don't know how she feels.' Prue was blunt as ever. 'It's you I'm concerned with, not her.'

Jodi would have understood if her mother hated her. She'd killed her husband. *Killed him!* It was there in her head, too terrible to think about, her thoughts darting around it, unable to dwell on it, unable to analyse the magnitude, the utter awfulness, of what she'd done.

Unlike the last hearing, Prue was more confident that bail would be granted this time around.

'The judge is very understanding. The Crown, although they're opposing, are sympathetic to the fact that you're just eighteen years of age. I think we have a reasonable chance; after all, you are not likely to reoffend or flee the jurisdiction. Hopefully the hearing will be more about agreeing on the conditions than anything else.'

Jodi whiled the days away, lying on her mattress, her mind flitting from one thing to another. She changed channels in her head in a way that she couldn't with the TV: Shirley, Tony, the surf club, the classes she was missing at university, Grandma, Bob, Shirley . . .

Mealtimes were like an interval from her thoughts. The food was mush, but the officer was a voice, a face.

'Two of the psych nurses are out sick,' he told her a few days in. 'There's nobody available to assess your mental state, so you'll be staying in this cell until your hearing. Consider yourself lucky.'

'But I'm not allowed to read or write,' Jodi pointed out with a great deal of frustration, 'and the noise from the TV is doing my head in.'

'At least you're safe.' He jerked his head backwards, in the direction of the main cells. 'A nice girl like you wouldn't want to be in the midst of that lot.'

Finally, the day of the Supreme Court hearing dawned. Jodi got dressed in the green tracksuit and was transported in a security van to the court. She was taken to the cells, then to an interview room for a brief chat with Prue, back to the cells, and finally to the courtroom. It was a small ordinary room in the bowels of the building, decorated with light green carpet and wood-panelled walls. The ceiling, set low, had dozens of inset lights that dazzled Jodi's eyes after the dimness of the cells.

Grandma and Marlene were there, sitting along the back wall, a sign overhead saying that the area was reserved for family members. Her dad was there too. He looked as if he had a stomach bug, his face sickly, his lips puckered.

Grandma smiled encouragement at Jodi. Her love, hard and unconditional, transcended the short distance between them and instantly boosted Jodi's spirits.

I'm going home today. I am. I am.

Grandma was the first and only witness to be called to the stand. She leaned heavily on her walking stick but, once in position, looked as formidable as ever. She spoke in her most austere tone, one that could still make Jodi quake in her boots.

'My granddaughter won't run away, I can assure you that,' she stated, staring daggers at the judge. 'She's a good, obedient girl, very studious and hardworking. She'll live with me until this is all sorted out. Her poor mother is in no condition to care for her.'

Grandma stepped down and the hearing became focused on the conditions of bail. Prue leaned forward in her seat as she spoke to the judge.

'Your honour, my client is a student and will need some

leniency in order to attend her classes. She is no threat at all to the community . . .'

The Crown, a woman with short dark hair who didn't look unlike Prue, didn't quite agree.

'Your honour, the Crown suggests that exposure to the community should be limited as this is an extremely violent crime. We strongly believe that a nightly curfew is appropriate in this case . . .'

For Jodi, it was like watching a play in which she was the central character, but she was mute and couldn't speak for herself.

The judge cleared his throat, anticipation falling across the courtroom at the sound. 'Bail is granted on the following conditions: daily reporting at Dee Why Police Station, and a 7 pm to 7 am curfew.'

Prue stayed poker-faced. Grandma and Marlene smiled shakily. Tony looked ready to keel over.

Jodi was told that she needed to return to the prison until the paperwork for the bail was complete. Prue had already warned her that this would be the case. She accepted it. She could cope with a few more hours.

After dinner, when all the paperwork was signed, Jodi was released from the prison. Marlene and Grandma came to fetch her. They took turns to hug her and check her over. Jodi hugged them back, vowing never to take their familiarity for granted again.

Marlene drove while Grandma ran through the accommodation arrangements.

'You're coming to stay with me, Jodi,' she stated, 'and Shirley is staying with Marlene.'

Jodi realised for the first time that the house in Lewis Street was a crime scene, no longer a home.

Shirley was waiting at Grandma's house. She stood up from her seat as they walked in. She looked like a skeleton of her old self, her cheekbones protruding, her eyes hollowed out.

'I'm sorry, Mum,' Jodi cried, afraid to step closer, afraid of what reception she would get.

Shirley shook her head, tears rolling down her face. 'I'm the one who should be sorry. Sorry that I wasn't strong enough to go to the court today, that I was blind to what was going on in my own house, that I didn't kill the bastard myself.'

They moved towards each other. Their embrace held nothing back: shock, sorrow and disillusionment melding them together. They cried in each other's arms until Grandma, thinking that they had cried enough, shepherded them into the kitchen for tea and sandwiches.

After the tea, Grandma suggested that Shirley and Jodi both get some rest. Shirley left with Marlene and Jodi went to Grandma's spare room. She crawled, exhausted, into the bed. The cotton sheets felt soft under her skin. The sheets in the prison were made of some special tear resistant fabric and had a plastic feel to them. These sheets were so much nicer. She nestled into them. But couldn't sleep.

She'd thought she was coming home to the familiar, but now she was beginning to realise that everything was irrevocably changed. Grandma's house was now her home. She liked its clutter and cosiness, but this bed wasn't where she was used to sleeping. Tomorrow she would have to report at the local police station, and she would not be permitted to leave the house between the hours of 7 pm and 7 am. The accommodation arrangements, daily reporting and curfew would be her new life until the trial, a year or so away. Then there would be more change, change she couldn't even begin to contemplate right now.

The door to the bedroom opened and Grandma shuffled in. The old woman lowered herself awkwardly to sit on the side of the bed and her hand reached out to stroke Jodi's eyelids shut.

'Sleep now, child. Everything is going to be okay.'

Jodi disagreed on two counts: she wasn't a child and she couldn't see how everything would be okay. But still the soft rhythmic strokes of Grandma's hand soothed her into the welcome respite of sleep.

Chapter 14

Jodi went back to university towards the end of September. Whilst Bob's death had been headlined on TV and radio, her name had been withheld so that potential jurors wouldn't be prejudiced. As result, the faculty and its students were utterly unaware that one of their own had been charged with murder. Obviously Alison knew, but she'd kept the shocking truth to herself. Jodi was thankful for her loyalty, and also thankful that nobody had spotted the small newspaper excerpts after the local and Supreme Court bail hearings and equated that Jodi Tyler with the girl in their class.

Once she was back, Jodi attended her lectures religiously, taking copious notes because her memory was shot to bits. She struggled with the assignments, finding it difficult to plan any task that lasted longer than a few minutes. Her concentration wasn't helped by the strain of having to report to the police station every day and the preparations for the trial.

'We're running two defences,' Prue informed her. 'Self-defence and diminished responsibility.'

'What's the difference?'

'Self-defence is a full defence. If you're found not guilty, then you walk out of the courtroom free. Diminished responsibility is only a partial defence. It would get the charge down from murder to manslaughter. It's our back-up if the jury don't buy self-defence.'

The threat of losing the trial, of prison, was never far away. It underscored every discussion with Prue.

'Is there a significant chance that self-defence *won't* be successful?' Jodi asked guardedly.

Prue was matter-of-fact. 'There's a possibility that the jury will find the level of violence you used wasn't reasonable for the circumstances.'

'Twelve people hearing all the gory details,' murmured Jodi. 'How humiliating!'

Prue's voice softened a little. 'The jury will be made up of people just like you. They will put themselves in your shoes, Jodi. They'll be sympathetic.'

The weeks slipped by until it was time for the end-of-year examinations. Jodi spent every waking hour studying. But to no avail. Her mind went completely blank during the first exam, Econometrics, a subject she had once found easy. She stared at the blackboard that had *Exam in Progress* written on it, at the windows with their grey roller blinds, and at the exam supervisors who surveyed the students from the top of the room. Inspiration didn't come.

The Accounting exam the next day was a little better. Until she realised, with a few minutes to spare at the end, that she had misread one of the questions. Frantically, she began to rewrite her answer, her haste making her handwriting no better than a scribble. But time was called and she was forced to put down her pen.

'I'm going to fail my first year,' she wailed to Alison.

'Don't be ridiculous,' Alison chided.

But five weeks later Jodi's dire prediction came true. She had indeed failed her end-of-year exams.

'What will I do?' she asked Alison on the phone.

'Resit the papers.'

'But I'm not sure I'd do any better if they did allow me to repeat. I seem to have lost my ability to concentrate.'

Alison took a moment to consider the dilemma.

'Go and see the dean,' she suggested eventually. 'Explain what happened – put yourself at his mercy. He'd have to be a hard ass not to give you a break.'

Much as she hated the idea, Jodi realised that she had no option but to tell the dean the truth. She phoned the university the next day.

'The dean is only just back from the UK. He's completely booked out this week.'

'Please,' Jodi begged the secretary, 'fit me in somewhere.'

The secretary sighed and Jodi heard the sound of a page flicking over. 'I could slot you in at five-thirty on Tuesday – what shall I say it's about?'

'I'd like to ask him for special consideration in relation to my exam results.'

'There's a form you can fill in for that,' the secretary stated, her tone indicating that she believed the dean's limited time would be better spent elsewhere.

Jodi had done her homework. 'I know. I've filled in the form. I just want the chance to discuss the – *unusual* – circumstances with him in person.'

The secretary begrudgingly agreed to book the appointment and hung up.

Tuesday was the hottest day of the summer so far. The temperature had peaked and was starting to edge its way back down when Jodi caught the bus to the city. Traffic was heavy right from the start and the bus came to a standstill at Spit Bridge. Too many cars filled with beach-goers were heading home at the one time. The bus took fifteen minutes to get past the bottleneck, and the rest of the journey was slow and jerky.

I'm going to be late, Jodi thought in despair.

The bus finally reached the city centre and Jodi raced up to Castlereagh Street to catch the 422. Sweat glistened on her face and trickled between her breasts. The bus took ages to come. It seemed that everything was working against her today.

It was after 6 pm when she reached the dean's office. The outer and inner doors were ajar. The secretary had left for the day.

'In here,' the dean called from his office.

In contrast to the bright sunshine outside, it was dark and gloomy in Professor Phelps' office. He sat behind his desk, his shirt sleeves rolled up and his tie loose around his neck.

She wetted her dry lips. 'I'm so sorry I'm late, Professor. The traffic was terrible.'

'That's okay.' He didn't seem to be annoyed by her tardiness. He seemed to be relaxed. Reachable.

'Thank you for seeing me,' she said and sat down on one of the seats.

He shrugged disarmingly. 'My door is always open for the students of the faculty.'

Unsettled, Jodi dropped her eyes. She noticed the fine dark hairs on his bare forearms. The slender fingers that curled around his pen. Her old crush returned. The full, unexpected force of it burned her cheeks.

'Would you like a drink?'

He had mistaken the reason for her heightened colour.

'Yes, please. Water would be great.'

He rose from his seat. His waist was narrow, his dark trousers belted with thin leather and a flat silver buckle. His body was lean. No fat. Unlike Bob.

He strode into the outer office. A few moments later he returned with two cans of Coke.

'Sorry. This is all that's left in the fridge. No clean glasses either.'

The icy-cold Coke felt good in Jodi's dry mouth.

'Well,' he said when he was seated back behind his desk, 'I presume you want to discuss your exam results.'

'Yes, Professor,' Jodi stammered. She paused to control the wobble in her voice. 'I was hoping that you would consider some special circumstances regarding my performance this year.'

He leaned forward, hands clasped, expression businesslike. 'I must say that I was very surprised to see you'd failed the annual examinations, particularly after the high marks you attained in the first semester. I would imagine that your six-week absence,' he looked down to check the notes in front of him, 'was not of any help.'

Jodi handed him an envelope. 'I hope this will help you understand . . .'

She'd written it down. It was all there: what had led up to the night of her eighteenth birthday; what had happened in the kitchen, in the court, in the prison; the bail, the curfew, and why she had found it so hard to concentrate on her studies.

She couldn't bear to look at him while he read the sordid truth about her life. Her eyes flickered around the room. She noticed an ice-pop wrapper strewn amongst rubbish in the overfull trash can, a reminder of summer in the dismal space that was his office. Over on the left a closet door was slightly ajar, giving a view of the spare shirt and tie hanging inside. Up on the beige-coloured walls, in the gaps between the cluttered bookshelves, there were various framed certificates, testament to the dean's academic achievements. The room seemed to be devoid of any personal photographs. Jodi would have been interested to see what his wife looked like.

'My goodness!' he exclaimed when he had finished reading.

It was such a British thing to say that Jodi nearly laughed. Nearly, but for the fact she was so close to crying.

'Was this in the newspapers? How did I miss it?'

'My name was withheld,' she explained.

Understanding dawned on his face. 'So there wouldn't be prejudice?'

He looked perplexed again. 'But why on earth didn't you come and tell me?'

Jodi, her face on fire, looked down at her hands. 'I didn't want anybody to know. I was ashamed . . . *embarrassed* . . .'

'My dear, embarrassed is the very last thing you should be.'

Jodi felt a surprising spurt of anger at him. 'How would you know? I don't want people to look at me and imagine what it was like –' She choked. She was in serious danger of crying, of humiliating herself even further.

'I'm sorry,' he said softly. 'I didn't mean to sound dismissive of your feelings.'

Jodi hung her head and tried to deny the tears that welled in her eyes. One or two escaped and crept stealthily down her face. It took her a few moments to find her composure.

'Professor,' she began, 'the problem is that even if you allow me to resit my exams I'm not sure that I can pass. I can't concentrate for more than a few minutes at a time, let alone complete a three-hour exam . . . I'm hoping there's some other way you can help me get into second year.'

'Let me think it over,' he replied.

'Thank you.'

As she stood up, she glanced at her watch: 6.40 pm.

'Oh no!' Her hand flew to her mouth. 'I forgot the time – my curfew – I'm going to be late.'

'I'll drive you home,' he said, his voice firm and allowing no room for argument. 'My car's right outside.'

Terrible thoughts ran through Jodi's head as they rushed outside to the professor's car. She'd unintentionally broken one of the conditions of her bail. Would she get caught out? Be sent back to prison? Would Grandma lose her house?

She felt sick at the thought of the possible consequences. She jumped into the car, buckled her belt and hardly spoke a word for the entire journey, other than to give the dean directions.

They pulled up outside Grandma's house as the clock on the dash turned over to 7.30 pm.

He touched her arm lightly. 'Don't worry. The police aren't here waiting. Nobody's going to know.'

She didn't tell him that her bail officer phoned the house on occasion to make sure that she was at home.

'I'll call you tomorrow to discuss your exams,' he said.

She nodded, thanked him, and hurried up the pathway to the house. Grandma had the door open before she got there.

'Where were you, child?' she asked, her voice sharp and anxious. 'Didn't you know the time?'

Jodi burst into tears. 'Sorry, Grandma. Did they phone?'

'No – lucky for you!'

'I'm so sorry. The bus was delayed getting into the city. I was so worried about being late for the professor that I forgot all about the curfew.'

Grandma ushered her inside the door. 'Well, you're home now and hopefully there's no harm done. I've saved your dinner for you.'

Jodi wasn't hungry but Grandma's fussing made her feel safe and reassured almost at once.

As promised, the professor phoned the following day. Grandma answered.

'Yes?' She listened. Then she handed Jodi the receiver. 'It's Professor Phelps.'

Jodi snatched the phone and gestured Grandma away. 'Hello, Professor.'

'Hello, Jodi.' His voice sent a shiver down her spine. 'I've given your situation much thought. It appears that the assignments you missed last August and September had a significant impact on your overall results. Hence, I've arranged a workshop for each assignment. The relevant lecturer will sit with you, one on one, and discuss the topic in question. At the end of the session he will ask you some basic verbal questions to confirm your understanding. On that basis, I will be satisfied to deem that you have passed your first year.'

Jodi breathed a sigh of relief. 'Thank you, Professor.'

'My faculty stands by its students. It's a matter I take great pride in.'

'Thank you,' she said again.

'When is your court hearing?' he asked after a brief pause.

'Sometime in June or July.'

'Goodness, these things take so long to proceed. Well, I can only assume that this coming academic year will also be very disruptive for you.'

'Yes.' Jodi bit her lip. 'My lawyer warned me the media will be all over the trial. Once it starts, my name will no longer be withheld.'

The dean was unfazed. 'Let's ensure we manage the situation better this time and make whatever arrangements necessary for you to pass your second year.'

Jodi attempted a joke. 'You never know, I may be studying long-distance from prison.'

'That's not even remotely funny,' he retorted.

Chapter 15

The clerk of the peace fixed the date for the trial: 15 July 1987. Once the date was set, time passed much like a ticking bomb.

'I'm organising for you to be assessed by a psychiatrist,' Prue announced one day on the phone. 'He's going to ask about your history – your childhood, your relationship with Bob, all the stuff you've told me already.'

Jodi had a number of discussions with the psychiatrist in his inner city rooms. He was kind and nonjudgemental. It was easy to talk to him.

Prue read his report and was pleased with it. She wrote to the prosecution to advise them that she would be relying on it in the defence. The prosecution wrote back and requested that Jodi talk to their psychiatrist.

'Not again!' Jodi protested to Prue.

'Look, I know how you feel. But it helps our case if you consent to talk to their guy.'

The prosecution's psychiatrist also had rooms in the inner city. The similarity ended there. He was a brittle man with an irritating cynical smile. Jodi found it much harder to open up to him.

Shirley put the house in Lewis Street up for sale and accepted the first offer that was made, not seeming to care that it was well below the market value.

'Are you going to buy somewhere new?' Jodi asked.

'I don't think we'll see much of the proceeds,' she replied. 'The legal fees are building up.'

'I'm sorry, Mum.'

'Don't be sorry, darl. That house brought me no happiness in the end. I'm glad to see it go. And Prue is worth every cent.'

Despite Shirley's assurances, Jodi felt enormously guilty. The guilt gnawed at her concentration, as did the worry about the trial. She began her second year at university much like she'd finished her first year: badly. The dean promised to organise more workshops and told her not to worry. But she did.

The week before the trial, Tony picked Jodi up and took her for a drive. He parked the car by Narrabeen Lake and cut the engine.

'Grace and I have talked . . .' he began. 'It's not fair on her or Cory to be caught up in this . . . they didn't ask for it . . .'

'Neither did I,' Jodi murmured.

'Of course . . . The thing is, we don't want Cory exposed in any way to the trial – he's only seven years old.'

'So what are you saying, Dad?'

'I'm saying that I think it's best I don't get involved – that I keep my distance – for Cory's sake. I'm sorry.'

Jodi had an epiphany as she sat in the silence that followed. Tony didn't have the strength of character to juggle her needs and Cory's; he was too weak, too shallow. He'd been struggling even before Bob's death. She should put him out of his misery, cut him loose.

'I understand, Dad. Can you drive me back now?'

He did, and their goodbye had an unmistakeable finality.

The day of the trial finally dawned. Jodi rose after a sleepless night. Apprehension rolled in her stomach, but she did feel a degree of relief that the waiting and dreading would soon come to an end. In three weeks, four at most, she would know what her future entailed. Twelve strangers would decide.

'The eyes of the jurors will be on you at all times,' Prue had warned. 'Twelve pairs of them, watching, *assessing*. You should glance over at them every so often, show them that you have nothing to hide – but don't stare. For the most part you should be looking at who is speaking, be it the judge or a witness or whoever.'

Prue had also given an outline of what to expect the first morning at court.

'The Crown prosecutor will present an indictment against you, to which you will reply "not guilty". The jury will be empanelled. Then the Crown prosecutor will make her opening statement.'

Jodi found it hard to believe that in less than two hours she would be pleading not guilty. She began to dress in the white cotton blouse and black trousers her mother had purchased for the occasion. She gathered her hair in a conservative knot and purposely refrained from putting on make-up or jewellery. Studying her reflection, she tried to see herself through the eyes of the jury.

Who is Jodi Tyler? A killer? Or a victim?

The mirror showed a young girl, defenceless and scared.

Grandma, Shirley and Jodi all piled into Marlene's station

wagon. They set off to the city, a dead silence in the car. What was there to say? Knuckles white, Marlene gripped the steering wheel; she wasn't used to rush-hour traffic. She scratched the wing of the car as she parked in the high-rise car park across from the barrister's chambers. Grandma offered to pay for the repairs.

Jeremy Horton, the barrister, and Prue were waiting in the chambers. Jodi had met Jeremy a number of times. He was a nice man, albeit a little abrupt. Today he wore a black gown and an imposing grey wig. He looked like someone from another era, more like a foe than a friend. Jodi was reassured to see that Prue wasn't wearing a wig and looked the same as ever in her customary short skirt and high heels.

Jodi walked alongside Prue in the short stroll to the court, unaware of how naive she looked next to the streetwise lawyer. Jeremy and his offsider walked immediately behind them. Grandma, Shirley and Marlene, three abreast, were next in the procession. Prue's assistant was last, arms full of files, struggling to keep up.

There was a crowd gathered on the steps of the court, many of them holding microphones or TV cameras.

Prue's plum lips pursed together. 'It's like a circus. Hold your head high, Jodi. Show them that you've got nothing to be ashamed of.'

Prue's fingers pressed into Jodi's arm as she steered a path through the rapid-fire questions. 'No comment,' was the only answer she gave.

Once inside the court, they went through the security gate and waited at the other side for Grandma, Shirley and Marlene. It didn't help Jodi to see that her family were shaken by the scale of the media attention. Just like her, they were clearly out of their depth. And the trial had not even begun!

In the courtroom Jodi was seated in the dock. She, along with everybody else, rose when the judge made his entrance. He sat down, his long face stern as his eyes swept across the courtroom. His gaze stopped at Jodi. It was all she could do not to squirm in her seat.

Grandma, Shirley and Marlene were seated at the rear and she had to turn her head to make eye contact with them. She turned once and caught sight of a familiar face in the back row. Was it the dean? No! He was a busy man, far too busy to have time to sit through the trial of an unfortunate student. She risked another glance. The man's lips moved in a slight curve. It was a smile of recognition, support and encouragement. It was him.

The judge began to address the jury panel. 'Ladies and gentlemen, I'm shortly going to ask the Crown prosecutor to briefly outline what this case is about and to give you a list of the names of the persons who are likely to be mentioned during the course of the trial or who may be called to give evidence. Please indicate to me if any of these people are known to you.' He paused and turned his head to emit a small cough. 'I have been informed by the parties that this trial is expected to last three to four weeks. If you think that you have a problem with sitting on the trial for that length of time, or if you have health or hearing issues, then please indicate them to me.'

About half of the panel asked to be excused at this point. Jodi watched them go, wondering if they would have been on her side. Jeremy and the Crown began to haggle over the remaining jurors. Prue had already explained that Jeremy would challenge any males of about Bob's age who might sympathise with him.

Finally, the jury box was complete, with seven females and five males. Three of them were of pensioner age, two looked like students, and the rest were aged somewhere in between. Jodi did as Prue directed and glanced their way every now and then. They all had the same reaction: they looked away.

The judge began to speak again, his tone grave. 'Ladies and gentlemen of the jury, I don't know whether any of you have ever sat on a jury before. Possibly some of you have. But in any event, it is appropriate at this point of time that I explain some things to you. I am the judge presiding over this trial. The barrister sitting closest to you at the bar table is the Crown prosecutor and she will be presenting evidence which she hopes will persuade you that the accused, who is sitting in the dock, has committed the offence for which she is accused. This is a criminal trial. It is alleged by the Crown that Miss Tyler murdered Mr Bob Jones, her stepfather . . .'

The jury sat straighter in their seats. Twelve pairs of curious, condemning eyes swung in Jodi's direction and crushed the little confidence she had left.

'Your role in these proceedings and my role are quite different,' the judge continued. 'I'm here to deal with the *legal* matters that occur during the course of the trial. However, you are the judges of the *facts* of the case. You are going to hear evidence from a number of witnesses about various factual matters over the next three weeks or so. When a person comes into the witness box, you are faced with the difficult task of making an assessment of that person and determining whether they are reliable, whether they are accurate, whether they are consistent, whether you think they are being truthful . . .'

Suddenly it became a massive burden to prove to these twelve strangers that Bob's death hadn't been intentional. The strain of the morning, of the whole year, began to take its toll. Jodi felt faint. Black spots dotted her vision. The judge droned on, telling the jurors not to discuss the case with husbands, wives, boyfriends or girlfriends. The spots before Jodi's eyes enlarged as the judge warned the jurors to be wary of the TV and newspaper reporters outside the building. Jodi willed Prue to look in her direction, to help her. But Prue was looking at the judge, just as everyone else was. From far away, Jodi heard him call a recess. That was the last she remembered.

Court was suspended for the rest of the day. Jodi was angry with herself. She shouldn't have fainted; everyone would be annoyed by the inconvenience: not a good start.

Grandma blamed lack of food and on the second morning she insisted that Jodi eat a big breakfast. Jodi did her best to force down the eggs and bacon, but it didn't make her feel any stronger.

'How is Jodi feeling?' asked the reporters outside the court.

'My client feels well today,' Prue answered abruptly.

Court began with the Crown making her opening address to the jurors.

'Members of the jury, just returning again to the charge . . .' She paused dramatically. '*The charge is one of murder.* The event took place on 8 July last year at 23 Lewis Street, Dee Why. I'd like to outline the sequence of events as they occurred, starting with Miss Tyler's eighteenth birthday party the night before . . .'

The jurors listened intently to the Crown. Jodi could see that they were in awe of the young woman wearing the old-fashioned wig. Once again she felt that the odds were overwhelmingly stacked against her. Only one thing kept her going: the dean was sitting at the back of the courtroom again. For some reason, that mattered more than anything.

*

'What's your full name?' asked the Crown.

'David Anthony Thompson,' replied the man in the witness box.

'And what is your occupation?'

'Detective Sergeant of Police in New South Wales.'

'Did you visit number 23 Lewis Street on 8 July 1986?'

'Yes, I did.'

'At what time?'

'I arrived at the house shortly after two-thirty in the morning.'

'Can you please describe to the court what you found on your arrival?'

'Bob Jones was dead on the kitchen floor with a stab wound on his neck. Miss Tyler was in her pyjamas, covered in blood. The weapon, a carving knife, was on the floor . . .'

'Can you please describe Miss Tyler's injuries?'

'Her lips were bleeding, she had bruising on her left arm, and some of her nails were broken.'

'What kind of mental state was she in?'

'She was emotional, but she was coherent and quite aware of what was going on . . .'

'Your full name, please.'

'Richard William Franklin.'

'And your profession.'

'Forensic psychiatrist – I was asked by the Crown to assess Miss Tyler.'

'For the benefit of the jury, can you please summarise the findings of your report?'

'I found Miss Tyler to be clear-headed and logical in all aspects of her life.'

'So, on the basis of your assessment, would you assume that at the time of the crime Miss Tyler was aware that her life was not at risk?'

'Your Honour, I object to this line of questioning.'

'I'll allow it, Mr Horton. Please answer the Crown's question, Dr Franklin.'

'Yes, I would say that Miss Tyler was aware that her life was not at risk.'

'And would you say that she was aware she was inflicting a potentially fatal wound?'

'Yes, I would say that Miss Tyler was aware that she was inflicting a potentially fatal wound.'

'Please state your full name.'

'Janine Jones.'

'And your occupation . . .'

'I'm on a disability pension.'

'And your relationship to the victim, Mr Jones.'

'His sister.'

'When did you last speak to your brother?'

'March 1986 on the phone.'

'Can you please tell the court what Mr Jones said during that particular telephone conversation?'

'Bob said that Jodi was a handful.'

'Was anything else said?'

'He said that she was very possessive of her mother – she wanted Shirley all to herself and became jealous whenever she showed any intimacy towards Bob. Well, she got what she wanted in the end, didn't she? Her mother all to herself and my poor brother in a grave –'

'Thank you, Miss Jones.'

*

The witnesses were questioned exhaustively, the process slowed further by the large number of objections made by both sides. Matters of admissibility were hotly debated and on a few occasions the jurors were asked to leave the room. The trial entered its third week. The jurors looked fed up and anxious to get back to their normal lives.

Once the first few days were behind her, Jodi became stronger and progressively more interested in the theatre that unfolded each day in the courtroom. She listened intently to the witnesses. She familiarised herself with all the evidence. She asked if she could read the court transcripts.

'Why?' Prue queried.

'Because the more I know, the more control I feel I have.'

'There's nothing in this process that you can control,' Prue replied plainly.

'I know that. But let me have the illusion.'

Jodi read the transcripts late into the night. She highlighted the parts she considered important. She kept a tally of what strengthened her case and what weakened it: neat bullet points listed on large sheets of paper stuck to her bedroom wall. Her court case: her project. It surrounded her. It consumed her. She allowed it to do so. She didn't know how else to get through it.

Grandma, Shirley and Marlene came to the court every day. The trips to and fro in the car were no longer silent. They talked about the weather, the family, what was on TV that night. They fussed. They bickered. Sometimes they even laughed.

When they got home from court, Grandma would make tea and they would sit around the table and analyse what had happened in the day. They would recap on the witnesses, the evidence, and surmise about various members of the jury. They sounded more like a group of lawyers than a family.

Sometimes Sue came to the court to show her support. She looked like a fish out of water with her tan and beachy clothes. The dean also made regular appearances. Jodi's heart always did a little skip when she saw him. It seemed a bit abnormal to still have a crush on him when she was going through something so awful. But what was normal any more?

'Please state your full name.'
　'Shirley Jane Tyler Jones.'
　'Please state your relationship to the accused.'
　'I'm her mother.'
　'And Bob Jones was your husband?'
　'Yes.'
　'Please tell the court what happened in the early hours of the morning in question.'
　'I was woken by a noise.'
　'What kind of noise?'
　'My husband shouting. My daughter screaming.'
　'What did you see when you went into the kitchen?'
　'My husband kneeling on the floor, blood everywhere . . .'
　'Did your daughter say anything to you?'
　'She kept on saying sorry . . . over and over . . .'

'Your full name, please.'
　'Alison Hobs.'
　'Your occupation?'
　'A student at the University of Sydney.'
　'How do you know the accused?'
　'Jodi is my friend.'
　'Did she ever talk to you about her stepfather, Bob Jones?'
　'Yes.'

'What did she say?'

'That he was in love with her. That he'd kill her if she told anyone.'

'Did she say anything specific on the night of the party?'

'She was worried about his drinking. I told her she could stay the night at my bedsit.'

'Did she often stay with you?'

'Yes, a few nights a week – as often as she could.'

'Why didn't she stay on that specific night?'

'She wanted to help her mother tidy up.'

'State your full name, please.'

'Jodi Ann Tyler.'

'And your occupation.'

'A student of Economics and Business.'

'Can you please describe to the court the events that occurred at 23 Lewis Street on the 7th and 8th July last year?'

'We had a party for my eighteenth birthday. The guests left around midnight. I helped my mother clean up, then we both went to bed. I woke an hour later, thirsty, and got up to get a drink. I was at the kitchen sink when my stepfather put his hand over my mouth. He started to pull me towards the back door . . .'

'What were you thinking at that time?'

'That he would rape me.'

'Can you explain to the court why you thought this?'

'He'd been sending me letters. They were very graphic.'

'You destroyed his letters. Can you please explain why?'

'I was afraid my mother would find them. He'd told me he'd kill us both if she ever found out . . .'

'So, when you were being dragged from the kitchen, you

believed that you were about to be raped and you also had a genuine fear that your stepfather might carry out his previous threat to kill you?'

'Yes.'

'Did you warn him before using the knife?'

'His hand was over my mouth. I couldn't speak.'

'Did you know in advance of stabbing him where the knife would penetrate?'

'No. I didn't have time to think that far ahead. I just grabbed the knife and used all my strength . . .'

'You told both Dr Franklin and Dr Barrett that you hated your stepfather. Are you sure you didn't wish him dead?'

'I only wished to be away from him. My mother had agreed earlier in the night that I could move out of home. I was happy with that. I didn't wish him dead.'

The truth was that she *had* wished him dead. Many, many times. But not in the way it had happened. Not at her hand.

At the end of the fifth week, the jury were sent out to see if they could reach a decision.

'It may take an hour, it may take a week,' said Prue.

As it transpired, it took only two hours. Jodi didn't feel good about how quickly they had come to their decision, and she knew Prue well enough by now to tell that she was also worried.

'Ladies and gentlemen of the jury, have you reached a verdict?' asked the judge.

The jury's representative was an elderly man who seemed quite at ease with being in the spotlight.

'Yes, Your Honour.'

'On the count of murder, what do you find?'

'We find the defendant not guilty.'

'Is this a decision with which you are all in agreement?'

'Yes.'

The room erupted. Shirley, Grandma and Marlene cried and hugged one another. Bob's sister shouted that it was a disgrace. The dean nodded his head in approval. Sue beamed.

Prue shook hands with her legal team before crossing to Jodi in the dock. 'It's all over, Jodi. You can put it behind you now.' Her eyes, the hardest part of her, were soft with emotion.

It *was* all over. The Crown couldn't appeal a jury verdict of acquittal.

'Thanks, Prue. Thanks for everything.'

'How do you feel?'

'Euphoric.' Tears glittered Jodi's vision but she was determined they wouldn't fall; she'd shed far too many tears as it was. 'I've made it through. Anything is possible now.'

'That's the right attitude,' Prue smiled. 'This is the start for you, not the end.'

Outside the court, Prue stopped to address the reporters.

'Miss Tyler and her family are very pleased with today's outcome . . .'

The cameras focused on Jodi.

'Any comments, Jodi?'

'As of today, I want to look forward, not back,' she told them. 'And I want to make the very best of my life from here on in.'

As she stood on the steps of the courthouse, Jodi experienced a surge of determination and ambition. She was going to study very hard and get the best degree that she could. Then she would get a job and work her way up until she was an executive of the highest level. She would earn a lot of money: enough money to be able to repay the legal fees to her mother, plus interest. She would have so much respect that this court case would cease to matter to her, or anyone else.

I have to make something of myself. I can't have come through the last year – the last seven years – to be nothing.

Sarah: Moving Up

Chapter 16

Summer 1989

Sarah's class scattered around the world that summer: Emma and Fiona to Australia, Tim back to New York, and some of the others to Europe. Sarah promised herself that next year she would go away too. She'd work out some arrangement with Brendan and Mary and head off to America. It was a full year away, but she was adamant that the last summer of her college years would not be spent behind the shop counter.

Nuala began dating a garda by the name of Colin. Colin's conversation skills were very basic and he had no compensating strengths that Sarah could see. He was tall and broad, his face dour and his movements slow. It was hard to imagine him running after a thief, or doing anything else that required a degree of agility.

Late one evening, as the sun smeared the sky with a bright orange sunset, Sarah went outside to put up the CLOSED sign at the entrance to the yard. She was dragging the sign across when a car pulled in. She pointed to the sign and mouthed, 'Sorry.' However, the driver continued on and drew up alongside her.

'Hi,' he said through the open window.

'Hello,' she replied. 'I've just closed. The pumps are switched off.'

'Okay.' He made no move to drive away. 'You don't remember me, do you, Sarah?'

Taken aback that he knew her name, she looked at him more closely. There was something familiar about his lazy brown eyes.

'You're the runner from the Mardyke?'

He nodded.

'I didn't recognise you without the hat,' she mumbled, taking in the scraggy brown hair flopping over his eyes. 'Sorry, I don't remember your name.'

'Kieran Murphy,' he said, extending his hand through the window.

She shook it, awkwardly hanging onto the heavy sign with her other arm.

'I haven't seen you at the track for a while,' he commented.

'During the holidays I do more cross-country than track,' she explained.

His mouth lifted in a smile that made Sarah feel funny inside. 'Ah! A country girl through and through.'

She didn't answer, couldn't think of anything to say. Her face began to grow inexplicably hot.

'Maybe we could run together sometime,' he suggested.

'Maybe . . .' she shrugged in a poor attempt at nonchalance.

'I'll be at the track on Saturday morning from nine. Bye, Sarah.'

He drove off before she had the chance to tell him that she had to work on Saturday. Her face still hot, she dragged the sign the remaining distance. Once in place, she stared unseeingly at the large black letters.

Something about Kieran Murphy unsettled her. Gave her butterflies.

Don't be stupid, she admonished herself before turning to go back inside. *You don't even know him.*

On Saturday morning Sarah parked her Fiesta outside the Mardyke complex. The clock on the dash flashed the time as nine-fifteen.

Why am I here? she asked herself.

Because I want to run, was the only answer she would believe.

She got out of the car before she could chicken out.

There were a few runners jogging around the track. Her eyes glanced at them one by one.

He's not here.

Deeply disappointed, and feeling very foolish, she togged off to her running shorts and began her stretches.

'You're late,' said a voice from behind.

Her heart somersaulted. 'You said you'd be here *from* nine,' she pointed out and continued with her stretches.

'Fair enough,' he replied, amusement sounding in his voice. 'Are you ready?'

She nodded.

He adjusted the peak of his cap and for a moment his sexy eyes were looking straight at her. She got that funny feeling again.

Side by side, they jogged onto the red clay. They didn't talk for the first few minutes. Sarah concentrated on her breathing.

'Okay?' he asked eventually, shooting a glance her way.

'Yeah,' she nodded. 'I suspect that I'm not in your league, though. You come here practically every day, don't you?'

'Yeah. You could too.'

'I'd like to, but I've too much on with work.'

'Ah!' He looked sympathetic. 'Your boss is working you to the bone?'

Because there was no point in keeping it a secret, she admitted, 'Actually, I *am* the boss. I own the petrol station – and the shop.'

He looked across at her, his lips twitching in a disbelieving smile. 'You're joking, right?'

'My grandmother left it to me,' she shrugged. 'But don't get too excited – I'm not *that* rich.'

He chuckled. Laugh lines grooved his face and creased the corners of his eyes. Sarah noted that Kieran Murphy had a good sense of humour, as well as those very sexy eyes.

'You're seeing him tonight?' Nuala asked, agog with all that Sarah had told her.

Sarah couldn't suppress her smile. 'Yep. In the Star.'

'You seem really keen on him.' Nuala's eyes narrowed with suspicion. 'You fancy him, don't you?'

Nuala's mother, with practised bad timing, bustled into the kitchen.

'Oh hello, Sarah. I didn't know you were here, love. Have you had a cup of tea?' Her beady eyes assessed the situation and established that no tea had been offered to the guest. 'Nuala! Where are your manners?'

'It's all right –' Sarah started to say but Mrs Kelly was already filling the kettle.

'She has her head up in the clouds, that one,' she declared with a nod in Nuala's direction. 'She can't remember the time of day since she started going out with himself.'

It seemed that Colin was already well known to Nuala's family. Sarah wondered what they thought of him. Did they think he was as dull as dishwater too? That Nuala's vivacity was wasted on him?

Mrs Kelly flicked the switch and the kettle hummed to life. Then she reached up to the highest shelf of the pantry and took down a tin of biscuits.

'Oh, lucky you, Sarah!' Nuala exclaimed. 'The chocolate biscuits are making a rare appearance.'

When the tea was made, Mrs Kelly bustled away to do some chores upstairs.

Nuala, her mother safely out of earshot, repeated her question of earlier.

'Well, do you fancy him?'

'Kieran?' asked Sarah, drawing her out.

'No, Bishop Casey,' she shot back.

They laughed and then Sarah came clean.

'Yes, as a matter of fact, I do fancy him.'

'Well, that's a relief,' said Nuala, taking one of the coveted chocolate biscuits from the tin. 'I was beginning to think there'd be no one but John for you.'

The Star was a casual pub and Kieran didn't seem the kind to get too dressed up. Sarah tried on a number of outfits before settling on a scooped black top and a pair of jeans. Her make-up was subtle but for a heavy coat of mascara.

Nuala, on her way to see Colin, gave her a lift to the city.

'Are you sure you don't want to meet up with me and Colin later on?' she asked.

Sarah shook her head.

'I'll give you a ring tomorrow,' she promised as she got out of the car.

The Star seemed a shell of its former self. With all the students on holiday, the summer patrons were a mismatch of young and old, grungy and smart.

She saw Kieran sitting at the bar, wearing a well-washed dark T-shirt and drinking from a pint glass of Guinness.

'Hi,' he smiled.

'Hi,' she echoed, sitting on the stool next to him.

'Your hair is nice down.'

To her horror, a blush started to spread on her face. 'Thanks. I always wear it up when I'm running.'

'What would you like to drink?'

'White wine, please.'

He added another pint of Guinness to the order and there was a small silence as they waited for the drinks.

Sarah's wine was a cheap chardonnay but it helped steady her nerves. Everything about Kieran Murphy set her on edge: his lazy yet assessing eyes, the untamed hair, the toned body beneath the baggy T-shirt. She was intrigued by the contradictions in him. His laid-back attitude seemed at odds with the discipline that spurred him at the running track. His appearance on first glance was scruffy, but on closer inspection the T-shirt and frayed jeans were Levi's.

'Do you live around here?' she asked in an attempt to get to know him better.

'I have a bedsit up in College Road,' he replied. 'I'm originally from Clonmel.'

Most students went home or abroad for the summer. Why did Kieran Murphy stick around, Sarah wondered.

'I have a summer job with an engineering company in town,'

he said, anticipating her question. 'My parents own a butchers in Clonmel. The lifestyle isn't me, I'm much better off spending the holidays here, getting work experience, living close to the track . . .'

A folk singer set up in one of the corners with his guitar and started to sing some traditional ballads. Sarah drank back her wine and ordered another round of drinks. She and Kieran listened to the familiar lyrics as they sat on the rickety stools. They spoke mostly through glances and smiles.

Hours flew by, swallowed by a haze of moving music and strong attraction. The singer packed up his guitar and the proprietor called for the patrons to finish up their drinks. Sarah's heart thumped in her chest. What now?

'What would you like to do?' Kieran asked, reading her thoughts.

'I don't know,' she hedged. 'What would *you* like to do?'

'There are two options that I can see,' he said, his voice soft. 'We can go on to a club – or we can go to my place.'

There was no mistaking the message in his eyes. Sarah knew well what would happen at his place. Was she ready for it?

'Option two,' she replied, her voice just as soft.

I won't sleep with him, she promised herself as she slid down off the stool. *I just want to kiss him.*

Kieran asked the proprietor if he could buy a bottle of wine over the counter.

'Trying to get me drunk?' Sarah asked.

His response was serious. 'Not if you end up regretting anything.'

His hand closed over hers and they strolled uphill to College Road. Having seen many students' digs over the years, Sarah prepared herself for the worst.

'This is nice,' she said in surprise when she saw the bedsit. Tucked away in the attic of a two-storey house, it had an unexpected charm. With three skylights set into the sloping roof, a clean galley-style kitchen and a double bed, it was way above the usual student accommodation.

Sarah sat down on the floppy sofa and Kieran handed her a tumbler of wine.

'Sorry I haven't got a proper wine glass – all of my guests to date have been beer drinkers.'

Sarah wondered how many of those guests had been girls who'd chosen the option of his bedsit over a nightclub. Like her.

He sat down, his thigh touching hers. His arm reached across her shoulders. He swigged his beer. She sipped her wine. A few minutes, charged with anticipation, passed.

Finally, he leaned across. His lips had a sexy Guinness taste. He stopped, removed the tumbler from her hand, and gathered her close. Jolts of attraction shuddered through her body as he kissed her again. She felt his hand slide inside her low-cut top and cup her breast. His thumb ran across the nipple. His movements were smooth, clearly a combination of practice and natural instinct. His mouth dropped casually from hers. She felt soft feathery kisses on her neck. Her chest. Her breasts.

'Stop,' she snapped, her voice sounding sharp, panicked.

He moved away, and she put her bra and top back into place.

'It's only our first date,' she said, feeling awkward, unworldly.

'It's okay,' he said, seemingly unperturbed. 'Whatever pace you want is fine with me.'

To prove his point, he picked her tumbler up from the floor and put it back in her hand.

*

A few weeks later Sarah acquiesced to Kieran's charms and had sex with him. All her worries, that it would hurt after the abortion, that it'd never be as good as it had been with John, that she didn't deserve to be happy, dissipated between the silky sheets of his double bed. She rediscovered passion. Rediscovered closeness. Rediscovered love.

They were very different to each other. She was intense: she worried about her studies, the shop, practically everything. Kieran was relaxed, and so hard to ruffle that she sometimes had the urge to shake him. But their differences were complementary and they generally brought out the best in each other.

They did have one major thing in common: their mutual love of running. They went to the track four or five times a week. They spurred each other on, empathised over their respective aches and pains, and applauded their individual achievements.

Gradually Sarah started to spend a few nights a week in Kieran's bedsit and he began to help out with the shop.

'If you're going to work here, then I should pay you,' Sarah said to him more than once.

'I don't want money,' he insisted. 'I enjoy it. I get to see more of you and some of the locals are a ticket.'

He chatted away to the customers as if he had lived in Carrickmore all his life. He managed to charm even the most cantankerous of them. Like Mr Glavin.

'There's a small tear on that box so I'll take twenty pence off the price for ya, Paddy,' he said.

From the look on the old man's face, it was as if he had got the cigarettes for free.

Mrs Burke, Peggy's old friend, also approved.

'That young man of yours could talk the leg off the table,' she remarked. 'And he's very handsome . . . in a scallywag kind of way.'

Nuala was wary of Kieran, though. For a start his scruffy appearance was in direct contrast to Colin's fastidiousness.

'He'd look a lot nicer if he cut his hair.'

'I like his hair just the way it is.'

Nuala's next remark was a little harder to brush off.

'Do you worry about . . .' Her friend paused. 'Do you worry about him staying faithful?'

Sarah followed her gaze to the other end of the room where two attractive girls were hanging on to Kieran's every word. She didn't know whether it was his muscled body, his sensual smile or simply an urge to comb the ruffled hair, but girls buzzed around him like bees to a honey pot.

Kieran caught her eye. He smiled slowly, sexily, making it obvious to all that she was his girl.

Nuala saw the exchange and backed off. 'Sorry. I'm in a catty mood tonight. You two make a lovely couple. Really.'

Sarah continued to stare across at Kieran. Then she spoke from her heart, something she rarely did, even with her best friend.

'For the first time in a long while, I feel anchored. I *matter*. And it's largely because of him, Nuala. He makes me happy. It's that simple.'

Chapter 17

Summer 1990

If Kieran makes me happy, then why am I leaving him?

Sarah stared out the window. Her first time on a plane, she should have been awestruck by the bulbous clouds skimming beneath the aircraft.

Because I promised myself this. One summer away.

Her final year at UCC was finished. It seemed like the perfect time to see some of the world. Leaving Kieran was the only downside. Usually so sunny and upbeat, he had become withdrawn as the date for her departure drew closer.

'Remind me again why you feel you have to go?'

Lying naked on his double bed, four days before she was due to leave, Sarah struggled to remember her reasons.

'Because I was always left behind. Not just at college, but all through school too. I've never had a holiday – not ever.'

There was a secondary reason, though, one that Sarah wasn't revealing. She wanted to test how strong she was, how confident, without Kieran. She wanted to test whether the depression had really gone, or if it was just waiting in the wings. It was a controlled test: she was doing the leaving, not someone else.

Kieran, lying on his back, rested one arm behind his head and stared at the sloping ceiling. If Sarah looked hard enough she could see patterns in the cracked white paint. She often gazed at the rivulets on the ceiling after she and Kieran made love, until she fell asleep. Now she waited for him to say what he was thinking.

'Three months is a long time, babe.'

Too long for you to wait? Is that what you're thinking?

'Remind me why you won't come with me,' she said, sounding flippant but not feeling it.

'You know why,' he all but snapped. 'You know well how hard it is to get a full-time job. So don't make me feel like I'm doing the wrong thing.'

Kieran's summer work had paid off with a permanent job offer on the completion of his degree. Tempted as he was by the idea of jetting away to New York, he was practical enough to see that turning down the job could have a negative long-term impact on his career. With graduates forming a growing part of the unemployment statistics, there was a real chance that he'd return to join the dole queues. Anyway, he didn't have a green card. Sarah did. Along with practically every other student in the country, she had applied for one. A lottery system, which didn't care for Kieran or her responsibilities with the shop, had selected her as a winner.

Sarah rolled on top of him, her face grazing his, her breasts hanging, waiting for his touch.

'Let's not spend these last few days together fighting,' she whispered.

His hands pulled her head closer and he devoured her mouth in an angry kiss.

For the rest of their time together, any discussion about New York ended in sharp words and those angry kisses.

The biggest surprise about JFK Airport was that it wasn't shiny new. It looked like an old train station. It felt grim.

Sarah walked along littered floors towards customs. There, a large mean-looking African-American scrutinised her passport and ticket.

'This ticket says you're going back home in the fall.'

'Is that a problem?' asked Sarah earnestly.

He frowned. He looked quite ferocious. 'Seems like a waste of a green card to me. Why are you going back?'

'I own a shop. In a place called Carrickmore. My staff can't run it indefinitely.'

He glared at her, beads of sweat lodged above his fat upper lip. The airport's airconditioning system was down. Staff and passengers alike were feeling the heat.

'Why bother coming here at all?'

'I want to work somewhere else. Try something new.'

'Who are you staying with here in NYC?'

In her growing intimidation, Sarah didn't know what he meant. 'NYC?'

'New York City,' he growled.

'Tim Brennan – a friend from college. He's meeting me outside.'

Finally, begrudgingly, he stamped her passport and let her through.

Tim was one of the first people she saw when she got to the arrival's lounge. His pale face was easy to pick out in the crowd.

He wore a white shirt, a light blue tie and black trousers. Sarah thought he looked very suave.

'God, I'm glad to see you,' she said and gave him a big hug.

He returned her hug with such warmth that it was obvious he was very glad to see her too. 'Come on, I'll show you to your hotel,' he joked.

Tim's apartment was in Greenwich Village. He shared it with his girlfriend of three years, Louise, and his mate, Charlie.

'Isn't there a lift?' asked Sarah as they trawled up endless flights of stairs.

'No – it's a walk-up,' Tim puffed as Sarah's suitcase bumped along behind him.

They got to the top. Tim bent over, hands on his knees, and exhaled slowly.

'Don't be shocked when you see inside,' he said when he caught his breath.

'Why?'

'Because in this city you don't get much for your dollar by the way of accommodation.'

'Oh.'

His warning was justified. Sarah's first impressions of the hallway were of peeling paint and badly fitted carpet. The kitchen was shabby and the bathroom looked like a converted cupboard.

'Where are the others?'

'At work.' It was 7 pm. 'I'm the only one who works nine to five around here,' he added.

'Are these the bedrooms?' Sarah asked, looking at two adjacent doors on the right-hand side of the hall.

Tim opened the first door. 'Louise and I are in here.'

Sarah had a quick glance at the unmade bed before he clicked the door shut and opened the next.

'Charlie is in here at the moment, but he's willing to move out to the living room if you want to take it.'

'There's no window,' said Sarah in wonderment.

Tim shrugged. 'That's not unusual in New York.'

Sarah turned back towards the living room. Despite the flaking paint and awful carpet, it felt comfortable. A murky brown sofa was the only piece of furniture; the TV was perched on a cardboard box and books in uneven stacks on the floor.

'How would Charlie fit in here?'

'He'd be happy down there.' Tim pointed to the end of the room and Sarah saw that it had an L-shape. 'It's quite private round the corner there. But, of course, the bedroom has a door, so there's more rent for it . . .'

'How much?'

'Six hundred a month.'

'I'd better get a job, then.'

Sarah was soon to discover that getting a job in New York was easier said than done. She scoured the advertisements in the newspapers, but nobody was looking for graduates. She phoned every recruitment agency in the directory.

'I'm looking for something with a bank,' she told them.

'You don't have any previous experience,' they replied and that was the end of the conversation.

She spent precious dollars printing out her CV and mailing it to all the banks in the city. A few days later she received dozens of replies in the post, saying thanks but no thanks.

Tim became her only hope. He worked in EquiBank, one of the most elite investment banks in the world.

'Did you give my CV to your manager?' she asked.

'Yes. But he says we're overstaffed at the moment.'

'How long before he starts recruiting again?'

'A few months, I'd say.'

'What will I do until then?'

'Wait tables,' Tim shrugged. 'Just like Louise, Charlie and everybody else in this city waiting for their big break.'

Tim knew what he was talking about. This was his third summer in New York and the first time he'd scored an office job. EquiBank was his big break and he was going to stay in New York indefinitely to make the very most of it.

Sarah took his advice and the next day she hit the streets looking for work. Just two blocks away from the apartment she happened upon Palazzio's, a busy café with a large sign on its window that read, *Staff needed. Apply within.*

It looked charming, with its green awning and square wooden tables.

'Is the manager around?' she asked one of the waitresses.

The girl, Mexican in appearance, jerked her head towards the back of the premises.

'His office is out there.'

Sarah walked past the kitchen and, from a quick glance, noticed that most of the kitchen hands were young women with smooth brown faces. They talked in a foreign language as they prepared the food.

The office was a desk in a room full of clutter. Amidst brooms, buckets and highchairs, the manager, a short, fat swarthy-looking man, talked on the phone. Sarah listened as he swore profusely at the unfortunate person on the other end.

'What do you want?' he barked at Sarah when he was through.

'A job.'

His sleazy eyes looked her up and down.

'You must wear black, be on time and pay for all breakages.'

'What if it's the customer's fault?' she asked.

'Don't care,' he snapped. 'It's five dollars for glasses, seven dollars for cups and plates.'

'What's the hourly rate?'

He laughed nastily. 'Zilch, zero, sweet fuck all. Your tips are what count – so you'd better use that Irish charm to the max.'

'Is that legal?' she asked, thinking that he surely had to pay his staff a minimum wage.

'Fuck legal,' was his reply.

Sarah was sorely tempted to respond with 'Fuck you' but she wanted the job. Not because of the money, although her traveller's cheques were running down, but more because she was dying to experience life in mainstream New York.

'What's your name?' he asked.

'Sarah Ryan.'

'I'm Lorenzo – and I take no shit. You and I will get along just fine if you remember that.'

He threw a black apron her way and that was how Sarah started work at Palazzio's. She worked from eleven in the morning till midnight, six days a week. She fetched coffees, ice creams, nachos and hoped that her big smile would earn a big tip. One day Al Pacino came in and left her twenty dollars. It went into the kitty to be shared with the other staff.

The longer Sarah worked for Lorenzo, the more she realised that he wasn't just unpleasant, he was actually a little crazy. He was having an affair with the head waitress and they would often retreat to his office to snort coke. The cops came in regularly and drank free coffee in return for turning a blind eye to

Lorenzo's illegally parked car. Their presence did not in any way deter Lorenzo from doing lines of coke out the back.

The long hours at the café, combined with the five-hour time difference, made it hard to find the right time to call Kieran. Sunday was the only day they could connect, but Kieran was usually hungover from the night before and not very communicative.

'Where did you go last night?' she'd ask.

'The Star – the usual.'

'Big night?'

'Yeah, feeling grisly this morning.'

'No training today, then?'

'No.'

'Me neither. But I'm going to join a running club as soon as I get a normal job.'

Then she'd tell him funny stories about the café and New York. But he didn't show much interest. All too soon, he'd say, 'Well, I'd better go. Have a few things to do.'

Sarah wondered what it was he had to do that was more important than talking to her.

Her phone calls to the shop were equally unsatisfactory.

'Everything's grand,' Brendan would say when she asked how things were going.

'Are the takings up or down?'

'A little bit down . . . but only a fraction.'

'Is Mary around?'

'She's out the back.'

In truth, Sarah was uneasy about Kieran and the shop. However, she knew only too well what would happen if she didn't keep her thoughts positive.

The next morning she got up extra early and went for a jog in

Central Park. She wasn't alone, the park was full of runners, and she felt like part of a greater group. She breathed in the nature all around, the leafy trees and abundant shrubs and flowers, and the tension eased away. She felt strong again. Confident. Regardless of what was happening at home.

Sarah asked Tim about EquiBank nearly every day.

'Still no vacancies,' he'd reply with a sympathetic shrug.

But one day he announced, 'The manager said he's put you to the top of the list – apparently he rates persistence highly.'

'I hope it won't be much longer,' Sarah sighed. 'I don't think I can stick it at Palazzio's.'

Not only were the hours back-breaking and the pay woeful, but Lorenzo was snorting coke as if it was going out of fashion. When he was high, he was greasy and overfamiliar with the female staff. When he was low, he was angry and abusive. Sarah didn't know which was worse.

In the end it was a row over tips, instigated by a group of German tourists, that brought a finish to her career as a waitress.

'They didn't leave a tip,' exclaimed Maria, the head waitress.

Sarah, already on shift for more than ten hours, shrugged wearily.

'I smiled. I gave them good service. I can hardly hold a knife to their throats and demand a tip.'

'Go after them,' Maria ordered.

'What?'

'Go! Go!' Maria waved her out the door.

Sarah ran outside. She spotted the tourists and sprinted after them, her apron flapping around her knees.

'Excuse me,' she panted, veering in front of them, blocking their way. 'I'm very sorry but you forgot to tip.'

Five pairs of eyes stared incredulously, making Sarah wish that she could climb into one of the nearby steaming manholes and disappear underground.

'It's not obligatory to tip in Germany,' said one of the group, a young man with Arian good looks.

'I know. But this is New York,' she explained, her face reddening with embarrassment. 'If you don't tip, I don't get paid.'

An older man shook his head. 'You shouldn't work in a job where you don't get paid.'

How could Sarah refute such logic?

'Yes, you're right,' she said. 'I'm sorry to have troubled you.'

She turned on her heel and headed back towards Palazzio's. Maria would be furious that she was returning empty-handed. The rest of the waiting staff would be furious that there would be less in the kitty to share at the end of the night. And Lorenzo would be furious because he didn't have any coke left.

Sarah, deeply mortified that she had sunk low enough to give chase for a tip, decided there and then that she'd had enough of Palazzio's. She strode straight past the café and kept going till she got back to the apartment. Then she rang Tim.

'I've just had to run after some German tourists because they didn't leave a tip,' she yelled. 'Tell your manager that he must give me a job. *He fucking must have something that I can do.*'

'Calm down, okay?' Tim replied. 'I'll ask him again. Give me a minute.'

She heard voices in the background. Tim's was forceful.

He came back on the line. 'The boss says you can start in the settlements department on Monday.'

Yelling obviously paid dividends in New York: you had to show attitude to be taken seriously, to get what you wanted.

'Thanks, Tim. I don't know what I'd do without you.'

*

Before starting her new job, Sarah decided to spend the last of her traveller's cheques on new clothes.

'I need to look the part,' she said to Louise, Tim's girlfriend. 'Want to come along?'

Louise's reply was short. 'No, thanks.'

Sarah had made many attempts to get to know the other girl better, but it seemed that living in the same apartment wasn't enough to forge even a superficial friendship.

'Whatever,' she shrugged and went shopping on her own.

From Tim's descriptions, Sarah knew that the dealers and their assistants spent a significant portion of their salaries on designer clothes. With this in mind, she went to Barney's, New York's quintessential department store. Feeling decidedly out of place amongst the impeccably groomed sales assistants and well-heeled customers, she tried not to gasp when she saw the price tags on the clothes.

'Can I help you, madam?'

'I'm starting a new job on Monday,' Sarah explained to the heavily made-up middle-aged assistant. 'It's in a bank . . .'

The woman nodded and took Sarah by the arm. 'We have a sale rack over here – it will be easy to find something to suit a figure like yours.'

An hour later, Sarah left the store five hundred dollars poorer. The sales assistant had assured her that the jacket, trousers and skirt were a 'steal' for that price. Sarah, having seen the prices before the markdown, had to agree with her.

Sarah got up extra early on Monday morning to make sure she had first call on the bathroom. She showered, blow-dried her hair and was halfway through her make-up when Tim knocked on the door.

'Are you going to be much longer?' He sounded grumpy.

'Coming,' she replied, hurriedly brushing some blusher across her cheekbones.

'I hope you're not going to take this long every morning,' he remarked, a towel slung around his neck.

'Sorry.' She shot him a smile. 'I just want to make a good impression on my first day.'

Back in her room, she slipped on the new knee-length black skirt and matching jacket. She studied her reflection in the mirror and, pleased with how professional she looked, told herself that the suit had been worth every cent.

Tim was in the kitchen. The shower seemed to have restored his usual good humour and he chatted easily while he downed a bowl of cereal.

Too nervous to eat, Sarah sipped a cup of tea.

'Ready to go?' he asked, pushing back from the table.

'Think so.'

The bank was a ten-minute ride on the subway. Sarah and Tim had just got on the train when they heard an ear-piercing scream. They, and all the other commuters, turned to see an enormous rat inside the doorway of the carriage. The whistle sounded and the doors started to close. The rat looked like he was planning to stay for the ride to the next stop. Tim stomped his foot at it. Once. Twice. Finally, the rat spun around and scurried out through the narrowing slit between the doors.

Sarah shuddered. 'That was disgusting.'

Tim hunched his shoulders as if it was no big deal. 'The subway is supposedly infested with them.'

The only benefit of the incident was that it made Sarah temporarily forget her nervousness. They got off at the World Trade Centre and emerged into the heart of New York's financial district. Sarah remembered how nervous she was.

'This is my first real job – what if I'm bad at it?'

'You've managed a petrol station and grocery shop.' He gave her an encouraging smile. 'This will be a piece of cake by comparison.'

'Do I look okay?' She paused outside the EquiBank tower.

He squeezed her hand. 'You'll knock them dead.'

The foyer was a vast marbled area and the security staff issued Sarah with an access card before Tim took her up in the lift.

'The boss's name is Josh Grimshaw. He's doom and gloom – his name suits him – but he's not the worst of them.'

They rode the lift to the nineteenth floor and Sarah used her newly acquired access card to open the glass security doors. Josh Grimshaw's office was the first inside, in prime position to keep tabs on who was coming and going. He was a slender man with stooped shoulders and deep facial lines. He was aged somewhere in his sixties, his thinning hair more white than grey.

'We settle the deals that are done upstairs.' He cast his bespectacled eyes upwards, as if the traders on the floor above were the bane of his life. 'We're a processing department – administration, bottom of the food chain.'

Surely all jobs in the bank, even administration, are important? Sarah thought.

Tim went to his desk and left Sarah with Josh. He introduced her to a handful of people before leading her to a long narrow room, its walls lined with filing cabinets.

'These are the deal tickets.' He pointed to a stack of paperwork on the table inside the door. 'You tear off the edges . . .' He demonstrated by tearing the perforated sides off one of the documents. 'Top copies go to the traders for signature, then on to the other party. Middle copy gets filed. Make sure you don't punch holes over any of the print. That's about all you need to know.'

Sarah's induction to EquiBank was thereby complete and Josh returned to his office.

The windowless room felt stifling and Sarah slipped off her jacket. She hung it off the back of a chair and flicked through the stack of deal tickets. She started to arrange them in alphabetical order, then changed her mind and re-sorted them by dealer name. It crossed her mind that she was probably the best dressed filing clerk in New York City.

Sarah's first venture onto the trading floor was something she would never forget: the buzzing phones, the clatter of voices, the flickering screens. Numbers were called out, phones hung up and keyboards tapped. People sat elbow to elbow, many of them with two phones going at once. Every few seconds someone would scream a string of expletives but nobody took a jot of notice.

Sarah momentarily forgot the reason she was there in the first place: to obtain the dealers' signatures on the deal tickets. A wolf whistle jolted her back to the present. One by one the dealers swivelled around on their seats, many of them still on the phone, and sized her up.

One called out, 'Who's the cute new chick?'

He directed the question to his colleagues.

'My name's Sarah,' she answered, projecting her voice above the racket. 'I work in settlements.'

He snorted. 'We won't hold that against you.'

His colleagues laughed. They all looked similar: young, white shirts, and oozing with so much confidence that one face looked the same as the next.

Anxious to escape their scrutiny, Sarah consulted her paperwork.

'Who's Joe Fletcher?' she asked.

'That's me,' one of them smirked. 'Must be my lucky day.'

Another round of laughter and wolf whistles swept across the floor. Sarah, a blush staining her cheeks, weaved her way towards Joe. His phone rang just as she got there and he scrawled his signature without making any further comments.

Sarah looked around for the next name on her list: Denise Martin. There was a woman amidst all this testosterone?

'Over here, honey,' a husky voice called out.

With her tailored white shirt and short hairstyle, Denise Martin blended seamlessly with her male counterparts.

'Just ignore them, honey,' she advised as she countersigned her name next to Joe's. 'They simply can't help it – their dicks are bigger than their brains.'

Later on that day, on the subway home, Sarah told Tim about her first experience on the trading floor.

'Denise was the only woman there,' she said. 'I don't know how she can put up with them carrying on like that.'

'She's tough – and very talented,' he replied. 'Managing directors are ten a penny in EquiBank, but Denise is different – you can tell she's destined to go to the very top.'

Sarah was in awe. 'I didn't realise she was a managing director – she seemed so ordinary.'

In the following weeks Sarah watched and learned what she could from Denise. She studied the other woman's unflappable composure, her authoritative phone manner, even the clothes she wore. The more Sarah watched Denise, the more she came to appreciate how she differed to the other traders. She didn't swear, or scream, or get overly excited. She didn't tell dirty jokes or smoke fat cigars. She possessed a deadly focus. When she found a stock, bond or commodity that she considered to be over- or underpriced, she'd rally those around her to buy or sell. People said she had a sixth sense and rarely made a mistake. She was by far the best trader in the company and her promotion to managing director hadn't diluted her effectiveness, as it had with others before her.

Often, as she was signing the paperwork, Denise would tell Sarah a little bit about the deal.

'The brokers kept the other party a secret – they always do – but I could tell who it was . . .'

'Bought US$10m on this one – just went on a hunch, honey . . .'

'Joe lost thousands on this – he really screwed up the calls . . .'

Downstairs, away from the flurry of the trading floor, Sarah scrutinised each deal ticket before filing it away. She promised herself that one day she'd have a job as exciting as Denise's.

Chapter 18

In September, just as Sarah should have been planning her trip home, Joe Fletcher got fired and the ripple effect caused her to re-evaluate her travel plans. Joe's departure brought about a promotion for one of the assistants; Tim got the assistant's old job; and Sarah was offered Tim's job: inputting the deal details into the computer. In reality it was every bit as boring as the filing, but nevertheless it was still a promotion and she rang Brendan to let him know she was staying on for a few extra months.

'Everything's under control here,' he told her. 'No need to rush back.'

'All the bills up to date?'

'Yep, do them every week.'

'Any over- or understocking?'

'No, everything's about right.'

'How's Mary?'

'She's grand.'

'Can I say hello?'

'She took off early today. She had something on, I can't remember what.'

Sarah hung up with all the usual niggles. She briefly considered asking Nuala to drive out there to check if everything was okay.

No, she dismissed the idea. *That would be spying. I've put Brendan in charge. I must trust him. I must think positive . . .*

That Friday night all the promotions were celebrated in a new nightclub down in Chelsea. The club was packed to capacity with stockbrokers and bankers. Music blared as skimpily dressed cocktail waitresses took drink orders from the designer-dressed clientele.

Sarah drank champagne with the girls from settlements while the dealers, including Tim and Denise, stood in their own circle and drank bottled beer.

A few drinks in, Denise broke ranks and came over.

'Congratulations, honey,' she said in reference to Sarah's promotion.

'Thanks,' Sarah replied politely, feeling that her job, promotion or not, was menial by comparison to Denise's.

Denise seemed to know what she was thinking. 'The best traders are the ones who start at the bottom and work their way up – you file, you do data entry, you learn. If Joe had started where you did, he wouldn't have made so many stupid mistakes and I wouldn't have had to fire his ass.'

Denise motioned to the cocktail waitress. Soon Sarah had a fresh flute in her hand and Denise was ready to impart some more career advice.

'Give them another thirty minutes and they'll be swarming all over you,' she said, inclining her head towards the circle of men. 'Looking for a squeeze for the night. You'll have had a few drinks too. You may be tempted – but don't do it. They'd never take you seriously again.'

Then, between sips of champagne, she confided that she was in her late twenties and already twice divorced. 'I got married too young, honey – childhood sweetheart – pity I didn't like the adult he became.'

'What about your second husband?' asked Sarah.

'Oh, that just lasted a few months.' She flicked her hand dismissively. 'A Brazilian – the most beautiful man you've ever seen – but all he wanted was a visa. People tried to warn me. Now I listen when my friends give me advice.'

As Denise predicted, the men began to integrate, sidling up, turning on the charm. Denise moved off and Sarah talked to Tim for a while.

'How was your first week in the new job?' she asked.

'Good – spent most of the time on the phone, confirming deals. I got a real taste for it.'

'Already dressing the part,' Sarah commented, noticing a new Armani tie around his neck.

He looked sheepish. 'I'm trying to disguise my cheap suit with a flashy tie, but I'm sure they have me sussed – those guys spend so much on clothes, they make me look like a street urchin by comparison.'

Sarah laughed. Tim was far from a street urchin. In fact, business attire really suited him. In the mornings, when he was getting ready for work, he went around the apartment in his white shirt, tucked in at the waist, open at the neck. The plain white emphasised his dark hair and eyes. Sarah, in the midst of her own morning routine, often found it impossible not to sneak surreptitious glances.

Rob Spencer, one of the foreign exchange dealers who was

designer-clad from head to toe and would have been good-looking if he wasn't so conceited, came over and slid his arm around Sarah's waist.

'Where are you going after here, Irish?'

Sarah gave him a polite smile as she pointedly removed his arm. 'Home.' Then she added, in case he hadn't got the message, 'On my own.'

He smirked. 'Playing hard to get – cute.' He leaned close to play his trump card. 'How about lunch at Bakka's next week?'

She hadn't heard of Bakka's but she could guess what it was like. The dealers were food snobs of the highest degree, patronising the city's trendiest restaurants, trying to outdo each other in securing the very best table.

She shook her head. 'I have a boyfriend.'

Rob frowned in puzzlement. 'What's that got to do with anything?'

Genuinely baffled, he swaggered off and soon he was hitting on another, more receptive girl.

Sarah rolled her eyes to Tim. 'Please don't turn out like him. Maybe your new Armani tie is the start of a terrible change . . .'

Tim stamped his feet. 'These are firmly on the ground,' he assured her, then drank back his beer. 'Come on, Sarah, I'm suddenly bored. Let's get out of here.'

Denise was the only one of the group who noticed when they left.

Sarah ran to the phone when it shrilled through the apartment early on Sunday morning.

'Sarah!' It was Nuala and she sounded very excited. 'Guess what?'

'You've won the lotto?'

'I wish. But nearly as good. Colin and I got engaged last night.'

Sarah was floored by the news. A noticeable silence stretched down the line as she tried to gather her wits.

'Congratulations.'

God, that sounded feeble. Surely I can do better?

Nuala didn't seem to notice anything amiss. 'Oh, you should see the ring, Sarah. It's a cluster of tiny diamonds. Colin got it in Keane's . . .'

Sarah only half listened as her friend gushed on about clarity and carats.

Colin's all wrong for you, she wanted to shout. *You can't marry him.*

She was vaguely aware of Tim coming out of his room. His hair tousled and Levi's hung low on his hips, he walked down the hall towards the kitchen.

'Of course, you'll be my maid of honour . . .'

Sarah couldn't think of anything more two-faced than signing her name to the marriage certificate. Didn't the maid of honour have to at least *like* the groom?

'When's the big day?'

'Christmas. Imagine if it snowed – a white wedding!'

'Isn't that a bit soon?'

'Why wait when you're sure?' Nuala was quick to respond.

When Sarah hung up the phone, she knew she had no hope of going back to sleep so she headed for the kitchen. There she found Tim pouring boiled water into a cracked mug.

He paused to ask, 'Want one?'

She nodded and sat down at the white plastic-top table. 'Did the phone wake you?'

'No, I've been waking at the crack of dawn for the last week. Was it Kieran?'

Sarah rolled her eyes to heaven. 'Some chance.'

Truth be told, she had thought it might be him when she'd dashed out of bed. But she should have known better. She'd almost felt like a liar when she'd told Rob Spencer that she had a boyfriend. Did a phone call every few weeks constitute a boyfriend-girlfriend relationship?

'No, it was Nuala. She's got engaged!'

'Jesus!'

Sarah grimaced. 'I know! I can't believe it either. Colin doesn't like going out, or doing anything that involves spending money. He can hardly hold a conversation, for God's sake. He'll squeeze the life out of her.'

'Have you told her what you think?' asked Tim, sitting down at the other side of the table. Sarah had an unhindered view of his toned chest with its pale skin and sprinkle of dark hair. Disconcerted, she averted her eyes.

'No way. Even though she's my closest friend, I feel I have no right to run down her boyfriend.'

Tim sipped his coffee, his eyes more broody than usual. Sarah had a feeling that the conversation was about to turn personal.

'Would you give an opinion to a friend who asked for it? Say, what if I asked you outright what you thought of Louise?'

'Don't.'

'I am.'

'Oh, Tim,' Sarah sighed. 'Let's not start this. What I think doesn't matter.'

'It matters a hell of a lot more than you think, Sarah,' he said darkly. 'Louise and I are on the verge of breaking up. It's because I –'

He stopped at the sound of movement from the lounge area. A few moments later a bleary-eyed Charlie leaned his shoulder against the kitchen's doorframe.

'Feckin' impossible to get any sleep in this gaff,' he declared. 'First the phone, then you two gabbing away . . . Is that kettle still hot?'

Louise moved out the following week. Tim, wisely, made himself scarce and went off somewhere with Charlie. Sarah, feeling sorry for the other girl, knocked on the door of her bedroom to ask if she needed any help.

'Not from you,' was her caustic reply.

Sarah didn't rise, understanding that Louise needed to lash out at someone. Clothes were strewn across the bed and Louise folded them roughly before placing them in her suitcase.

'I'm really sorry about you and Tim,' said Sarah quietly.

'Sorry?' Louise stopped folding to spit out, 'God, you've some cheek.'

Sarah knew she was hurting but her animosity seemed rather extreme. 'Excuse me?'

'He's all yours now,' said Louise in a brittle voice. 'I'm sure you'll make a lovely couple.'

Sarah frowned. It seemed that Louise had got her wires crossed somewhere.

'You're wrong –' she began.

Louise cut her off. 'Stop acting like Little Miss Innocent. You've been stringing him along for years, pretending to be his friend, making him fall for you.'

'Tim *is* my friend,' Sarah told her, her voice clipped. 'Nothing more.'

Louise laughed bitterly. 'God, you must think I'm really

stupid. Now, get out of here and leave me alone.'

Sarah did as Louise bid and clicked the door shut. Seeing the splatter of rain on the window, she grabbed her raincoat and stomped down the stairs.

Have I been stringing him along? She pulled up her hood. *Is Louise right?*

The rain was cold and Sarah walked with her chin burrowed into her chest, down West 3rd Street, left along Mercer and then back through Waverly. Her sneakers squelched through puddles and damp seeped into her socks. Peggy came into her thoughts and a lump caught in her throat.

'*Jesus, Mary and Joseph*,' Sarah could hear her say. '*Get in out of the rain before you catch your death.*'

Sarah ducked into a café and ordered a latte. The waitress gave her a big smile, the kind of smile that Sarah used to give when tips made up the sum total of her pay packet.

As Sarah sipped the weak coffee, she finally admitted the truth to herself. She had known for a long time that Tim was a little bit in love with her. She couldn't, however, figure out how she felt about him.

Chapter 19

The onset of the cold weather brought many obvious changes to New York: the big old trees lost their rich greenery, the morning air cut like glass down Sarah's throat, and the city was lit up in all its glory when she left the office in the evenings.

Sarah was also struck by other, more subtle changes. The commuters became faceless, their features hidden by the raised collars of their heavy overcoats. And it seemed like the dark evenings brought with them an increased propensity for violence, the atmosphere in the subway tense with wary glances between the passengers. Yet the most disturbing difference was the homeless: hundreds more than the summertime, congregating on the street corners, some with scrawny dogs, some with cardboard signs reading, *I'm hungry and homeless. Help me.*

At work Sarah was focused. She updated the deals on the computer as quickly as possible each day so she could go to where all the excitement seemed to happen: the trading floor.

'Anything I can help with here?' she'd ask Denise. 'It's quiet downstairs.'

Sometimes Denise would allow her to call the brokers to confirm the deals. Sarah appreciated her trust. Because she was a director, Denise handled only the biggest deals, some in excess of ten million US dollars. Sarah returned her trust by taking extreme care on the phone.

Sarah was constantly propositioned with drinks, lunches and dinners. Whoever it was always made a point of mentioning the establishment he wanted to take her to, as if the name alone would make her swoon. Most of them were married or engaged. Sarah wondered if the wives and girlfriends had any idea how faithless their men were.

Time and time again she told them she wasn't available, that there was a boyfriend back home. Her morals were a source of bafflement to them and she started to question herself. Was she the crazy one to stay true to Kieran? When had he last called her? Last told her that he missed her? He hadn't written a single letter. Not one.

Tim was a personal dilemma of another kind. With Louise's departure, their easy friendship had developed an edge. They were often alone in the apartment as Charlie worked antisocial hours. If Sarah looked too long, she'd catch an odd expression on Tim's face. As if he was holding something back. Something that would change things forever if said out loud. Something she wasn't ready to hear.

Nuala's wedding became the new benchmark for Sarah's return home. As the weeks counted down to December, the trees became completely bare, the daytime bitterly cold, and the homeless even more prevalent. Sarah couldn't pass them.

'What did you do that for?' Grant Forbes, Tim's boss, asked incredulously when he saw her drop a çoin into a beggar's polystyrene cup.

'Because he's homeless.'

'He's homeless because he's too lazy to get off his ass and get a job,' Grant declared. 'And it makes it all too damned easy when people like you give him cash for nothing.'

Sarah, disgusted, quickened her pace and caught up with Tim. They were all on their way to a club, the usual Friday night out where the cost of a cocktail would feed the beggar for a couple of days.

Once in the club and propped with their expensive drinks, the traders began to talk about the subject matter at the fore of their minds: the annual bonus. With the end of the year approaching, speculation had begun in earnest.

'If they don't pay me three hundred thousand, I'm going to Merrill Lynch . . .'

Sarah's mouth gaped when she overheard the enormous sums of money these young men, some only a few years older than her, expected to earn.

'That bastard better not get paid more than me . . .'

Rivalry fuelled their greed. It seemed that no matter how big the bonus, it would not suffice if it was less than someone else at the same level got paid. Sarah wondered what was on their shopping list. How much would they whittle away on designer clothes and eating in the city's best restaurants? How much would they spend on sensible things like real estate or other investments? One thing she was sure of, after Grant's callous attitude to the beggar, little of the money would go to charity.

Much later on that night, when he had finally tired of talking about his bonus, Grant whispered in Sarah's ear. 'How's Mother Teresa?'

'Fuck off.'

His breath was warm as he slurred, 'Come on, let's go somewhere quiet.'

'Fuck off,' she repeated again.

Grant, oblivious that she despised him, stroked his hand down her waist-length hair.

He cocked his head to one side. 'Forget Mother Teresa – I'm going to call you Rapunzel.'

Sarah pointedly removed his hand from her hair and went to find Tim.

Grant's comment goaded Sarah into getting her hair cut. She chose Fred's Hair Salon simply because she passed it every day on the way to work. When she saw the inside, with its old-fashioned décor along with two elderly ladies sitting under dryers, she quickly turned on her heel to leave.

'Hold on.'

A hand gripped her arm, its long talon-like nails stained with dye. Her gaze moved up to the hand's owner, a middle-aged man with bleached hair and a sun-bed tan. She presumed he was Fred.

'I was mixing dye out the back when you came in. Sit over here.' He propelled her towards a seat and then ran his talons through her hair as he assessed its thickness and condition. 'This style is medieval – you look like Rapunzel.'

Sarah bristled. 'That's why I'm here – I want something more modern – something that says "don't mess with me".'

'How about colour?'

'What's in?'

'Streaks – I could do a few blonde ones down the parting.'

Sarah shot a worried glance at the old ladies and prayed that Fred knew how to do more than blue rinses.

'Okay.'

He shampooed and conditioned her hair without making any further conversation.

Across the room, one of the old ladies croaked, 'It's getting hot under here.'

He didn't seem to hear.

A few minutes later the other woman called out, 'How much longer, Fred?'

He didn't respond.

Sarah, watching his expression in the mirror, saw his lips twitch ever so slightly. He could hear perfectly well.

With several silver foils sticking out at angles from her head, she was at his mercy, just like the old ladies.

'Sassy,' Denise commented approvingly when she saw Sarah's hair.

Sarah was pleased. Despite her misgivings about Fred, she liked the shoulder-length cut and the careless layers on the sides. He'd also done a good job with the colour, the blonde streaks complementing her natural chestnut.

'Sex-y,' Rob Spencer remarked when she reached his pod.

Sarah didn't blush; she was used to him by now. She opened her folder at the allotted place.

'Sign on the dotted line, please, Rob,' she instructed in a businesslike tone of voice.

She continued on around the floor, obtaining all the necessary signatures whilst turning a deaf ear to the wolf whistles and suggestive remarks about her new hairstyle. She was just about finished when Denise, who had been staring at her screen for the last while, suddenly jumped up and shouted, 'Calls!'

Pandemonium followed. All at once, everyone was on the phone.

'Fifty-two, fifty Sterling,' someone yelled out.

'Take ten,' Denise shouted back.

Sarah's eyes widened as she realised that 'ten' meant ten million dollars.

'Fifty-two, forty-nine,' was the next response.

'Take twenty,' Denise instructed without pausing to think.

'Fifty-two, fifty-two.'

'Nothing there.'

In awe, Sarah watched the ping-pong between Denise and those on the phones. Tim was in there too, his shirt sleeves rolled up, shouting his prices loud and clear.

Sarah felt both proud and envious of Tim. She longed to have a part in the action. This was the coalface of investment banking, where millions could be gained or lost in a matter of minutes. With a sigh, she acknowledged that inputting the chits onto the computer system was the closest she would get to any action. For now.

Sarah began to look forward to going home. New York was so vastly different to Ireland that for most of the six months it had been hard to visualise anything from her old life: Kieran, the shop, even Carrickmore itself. Now, with her departure imminent, Ireland came back into focus. She looked forward to hearing the soft accents. To seeing the lush green fields. To being back with Kieran.

He wasn't one for long-distance relationships, that much had been proved. Phone calls or letters weren't his mode of communication. Kieran needed to see and touch. There was no one better when it came to support with the shop, or encouragement with her running, or making love. Now that she had him figured out, she was excited about being with him again and regaining the closeness they'd had before she went away.

Although Sarah was ready to leave the brashness of New York, she wasn't ready to leave the banking world. Even the most mundane aspect of her current job, the data entry, was a thousand times more exciting than ringing up sales in the shop. She couldn't imagine what it would be like to deal with pounds and pence again, she'd got so used to the millions flying around the trading floor. Her daily interaction would be limited to friendly yet unstimulating locals, a far cry from Denise and the traders. She knew that some difficult decisions about the shop lay ahead.

On her last day the dealers surprised her with a male strip-o-gram, a muscled hunk in tight leather pants that he quickly removed to reveal a leopard-skin G-string. Sarah didn't even blush when he danced his crotch into her face. She'd come a long way.

Later that night, in a club called Rascals, Denise handed her an envelope.

'It's a reference,' she said.

'For what?'

'For EquiBank in Dublin – I've told them that you'll make a great assistant.'

'Thank you so much, Denise.' Sarah smiled at the woman who'd been a wonderful mentor over the past few months. 'For everything.'

'No problem,' Denise shrugged, her tone matter-of-fact. 'This business is tough for women. We have to look out for each other.'

Carefully, Sarah put the envelope in her handbag. Now was not the time to think about what she was going to do with the reference, or with the shop. The music was too loud and her head was starting to swim from all the champagne. She'd lost count of how many times the cocktail waitress had been around.

Tim came over.

'Are you really sure you want to go back?' he asked.

'Yes. It's been great, but New York isn't where I want to live forever.'

'I'll miss you,' he said, his voice barely audible above the music.

Sarah kept her tone light. 'And me you.'

An uneasy silence stretched between them and Sarah was as confused as ever about her feelings for him. There was something there. Attraction, for sure. Admiration too. On a few occasions, mostly after Friday night drinks, they'd almost transgressed the line of friendship. Nights where it seemed they had the same ambitions, the same sense of humour and the same perspective on the world. Nights where, both a little drunk, they would look at each other in a way that friends shouldn't.

But somehow Sarah had resisted the temptation. She didn't have it in her to cheat on Kieran. She knew only too well what it was like to be the one at home. Waiting. Trusting.

The music changed and INXS, Tim's favourite band, blared out over the speakers.

'Let's dance,' he suggested suddenly.

She nodded, set down her glass of champagne, and let him take her hand. He led her through the throbbing crowd. They danced right under the rotating disco ball. Every few seconds pure white light illuminated his face and Sarah would steal a look at his dark flashing eyes and ruffled hair. Other girls looked too.

The track changed. More rock. They stayed out. The beat mixed with the champagne and with all the odd emotions that swirled inside Sarah. As the music reached a high, Tim crushed her to him as if he would never let her go. She could feel every line of his body. The light sweat on his back. The heat of his arousal. The music pulsated through their bodies, fusing them together.

Far, far away she heard the voice of reason.

Stop now. Before it goes any further.

Sluggishly, she pulled away from his embrace.

'Better get back to the others,' she said shakily.

Quickly, Sarah lurched through the crowd, terrified that if she stayed another moment she would completely disregard that nagging voice of reason.

Chapter 20

A northerly wind gusted across the runway at Cork Airport and Sarah hugged her arms around her as she ran towards the terminal. Once inside, she couldn't help noticing that passport control was a mickey-mouse affair in comparison to JFK.

Don't turn into one of those unbearable people who are always comparing Cork to some bigger and better place, she chided herself.

Hoisting her bags onto a trolley, she headed towards the arrivals' lounge. Only one person knew she was coming home. It looked like he wasn't here to meet her.

'Sarah, over here.'

The voice sounded familiar but the person who owned it wasn't.

'Kieran?'

His gorgeous tangly hair had been cut in a short back and sides, and a tie hung loose around the collar of his blue shirt.

The stranger caught her up in a hug and then took charge of her trolley.

'Come on,' he said, walking briskly towards the exit. 'Let's get out of here before the rain comes.'

Even his car had changed.

'Very nice,' she commented as she sat into the passenger seat of the brand new Peugeot. 'Your job must be going well.'

'I've landed on my feet all right.'

Once out on the main road, he showed her just how fast the Peugeot could go. She asked him more about his job. He asked her about New York. It was all dreadfully polite.

A half-hour later, when he pulled up outside the shop, nothing of significance had been said. He turned off the engine. The awkwardness grew. She made it easy for him.

'You want to finish it, don't you?'

Even though he didn't say yes, or even nod, there was acquiescence in his eyes.

'You've met someone else?' she asked.

'Sorry.' His voice was so quiet that she almost didn't hear the apology.

'It was the risk I took.' She used a falsely bright tone. 'It's not surprising that someone else grabbed you up while I was away.'

He grinned. Some of the awkwardness dissipated.

'We can stay friends, can't we?'

'Yeah,' she replied but didn't believe they would.

'Let me bring your bags inside,' he said, looking keen to get away.

'It's okay. The suitcase has wheels. Just pop the boot open for me.' She leaned across to kiss his cheek. 'Bye, Kieran.'

Tears threatening, she quickly got out of the car.

Sarah stood in the yard and tried to steady herself before going inside. Kieran was gone. He'd met someone else. Just like John. Deep down she'd known. All the signs had been pointing that way: the sparse phone calls and, when they did talk, the evasive replies to her questions. But towards the end she'd glossed over all the warning signs and fooled herself into believing that distance was the only thing keeping them apart.

We weren't meant to be together forever. We're too different.

True, but it didn't make it any easier. Driving away in that car was someone who'd made her feel happy. Now she was on her own again. Unanchored. Without the buzz of New York to offer distraction. Would she be okay?

After a few deep breaths, she started to become more aware of her surroundings. Something was different. Not the kind of different that comes from seeing everything with fresh eyes after being away. Sarah glanced around, trying to pinpoint what it was. Her eyes rested on a crumpled tin can over by the second pump. Then they were drawn to a wrapper, buoyed by the wind, skipping across the yard.

Litter!

Having identified what it was, she could see it everywhere.

Grabbing her suitcase by its handle, she strode across the yard. As the glass doors slid open, she saw that they were smudged with fingerprints. Boxes cluttered the aisles inside, grime coated the linoleum flooring, and dust was thick on the shelves. Rage surged through her when she saw Brendan behind the counter, reading the newspaper. He didn't even bother to look up at the sound of the door.

She cleared the rage from her throat. 'Hello, Brendan.'

His head shot up. Guilt flooded his face.

'Sarah,' he spluttered. 'What are you doing here?'

'Thought I'd surprise you,' she said in a sharp staccato. 'Where's Mary?'

'She's not here,' he mumbled.

'I can see that. Has she got the day off? Is she sick?'

'Actually, she doesn't work here any longer – I had to let her go.'

Sarah's eyes narrowed. 'Since when was that *your* decision?'

He floundered. 'You weren't here –'

She cut him off. 'I was a phone call away.'

He continued to dig himself deeper. 'Me and Mary weren't seeing eye to eye –'

'About what?' Sarah interrupted again. 'About keeping the place clean? About taking the stock out of the boxes and putting it on the shelves?'

He bristled to his defence. 'Listen, I've been on my own these last few weeks, I obviously couldn't do everything . . .'

Sarah saw a car pull up outside and realised that soon a customer would have a ringside seat to their quarrel.

'Take the rest of the day off, Brendan,' she said, approaching the counter. 'We can finish this discussion tomorrow.'

'I want to stay,' he objected, his spindly fingers hanging onto the counter edge, intimating that she'd have to drag him away.

'*I* want you to go,' she snapped, her eye on the customer who was getting out of his car.

Brendan still didn't budge.

She used a softer tone. 'You said yourself that you're overworked, Brendan. Go home. Have a rest. We'll both be in better form when we talk tomorrow.'

Her logic was hard to refute and reluctantly he let go his grip on the counter. He pulled his apron over his head. He and the customer passed each other at the doorway.

Sarah stayed up all night. She reconciled the bank statements to the cashbook and the totals from the till. Methodically she worked through every day of the six months she had been away. The differences at the start were irregular and, when they did occur, the amounts were insignificant. But by the time Mary had been 'let go' at the end of the third month, the discrepancies became both regular and significant. As dawn started to break, Sarah totted up almost five thousand pounds of missing cash. She didn't doubt that the missing fifty on the day of her grandmother's death had gone into Brendan's pocket too.

How could he cheat me like this?

She buried her face in her hands. Who in the world could she trust? Not Brendan. Not Kieran.

You can count on yourself. You're strong. You can cope with this.

Brendan came in shortly after seven. His face grey and shoulders hunched, he put a brown envelope on the counter.

'There's nearly a thousand pounds in there. I have another thousand in the bank that I'll withdraw later on. I'll have to work for the rest of it.'

She pushed the envelope back towards him. 'Keep it and let's call it quits.'

Shock registered on his narrow face. 'Are you firing me?'

'I'm letting you go,' she said, using the words he'd used for Mary.

'Please!' He looked close to tears. 'Please, I'm begging you, don't bring my disgrace down on my family. I promise you –'

'Why did you do it?'

His answer was ready; it was clear that he'd analysed his reasons many times before. 'I was just trying to get a small bit ahead. All my life I've teetered on the brink of unemployment, lived hand to mouth. I wanted to have some money in my pocket, for once. I knew it was wrong . . .' He broke down crying.

'I won't mention this to anyone,' she said. 'I just want you to go – quietly.'

He left. Quietly, as she'd asked. In his wake she felt shaken. But strong. Her experiences on EquiBank's trading floor had hardened her.

Later on that day, just as Sarah was about to lock up, the door flung inwards and a familiar voice called out, 'Sarah Ryan! Come here and give me a hug!'

'Well, if it isn't the bride-to-be!' Sarah grinned. 'Nuala Kelly.'

They hugged then stepped back to examine each other.

'You're positively glowing,' said Sarah in admiration.

'It's all the facials I've been having in preparation for the big day.' Nuala touched Sarah's hair. 'Those highlights are mad. What was it like getting your hair done in New York?'

'Crazy. Just like everything else there.'

Sarah told Nuala about Fred's Hair Salon as she locked the door and turned off the lights.

'Do you want a cup of tea?' she asked as they walked through to the house.

'Go way with your tea!' Nuala gave her a small shove. 'I haven't seen you for six months.'

'I don't have anything stronger in the house, sorry.'

'Let's go across the road then,' said Nuala, as if it was that simple.

'To Delaney's?'

'Don't tell me you haven't ever had a drink there?'

'Not since John,' Sarah admitted.

'Then it's well and truly time,' Nuala declared, grabbing her by the arm.

Delaney's hadn't changed at all in the four years since Sarah had last set foot in there. The same old faces lined the bar. The lounge, although practically empty, was clouded with cigarette smoke.

John's father was behind the bar.

'Sarah, you're back.'

Tall like John, with thinning hair combed neatly to the side, his smile was warm. Sarah had always liked Mr Delaney much more than his wife.

'Yes,' she replied. 'I got home yesterday. This is my friend Nuala.'

Mr Delaney smiled again. 'Hello, Nuala. Sarah here was gone so long that we were thinking she had no notion of coming home at all. Now, what can I get you?'

'A glass of white wine and a Heineken, please,' said Sarah.

He turned to get glasses from the shelf behind.

'How's John keeping?' asked Nuala brazenly.

'He's doing grand,' replied Mr Delaney, pouring tawny Heineken from the tap. 'He's been in Canada for the last few months. A famous pianist invited him over for an extended visit – I can't remember the fellow's name, though. It all goes in one ear and out the other with me. John gets his talent from his mother's side.'

'Where is he going after Canada?' Nuala ignored Sarah's nudge in the ribs. 'Back to Paris?'

'No, he's finished there. He says he'll go wherever he gets invited to play. Like a tinker with no home, said I,' Mr Delaney chortled. 'His mother didn't find it funny, though.'

The drinks ready, Sarah opened her purse to pay.

'On the house, love,' said Mr Delaney, waving away the money.

The girls thanked him and made their way to one of the far tables.

'Why did you ask him about John?' Sarah hissed once they were sitting down.

'Because I knew you wanted to know,' Nuala replied airily.

Chapter 21

Nuala's wedding day dawned with a cold blue sky. Sarah woke, her knees cramped.

'Sleeping beauty awakens,' Nuala commented by her side.

'Morning,' Sarah grinned. 'Did you sleep okay?'

'Not a wink.'

'Nervous?'

'Yeah.'

Sarah propped herself up on her elbows. 'Too early to use champagne to calm the nerves. How about a strong cup of tea?'

Nuala shook her head. 'Let's just lie here and talk for a while.'

'Okay. What do you want to talk about, bride-to-be?'

Nuala usually smiled when Sarah called her *bride-to-be*. Not this time, though.

'Let's talk about whether I'm making a huge mistake or not,' she replied in a serious tone of voice.

'Oh, don't be silly,' Sarah admonished. 'Of course you aren't making a mistake.'

'You don't like him, do you?'

'Colin? Of course I do –'

'No, you don't,' Nuala cut her off. 'Come on, admit it.'

'I'll admit no such thing.' Sarah was firm. 'This is the morning of your wedding, for God's sake. Why do you want to start an argument?'

'I don't want an argument,' Nuala insisted. 'I just want you to be honest, that's all.'

'You're the one getting married, not me,' Sarah pointed out. 'You're the one who needs to be honest with yourself.'

A tense silence filled the small bedroom. Sarah heard the creak of a door and some footsteps on the landing. The rest of the household was starting to rise. She needed to address Nuala's doubts quickly.

'Just remember what you love about Colin,' she told her friend. 'That's what's important – banish the rest of the fanfare from your head.'

A knock sounded on the door and Nuala's mother bustled in.

'A lovely crisp day, it is,' she exclaimed as she drew back the curtains. 'Now, you'd better hop out of bed, Nuala. The hairdresser will be here at nine.'

Nuala peeled back the covers and her mother rushed off to begin breakfast.

'Problem is, I can't remember what it is I love about Colin,' she said in a matter-of-fact way as she tied the belt of her housecoat.

Breakfast, hairdresser and make-up followed in quick succession. Nuala smiled and laughed through it all, and nobody but Sarah noticed that she was a little detached.

The bride's dress was rich cream brocade with a scooped neckline and long sleeves. She looked like a medieval princess. Sarah's burgundy dress was of a similar style.

'Are you okay?' Sarah whispered when they had a brief moment alone before going downstairs.

'Yeah,' Nuala replied vaguely.

The heating in the church was patchy and Sarah felt blasts of cold air as she walked down the aisle. Nuala followed close behind with her father. In what looked like a brisk interchange, the bride's father handed her to her future husband and the service began.

The priest, old and doddery, referred to Colin as Colm and gave a rambling sermon on the sanctity of marriage. More than an hour later, the wedding party smiled and posed in front of the altar. Cameras flashed, and permanently recorded the forced smiles of the bride and groom.

Later, after the meal and speeches, Sarah had token dances with the recently married best man and Nuala's brother, who now had a steady girlfriend. For the rest of the night she hopped from group to group, talking, laughing, but feeling a little on the outer. It would have been nice to have had Kieran there, to dance with and talk to. *There's nothing quite like a wedding to make you feel lonely,* she thought.

In hindsight, the decision to sell the shop had been inevitable since the moment Sarah arrived back from New York. She missed the exhilaration of EquiBank's trading floor and found the day-to-day management of the shop hopelessly dull by comparison. She missed the big-city buzz, the honking horns and pushing pedestrians. She couldn't visualise her future in Carrickmore. No matter how hard she tried.

Even before she recognised the decision as final, she started to prepare for the sale by getting the books in order, doing a full stocktake and arranging for the exterior to be painted.

'I can't believe you're going through with it,' said Nuala when she saw the advertisement in the *Cork Examiner*.

Sarah shrugged. 'EquiBank Dublin have an opening in the fixed interest desk and, thanks to Denise's reference, I've been offered the job.'

'Oh. Congratulations.'

'At least *try* to sound like you're excited for me.'

'I am,' Nuala said, but not very convincingly. 'But I don't understand why you have to sell the shop. Why don't you put someone in charge?'

Sarah arched an eyebrow. 'I tried that before, and look where it got me.'

'Brendan was just bad luck – it would work if you found the right person.'

Sarah shook her head, quite determined. 'I don't want the worry of it. I learned in New York that you can't do investment banking fifty per cent – it's all or nothing.'

'You know, I envy your ambition,' Nuala sighed. 'I wish I had your drive. You decide something and you go for it – college, New York, now Dublin. Me, I just float along . . .'

She sounded very disillusioned. In fact, since the wedding she often had a resigned expression on her face. However, she'd never mentioned again that she couldn't remember what it was she loved about Colin.

Sarah put an arm around her friend's shoulders. 'You can visit me heaps when I get my new place.'

'Colin doesn't like Dublin – he says the crime up there is something terrible.'

'Well then, you'll just have to come without Colin,' Sarah replied tartly.

Her suitcases packed and loaded in the car, Sarah dashed across the road for one last visit to the cemetery before the drive to Dublin. The white metal gate squeaked on opening. Mr O'Hara, bent over as he yanked stubborn weeds from the grassy verge, was midway down the main path. He straightened and touched two fingers to his cap in salute.

'You're off then,' he said.

'Yes. I'm hoping to get there before the dark –'

'Just take your time, girl,' he advised. 'Better for it to be dark than you rushing and taking unnecessary risks on the road.'

Sarah smiled at his fatherly tone.

He inclined his head in the general direction of the shop. Like all the residents of Carrickmore, he was curious about the SOLD placard at the front of the premises.

'It didn't take long to go,' he remarked in a conversational tone.

Sarah's answer was noncommittal. 'No, it didn't.'

Much as she liked the old fellow, she was reluctant to discuss the details of the sale with him. It seemed a foregone conclusion that Mr O'Hara and the other villagers wouldn't approve of the buyer, a supermarket chain that had plans to bulldoze the house and build a new, larger premises. Sarah could put her sentimentality to one side and see that the plans made good business sense. New homes were springing up in the area and the population was on the rise. The supermarket chain was building for the future. The villagers, though, were entrenched in the past.

'Will you watch the grave for me?' she asked.

'Of course, I will.'

She slipped a fifty-pound note into the palm of his weathered hand.

'Ah, go way outta that,' he protested, trying to give it back.

'Keep it, please.' She waved it away. 'I'd be very grateful if you could put flowers on the grave every now and then.'

Reluctantly he stuffed the money into the inside pocket of his anorak, and Sarah, her boots scrunching on the gravel, walked on towards the grave.

'You don't mind, do you?' she asked Peggy as she crouched down next to the marble headstone.

She'd sought her grandmother's counsel on the sale a hundred times before. As always, there was no clear answer to her question, only a deep sense of peace. The supermarket chain had paid good money. Peggy was a businesswoman: Sarah had her blessing.

Chapter 22

In many ways Dublin was similar to New York: the streets brimming with rushed preoccupied-looking people; the congregating homeless on street corners and wide doorways; the beeping horns, screeching brakes and revving engines combining to create an urgent, familiar anthem.

Initially Sarah shared a house with two commodity brokers, George and Sam. However, it soon became apparent that they regarded her as their live-in housekeeper, leaving the bathroom sink grimed with their stubble, the kitchen sink overflowing with dishes, and the living room littered with mouldy coffee cups. Sarah cleaned up after them for a few months before deciding that enough was enough. She placed a cleaning roster over the kitchen sink, the main crime scene. George and Sam nodded and made all the right sounds when she ran through it.

'So, I'm on Thursdays and Fridays. That should be okay.'

'Tuesdays and Wednesdays for me – no problem.'

A week passed by, the roster totally ignored by the boys.

'Tough few days at work. Couldn't get to it.'

'Too tired. Maybe next week.'

Sarah went on strike and refused to do any cleaning at all until they pulled their weight. The house was bordering on unliveable when Emma, her old college friend, phoned.

'I've got a job with Irish Life – I'm moving to Dublin too.'

'That's great news, well done.'

'Want to share a flat?'

'Yes!' Sarah replied emphatically. 'I can't live in this disgusting mess a minute longer.'

The girls moved into an old-style two-bedroom flat in Rathmines. It had battened windows, ornate cornices and a period fireplace.

'I'll give you my share of the bond as soon as I get a few pay packets into my bank account,' Emma promised. She was broke after a year of inter-railing around Europe.

'Don't worry about it.'

Sarah felt guilty that she was so well off in comparison to her friend. The money from the sale of the shop, still largely intact, sat in a term-deposit account and had already earned interest that amounted to three times more than the bond. Sarah also earned a good salary. She had to work hard for it, though. She supported four male dealers who, just like their counterparts in New York, had an oversupply of testosterone and an undersupply of morals. While they swanned off to extended lunches in Dublin's most exclusive restaurants, Sarah was left to settle the bonds that were due and to borrow for any shortfalls. She also had to balance the portfolio and make everything square for the day. She worked twice as many hours as the dealers, but that was just the way things were.

The trading floor had a distinct pecking order. At the very bottom were the assistants, like Sarah. Next came the dealers, young men who earned quarterly bonuses that were enough to retire on. Those who didn't retire young, or burn out, became associate directors. A few years later, if they *still* hadn't retired or had a nervous breakdown, they became fully fledged directors.

Eric MacDonald, the chief dealer, presided over the directors, associate directors, dealers and assistants. Eric was a burly man with gold-framed spectacles that seemed far too delicate for his big face. He had a glass-walled office on the mezzanine level where he could keep an eagle eye on the happenings of the entire floor. He was not one to hide away in his office, though. Three to four times a day he would walk the floor, looking over shoulders and proffering advice. He regularly mixed up names, getting them wrong every other time.

'There's no future in long-term bonds at the moment, Tony.'

'It's Robert.'

Eric would roll his eyes and continue on without apology. 'Go short for today,' he'd say, tersely.

Being one of only a handful of females had its benefits. Eric knew Sarah's name right from the start.

'Here on your own, Sarah?'

'The guys are out to lunch with Bank of Ireland,' she told him. 'They're hoping to borrow two million – we've a lot of bonds maturing this week.'

Seemingly satisfied with her response, Eric continued on with his rounds, his hands clasped behind his back, his tiny glasses perched on his oversized nose.

One Friday afternoon, when there wasn't a lot happening, he was more chatty than usual.

'Do you like working here, Sarah?'

'Yes.'

'What do you like the best?'

'Balancing the portfolio.'

He nodded as if he approved of her answer.

'What job do you want to do after this?'

Sarah saw his question as one of the most important opportunities of her career and was appropriately careful in her response. 'I sometimes used to help out by confirming the FX deals in New York. I found it really interesting and –'

Before she could finish, Eric was distracted by a commotion over at the corporate bond desk. He hurried away to deal with whatever crisis was unfolding. Sarah sighed at the untimely interruption, and returned to the task at hand.

A few months later, Eric called Sarah into his office and informed her that she was being transferred from the fixed interest desk.

'You're going to Foreign Exchange – just as you asked.'

She broke into a delighted smile. 'Thank you, Eric. I really appreciate this opportunity you're giving me . . .'

'Just watch and learn,' he replied gruffly. 'Make sure you ask questions if you don't understand something.'

She tried to take his advice but, with multiple currencies on the move, the FX desk was a frantic place. Nick and Peter, the dealers, had little time or patience for questions. After getting her head bitten off more than once, Sarah learned to ask only what was essential.

'They tell me you're getting on well,' Eric commented one day. 'That you're very fast with numbers.'

She smiled. 'I was practically still in the pram when my grandmother had me working in her shop. We didn't have a cash register in those days – I did a lot of addition in my head.'

'Does your grandmother still have the shop?'

Sarah felt a familiar pang of loss as she replied, 'No, she died three years ago.'

'How about your parents?'

She shook her head. 'They passed away when I was a small child.'

Eric began to take Sarah under his wing. If things were quiet, he'd sit on her desk, one leg hanging, and coach her on how to watch the markets.

'You have to be able to do the maths – split-second calculations are often all that stands between a gain or a loss.'

Over time, Eric revealed more about his personal life. He had been married to Patsy for twenty-eight years; their daughter, Laura, was engaged to Mark. Eric adored his strong-minded wife and daughter and was also rather fond of Mark.

'That young man is far too submissive for his own good,' he sighed one morning.

Sarah smiled. 'Ah, so Laura wears the pants.'

'Just like her mother,' Eric grinned. 'Speaking of Patsy, she wants to know if you'd like to join us for Christmas dinner.'

Sarah was caught off guard. She had no set plans for Christmas. Nuala had extended an invitation, as had Emma. But Nuala came with Colin, and Emma with her valium-popping mother. Neither prospect appealed. But was having dinner with virtual strangers any better?

'We don't bite,' said Eric with a smirk.

Sarah laughed. 'Okay, I'll come then.'

The MacDonald residence was in Blackrock. Set well back from the road, its imposing two storeys were coated with dark green ivy, and it looked like a fitting abode for EquiBank's chief dealer.

I'm going to be a fish out of water here, thought Sarah as she drove up the sweeping driveway.

'Ah, you must be Sarah.' The woman who opened the door had a loud voice, a big bosom and a friendly smile. 'I'm Patsy – Eric's better half.'

She ushered Sarah inside, took her coat and handed her a glass of mulled wine.

'Laura, is everything ready on the table?'

'Mark, get some music on.'

'Eric, check on the turkey, would you?'

Once her instructions were dispatched, she emitted a raucous laugh.

'Eric might be the boss at work,' she told Sarah, 'but he's got no clout in this house – *I* call the shots around here.'

After Christmas Sarah was often invited over to the MacDonald household and eventually she came to know them so well that she would call unannounced. She felt at home there. It was as if there had always been an empty seat around their family table with her name on it.

'Why do you hang out with them so much?' asked Emma, perplexed by the unlikely friendship. 'They're nearly three times your age.'

'Patsy's like a mother – she fusses over what I eat, what I wear, my health – and Eric's like a dad . . .'

Emma smiled wryly. 'Maybe I'll leave Mum to her valium and ask the MacDonalds to take me in as well.'

Sarah did nothing to hide the friendship at work, and it was a rude awakening when she overheard a conversation that was going on inside the smoking room.

'Every time I turn around he's there with her, showing her this, showing her that.'

'That's not all he shows her, I bet.'

Sarah recognised the sniggers: Nick and Peter. Deeply upset, she returned to her workstation.

Eric came around later that day and sat on her desk while he talked about the dip in the US dollar. Sarah tried to talk to him as normal. She felt as sorry for him as she did for herself that people would misinterpret their friendship.

The following year Sarah got promoted and became a foreign exchange dealer. She had finessed her natural instinct for the market and the promotion was one hundred per cent merited.

Nick and Peter were put out that she was now on the same level as them.

'Anybody can get ahead if they're sleeping with the boss,' she heard Nick mutter under his breath.

'What did you say?'

He was too cowardly to repeat it out loud. 'Nothing.'

'I've worked damned hard for this promotion,' Sarah informed him in a stony voice. 'If I ever hear you insinuate again that Eric is more than my friend, I'll tell him – and I think you're smart enough to know what that will mean for your future here.'

With a grunt, Nick swung around in his seat and went back to work. Seething, Sarah continued to stare daggers at his back. It had been Denise, in New York, who had first set the standard. Then Eric. Sarah was very grateful to them both for helping her establish the direction she wanted her career to take. She was aiming for the very top. Nobody, least of all Nick, was going to stop her.

She'd never felt more confident, more sure of herself and her place in the world. She still had dark moods, like everybody else, but they usually passed. If they lingered, she had coping strategies: running, keeping her thoughts positive, focusing on her achievements at work. She was often amazed by how effective her strategies were, by the way she could change her thought patterns and lift her moods. An ocean of tears could have been saved if she'd known all this at the time of the abortion and her grandmother's death.

Jodi: Moving On

Chapter 23

1990

Jodi finished her degree with second-class honours. It wasn't what she'd initially aimed for, but it wasn't a bad result considering.

'When's your graduation ceremony?' asked Shirley.

'I'm not going, Mum.'

'Oh, darling, why not?'

'Because the sooner everyone forgets my face and name, the better for my career.'

After the trial, Jodi had been the subject of much curiosity at the university. She had tried to ignore the stares and nudges and whispers, and now that her degree was finished she had no desire to extend her notoriety to the graduation ceremony.

Shirley didn't argue and Jodi returned the paperwork to the university, electing not to attend the ceremony.

The dean phoned the house the next day, sounding very displeased.

'Your form says that you're not attending the graduation ceremony. May I ask why?'

'Because all the graduates will be pointing me out to their relatives – that's the girl who stabbed her stepfather.'

'That's not a worthy reason –'

'Yes, it is, Professor,' Jodi cut him off. 'The ceremony will be full of business mums and dads – bankers, accountants, economists, potential employers. I don't want to remind them that Jodi Tyler is on the job market. I don't want to prompt them to warn their recruitment departments about me. "Whatever you do, don't hire that girl, she's dangerous, she could go on a stabbing frenzy in the office some day . . . "'

'You're being ridiculous,' he snapped. 'This graduation ceremony marks a momentous occasion for you and the faculty. It's a testament to how we worked together. It sets an example for every other struggling student.'

'I'm not interested in setting an example! I just want the best possible start to my career – which is to be as anonymous as possible.'

'Now you're being selfish . . .'

Jodi flared up. *'No, I'm not!'*

Suddenly he was angry too. 'For goodness sake, Jodi, grow up.'

'I *am* grown up – and I don't have to listen to you patronising me.'

She crashed down the phone and fled to her room.

Grandma, who had overheard the yelling, made to go after her but changed her mind.

They'll sort it out themselves, she thought.

Grandma was wrong: they didn't sort it out, even though Jodi tried to. A few weeks after their argument, she was offered a job in ComBank. It presented the perfect opportunity to phone the dean's office, to tell him the news, to make amends.

'The dean is overseas,' said the secretary.

'When will he be back?'

'We don't know.' The secretary lowered her voice. 'You never know how long family problems take to resolve, do you?'

Jodi hung up with an odd mix of emotions: curiosity about the professor's 'family problems', regret that she had waited so long to phone him and, the most acute of the emotions, loneliness. One way or another, Professor Phelps had been a constant in her life for four years, a formidable ally, helping her through the trial and her degree. She missed him.

Jodi's new job consisted of processing changes of address in the unit trust department. It was soulless work, data entry peppered with a few phone calls.

Think of this as a stepping stone, she told herself over and over.

The notifications of address change came in the mail and Jodi was one of four administrators who processed the data onto the system. Jodi's colleagues were pleasant in a remote, disinterested kind of way. They talked about weekend plans and the weather. They never asked Jodi anything about her personal life. They were too self-absorbed to follow world or even local news, and didn't have a clue that three years previously their new colleague had been on the front page of every newspaper in the country.

They were just as insular when it came to their work, tapping away on their keyboards and muttering under their breath if there was anything slightly out of the usual with a customer's request.

The supervisor, a hefty woman called Mary, was consulted on every minor deviation from the norm. She would give instructions on how to proceed, a sigh in her voice.

'Phone the customer.'

'Enter a file note.'

'Ask for further evidence.'

Mary gave the same advice over and over but none of the administrators took the initiative to retain it. Jodi saw an opportunity to make her mark. Initially this meant bothering Mary with even more questions. At five o'clock, when the others had scarpered from their desks to make their train or bus home, Jodi would type up her notes. It took three weeks to put the standard operating procedure together, but she felt a great sense of achievement when it was done.

She put the final copy on Mary's desk.

Please, Mary, give me a promotion – before I go insane.

The next morning, when Jodi was opening the mail, she saw Mary approach. She didn't look particularly happy. She reached Jodi's side and put her hands on her ample hips.

'Are you trying to put me out of a job?'

Then, to Jodi's relief, her broad face broke into a smile.

After that, Jodi's promotion was swift; in less than a month she was moved to the application processing area which was also under Mary's supervision. In her new role she was responsible for handling applications to join the unit trust fund. This involved setting up new clients in the unit holder registry system and creating a purchase of units. She had to prepare a deposit slip for the cheques that came in with the application forms. Sometimes she liaised with other areas, like the funding department where the price for each unit was set. This was how she met Andrew Ferguson, a fund accountant from the UK.

'How do you set the price?' she asked him one day.

'Easy,' he replied and opened a spreadsheet on his screen.

'First, we value all of the assets. Then we add on the known income receivable. And divide by the number of units. Basic maths, really.'

Jodi was fascinated. 'How do you value the assets?'

'We upload the share prices from the night before.'

'What happens if you make a mistake and work it out wrong?'

'We check everything very carefully.' Andrew regarded her from behind his silver-framed glasses. 'Look, if you're that interested, we can go for a drink after work and I can bore you with all the details . . .'

Jodi was on the verge of turning him down, but she stopped. Andrew was quite good-looking with his boyish face, gentle brown eyes and dimples at the corners of his mouth.

'Okay,' she shrugged, as if it was no big deal.

'Dates are more about the preparation than the actual event,' Alison had once said. 'It's so much fun picking what to wear and doing your hair.' Which in Alison's case meant changing her tresses to a bright orange or, one time, electric blue. 'Then there's all the anticipation mixed in with the nervousness. No wonder it's often an anticlimax when you actually meet the guy.'

My very first date at the ripe old age of twenty-two, Jodi thought as she touched up her make-up in the office toilet. *Well, better late than never, I guess.*

Her white shirt and pinstriped skirt looked very ordinary and the last thing she would have chosen to wear had there been more notice. She opened an extra button on the shirt, revealing some of her year-round tan.

Andrew was waiting in the foyer. Jodi had only ever seen him sitting down and was surprised at how tall he was. His light brown hair was spiked, as if he'd run some water through it, and his jacket was slung over his shoulder.

'Well, you know this city a lot better than I do,' he grinned. 'Where can we go to have a nice chat about fund accounting?'

Jodi laughed. 'Let's try the Hilton.'

Outside, a gusty wind whipped down George Street and Jodi pulled the lapels of her jacket together.

'Gosh, it's cold,' she said with a grimace.

'Cold?' He looked amused. 'This is positively balmy next to London.'

The Hilton was only a block away and they were soon descending the marble steps into the bar.

'What would you like to drink, Jodi?'

'Well, I'm the one who wants to pick your brain, so maybe I should get this,' she replied.

'You can get the next one.'

'Oh.' She felt tremendously pleased that it wasn't going to be just a quick drink. 'I'll have a beer, please.'

She found two spare stools while he was at the bar. She didn't take off her jacket. Despite what he'd said, it *was* cold. He came back with the drinks and his knee brushed against hers as he slid onto the stool.

'Cheers.' He raised his glass of lager and took a sip. 'Now, what do you want to know?'

Jodi asked him about his family, his life back home and what he liked to do in his spare time. She asked him about his travels, his friends and what kind of music he listened to. In fact, she asked him about everything but fund accounting.

On the steps of the Hilton Hotel, on their way out, Andrew's hand cupped the underside of her chin and tilted her face upwards. His lips were warm and tender. Jodi returned his kiss with a passion she didn't know she was capable of. He gathered her closer, kissed her harder. Carried away in the moment, they temporarily forgot where they were.

'Move along from the steps now,' the bouncer said gruffly, trying to hide a smile.

Up on the street, the cold wind brought a gush of reality.

He wouldn't want to kiss me if he knew the truth.

Andrew, feeling the cold this time round, put on his jacket.

'How do you get home?' he asked.

'Bus.'

'Come on, I'll walk you.'

Her hand felt warm in his grasp as they walked down the street. Leaves and the odd piece of litter blew against them. Jodi's hair streaked across her eyes and, after many futile attempts to tuck it back behind her ears, she let it be. She walked slowly, not wanting the night to end or reality to intrude again.

'That bus says *Dee Why*,' said Andrew, his pace quickening.

'Oh.'

The buses were usually a half-hour apart. How unlucky that there was one about to leave!

Andrew bounded onto the bus.

'What are you doing?' she giggled. 'You live in the opposite direction, you big idiot.'

He handed the driver the fare. 'Thought I'd come along for the ride.'

They sat down the back, his arm resting across her shoulders. The bus rattled its way down Military Road and over Spit Bridge. Jodi gave Andrew, who'd never been north of the city, some orientation.

'This bridge opens up to let the yachts through. The road traffic has to stop and wait.'

'I wouldn't mind living here,' he said, eyeing the houses on the harbourside, 'and causing a traffic jam with my yacht.'

'All you need is a few million,' Jodi quipped.

He squeezed her shoulder. 'Well, we do work in investment banking – another few years and who knows?'

The bus chugged up the hill and after that it was an easy run to Dee Why.

'This is my stop coming up,' she said, making a sad face.

Andrew leaned down to kiss her and once again Jodi forgot where she was. In the distance were the grinding brakes of the bus, the lurching stop, the bang of the doors as they opened.

Finally she pulled away. 'I'd better go.' She stood up, feeling decidedly starry-eyed. 'Enjoy the ride back to the city.'

He winked. 'I will.'

Jodi was apprehensive about going to work the next day.

What if he ignores me? Acts like nothing happened?

She walked into the office, settled at her desk and logged onto her computer. Andrew's desk was at the other end of the floor. She didn't need to see him until she required the unit price for the day. She could drag that out for another hour.

'Good morning.'

She jumped at the sound of his voice. A blush invaded her face. Luckily, her colleagues weren't watching.

'Hello, Andrew.'

She noticed that his face was a little red too.

'Jodi . . .'

'Yes?'

'Will you go out with me again?'

'Okay. Yes.' She nodded, her head bobbing like a fool.

'Friday night?'

'Okay.'

'Same place?'

'Let's try the other end of town: the Rocks.'

He made a move to return to his desk.

'Andrew ...'

'Yes?'

'Do you have the unit price for today?'

This time Jodi could fully enjoy the anticipation of the date. For three days she deliberated about what to wear before she decided nothing in her wardrobe was good enough and dragged Alison out on a last-minute lunchtime shopping spree.

'Gosh, you must be keen on him,' Alison remarked when they met up outside her office. Now that she was part of the work force, her hair was toned down and her nose ring an accessory she wore only at weekends. 'This is so not like you.'

'I know,' Jodi hurried her across the road to a busy shopping mall, 'but I was dressed in my absolute worst the last time we went out – this time I want him to see me at my best.'

With only an hour at their disposal, they raced in and out of chain stores and boutiques. Eventually Jodi settled on a pair of bootleg jeans and a low-cut white top.

'Phone me tomorrow,' Alison instructed before rushing back to work.

Jodi went back to her desk and pretended to work. In her head she played out their date: meeting at the Orient Hotel, laughing and talking over drinks, and finally the walk to the bus. Funny that it was the end of the night she was most looking forward to, when they were alone, holding hands, kissing. Maybe he'd get on the bus again.

She got changed at work. In the harsh lights of the bathroom she thought the white top didn't look half as flattering as it had in the shop. Her hands shook as she applied her mascara. A black blob smeared her eyebrow and she wiped it off with some tissue.

The walk down George Street calmed her. She arrived at the Orient, scanned the crowd and realised he wasn't there.

A stool freed up at the bar and she put her jacket on it. She ordered a drink and had taken a few sips when she saw Andrew weaving through the crowd. She waved, beamed a happy smile at him. He made for her direction, but didn't return her smile.

'Hi.' She greeted him with a kiss and, when his response was lukewarm, wondered if she had been too forward. She gestured to her drink. 'What would you like?'

'Nothing for now.'

He took her arm and guided her away from the bar, to the gaming room, where it was quieter.

'What's wrong?' she asked.

'This.' He reached into his trouser pocket and took out a folded page.

Jodi quickly glanced at the copied newspaper article and accompanying photograph. All the happiness poured out of her.

'Why didn't you tell me?'

'We've only had one date, Andrew. Obviously I would have told you at a later point . . .' Jodi swallowed a lump in her throat. 'Where did you get the article from?'

'One of the blokes in the office gave it to me,' he answered flatly. 'I told him that I had a date with you – he gave me an odd look at the time, then handed me this today.'

Jodi shook her head, tears smarting in her eyes. 'I thought that nobody knew. They never said anything to me.'

Andrew's reply was harsh. 'Everyone knows – everyone except *me*.'

'Sorry,' she mumbled. 'I'm so sorry.'

Then she fled the dark room with the flashing poker machines and zombie players.

'Wait a minute,' she heard him call but she kept going, through the overheated bar, out into the crisp night. She shivered. She'd left her jacket behind. But there was no going back.

'Excuse me.'

'Sorry.'

On she went, bumping shoulders, apologising, ignoring the curious stares at her tear-streaked face.

A while later she found herself climbing the steps to the Harbour Bridge. The exertion slowed her and numbed the hurt she was feeling. She walked along the pathway, alongside other pedestrians: people who came from normal families; people who'd never had their photograph in the papers; people whose colleagues had no reason to gossip behind their backs. She wondered what she had done to deserve being so different to them.

Down below, the harbour was black and swirling. Barbed wire arched over the railing to prevent desperados from jumping in. But she could scale it. If she wanted.

Jodi dismissed the thought as soon as it entered her head. She wasn't a jumper, she was a survivor.

She walked as far as Neutral Bay and caught the bus from there. Grandma was watching TV when she got home, a cup and saucer balanced on her knees. She frowned disapprovingly at Jodi.

'You'll catch your death, girl.'

'I left my jacket in the pub.'

Grandma sighed and lifted the cup, her lips pursed in anticipation of the sugar-laden tea.

'That top doesn't leave much to the imagination at all,' she declared, the cup rattling against the saucer as she set it back down.

She resumed watching the quiz show on the TV, completely unaware that she'd said those same words about Jodi's dress on the night of her eighteenth birthday.

When the alarm started to beep on Monday morning, Jodi fleetingly considered not going to work. Rain that had lingered on from the weekend splattered her window. She felt warm, sleepy and in no way ready to face Andrew and her other colleagues.

She yawned widely and pulled back the covers. She needed the job. Liked the job. It had given her a much-needed foot in the door of the banking business and she could see the possibility of further promotions. The harsh reality was that she'd been foolish for thinking she could keep her past a secret.

The day started with the usual half-hearted enquiries about the weekend. 'Do anything special?'

Jodi was about to reply in the negative when she thought the better of it. 'I had a date with Andrew Ferguson on Friday night.' Their jaws dropped at her announcement. They neither wanted nor expected to hear specifics about her life. She continued on cheerily, 'He wasn't too keen when he found out about my stepfather, though. Pity – I kind of liked him. I've never had a boyfriend, not even a date, really – I think men are quite scared of me . . .'

They didn't know where to look or what to say. Jodi found it hard not to laugh.

Then Celia, one of her older colleagues, cleared her throat. 'The weather is shocking, isn't it? We need the rain, though.'

They all murmured their agreement, relieved at the change in subject, and then their fingers became busy on their keyboards.

Jodi, her lips twitching in a smirk, opened the mail, sorted out all the cheques and began to update the cashbook.

'Jodi?'

Her heart missed a beat at the sound of Andrew's voice. She didn't let it show, though, as she swung around brazenly in her seat.

'Yes?'

'Today's price is four dollars and ninety-eight cents.'

For a moment she was slow to cotton on.

Oh, the unit price, she realised. *Stupid me! Why else would he have come around?*

'Thanks,' she snapped, aware of the sidelong glances of her colleagues.

Andrew backed away at her tone and Jodi returned to her work, sorry that she'd been so abrupt. It wasn't Andrew's fault. Of course he'd been horrified when he'd found out the truth. She was horrified herself on the occasions she allowed herself to think about it.

The morning dragged on, the monotony broken only by a soggy trip to the bank to deposit the cheques. Jodi was on her way back to the office when she ran into Andrew again.

'Sorry about earlier,' she said, pushing her damp hair back from her face.

'I'm sorry too,' he mumbled. 'I shouldn't have put you on the spot like that on Friday night. It wasn't fair.'

Jodi chewed her lip, the awkwardness rendering her speechless.

'I came after you,' he said, staring down at her, 'but you were nowhere to be seen.'

'I –' The intensity of his gaze brought a blush to her face. 'I took a detour, then I got a bus home.'

He slid his hands into his pockets and hunched his shoulders. 'Will you go out with me again?'

It seemed that Andrew Ferguson didn't scare easily.

'I really like you,' he added when she didn't respond.

It also seemed that he wore his heart on his sleeve.

He stared, waiting for her answer. It was a defining moment: one that Jodi knew would change the rest of her life.

'Yes, okay,' she replied in a croaky voice.

They both realised that she'd have to tell him everything. So she did. In the Hilton Hotel, he with a lager, she with a glass of red wine, sitting on the hard wooden bar stools. Even though they'd only been there once before, it felt like a comfortingly familiar setting in which to bare her soul.

Jodi talked in a slow and measured manner about her father leaving, her mother marrying Bob, the letters that shadowed her teen years, the knife, the court case, the media. A weight lifted off her as she recounted details that no one else knew, trivia that was incidental to the court case but still impacted her daily life.

'I have an aversion to the colour pink because of him – apparently the girlishness of it turned him on. So I got rid of everything that was pink – hair clips, bangles, sheets – made my room as sterile as possible. I thought it might keep him away.' She looked at Andrew's face, the softness of it, the boyishness. It was the polar opposite of Bob's. She needed that. 'I still see his face in my head – the bulging eyes, the leer . . .'

'What did the rest of your family think of him?' Andrew asked perceptively. 'Did they like him?'

Jodi recalled the family barbecues and other get-togethers. 'Yeah, I guess they did. Bob had his act down pat, always declaring how lucky he was to have Mum, kissing and cuddling her, making a show of how much he doted on her. Grandma and the rest of the family were happy to see Mum happy . . .'

'What about his family?'

Jodi grimaced. 'Bob's parents died a long time ago and he didn't really keep in touch with his sister – not even Christmas cards – both too lazy to make the effort. Yet at the funeral and in court you'd swear Janine, that's his sister, had lost her right arm. All she could say was, "My brother didn't deserve an end like that". Over and over she'd say the same thing, sobbing into a big dirty handkerchief. She loved the TV cameras outside the court – she was the only one who'd talk to the reporters. The rest of us tried to ignore them.'

It was very late when they left the Hilton. Jodi was exhausted, all talked out.

'Now that you know everything, can we put it behind us and not discuss it again?' she asked quietly as they strolled towards the bus.

He squeezed her hand in his. 'If that's what you want.'

Over the following months Jodi and Andrew became closer. They went for quiet drinks and never ran out of things to say. They went to the cinema, usually on Tuesdays when the tickets were half price, Andrew laughingly calling them cheapskates. And, as the weather became warmer, they went to the beach. At Andrew's encouragement, Jodi decided to lay an old ghost to rest and compete in the Ironwoman Series. She began to train, running at dawn, swimming at dusk. She didn't have anywhere near the same speed or agility she'd had when she was seventeen, but it felt gloriously good to be back, running barefoot on the sand, swimming through waves, in the club's family fold, with Sue as her coach, mentor and friend.

On the weekends Andrew came to watch and cheer her on. He was a distraction more than anything, but she loved having him there. When her training was finished, she would give him a surfing lesson. He was hopeless, had no sense of balance. Nevertheless, it became his favourite pastime, laughing uproariously when he got dunked, proud as punch on the rare occasions he managed to stand up on the board.

Jodi didn't expect it to happen so quickly: falling in love. She thought she'd be more guarded, slower to open up. But it wasn't like that at all.

'Jodi . . .' Andrew began, one sunny October afternoon when they were laid out on their beach towels, the salt from the sea dried into their skin.

'Yes,' she replied sleepily.

'When are you going to introduce me to your family?'

She opened her eyes warily and raised herself up on her elbows. Andrew's brown eyes were waiting intently for her response.

She licked her dry lips, felt a taste of salt.

'Gosh, I'm thirsty.' She reached into her backpack for her water bottle.

He watched her glug it back.

'Finished avoiding the issue?' he enquired.

'I'm not –'

'Yes, you are,' he interrupted calmly. 'What are you so afraid of?'

Jodi pulled her knees up, rested her chin on them, and answered him honestly. 'Of you not liking them – or them not liking you. I don't want anything to ruin what we have.'

'It's what normal couples do – meet the families.'

'We're not normal,' she answered tersely, then corrected herself, 'I mean *I'm* not normal.'

Andrew pushed her backwards so she was lying flat on the towel. He rolled on top of her, impervious to the curious glances of the sunbathers around them. He pulled a face that was meant to look fierce but, with his baby face, fell woefully short.

'Right! I'm going to keep you here until you concede to my reasonable request.'

Laughing, she tried in vain to push him off.

'Grandma can be a bit of a battleaxe . . . and Mum's paranoid after everything that happened . . .' she warned him.

'Well, my family's not that crash hot either,' he answered.

'They can't be as bad –'

'Oh yes they can. Anyway, families are kind of a necessary evil. Especially when you love someone . . .'

Jodi's heart stopped.

Love? Does he mean it?

He saw the question in her eyes and became serious.

'Yes, I do love you, Jodi Tyler.'

Jodi wrapped her arms around his neck and stared deep into his eyes.

'I love you too,' she whispered.

Their lips met in a long sensuous kiss that caused some onlookers to tut disapprovingly and others to reminisce fondly about young love.

Grandma was nothing less than charming when she met Andrew. She dressed up in her best frock and chatted in a soft cultured voice that didn't sound at all like her usual broad tones.

'My own parents were from Liverpool,' she told him confidingly. 'They got the boat out – I was born here. Mother and Father never went back, never saw their families again. Of course, you young folks can fly to and fro at the drop of a hat. Would you like a scone, Andrew?'

'Yes, thank you.'

'Jodi, can you pour Andrew's tea, please, dear?' Grandma asked.

Jodi held back a fit of the giggles and obediently reached for the teapot. Her grandmother, usually as tough as old boots, made an unlikely lady of the manor. Yet here she was, a splendid Devonshire tea laid out and a seemingly wide repertoire of polite conversation topics to while away the afternoon.

Shirley, on the other hand, didn't say much. For the first half-hour she sipped her tea and smiled absently on the occasions that Grandma stretched the truth. As a consequence, it brought a jolt to the conversation when she did find her voice.

'How long are you here for, Andrew?'

'A year in all,' he replied. 'It'll be up in January.'

'So, you're going home in the New Year then?'

'Well . . .' Andrew looked a little uncomfortable. 'Yes, I am.'

Grandma quickly smoothed over the awkwardness. 'Won't it be lovely to see your family again?' she asked brightly, and then tried to persuade him to have another scone.

Later in the evening Jodi walked with Andrew to the bus stop.

'I think your Grandma likes me,' he grinned.

'She's smitten,' Jodi laughed. 'I've never seen her like that before – the social butterfly – usually she's stamping her stick and keeping everyone in line.'

'I don't think your mum is quite as smitten though.'

Jodi shrugged. 'Oh, she's just worried that I'll get my heart broken when you disappear into thin air next January.'

Up until now they hadn't talked much about Andrew's return

home. It was out there, a dark cloud looming, but still far enough away to pretend it wasn't a problem.

Andrew stopped midstride and turned Jodi to face him.

'I could have told your mother that I don't want to leave you . . . that I'd like you to come back with me . . .'

Jodi cocked her head. 'Oh, really?'

'Yes, but I thought I should ask you first . . .' He paused and affectionately swept a stray strand of blonde hair from her eyes. 'So, will you come back to London with me, Jodi?'

She didn't need to think twice. 'Yes, Andrew. Yes, I will.'

They kissed as though it was the first time. With tenderness and hope. Their future a blank page full of possibility.

'I can't go until after the Ironwoman Series,' she said softly. 'I've waited four years to compete in that competition.'

'Of course,' he replied. 'That's a given.'

With their commitment firmly in place, Jodi finally felt ready to take their relationship to the next level. Despite some very passionate moments, Andrew hadn't seen her naked and they hadn't made love. He'd been the proverbial gentleman and hadn't pushed the issue.

A week after Grandma's tea party, their bodies entwined on Andrew's sofa, their clothes half off and lips devouring each other, Jodi whispered to him that she was ready.

He stopped, looked down with desire-darkened eyes, and asked, 'Are you sure?'

She nodded.

He seemed to need further reassurance. 'I'm kind of scared,' he admitted hoarsely. 'I don't want to make you remember –'

'Ssh,' she put a finger to his lips, 'all I'm thinking about right now is you.'

She wasn't telling the truth. Bob was on her mind. Of course, he was. But she was hoping that a normal sexual relationship would release the last stronghold that Bob had over her life.

With a slight tremor in his hands, Andrew unbuttoned her Levi's. Gently he edged the denim over her hips and she reached to undo his belt. Moments later they were fully naked. Andrew laid his body over hers and held her tightly against him. His body heat seared them together. Jodi felt an ache within her and, seeming to feel her need, his hand touched between her legs. His fingers breezed over her, tantalising, not enough.

'I really need you . . .' she whispered, pressing hard against him.

'We've lots of time,' he replied. 'There's no rush.'

He didn't know it, but there was a rush. Jodi wanted to do it now, while thoughts of Bob had retreated.

But Andrew refused to hurry. He seduced with his hands and mouth until Jodi forgot time and the race against her memories. Finally, he braced against her hips and entered her fully. She caught her breath. Then followed his rhythm.

Afterwards, while she lay cocooned in his arms, she wondered at everything about him: his boyish good looks, his understated intelligence, his keenness to debate every topic under the sun, the way he loved the outdoors and had helped her to remember that she did too, the many ways he showed her how much he loved her. She'd heard Alison talk about boys who'd lied their way into her bed. Boys who played games and broke hearts. Jodi knew Andrew wasn't one of those guys. He didn't play games and his emotions were plain for all to see.

It's like I've struck gold, she thought, then recoiled in horror as she recalled that was exactly what her mother used to say about Bob.

Chapter 24

London, 1991

London in January was cold and unwelcoming, just like Andrew's family. His mother, Janice, lived with her second husband and stepdaughter in a suburb called Harrow.

'You can stay until you find your own place,' she informed them in a curt voice. 'But I don't want any long-term lodgers.'

Janice was openly keen for her children to leave the nest. However, Tracey, her stepdaughter, wasn't showing any such intentions. Janice felt she was going backwards with Andrew staying too, no matter how temporarily.

The two-storey house was identical to all the others in the street: white dashed walls and a bay window that jutted into a small concrete front yard. Andrew, carrying a suitcase in each hand, ascended the narrow staircase in the hallway and entered the first doorway on the landing. The square wallpapered room was not quite big enough for the double bed that was pushed up against the window.

'Was this your bedroom?' Jodi took in the old-fashioned floral bedcover and the gilded doorknobs on the white wardrobe.

'No.' He lifted one of the suitcases onto the bed. 'I've never lived in this house. I moved out of home when I was eighteen. Mum married Simon the following year.'

'Do you get along with Simon?' Jodi asked, wondering why she hadn't thought to question Andrew closer about his family before moving in with them. She'd known that his real father had died when he was ten, and that he'd acquired a stepfather and stepsister when his mother remarried. That was the sum of her knowledge until now.

'Oh, Simon's okay – a bit miserable, but okay.'

He propped the second suitcase up against the wardrobe and there was hardly standing space in the room. Feeling claustrophobic, Jodi crawled across the bed to reach the window. She opened it wide and a blast of cold air stung her face. On the street below she saw children with woollen hats and bulky jackets. Their faces looked pinched and bored as they kicked at yesterday's puddles of rain. Jodi turned away from the window feeling rather despondent. It was hard to believe that only a few days ago she'd swum under a dazzling sun and run across piping-hot sand to come twelfth place in the Iron-woman Series.

'Don't worry,' said Andrew reassuringly. 'You'll feel different when we get our own place nearer the city. You're going to like London, I know it.'

Janice and Simon worked demanding jobs and were out of the house for the greater part of the day. In the mornings they ate a hurried breakfast before heading off in their mud-splattered ten-year-old BMW. Simon dropped Janice at the tube station before continuing on to his own job which was located further out of town.

Tracey, a science student who seemed to have very few classes, had a more relaxed schedule. She ate cereal, not just for breakfast, but for lunch and dinner too. She watched a lot of TV and muttered monosyllabic replies whenever Jodi tried to make conversation.

Every day Jodi and Andrew went to the local library to sift through the work advertisements in the daily newspapers. They used the library's copying machine and computer to complete their job applications. Then they would read through the ads for rental accommodation and daydream about living together on their own.

After two weeks, Andrew was called for an interview in the city. Jodi went with him for moral support. It was a forty-minute ride on the tube, initially on an overground track. The stations they passed through had large billboards saying things like: *We're now on the internet, you can make your application online* or, *Visit our new website to see a full range of products and services.*

'The internet boom seems a lot more prominent here than it was in Sydney,' Jodi commented.

'Maybe that means there's a strong job market,' Andrew replied, his thoughts on his upcoming interview.

The tube went underground as it neared the city centre. It whizzed through black tunnels, Jodi staring unseeingly out of the window. She was nervous for Andrew. They were both desperate to move out of his mother's house and into their own place. Hopefully he would get the job and they would have the means.

They changed trains at Oxford Circus and had a short ride to Cannon Street Station, where they finally disembarked. The escalator up to the street went on forever; it seemed as though they were emerging from the very depths of the earth. The sky threatened rain as they walked through the inner square mile, where all the prominent banks and blue-chip companies had their offices.

'Good luck.' Jodi pecked a kiss on his mouth when they got to their destination. She straightened his tie and pointed to a café across the road. 'I'll wait in there.'

Inside the café, she unwound her scarf and sat at a table next to the window. There was only one other customer, a man in a suit who looked as if he'd just received some bad news. The waitress, however, had a friendly face.

'Where's that accent from?' she enquired as she took Jodi's coffee order.

'Australia.'

'Ohhhh, how I would love some sun right now!'

The waitress had caramello skin and dark exotic eyes. She chatted for a while, until a male voice called from the kitchen, 'Seeta!'

'My father,' Seeta explained, throwing her eyes to heaven. 'He doesn't like me fraternising with the clientele.'

When she'd gone, Jodi thought that her friendliness made a pleasant change from Andrew's family. Now that she was alone for the first time in two weeks, she had time to gather her thoughts. They weren't positive.

It's so bleak here, she thought, looking out at the heavy sky. *Maybe that's why his family don't laugh or seem to enjoy life.*

A feeling that had been nagging her since the day she arrived reared its head high enough for her to be able to put a name to it: homesickness. She missed her mother, who still managed to smile despite the unlucky hand she'd been dealt in life. And she missed Grandma, her toughness, her softness, her wheezy cackle, and the walking stick that was practically part of her anatomy.

Seeta came along with the coffee and another friendly but brief chat. Jodi cupped the mug with her hands. Trying to feel warm. About London.

If neither of us gets a job, then we'll have to go back to Sydney.

An hour later she saw Andrew striding across the street. She could tell from the grin splitting his face that the job was in the bag. That they would be staying in this cold intimidating city.

Andrew's letter of offer came in the post three days later. On the promise of an upcoming pay packet, he promptly borrowed six hundred pounds from his mother for the bond on a maisonette in West London. The maisonette had a kitchen and living area downstairs, and a large bedroom and bathroom upstairs. The carpets were dark green, not a colour that Jodi would have chosen, but they were brightened by the fresh white paint on the walls.

'There's so much space!' Jodi exclaimed excitedly as she ran from room to room.

She stopped in her tracks, suddenly realising why the rooms seemed so vast. 'We have no furniture!'

Andrew laughed, amused that the obvious had only just occurred to her. 'We need to get some money in the bank first.'

'What'll we sleep on?'

'A mattress, I suppose. We should be able to pick up a second-hand one.'

Jodi giggled. 'We'll be like squatters.'

'Well,' he gave her a suggestive look, 'I must admit that I find the idea of squatting with you rather sexy.'

They moved in and Andrew started work. Jodi went for a few

interviews but the jobs weren't what she wanted. She had no desire to get another beefed-up administration job. She wanted something that would catapult her into a real career.

Two of the interviews turned into job offers, which she declined.

'Do you think I'm being too picky?' she asked Andrew.

'No. Hold out another while – everyone is saying the market's hot. Sooner or later someone will be desperate enough to over-look your inexperience.'

She smacked his arm. 'Desperate? Thanks very much!'

He grinned lopsidedly. 'You know what I mean.'

She pointed her finger. 'You watch out, Andrew Ferguson. Soon I'll be bringing in the big bucks and I'll be wearing the pants around here.'

He leered. 'To be honest, I like it best when you wear no pants at all.'

She rolled her eyes. 'You've got a one-track mind.'

Andrew was right. In the end someone did get desperate and Jodi got a phone call.

'One of our temps has gone AWOL.' The agent at the end of the line sounded stressed. 'We need someone to go in straight away or we'll lose the account.'

'What's the role?' Jodi asked.

'Business analyst,' was the harried reply, 'with unit pricing and reconciliation experience.'

Jodi's experience of unit pricing was limited to the questions she'd asked Andrew when they first met. She bit her lip while she contemplated the risk of putting herself forward for a role for which she had absolutely no experience.

She made her decision. 'Where do I need to go?'

'Liverpool Street. And as soon as you can. We'll pick up the taxi fare.'

The agent stayed on the line to give some further details. As soon as she hung up, Jodi raced upstairs to change into a suit. At last she was going to be part of London's work force. She would commute in a packed train, maybe buying an overpriced coffee to kick-start the day. She'd have deliverables and deadlines, a new boss and colleagues. And maybe, just maybe, she might see a more appealing side to this great big city.

Invesco had their offices in an old-style redbrick building. The lift was slow and creaky; it sounded like it needed maintenance. Jodi took a steadying breath when it finally shuddered to a stop at the fifth floor.

'I'm from ABC Recruitment,' she introduced herself to the receptionist. 'Jodi Tyler.'

The receptionist nodded and punched some buttons on her telephone system. 'She's here,' she announced to whoever was at the end of the line.

She hung up with a grimace. 'They're all in a flap back there! Some of the funds, the ones the temp was working on, haven't been valued yet this morning.'

'Oh.'

Jodi tried not to look worried at the prospect of being asked to value a fund the instant she set foot on the premises.

The doors leading to the back office slid open to reveal a forty-something woman with short frizzy fair hair and faded lipstick.

'Come through,' she barked, holding one of the doors open with her foot.

Jodi approached, holding out her hand. 'I'm –'

'I know your name.' She snatched her hand away after a mere

touch. 'It's about the only thing that agency is capable of getting right. I'm Gretel – the boss.'

Jodi followed her down a long corridor that had glass-panelled offices on both sides.

'You're sharing with me,' Gretel declared, turning into an office that looked just like all the others. 'We're short on space.'

The office was cold, the thermostat on the wall turned down low. Two desks, each with a computer, were positioned perpendicularly. Jodi put her handbag down on the smaller one. The office was generous in size, with more than enough space to accommodate two people. Nevertheless, it would be extremely difficult to share if Gretel was half the dragon she appeared to be.

'Now,' Gretel began menacingly, 'let's get a few things straight. I don't mind you being late on the odd occasion – I know that happens to the best of us – but I can't stand being let down like I was this morning. If we don't value our funds on time, then other departments can't do *their* jobs. It's like a production line – one person can impact ten others. So, if you can't come in – you're sick, or you've been run over by a bus, or whatever – then please call me. I'm here from 7 am. Once I have notice, I can avert most disasters. Understand?'

'Yes,' Jodi nodded. 'I won't let you down, Gretel. This is my first job in London and I really want to do well.'

'Good.' Gretel seemed to relax a smidgeon. 'You'll be responsible for valuing five of our funds. I'll run through them with you now . . .'

'Okay.' Jodi did her best not to look daunted. 'Do you mind if I take notes?'

Gretel shook her head. 'You'll find a pen and paper in the desk drawer.'

Jodi opened the drawer and found a half-used notepad and a pen with a chewed top. Gretel rolled her seat over and showed her where the valuation files were saved on the computer. She explained the process thoroughly, her voice becoming calmer as she went on. Jodi listened carefully, took copious notes, and then, under Gretel's watchful eye, began to update the data. After a while she felt confident that, despite her inexperience, she would master the job. She was also pretty sure that she'd get on okay with Gretel. Once she didn't let her down.

Andrew came out of the building deep in thought. His hands shoved in his pockets, his head down, he didn't notice Jodi standing there.

'Hello.' She waved an arm across his path. 'It's me.'

His face broke into a smile. 'What are you doing here?' He looked her up and down, admiring her short pinstripe skirt. 'Nice legs! Did you have an interview?'

'Not exactly. I got a job – as business analyst for Invesco – just round the corner from here.'

'That's great.' He lifted her up and swung her around. 'We'll be able to get the tube together and meet for lunch.'

'I know! And we'll be able to afford furniture . . .'

'And something other than noodles for dinner . . .'

They gazed at each other, delighted at the thought of enjoying two incomes.

'Let's celebrate – go out for dinner,' he suggested.

'Should we? I mean, I haven't got paid yet.'

'Of course we should. This is the job you've been waiting for since you graduated. It's what you deserve.'

They went to a small Indian restaurant with a reasonably priced menu and toasted each other with glasses of watery house wine.

'To the future.'

They held hands across the table while they waited for the food. Jodi felt deliriously happy. Not only did she have this gorgeous man who loved her as much as she loved him, but she finally had a job that was befitting of her abilities. For the first time since her parents' divorce, she felt that the good in her life outweighed the bad.

Later on that night, tipsy from the house wine, they caught the tube home. The rush hour over, the station felt eerie. The commuters were rougher and had shifty eyes. Jodi clasped Andrew's hand tightly, glad to have him by her side.

Jodi, anxious to prove herself to Gretel, worked very hard over the following weeks. She began work well before the official 9 am start, building in extra time to consult her notes and check for errors. Some days, if there was a delay in the availability of the price feeds, she worked through lunch. She learned to dress warm as Gretel liked the temperature of the office to be on the chilly side.

The job eventually became more familiar. Jodi was able to do without her notepad and wasn't slowed down by errors. However, she continued to come in early. Sometimes she picked up a coffee for Gretel along the way.

It didn't take Jodi long to notice that there was a lack of consistency in the daily processes she was required to perform. She had five funds and three different valuation processes.

'The company has a history of mergers and takeovers,' Gretel explained. 'Nobody had time to integrate the systems when the new companies came on board, and now we're left with all these higgledy-piggledy processes.'

Gretel didn't have enough hours in the day to worry about

standardisation. She had senior management meetings to attend, over thirty staff to manage, and dozens of daily operational fires that needed putting out.

'I'd like to have a try at making things more consistent,' said Jodi. 'I have a good head for process and getting it down on paper.'

Gretel looked up from the thick report she was reading and emitted one of her weary sighs. 'Look, Jodi, the last thing I need right now is to have to train someone else in your job.'

'I'll still do my job,' Jodi assured her boss. 'I promise you won't have to worry about that.'

Gretel smiled cynically. 'I don't think you have any idea how big and complex a mess it is.'

Jodi knew her well enough by now to be able to negotiate. 'How about you give me a week? Just to see if I can at least work out an approach to the problem. Then, if I can't convince you to proceed, I'll drop it.'

Gretel shrugged. 'Don't say I didn't warn you.'

She went back to her report having given an assent of sorts.

Jodi started with her own job and mapped the top-level steps of each valuation process onto a flowchart. Then she talked to the team leaders who worked for Gretel and mapped their valuation processes in a similar manner. She used sheets of A3 paper and drew the flowcharts in pencil so that it was easy to make changes. Once the mapping was complete, she collated and summarised her initial findings.

'We have fourteen different valuation processes,' she informed her boss.

Gretel grimaced. 'I guessed it would be something of that order.'

'I think we could get down to eight processes with minimal

effort,' Jodi continued. 'Then, with a little more planning, we could half that again.'

Gretel ran a hand through her short frazzled hair. 'You mean four processes in total?'

'Yes.'

Gretel asked to see the flowcharts. She laid the large sheets of paper across her desk and read each one, absently biting on her thumbnail as she did so.

'You're right!' She looked up. 'You do have a head for this, Jodi. I'm quite amazed that you got all of this down on paper in just one week.'

Jodi smiled proudly, knowing that Gretel wasn't one for doling out praise willy-nilly.

'So you're suggesting a two-phase approach,' Gretel went on. 'First, the quick wins. Then, a few months down the line, the integration of the remaining systems and processes, perhaps combining the best of each to come up with a new best-practice method of valuation. Integration and process improvement all at once – cutting cost, saving headcount . . .'

Jodi lost her smile. 'You mean people may lose their jobs?'

'Welcome to the real world,' Gretel replied, her tone harsh. 'You'll need to toughen up if you're to project-manage all of this. By the way, ring that stupid agency and tell them to send in someone to do your job – someone with experience this time, please.'

Andrew was also getting ahead in his job. He was promoted when his boss left for a better paying position. His work hours extended dramatically but Jodi still commuted with him whenever possible. Sometimes it was as late as 9 pm when they caught the tube home together.

'You should go home earlier,' he chided. 'You shouldn't wait for me.'

'I hate going home without you.' She snuggled up against him on the grimy plastic seat. 'Anyway, I have lots of work to do on my project so I don't mind staying back.'

The carriage had only a few people at this time of night: a man in a dark overcoat reading a paper, a woman – maybe a nurse – who was wearing a blue uniform under her jacket, and a lanky teenager with a vicious stare. Jodi was careful not to look his way.

Once they got off the train, they had a ten-minute walk. Too often it was raining and cold, spring bringing little improvement to London's weather. Whatever the conditions outside, the maisonette was warm and welcoming. The living room was starting to take shape with a round mahogany dining table and chairs, an antique coffee table and beige lounge. They had found a large patterned rug to brighten up the carpet. Various artefacts, picked up on weekends of meandering around bric-a-brac shops, created the room's character: a blend of Jodi's and Andrew's personalities: a home.

Too late and too tired for dinner, Andrew made toasted cheese and ham bagels and they ate them on the sofa, plates on their knees, while they watched TV.

'Must try to get to see Mum at the weekend,' he said, putting his plate down with a yawn.

Jodi didn't enjoy the visits to Andrew's family and her lack of enthusiasm must have showed on her face.

'Look, I know it's painful,' Andrew squeezed her shoulders, 'but I owe it to Mum. I'm afraid that she'll totally lose her sense of humour if I leave her alone with Simon and Tracey for too long.'

'You left her alone for a full year when you went to Australia,' Jodi pointed out.

'I know. And I see a huge change in her. Simon's miserableness is dragging her down. She used to be quite fun.'

'Do you think that will ever happen to us?' Jodi turned to face him. 'Do you think that one day we'll be miserable and get on each other's nerves?'

'No.' He caressed her cheek with his hand. 'Never.'

'How can you be so sure?'

'Because I am.'

He kissed her. Jodi felt her tiredness fall away. A familiar heat rose in her body as her mouth opened under his. The phone rang. They pulled away with resigned grins.

'Your grandma,' he said, 'with impeccable timing, as usual.'

Grandma phoned regularly, always late at night, and it wasn't the first time she'd interrupted their love-making.

'I could ignore it,' Jodi suggested feebly.

'It's okay.' He stood up and stretched his arms over his head. 'I'm tired anyway.'

Jodi picked up the phone.

'Hi, Grandma . . . Yes, Andrew's fine . . . We were just watching TV.'

The next day began unremarkably. Jodi and Andrew left the apartment at 6.30 am, both carrying umbrellas to shield the heavy rain. Due to the bad weather, the tube was even more packed than usual. They squeezed into a carriage and wrinkled their noses at the damp smell inside.

Jodi kissed Andrew goodbye when they reached Liverpool Street Station and hurried to work. She was preoccupied with an important project meeting that was scheduled for tomorrow.

She had a lot of preparation to do for the meeting; the entire management team would be present.

The day flew by. She had lunch at her desk whilst trying to finalise her presentation. In the afternoon she ran the content by Gretel, who seemed pleased enough with it.

'Just make the introduction more succinct,' she advised. 'And do try to speak slowly tomorrow – some of the older members of the management team find it hard to keep up.'

Jodi took her advice on board and, when Gretel had gone home, she practised the presentation out loud.

At five minutes to nine, knowing the presentation off by heart, she slipped on her jacket and picked up her umbrella. Outside the footpath was waterlogged after a day of steady rain. She angled her umbrella against the wind and walked quickly, thinking that soon she'd be curled up on the cosy sofa in the maisonette.

Andrew wasn't waiting at their usual spot. It was sheltered and Jodi was able to put down her umbrella. Twenty minutes passed.

Where are you, Andrew?

The only phone box in sight was out of order.

A man and woman started arguing nearby. They looked rough.

'Don't you walk away from me,' the woman screamed and tugged on the man's hood.

'Let go, you bitch,' he shouted and tried to shake her off.

'Fuck you,' she spat at him.

He continued to try to shake her off but she had hold of him at an awkward angle and he was flailing at thin air. She was making him look like a fool. Frustration glinted in his eyes. Then he had a knife. He swiped at her. Missed.

'Let go, you stupid cow.'

Jodi got out of there. She ran towards the escalator and it carried her down into the earth, away from the frightening scene above. A train was waiting and, her heart beating hard, she jumped on.

At home she tried Andrew's work number but it rang out. She got out of her wet clothes and put on her pyjamas. She tried Andrew's number again: no answer. She ate some tinned soup in front of the TV. Then tried him again.

The doorbell rang at half-past ten. She skipped down the stairs, thinking it was him, that he'd forgotten his keys.

It wasn't him. As soon as she set eyes on the police officers with their black raincoats and grave expressions, she knew that Andrew would never be coming home again.

Chapter 25

Of course, Jodi missed the all-important project meeting the next morning. She phoned Gretel to let her know she wouldn't be there, a faraway part of her brain recalling that her boss didn't like to be let down. Jodi couldn't remember the conversation she'd had with Gretel, or with Andrew's boss, or Shirley. Shock, hers and theirs, was all she could remember.

The phone call to Janice was the only one she could recall, maybe because it was the first. The kindly sister at the hospital had offered the use of the phone in her office.

'Andrew's been hit by a car.' Jodi's hand trembled as she held the receiver to her ear.

'Is he okay?' The dread in Janice's voice was palpable.

'No.'

Jodi's body heaved with pain and the receiver fell hopelessly from her hand. The sister picked it up and spoke consoling words to Janice before putting the phone back in its place. Then she held Jodi in her strong ample arms for a long, long time.

Andrew was buried after four blurry days. The pastor peppered the service with his name. Jodi's stomach clenched with each mention, unable to digest that it was her Andrew lying in the varnished casket in front of the altar. Yet the people gathered to mourn his passing were evidence that he was indeed gone: men with slick hair and dark suits from his work; Simon and Tracey, looking more dour and miserable than ever; Gretel, meek and nothing like the dynamo she was in the office; members of the extended Ferguson family, cousins, aunts and uncles whom she hadn't met until today.

Sitting next to Jodi, holding her hand, was Janice, her face ghostly, her eyes red-rimmed. The magnitude of their grief drew them together and they held hands for much of the service.

The day after the funeral was the worst. Andrew was not only dead, he was buried. Deep beneath the earth. Gone. Yet shadows followed Jodi around the maisonette, tricking her into believing he was just a few steps away. She'd jerk her head around each time it happened. 'Andrew . . .' she'd begin out loud, genuinely forgetting. Silence would answer. Then she would remember.

She wandered aimlessly around the apartment, touching this and that, but doing nothing. Seconds ticked by at a snail's pace, five minutes an infinity. How could she get through the day? All those seconds, minutes and hours to be filled. With what? After her eyes glanced dangerously off the container of sleeping pills the doctor had prescribed, she knew she had to get out. There was only one place she could go to escape the nothingness: work.

She went upstairs and changed into the pinstriped suit that Andrew had thought so sexy. She wavered at the memory and felt a fresh wave of grief.

Keep busy. Keep busy. Keep busy.

She blanked her mind and continued to ready herself to face the world.

If people thought it strange that she returned to work so soon, they didn't say so. They showed their concern in other ways, mainly sustenance. Gretel would buy her lunch, knowing that she didn't have the interest or appetite to do so herself. And Joanna, one of the team leaders, brought in a plated dinner a few times a week. Jodi thanked them for their kindness, reassured them she was coping, and got back to work.

Keep busy. Keep busy. Keep busy.

With her undivided attention, the project steamed ahead and soon they were implementing phase two. The surplus processes were made redundant and Jodi personally trained each staff member on the new procedures. As the evenings stretched with the onset of summer, she stayed back in the office to type up the training manuals.

Keep busy. Keep busy. Keep busy.

But at home, alone in bed, it was much harder to hold it together. Andrew was dead. She'd never see his lopsided smile again. Or hold a gaze with his soft brown eyes. Or debate all the big issues of life with him. Yes, she realised that the memories weren't all rosy. Yes, they'd had their petty arguments: sometimes he'd annoyed her when he'd left damp towels on the bathroom floor and teabags in the sink. But that was the extent of their disagreements. Everything else was perfect, *had been* perfect.

Can you see me? she'd ask the dark, tears streaming down her face as she lay unsleeping. *Can you see what a mess I am? I can't hold it together without you. I need you to come back from wherever you are.*

At some point, when she'd accepted yet again that he wouldn't be coming back, she'd lean across the bed and take two of the sleeping pills. She'd wait for the drugs to heavy her eyes and bring about a falsely deep sleep before starting another day.

London embraced summer enthusiastically. Girls wore short skirts to work; builders bared their pale torsos to the sun, and the city moved to a whole new beat. Everybody, from the commuters to the shopkeepers, seemed to be more jovial. Jodi felt like an impostor in their midst.

She trekked to and from work, Gretel's chilly office preferable to the stinking hot maisonette where the stand-alone fan did nothing at all to relieve the humidity. As the temperatures soared, Jodi longed for the beach, for Sydney. But she was too afraid to leave London. If she didn't come home to the maisonette every day, see the furniture they had bought together, and sleep in the bed in which they'd loved each other, then her memories would lose their edge and Andrew would surely fade away. She couldn't bear to lose him completely so she kept everything as it was: the furniture, his clothes and their conversations.

The doctor, whilst renewing her prescription for the sleeping pills, had encouraged her to talk to Andrew.

'Better out than in,' he advised. 'It's wonderful therapy – and who knows, he may be able to hear you.'

Jodi tried it out. First, she'd just whisper as she told him about her day. Then, because it seemed so natural and right, her voice became louder, as if this were a normal conversation. She could even hear his response. They talked about everything, even the fact that part of her wanted to leave him and go back to Sydney.

'You still don't like it here, do you?' he asked.

'Not as much as you do,' she replied softly.

'I'll go back to Sydney with you if you want.'

'Do you mean it?'

'Of course I do.'

His smile was so real. But when she reached to touch it, her fingers brushed air.

Suddenly angry, she swung to the other extreme, from denial to harsh acceptance.

Stop talking to yourself. He's dead.

Anger felt good, much better than the dull ache of grief or the bitter-sweet conversations. But it never stayed around for more than a few minutes.

If only I'd arranged to meet him earlier.

If he'd been crossing the road a minute earlier, even five seconds earlier, he wouldn't have been hit. It would have been someone else, one of the people at the side of the road, looking on at the accident and counting their blessings at their near miss.

If only it hadn't been raining so hard.

The road wouldn't have been so slippery. The tyres would have had some traction. The car wouldn't have pirouetted out of control.

If only the driver hadn't been going so fast.

The force of impact wouldn't have thrown Andrew up into the air. His shoes wouldn't have gone flying from his feet. He wouldn't have crashed down, his beige trench coat blanketing his broken body.

Grandma's nocturnal phone calls ceased.

'She's devastated for you,' Shirley explained. 'She was so sure you were going to be happy with Andrew. This has floored her – aged her ten years.'

'I think it's obvious by now that my life plan doesn't have happy-ever-afters in it,' Jodi replied bitterly.

'Will you come home?' Shirley implored for the umpteenth time. 'Let her see for herself that you'll be okay. And let her, and me, help you through?'

'I can't . . .' Jodi choked on a sob. 'I'm sorry, Mum. You see, Andrew's still here, around me. I can't leave him.'

'Don't cry,' Shirley urged with a catch in her own voice. 'It's okay. Stay there if that's where you need to be. Grandma will be fine.'

Despite her mother's assurances, Jodi was filled with terrible guilt. She'd caused her grandmother a lot of pain: Bob's violent death, the murder trial, Andrew's accident. Grandma was a victim too: robbed of her right to a peaceful old age.

'Tell her I'll come home for Christmas,' she promised impulsively. 'That should give her something to look forward to.'

Jodi hung up and hugged her knees to her chest. She was convinced that Andrew's death was linked to Bob's. She had taken a life and, in return, Andrew had been taken from her. An eye for an eye, so to speak. Was God even with her now? Had justice been done? Would Grandma be able to live the rest of her days in peace, without further tragedy?

Janice called around once a week, on Thursdays. Jodi would cook a meal, one of the few nights she bothered, and they would share a bottle of wine. Janice talked about Andrew, her memories flitting from when he was a baby to a teenager. Jodi loved to hear things she hadn't previously known about him. She could almost fool herself into thinking he was still alive.

Inevitably, though, the night would end in tears. The comfort that the memories brought reached a saturation point and hopelessness and loss took over. Sometimes Janice was too upset and too tipsy to begin the journey back to Harrow and she'd sleep on the sofa. Jodi didn't mind. Janice had become a friend. Someone with whom she could share a meal and a glass of wine. Someone with whom she could cry.

All too soon it was autumn and leaves fell inch-deep, cluttering the footpaths and gutters. They were brown and dry and would crunch underfoot, until heavy rain at the start of October turned them into soggy mulch. At first it had been seconds, hours and days that had passed by without Andrew. Now it was seasons.

Janice turned up one night looking different. Her hair had been trimmed and coloured, and the boots she slipped off at the door were high-heeled and stylish.

'I've left Simon,' she announced as she set her contribution to dinner, a bottle of shiraz, down on the dining table.

'Oh.'

Jodi was taken aback at the news. Janice rarely spoke of Simon and had given no clue that she was about to take such a drastic step.

'Should have done it years ago,' Janice declared. 'I knew early on that I'd made a mistake, but I thought I'd made my bed and had to lie on it. Life's short, though, isn't it? Too short to be unhappy. What's for dinner?'

'Beef curry,' Jodi replied woodenly.

'Great. I'm famished.'

Janice did most of the talking throughout the meal. She had the confident air of a woman who was getting her life back together.

'What's up with you tonight?' she asked, looking closely at Jodi's face.

'You,' Jodi answered honestly.

'What have I done?'

'You've left Simon, got your hair done – which is lovely, by the way . . .' Jodi trailed off, fearing she sounded churlish.

Janice didn't need to have it spelled out for her. 'This hasn't been easy,' she confessed, her eyes glazing over, 'but I'm trying really hard to pull myself together. That's me, though, not you. Let your grief run its course, Jodi. I'm here for you regardless of how long it takes.'

Suddenly they were both crying and it was just like every other Thursday night.

Jodi dutifully went through the mechanics of fulfilling her promise to Grandma. She booked a flight to Sydney, organised leave from work, and tried to dismiss the panic she felt at the thought of leaving London, albeit only for two weeks.

'I know you're scared,' Janice was understanding, 'but this is the right thing to do. It'll be hard at first, like opening a wound, but you have to do it to move on. Don't worry about the apartment while you're gone – I'll keep an eye on it.'

It seemed that Janice was now joining her mother and grandmother in the push to get her out of London. It felt unfair, especially when Janice had told her to 'take her time' with her grief.

Jodi browsed through Harrods for gifts to take home. She chose an expensive silk scarf for Grandma and a leather purse for Shirley. She found herself smiling at the thought of being scolded by Grandma for her extravagance.

The week before Christmas, just as Jodi was beginning to come to terms with the emotional consequences of the trip, Invesco provided her with a way of bowing out. The CEO announced

a major strategic initiative: the expansion of the existing investment management business into the institutional pension-fund
market.

'We're designing a portfolio of institutional pension funds
that will compete favourably in the market,' Gretel told Jodi
after the initial announcement had been made. 'The funds
will be designed by a product-development project team.
You – because of your unit pricing experience as well as your
aptitude for process change – have been selected as a senior
lead in the project.'

'How senior?' Jodi asked.

'Reporting to the project director. Essentially, you'll be
second-in-command in the most significant strategic project in
this company since my time here.'

With Gretel's service period closing in on the twelve-year
mark, that was no small statement.

'Will I still be able to take my holiday?' Jodi asked, though she
already knew from the urgency in Gretel's tone what the answer
would be.

Gretel shook her head. 'The pension funds must be ready
for April, the new financial year. Work will have to start
immediately.'

'Have I got time to think it over?'

'No.'

'Can I turn it down?'

Gretel glared. 'Certainly – if you don't give a toss about your
career.'

Gretel had worked too long in the hard-nosed investment management world to know when she was being unreasonable. Even
her stance, hands on hips and legs apart, was uncompromising.

'I'll have to take the risk with my career, then,' Jodi answered evenly. 'I made a promise to my grandmother, and, by all accounts, this trip is important for my healing process. Sorry.'

Gretel shrugged. 'Your decision.'

For Jodi it was a calculated risk. She was sure that Gretel would come round and hold the job open until she came back.

'It's real silk,' Grandma said as she rubbed the scarf between her callused forefinger and thumb.

'Yes,' Jodi affirmed. 'I got it in Harrods.'

'You shouldn't waste your money.'

'It wasn't a waste.'

Jodi had woken at dawn. She'd stayed in bed, enjoying the feeling of being back in her old room. Then she'd heard her grandmother moving about: the old lady started her day with the birds. The shuffling footsteps and pottering sounds from the kitchen had lulled Jodi back into a light sleep that lasted till midmorning.

'Your present is there – it's the big one.' Grandma used her stick to point towards the fake Christmas tree with its bald-looking branches and tawdry baubles.

Grandma looked well. Her hair was whiter and her face thinner, but her eyes were as alert as ever.

Jodi knelt in front of the tree. Grandma had a dozen or so presents under there, all neatly wrapped and labelled. The rest of the family were coming to Christmas lunch and she had ensured nobody would be forgotten.

The gift with Jodi's name was large and heavy to lift. She tore back the wrapping.

'It's lovely,' she exclaimed when she saw the oval-shaped serving platter. 'But I'm not sure I'll be able to get it back to London in one piece.'

The old lady's face fell. 'I was hoping you wouldn't be going back there . . .'

Jodi laughed, trying to make light of her grandmother's naivety. 'I've just got a big promotion, I have to go back.'

The promotion wasn't quite in the bag, but Jodi was fairly sure it would be hers when she got back.

'Life's not all about work and promotions,' said Grandma plainly.

'True,' Jodi felt a pang of pain but kept a smile on her face, 'but work helps me keep going.'

Grandma wasn't going to give up easily. 'You have a family who loves you here –'

She was interrupted by the sound of the front door being opened.

'Happy Christmas,' Shirley shouted out in a chirpy voice. Her heels clacked down the hall and she appeared in the back room wearing a white and red summer dress and glossy lipstick. Her hands clutched bulging carrier bags of food for lunch.

'You look great, Mum,' Jodi remarked.

'Thanks.' Her face took on a self-conscious expression. 'I thought I should make an effort at least once a year. Did you sleep okay?'

Despite the longhaul flight, the emotional reunion at the airport, and the catching up that had gone on late into the night, Jodi had slept surprisingly well. 'Yes. Better than I have in ages.'

Shirley went to dump the carrier bags in the adjoining kitchen and Jodi got up to help.

'Where's Marlene?'

'She's running late,' Shirley replied, opening the door of Grandma's fridge and frowning when she saw how little free space there was. She began to rearrange the contents. 'She couldn't prise the toys from the younger ones and the older lot are glued to some computer game.'

'Why don't you move in here with Grandma?' Jodi asked in a low voice, so the old woman wouldn't hear from the next room.

Shirley giggled into the fridge. 'We'd kill each other, that's why. No, I'm saving for a deposit on a place of my own – a nice apartment not far from the sea. I was hoping I'd be able to buy something this year, but the prices keep going up and up and up.'

Jodi took the perishable items from the bags and handed them to Shirley for fitting in the fridge. She wanted to buy the apartment for her mother. She owed it to her: a modern, two-bed apartment with a large balcony and sea views; a replacement for the house in Lewis Street: a home. She just needed another few promotions to make it happen.

Alison had acquired a live-in boyfriend while Jodi was away. His name was Jack. He was a massage therapist.

'I can't wait till you meet him,' she grinned excitedly when she met Jodi alone for a drink. 'I've told him all about you. Well,' she pulled a face, 'not *everything*, of course.'

They were perched on bar stools in a trendy inner-city hotel, the kind of place Alison would have once made fun of. Alison looked every bit as sophisticated as the rest of the clientele. Her hair, now a respectable shade of mahogany, had grown to shoulder length and her fingernails were painted a nonoffensive shell colour. She wore a V-neck top inside her two-piece trouser suit. Jodi wondered whether it was Jack, her new boyfriend, or her job, where she was now a manager, or a combination of both that had tamed her appearance so much.

Later on in the night, when Alison invited her back to her

apartment, she got to meet Jack and find out for herself. He was a hunk of a man with hands so large that Jodi feared they would inadvertently crush rather than massage his poor clients. Alison, tipsy from a few too many beers, gave him a wobbly kiss and his big muscled arm steadied her against his waist.

'Jodi, can I get you a drink?' he asked, his voice surprisingly soft for a man of his size.

'I'll have a red wine, if you have it.'

'Me too!' Alison chimed.

He looked down at her, his face taking on a look of mock sternness. 'You'll regret it in the morning . . .'

Alison giggled. 'You know me – play now, pay later!'

He laughed, squeezed her waist, and went off to get the drinks.

'Well, what do you think?' Alison asked, plopping herself down on the sofa. She immediately checked herself. 'No, I didn't mean to ask that. Because it doesn't matter what you, or anyone else, think. Just me and Jack.'

Jodi answered her anyway. 'I think he's big and handsome, with an emphasis on the BIG, and I think that he obviously loves you as much as you love him.' Then she added, 'You look so different, your hair, your clothes . . .'

Alison's reply was considered. 'Work demands a certain standard. I'm management now – have to look the part. But outside of work I don't need to make a statement. There's no need to do the gothic look or have a nose ring – Jack gets who I am no matter what I wear.'

Happy as she was for Alison, Jodi's own loss suddenly seemed unbearable. Tears, which she had held back through all the Christmas festivities and the well-meaning enquiries of her relatives, suddenly came gushing out.

'Oh, Jodi.' Alison hugged her tightly. 'I'm sorry. I didn't mean to rub your face in my happiness.'

Jodi tried to tell her it wasn't her fault but found it hard to utter anything remotely coherent. She cried for the memories of last Christmas. She cried because it was a brand new year and all she could see ahead was loneliness. She cried because she feared she would never again find someone who would *get who she was*. She didn't notice when Jack came back with their drinks. Or the look of concern he shared with his girlfriend before making himself scarce.

Jodi watched Sue from afar as she organised the little nippers for the flag race. The kids were lying down on the sand. At the sound of Sue's whistle they scrambled to their feet and their short legs raced up the beach, sand billowing in their wake. At the halfway mark some of the children were already well ahead as they grabbed their flag, nothing but a length of garden hose, and turned back. The slowest children found there was no flag left for them to take and had to return empty-handed and, devastatingly, eliminated. Sue called encouragement to each child as they crossed the finish line, managed to keep tears at bay and lined up the kids who'd made it to the next round.

This time the fact that there were fewer flags than kids went less smoothly. A little girl turned back against the flow to double check. The other kids bumped into her and there was a pile-up on the sand.

'Need help?' Jodi asked, coming forward.

Sue's face was a picture of surprise before it broke into a big smile. 'Jodi! Your mum mentioned you were coming back.' A few of the children were wailing and she paused to pat some shoulders. 'Yes, I do need help. Can you organise an activity for those out of the race?'

'Sure.'

Jodi kicked off her flip-flops and grabbed a ball from Sue's box of equipment.

'Okay, kids.' She smiled at the group of young children, some with tear-stained faces. 'My name's Jodi. Enough of racing, we're going to play ball. Who wants to get wet?'

'Me,' they all screeched in reply.

She lined them up in the shallow water and played some simple throwing games. Soon the children were laughing and splashing as they dived to catch the ball, their earlier disappointment at being eliminated from the flag race forgotten.

An hour flew by before Sue called an end to the activities. Jodi's shorts were soaking and sand was caked to her bare legs. She felt good, though. Better than she had for a long, long time.

She borrowed a sarong from Sue and they went across the road for a coffee. They managed to get a seat outside one of the buzzing cafés and they made small talk in the long wait to be served.

'How does it feel to be back?' asked Sue when she finally had a coffee cupped in her hands.

Jodi spooned the froth from her cappuccino. Rich and soft, it melted on her tongue. She spooned some more and realised that the cappuccinos in London were no match.

'The same and not the same,' she answered. 'The people, the perfect weather, the beach today – they're all wonderfully familiar. But me, I'm different.' She paused, sipped from her cup, and then added darkly, 'Very different.'

Sue reached over and covered Jodi's hand with hers. Her

freckled face was deeply sympathetic as she said, 'I'm so sorry about Andrew. It was such an awful tragedy . . .'

Her voice faded. Jodi didn't say anything. She had a lump in her throat that she didn't trust. Conversation babbled on around them as they sat in silence; women in beach dresses, men in singlets and shorts, children with ice-creamed faces, all with so much to say. Summer permeated the air. Not heavy and humid, like in London, but breezy and carefree.

Yes, I do miss this, Jodi thought. *The warmth of the sun on my skin, the feeling of sand between my toes . . .*

She came back to the present. A man had stopped by their table and was looking at her quizzically.

'I know your face,' he mused. 'I just can't place it.'

She shrugged as if he must be mistaken but in her mind's eye she could see it coming to him later on. He'd snap his fingers, startling his wife, and exclaim, 'I've got it! She's the girl from the court case – you know, the one who stabbed her stepfather.'

That was one of the few benefits London had to offer: anonymity. Jodi realised that she had lived with a desire to be anonymous, to disappear, for most of her life: during her parents' divorce, while she'd lived with Bob, the court case and its aftermath, even today with this man who thought he knew her.

Who is Jodi Tyler? Other than the girl who wants to disappear?

She didn't know. All she knew was that London was where she needed to be. For now.

Chapter 26

1992

Gretel did hold the job open and Jodi threw herself into it whole-heartedly when she got back to London. Her new boss, Ian Flynn, had very definite ideas and such a strong personality that Gretel seemed like a pussycat in comparison. His deliver-or-die style was good for the project but didn't win him any popularity points with his staff.

'What he gained in the good-looks department, he lost in personality,' Rachel, one of the juniors, complained.

He was certainly good-looking: wiry brown hair, a strong angular face and intense blue eyes. He was also very good at his job, with a knack for thinking outside the box.

'Rachel, have you tried asking the marketing team to see if that feature is totally necessary?'

Of course Rachel, whose attention was more focused on her social life than her job, hadn't thought to ask marketing.

'I didn't think that was part of my job,' she replied, a sigh in her voice.

Ian's expression became harder than it already was. 'Well, if you don't expand your limited conception of what your job entails, then I'm afraid you won't have one for very long.'

Rachel, panicked at the thought of losing her job and not being able to afford London's social scene, jumped to her feet at the warning. Ian Flynn was not one to make idle threats.

Jodi learned a lot in her quest to meet his exacting standards. She learned not to go to him with half-cooked ideas. She learned not to escalate issues until she had turned every stone in the attempt to resolve them. She learned that the IT department always said no at first, but if she persevered she could *almost* get what she wanted from them. All in all, she enjoyed the satisfaction of creating something new and was grateful to be preoccupied with the project as the anniversary of Andrew's death came closer.

Thanks to Ian's meticulous management, the new pension system was right on schedule as it moved from development to testing. The project team waited with bated breath while the testers checked the functionality and viability, everybody only too aware that this was make or break for the April deadline. Thankfully, the system needed nothing more than a little tweaking here and there. Invesco was now perfectly positioned to take the pension market by storm.

With the project entering its final phase, Jodi's job changed and took on more of a marketing emphasis. Ian was regularly asked to present the new pension products to blue-chip companies with a view to securing their investment. Jodi helped put the presentations together and went along to provide technical support that Ian rarely needed. During the presentations, Ian exuded charm as he tried to sell the unique design of the products. Jodi saw a completely different side to him.

She found that she, too, liked being face to face with customers. The more experience she acquired, the more Ian allowed her to be involved. He was an excellent role model and coached her on when to push and when to pull back. Together they brought their two-part act to boardroom after boardroom, doing their level best to win their first client.

Finally their efforts paid off: the board of IBM's pension fund agreed to invest. Other large companies were sure to follow suit. Ian was euphoric.

'This calls for champagne,' he declared to the team and Rachel's face brightened at the thought of a night out on the company.

In truth, a night out was the last thing Jodi felt like. Tomorrow, 10 April, was the anniversary of Andrew's death. Her mind kept drifting back. The police on her doorstep. The hospital afterwards. The all-too-vivid images of him being thrown into the air, crashing down, dead on impact.

'Jodi?'

Ian was staring. He'd obviously noticed that she wasn't as enthusiastic as the others about celebrating their success.

'You are going to join us, aren't you?'

His tone implied that he wouldn't take no for an answer. Jodi was suddenly sick of him and his bullying ways.

'No, I'm not, Ian.'

Drinking champagne on the eve of Andrew's anniversary was too much to ask.

Ian frowned. 'This is an important milestone for the team,' he informed her in his iciest of tones.

He had a point, of course. Securing IBM as a client was a major coup that guaranteed the long-term success of Invesco's venture into the pension-fund market. Definitely a cause for celebration for the project team who had worked so hard to pull it off. If it wasn't for the cold horrible truth that Andrew had been dead a whole year.

'Sorry, Ian.' Jodi reached for her jacket. She slipped it on and defiantly buttoned it up. 'Hope you all have a good time.'

The next morning dawned with unexpected brightness. Jodi pulled back the curtains to reveal a perfect blue sky that urged her outside. She followed its calling, dressing in casual jeans and a warm sweater, and walked a familiar route to a nearby park. A fresh breeze fanned her face but it wasn't cold. At the park flowers had begun to blossom in an array of vibrant colours. Spring had, belatedly once again, arrived in London.

Jodi sat on one of the weathered benches. She took deep breaths of the scented air as she watched the antics of the children playing around her. Surprisingly, there weren't any of the usual squabbles and tantrums. Only smiles and rings of laughter. This wasn't a day of sadness. It was a day of happiness, of new beginnings.

Sitting on the bench, Jodi began to make some decisions. Firstly, it was time to make some friends in this lonely city. This would involve going out socially and letting other people into her life. Another change would have to be the Thursday-night rendezvous with Janice. Yes, they could still continue to meet, but somewhere public where they'd have to hold it together. Lastly, and most difficult of all, came the decision to move out of the maisonette.

Her mind made up, Jodi didn't stay around to dwell on her decisions. She got to her feet, waved at a friendly toddler who was smiling her way, and left the park. Before she could change her mind, she walked to the office of the real estate agent who managed the maisonette.

'Can we help find you somewhere new to live?' the girl at the reception asked.

'No – I'm moving to another suburb.'

On Monday morning Jodi went to work and listened to all the talk about Friday's big night out.

'Ian put his credit card behind the bar,' Rachel told her. 'Champagne was literally flowing . . . and Ian was so relaxed – like a different person.'

Jodi smiled to herself. Rachel had undoubtedly drunk a lot of champagne and got herself into a state where everybody, even Ian, was her best friend.

However, when Ian arrived at work Rachel did actually smile at him and politely enquire how the rest of his weekend had been. And he did give her a civil answer, which led Jodi to believe that they were, at long last, on friendlier terms. All thanks to some free champagne.

Ian put down his briefcase and hung his suit jacket on one of the hooks by the door. He wore a crisp white shirt that enhanced his tan. His face was unsmiling as he turned to speak to Jodi.

'Multimedia asked if we could go see them today,' he informed her in a terse voice. 'They've apologised for the short notice and understand if we can't make it.'

'What time?'

'Eleven.'

Jodi bit her lip. That left very little time for preparation. 'The usual sales pitch?'

'Yes, but without the benefit of being able to study what pension fund they have at the moment and how we can differentiate from it.'

'Going in blind,' Jodi muttered half to herself.

'Yes.'

She tapped her pen on the desk while she thought it over.

'I think it's a bad idea, Ian. It would make us look cheap – running in at the drop of a hat and trying to sell our product without knowing what we're pitching against.'

Ian nodded. 'I agree. I'll tell Gretel the answer is no.'

Still no smile. Jodi got the feeling he was still angry that she hadn't gone for drinks on Friday night.

While the rest of the team prepared to transition IBM, Jodi and Ian were focused on wooing more big-name customers. They travelled all over the city, their mode of transport varying from the tube, to the infamous black cabs, to Ian's Saab convertible, which they used when their destination was out of town. The car would glide along the motorway as if on wings. Conversation was impossible as Ian liked to drive to loud music. He played U2 the most often, their original sound and edgy lyrics booming from the speakers. Jodi would lean back into the soft leather seat and allow the music to infuse her soul. She liked the band every bit as much as Ian. Not that she told him.

Fifteen or so minutes before they arrived at wherever they were going, Ian would turn down the music and run through the presentation one last time. He would reiterate the names of all those expected to be present and what he knew of their roles and personalities. Once there, he'd straighten his tie, run a hand through his wiry hair and adopt a businesslike expression. You would never guess he liked to listen to loud rock-and-roll in his car.

The presentations usually took about an hour. Sometimes, if the timing was right, Ian and Jodi would go for lunch afterwards and discuss how things had gone. Conversation was mostly based on business; Ian didn't talk about his private life and neither did

Jodi. The sum of her knowledge about Ian was that he lived in Notting Hill and had a sister named Gemma.

Their second big win was a medium-sized manufacturing company out at Windsor. The chairman of the board, an old fogy who looked like he would be better placed drawing his pension than deciding where to invest the firm's funds, had good news to impart.

'My colleagues and I have decided to transfer the management of our pension fund to Invesco.'

The fund was in excess of sixty million pounds and Ian was grinning like a Cheshire cat as he slid in behind the wheel of the Saab. He pressed PLAY on the stereo before pulling out onto the road. 'Angel of Harlem' boomed in the confines of the car as they drove along the tree-lined roads. Ian's fingers drummed the steering wheel. Jodi felt an unexpected surge of happiness.

Jodi sold the maisonette's furniture on *Loot* and Janice helped her move two suitcases of clothes and a few boxes of kitchenware to her new one-bedroom apartment.

The move took only one journey in Janice's little red car; however, the traffic was so bad that the maisonette seemed like a blurry memory by the time they finally reached their destination.

Janice helped Jodi unpack and organise the kitchen cupboards. The kitchen had new white fittings made from low-quality material. Linoleum covered the floor, also new, and just as cheap looking as the fittings.

'Anything else I can help with?' asked Janice when everything was stored away in the cupboards.

'No.' Jodi gave a forced smile. 'The clothes can wait.'

Janice lingered for a while longer, wiping down surfaces and picking up grey balls of fluff from the new carpet in the living room. Finally, she kissed Jodi's cheek, made arrangements to come again during the week, and took her leave. Jodi's brave face fell away as the door clicked shut. The place had none of the character of the maisonette. And none of the precious memories. There was an emptiness about it that couldn't be filled with any amount of furniture. She sank down on the thin grey carpet and put her head in her hands.

What on earth have I done?

Then she had a thought: maybe the maisonette hadn't been rented out yet. Maybe she could go back. She'd lose a month's rent on this place, but that didn't matter.

She stumbled to her feet. The apartment's phone wasn't yet connected so she'd have to find a pay phone. No problem. She searched her pockets for change, made sure she had a key, and pulled the door shut behind her.

She found a phone box a short walk away. She could hardly contain her impatience as she waited in the queue. She shuffled from foot to foot and mumbled replies to the inane comments of the woman ahead. Three people and ten minutes later it was her turn.

'Sorry, the maisonette was snapped up straight away.' The receptionist at the estate agent's office dashed her hopes. 'The tenants are moving in tomorrow. Two levels, big windows, nice carpet – places like that always go quickly.'

Jodi hung up without commenting that the carpet was dreary green and better covered with a rug. She felt tears prick her eyes as a man, looking every bit as impatient as she'd been earlier, brushed past on his way into the box.

The maisonette was going to be someone else's home. That was that. No going back now.

*

'Jodi, a word please?'

Jodi looked up at the sound of Gretel's voice. Their office-sharing days had ceased when Invesco trimmed its work force and freed up space on the main floor a few months earlier. Now Jodi worked at a small workstation and Gretel had to come looking for her if she had something to discuss.

Jodi saved the file she was working on before following Gretel to her office.

'Sit down,' Gretel commanded with an abrupt nod towards the closest free chair. Gretel didn't usually waste time by asking her visitors to sit.

Jodi sat obediently, crossed her legs at the ankles and tried to suppress the worry that she might be the next redundancy at Invesco.

'As you know, the company has been reducing its costs . . .' Gretel began.

Jodi's heart sank. This didn't sound at all promising.

'And, with the new pension funds, increasing its revenue. Less costs and more revenue mean . . .'

Gretel paused, looking to Jodi to finish her sentence.

'More profit,' said Jodi obligingly while her mind was thinking over how long it would take to find another job and how many weeks' rent she could pay from her savings.

'Yes,' Gretel nodded, 'and more profit means greater earnings per share and greater . . .'

'Share price,' Jodi said on cue.

'Exactly!' Gretel gave another nod for the second correct answer in a row. 'Which means Invesco's shares are worth a lot of money.' She stood up and extended her hand. 'Congratulations – the company has awarded you with one thousand shares.'

Jodi's mouth dropped open. 'You mean I'm not being made redundant?'

Gretel cackled, highly amused. 'Of course not! We see a lot of potential in you. The shares are testament to our commitment to your future with us.'

Gretel's hand was still outstretched. Jodi raised her own and they shook on it: one thousand shares and her future with Invesco.

As soon as she got back to her desk, she looked up the share price on the system. It was around the thirty pound mark. Gretel had just given her a thirty thousand pound bonus.

A few months later Jodi was called to Gretel's office again. This time it was a promotion. Ian was leaving, moving to greener pastures. Gretel offered Jodi his job: manager of client and product development.

'What's the salary?' she asked when Gretel noticeably neglected to mention it.

'Well, obviously you don't have as much experience as Ian,' Gretel began, 'and the company is continuing to keep a close eye on costs . . .'

'What are you trying to tell me?'

Gretel shrugged and looked apologetic. 'There's no salary increase, Jodi. Not for now, anyway. Maybe at the end of the year . . .'

Jodi thought it over. She was already well paid as it was. However, if she accepted the promotion without an appropriate salary increase, how would that make her look? Like a doormat: someone who could be pushed around, someone who had no bargaining power.

'Sorry,' she said to Gretel in a firm voice. 'I can't accept the offer as it stands. I want the same pay as Ian.'

Gretel looked somewhat relieved. 'I'll relay the message.'

Jodi left Gretel's office with the strong suspicion that the reason she hadn't been offered a salary increase was more to do with her being a woman than anything to do with cost control, and with the feeling that Gretel had to fight the same battles.

As Ian was moving to a competitor, he wasn't required to work out his resignation. Farewell drinks were hurriedly organised in a nearby pub after work.

'Are you coming?' Rachel asked as she unselfconsciously applied a fresh coat of lipstick in the middle of the office.

'Yes, I'll follow you down,' Jodi replied vaguely.

She had been out a few times since her resolution to be more social. But she still needed to psych herself up to drink, chat and laugh the evening away. She could put on a good show of having a great time. Inside, though, she was detached from all the merriment. Remote. Maybe a little dead.

An hour later she packed up her desk and put on her heavy woollen coat. It was hard to believe that it was the onset of winter again. Summer had been a flash-in-the-pan affair. Outside it was sleeting and bitterly cold. She was actually relieved to step into the warmth of the pub.

'You came!' Ian looked surprised when she joined their circle.

'I said I would,' she replied defensively.

'Can I buy you a drink?'

'No, my call. You're the one leaving, after all.'

She pushed her way through the crowds to the bar. A good-looking guy, who was waiting his turn to be served, started to chat.

'Do you work around here?'

'Yes.'

'Which building?'

'Invesco,' she answered reluctantly. She hated the personal details you were expected to impart to perfect strangers in the name of being social.

'I'm in Mutual Trust, just a few doors down.' He grinned as though it was an amazing coincidence they worked so close to each other. 'I'm Nathan.'

'Jodi.'

The barman, who looked flushed and run off his feet, asked Nathan what he wanted.

'The lady can go first.'

Jodi flashed him a grateful smile. 'Pint of bitter and glass of red wine, please,' she said to the barman.

She watched him take a narrow-stemmed wine glass from the rack over the bar.

Nathan began yapping in her ear again. 'You're not from these parts, are you?'

'No.'

'Where are you from?'

'Sydney,' she all but sighed because she suspected this titbit of information would start him rattling off the names of every single person he knew who'd ventured south of the equator.

'My mate, Jim . . .'

And he was off. After what seemed like an age, the barman put Jodi's order on the counter. She handed him a fiver.

'Keep the change.'

She grabbed the drinks and turned to go.

'Hold on . . .'

Nathan caught hold of her arm.

'I have to go back to my friends,' she said pointedly.

'Oh.'

He took his hand away and extracted a business card from his shirt pocket.

'Here.' She caught a glimpse of blue embossed writing on a white background. 'My phone number's there. Maybe we could go for lunch sometime, seeing as we work practically next door.'

Jodi looked at him objectively. She supposed his untidy curls were kind of cute and, going by the business card, he wasn't an axe murderer. All he had been trying to do was make conversation; the fact that she'd found it annoying was more to do with her state of mind than anything he'd said.

She raised her hands, showing him she had a drink in each and no means of taking his card. 'Can you slip it in my handbag?'

'Sure.'

He carefully unzipped her bag from where it was hanging by her side, popped in his card and zipped it back up again.

'Don't forget to call, now,' he grinned.

'Okay,' she said but had no idea whether she would or not.

She pushed her way back through the crowds and slopped some of Ian's pint on her hand in the process.

'Sorry,' she said as she handed him the less-than-full glass.

'No problem.' He tilted his head back as he swigged down the tawny-coloured bitter. Jodi saw the lump of his Adam's apple and the smattering of light brown hair where his Ralph Lauren polo shirt opened at the neck.

'Looks like you made a friend at the bar,' he commented.

She screwed her face in a grimace. 'I really don't know why I took his card. I'm not in the market for a boyfriend.'

She felt the weight of Ian's gaze and felt compelled to look up to meet it.

'I'm sorry,' he began, 'if I seemed insensitive that time . . .'

His voice trailed off without specifying which time he was referring to. Jodi knew, though, that it was the time they'd won the IBM deal, the time she hadn't gone to the champagne celebration, the time of Andrew's anniversary.

'Gretel explained later,' Ian continued, clearly uncomfortable. 'She told me about your boyfriend.'

'It's okay,' Jodi assured him as she inhaled a deep breath. 'You weren't to know.'

A silence fell between them. It wasn't uneasy, they'd had many spells of quiet in his car. Jodi finished her glass of wine. Someone handed her another. Then another. She began to feel a little light-headed.

'I really shouldn't drink too much,' she giggled to Ian.

He raised his eyebrows. 'You've only had three glasses of wine.'

'I know, but I don't have a very good history with alcohol.'

Then, totally out of the blue, she told him about the time she'd passed out at the university function and woken up in hospital. He laughed and so did she. It was kind of funny, in hindsight. She didn't know why she'd kept it a secret for so long. Force of habit, maybe.

Rachel left to join a friend at some other pub and eventually everybody else went their separate ways too. Jodi and Ian sat on the seats that were freed up by those moving on.

'Who would have thought I'd be the last to leave?' Jodi laughed.

Then her ears caught the opening bars of 'With Or Without You' coming from the pub's sound system. Ian's eyes lit up and his lips mouthed the words. Jodi realised, with a jolt, how much she would miss him and those journeys where little had been said above U2's lyrics.

Before she knew it, she had leaned across and kissed his lips. Not quite a friendly peck. Something a little bit more. The kiss felt good. It stirred something deep, deep inside her.

He looked stunned. 'Jodi . . .' Their lips were very close and this seemed to distract him from what he wanted to say. He pulled back. 'I have a girlfriend. In fact, we're engaged.'

Engaged? Now she was the one who was stunned. Of course, she knew nothing about him. And now she'd made the biggest fool of herself.

'I'll miss you – that's all I was saying with the kiss,' she said in an airy voice that had a telltale wobble.

'I'll miss you too,' he put in quickly to cover the horrible awkwardness.

They finished their drinks in record time. Said goodbye at the door. Exchanged another kiss, this time on the cheek. The worst part of the whole fiasco was the look on his face as he turned to go: pity.

Chapter 27

1993

Eventually, begrudgingly, Jodi was offered the role at a salary that was just shy of Ian's. She accepted and got on with proving she was worth the money. Over the following months she followed up every sales lead, never giving up, no matter how slim the chance. She wined and dined directors, chairmen and other decision makers. Her only impediment was her mode of transport: taxis and trains could get her only so far. What she really needed was her own set of wheels. First, though, she had to learn how to drive.

She feared she would be one of those nervous drivers who crawled along at ten kilometres an hour below the speed limit and stopped twenty metres before traffic lights. It turned out that she was quite the opposite. She loved the feeling of being behind the wheel. Shifting the gearstick, pressing on the accelerator, manoeuvring the instructor's car into London's impossibly tight parking spaces, all brought a rush of pleasure. She passed her driving test on first attempt. Then she asked Gretel for a company car.

'We've only just given you a big pay increase,' was Gretel's reply. 'Not to talk about the company shares. Can't you buy your own car?'

'No.' Jodi was matter-of-fact. 'You know as well as I do that image is everything in sales. I need to have a car that's comparable to the vehicles of the board members I'm trying to sell to. I can't very well arrive in a Mini or Starlet and expect them to take me seriously. Organise the car and I'll promise you an extra three hundred million of new business. Deal?'

Gretel took the deal. Jodi got her car: a sporty Mercedes-Benz. She adored everything about it: the silver metallic paint, the plush leather seats, the sunroof that slid open at the touch of a button; but mostly she loved the fact that it enabled her to spend more time on the open road rather than being stuck in an overheated office talking to a client who was a hundred kilometres away, not only in terms of distance but also in terms of buying into the pension fund.

Invesco appointed a new CEO in the New Year: Brian Hughes. He was a balding, arrogant man who was small in stature but big in voice. He bellowed his commands and opinions across meeting tables. It was even worse when his booming voice was channelled down the phone, Jodi having to hold the receiver back from her ear, everyone around being made privy to what he was saying.

Within a few weeks Brian had embarked on a cost-cutting and redundancy frenzy. Unfortunately, Gretel was one of the first casualties.

'I don't mind,' she confided to Jodi. 'I got a good payout – means I can stay at home for a while, be a real mum.'

But Jodi couldn't help thinking that Gretel was putting on a brave face. This was the woman who had worked her heart out as she'd fought to become the first female on the company's executive management team. Thirteen years of slog, all for Brian Hughes to decide, a mere four weeks into his tenure, that her services were no longer required.

Jodi kept her head down, worked hard, and tried to stay on the right side of the new CEO. The last thing she needed was to lose her job. She needed another year in this role to cement her experience. She needed to prove that she could bring in the extra three hundred million pounds of business she'd promised, even though Gretel wasn't around to hold her to it. And she needed to save another fifty thousand dollars to buy her mother that apartment by the sea.

Jodi made a concentrated effort to join the crowd in the local pub after work on Fridays. At first it was like something on her to-do list at work, a chore. But it got easier. Friendships developed with some of the girls. Shopping days and other social gatherings came about as a result and life was less empty.

She was at the pub one Friday evening when she saw a familiar face. He was laughing, head back, that's what made her look his way in the first place. Quite good-looking with longish untidy curls that many men wouldn't be able to carry off. She couldn't place him, though.

Later on she felt a touch on her shoulder.

'Jodi, isn't it?' he asked.

'Yes,' she replied, frantically trying to remember how she knew him.

'We met last year. It's Nathan.'

'Oh.' The guy who'd given her his business card at Ian's farewell. The one she hadn't called.

'Still working around here?' he enquired.

'Yeah. You?'

'Yeah. Different firm, though.'

An awkward silence followed.

'Can I get you a drink?' He glanced at her almost empty glass. 'Or should I simply take the hint from the fact you didn't call?'

Jodi wet her lips. 'A drink would be nice.'

He left to go to the bar.

Rachel was over in a flash. 'Who's he?'

'Someone I hardly know.'

'I think you should get to know him, then.' She eyed him as he stood at the bar. 'Very s*exy*!'

Rachel was right. Nathan was very sexy. Jodi felt a silly blush rise on her face.

'You're going red,' Rachel observed gleefully.

'No, I'm not.'

'Yes, you are. You like him, don't you?'

Well, something was happening. Her stomach felt a bit mushy. And her face was flaming red.

'Oh stop it,' she hissed to Rachel. 'He'll be back soon and I'm going to look as red as a . . .' She struggled to find an analogy. 'Traffic light,' was the best she could come up with.

Rachel laughed uproariously. So loud that Nathan turned around from where he was standing at the bar.

Jodi shot her a filthy look. 'Keep it down, would you?'

'Okay, okay.' Rachel held up her hand in a truce. 'I'm leaving now anyway. Meeting a friend over at the Arms. Call me tomorrow, though. Let me know what he's like in bed.'

'Rachel! I've absolutely no intention of . . . Oh, just go.'

Jodi saw Nathan making his way back, willed her face to return to normal and tried not to think what he'd be like in bed.

'Thanks.'

She took a long sip of her drink. Dutch courage.

Conversation was stilted at first. They talked weather, work and world news. Nothing too heavy or personal. Lots of punctuating silences.

Jodi learned that Nathan was a marketing consultant. This surprised her. He didn't look glossy enough. Later he mentioned that he played rugby at the weekends. That fitted better: his rough-and-tumble good looks had the markings of a man who liked to scrum.

She told him about her job, her beloved car and some bare details about her family back home. The night ticked away. Closing time was called.

'Do you want to go on to a club?' Nathan asked.

'No.' Jodi looked down at her feet. 'Two left ones. No rhythm.'

Nathan laughed. 'That makes two of us. How about a coffee at my place?'

'Okay.'

She finished up her drink and put on her jacket. She wanted to go quickly. Before she chickened out.

Outside the night was drizzly and taxis were thin on the ground. They walked along the roadside, keeping their eyes peeled. After a few minutes they got lucky when a cab pulled in across the road to drop someone off. Nathan clasped her hand and they sprinted towards it before anyone else could get in ahead of them.

'Hammersmith,' he said to the driver.

Jodi nearly mentioned that she lived close by in Shepherds

Bush but decided that the less he knew about her the better. They sat apart in the taxi. Her hands were crossed, his rested on his knees. No holding.

'Do you live alone?' she asked when he turned the key in the door of his apartment.

'No.' He flicked on the light. Jodi saw a spacious living room with neutral carpet and a corner lounge suite. An oversized TV was centred on a wall unit, books and CDs crammed in the shelves around. A guitar was propped on a stand in one of the corners. 'I have a flatmate. Casey. She travels a lot . . .'

He switched on a lamp at the far end of the room. Its seductive glow combined with the light from the hall. Jodi walked over to the guitar and strummed her fingers across the strings.

'Who plays?'

'Me.'

'I thought you said you'd no rhythm?'

'That's my feet.' His face broke into a smile that made her heart do a little flip. 'My fingers keep the beat okay.'

'Would you play something for me?' she heard herself ask.

He took the guitar from its stand and sat on the lounge, one knee jutting out. Gently, reverently, he strummed the strings with a few warm-up chords, then stronger ones that heralded the start of something. He began to sing, his voice hoarse, its timbre sending a shiver up her spine. She didn't recognise the song. The lyrics spoke of finding love. His eyes closed intermittently and she could stare, without being found out, at the emotion on his face.

She was in awe by the time the song whispered to a finish. 'You wrote that, didn't you?'

'Yeah,' he shrugged, looking self-conscious as he leaned over to put the guitar back in its stand.

'It was really good.'

'Thanks.' He looked a bit sheepish, as if he didn't quite believe her praise.

'No, it really was,' she insisted.

His hand reached out and drew her in to sit alongside him. Her heart hammered. The unexpected serenade had temporarily distracted her from the reason she was here in the first place.

'Your hair's wet,' he said softly as he stroked his hand over it.

'So is yours,' she replied, her eyes taking in sparkles of water glistening on his mop of curls.

His lips touched hers. She felt a jolt of chemistry.

Yes, this is the right thing to do.

She opened her mouth and the kiss deepened. Easy. Her lips seemed to remember what to do of their own accord.

His hand, damp from her hair, followed the line of her neck and slid inside her top to rest on her bare shoulder, cold against her warm skin. More kissing. Two hands under her top now. A thumb brushing across her nipple. Another jolt of chemistry or lust or whatever this was.

Yes, I'm okay with this.

Bravely, she unbuttoned his shirt. His muscled torso looked exactly as the outline of his shirt had promised. The kind of torso that had to be strong and solid enough to take the driving shoulders of the rival rugby team. Her hands spanned the breath of his chest. His kisses became more urgent. She stopped thinking.

Jodi lay wide-eyed in the dark. The flashing red of the alarm clock noted the time as 5 am. She'd watched it tick over the last two hours. She hadn't slept.

Next to her, in a deep slumber, Nathan's body was relaxed and his breathing even. She, on the other hand, lay in a tight little ball, her knees hugged in, her breathing jagged. Sleep wasn't going to come.

Cautiously, so as not to stir Nathan, she slipped out from under the blankets. She gathered her clothes from the floor and tiptoed out to the living area where she got dressed. Then she took small soft footsteps to the door, stealthily pushed the handle down, and left the apartment.

It was still drizzling outside. She deliberated for a moment on whether to hail a taxi. The rain was soft and home was only twenty or so minutes away. She decided to walk.

She imagined that Nathan would be quite relieved that he wouldn't have to dispose of his one-night stand in the morning; a good-looking guy like him would probably sleep with a different girl every other weekend. Must make it a lot easier if they weren't around the following morning, hoping for another date, or even a relationship.

Jodi was just grateful that it had been a positive experience. She'd really enjoyed Nathan's company and the sex had been powerful enough to make her forget that it was meant to be just another milestone. Now she could tick the box SLEEP WITH ANOTHER MAN. She was further down the road of recovery. And so she should be. Andrew was dead two years last week.

On the following Monday morning Jodi was informed that she was to lose two people from her team. The notice came by way of email. It seemed that reducing headcount was Brian Hughes's favourite pastime. Jodi went straight to his office to protest.

'I can't do without these people.'

'Of course, you can.' He dismissed her with a demeaning wave of his hand. 'They're only admin.'

He made the word *admin* sound like it was something dirty. Jodi tried to control the wave of anger rising inside her.

'Rachel coordinates the implementation of new customers,' she informed him in a stony voice. 'She inputs the employee details on the system, irons out any problems and makes sure it's all a smooth experience for the client.'

Brian's fat little face was unmoved. It was very evident that he didn't give a damn what Rachel did all day.

Nevertheless, Jodi continued on. 'Eileen handles all my correspondence. She makes meetings, cancels meetings, reschedules meetings, makes reservations, unmakes reservations, and does whatever is necessary to get me and the clients together at the same place and time.' She stopped for a quick breath. 'Brian, you must believe me, losing Rachel and Eileen will negatively impact our clients – it'll be bad for business.'

Brian regarded her from under his bushy eyebrows. He looked as if he had begun to contemplate her arguments.

'Paula,' he shouted to his secretary, who was sitting outside at her desk.

'Yes?'

'Can you book a table at Franco's?'

'How many?'

'Two.'

Jodi stared at him incredulously. So that was the end of it? Rachel and Eileen were to lose their jobs without any further discussion?

Brian leaned forward in his seat. His puffy lips parted to bare yellowed teeth. Jodi hadn't seen him smile before. If possible, it made him even less attractive.

'Let's talk about it over lunch,' he said in a voice that was low for him.

'Pardon?'

'You and me. Lunch.' The smile had transformed into a leer. 'Franco's is one of the best places in town,' he declared as if she should be honoured. 'Mondays are quiet there – we'll have some privacy, time to get to know each other a little better, eh?'

His leer widened, taking over his whole face. His intentions were quite unmistakeable and nothing to with Rachel and Eileen's jobs. Shock froze Jodi to the spot.

Brian heaved his fat little body up from his chair. He straightened his tie and squeezed his arms into his suit jacket. Coming around from the desk, he noticed an untied lace and stooped to fix it.

'I'm busy,' Jodi mumbled.

'What?' He straightened, his face red from the rush of blood, thinking perhaps he had misheard.

'I'm too busy to take lunch today,' she said, her words hurrying out.

Abruptly, she swung on her heel and practically ran from his office. Paula, the secretary, didn't even look up as she passed. Maybe she was used to women hurrying out. How many cosy lunches for two had she booked at Franco's before today?

Jodi flew down the corridor and, coming out at the foyer to see she had just missed a lift, decided to take the stairs. Down she went, flight after flight, her heels clicking on the bare grey concrete. She was trembling, her hands, her knees, her insides, everywhere. Why had she not seen it before? How like Bob he was? The fat face, the bullying ways, and now the misdirected desire?

What is wrong with me? Why do men like that think I'm an easy touch?

She had no answers. She walked around the surrounding

streets and tried to calm down enough to look at the situation objectively. She went back over everything in her head. Was it possible she had mistaken Brian's intentions?

No. He said Franco's was private and we could 'get to know each other'. He mentioned nothing more about Rachel and Eileen. And I know the look he had on his face.

The next most pertinent question was why hadn't she stood up to him? Let him know in no uncertain terms that she wasn't up for any hanky-panky or whatever else he had in mind?

Because I was petrified. So scared I couldn't think straight. All I could see was Bob in front of me.

Jodi heard a horn beep furiously and realised she had unwittingly crossed a side street without looking for oncoming traffic. She raised an apologetic hand to the driver and hurried along to the safety of the footpath on the other side.

Her thoughts reverted back to the problem at hand. Could she go back to the office and act as though everything was okay? Could she fool herself that Brian didn't look like Bob and history wasn't about to repeat itself?

I have a job that I love, a fabulous car and shares in the company. I'll be damned if Brian Hughes is going to scare me away from Invesco!

Jodi returned to the office and got on with her work.

The following day she received another invitation for lunch. The email read: **Paula can get us into Franco's at 1 pm. Please confirm.**

She typed a response.

Sorry, Brian. I should have explained that I don't go to lunches or dinners with the boss. I had a bad experience in the past. I know that you wouldn't take advantage, but I'd prefer for all our dealings to be here in the office. Thanks for your understanding.

Her lips twitched as she pressed SEND. Brian might be frighteningly like Bob, but she wasn't at all like the old Jodi. She'd come a long, long way.

Sarah: Old Love

Chapter 28

Dublin, 1997

Sarah strode into her office and put her briefcase on her desk. She'd inherited the office from Eric who had retired two years ago. Perched on the mezzanine level, it had glass walls on three sides. She could see everything that was going on down on the trading floor, and everyone could see what was going on in her fishbowl: her visitors, her moods, her every move. It was the one thing she didn't like about being chief dealer.

She unwound a cashmere scarf from her neck, unbuttoned her heavy winter coat and hung both items in the closet behind her desk. Sitting down, she took a moment to savour the sweet silence. The phone hadn't started to ring and there was nobody waiting at her door for a word of advice. Not yet, anyway. Give it ten minutes and there'd be the usual bedlam.

Closing her eyes, she inhaled over three seconds, held it for three and then slowly exhaled. She'd read about the breathing technique in a magazine last year and found it very effective, particularly at night when she needed to wind down from a manic day in the office.

After a few minutes of deep breathing, she turned on her computer. While it was loading up, she read the pink telephone-message slips that had been left on her desk. They were mostly trivial matters that could have been dealt with by any one of her staff. However, it was a frustrating fact of life that the richest clients wanted to deal only with the boss. If those clients were a little less self-important and a little more flexible, Sarah would not have to work twelve-hour days.

She had just started to read her emails when her secretary, Linda, popped her head around the door.

'The usual?' she enquired.

'Yes, please.'

A black coffee was exactly what Sarah needed to warm up on this chilly December morning where gardens, rooftops and windscreens had been coated with a sparkling layer of frost, leaving the city as pretty as a picture, until the sparkle melted away and revealed the greyness beneath.

Sarah quickly scanned through the messages in her inbox. They were all flagged urgent, but then what wasn't urgent in a business where the market could drop five per cent in as many seconds? Every message had to be read and resolved, or delegated. Quickly.

Sarah had a recurring nightmare in which she couldn't get to the end of her inbox. She'd read a message but five more would replace it. While she read the next, the new ones multiplied to twenty. She'd wake in a sweat, realise it was just a nightmare, but fail to go back to sleep because it was so damn close to the truth.

A new message highlighted on her screen.

Tim Brennan.

The sight of Tim's name always brought a funny feeling, a twinge. She saw him very rarely these days. They would meet up whenever she visited EquiBank's New York headquarters. They'd go for dinner or a drink. Catch up on what was happening in their respective lives and careers. Give each other a chaste kiss goodbye till next time. Walk away with a nagging sense of regret. Or at least Sarah did. She couldn't tell if Tim felt the same.

She clicked on the message to open it.

Hi Sarah, hope all's well with you. Big news here. I'm moving back to Ireland to take over the running of the farm. Obviously, I've resigned from EquiBank. Will give you a call when I get back.

Tim

Sarah's mouth dropped open as she read the message. Tim had resigned! He sounded so blasé about it. As if it was no big deal to go from being a vice-president to a farmer. As if it was an everyday thing to trade in a penthouse in Manhattan for an old farmhouse in Cork. Sarah had last seen him at his father's funeral in March. He had been shocked and sad, but had given no indication of stepping into his father's shoes.

Sarah hardly noticed that Linda was back with her coffee. Her secretary cleared her throat and began to run through Sarah's commitments for the day.

'You have a management meeting at nine . . . Lunch is at Gardenia's . . . I've allowed thirty minutes' travel time . . .'

Linda was under the false impression that Sarah was incapable of remembering what was scheduled for the day. Each meeting or lunch or dinner entailed such meticulous preparation that

Sarah was very unlikely to forget. But she kept mum; she quite liked Linda telling her what she already knew. It was the only constant of her day.

'You have back-to-back meetings for the entire afternoon, then you're meeting Eric MacDonald for dinner – 8 pm sharp. I've allowed fifteen minutes' travel time.'

Sarah's phone began to ring. She answered it and Linda, who had finished her recital, closed the door softly on her way out. The bedlam had begun.

Twelve hours later, Sarah finished her last phone call of the day and began to shut down her computer. She had a clanging headache and was in no mood for the dinner ahead. She briefly considered cancelling but dismissed the idea almost straight away. She couldn't let Eric down like that. The dinner was in honour of his sixty-eighth birthday. All the family would be there and her presence would be missed.

There were still people at their desks when Sarah walked through the floor on her way out. She saluted them as she passed but didn't feel guilty. She had done her time in the trenches, where working till 10 pm was quite the norm. If you didn't like it or couldn't stand the pace, then a career in investment banking wasn't for you. Simple.

A cruel wind lifted wisps of her hair as she scanned the street for a taxi. She stared to her right, where the flow of traffic was heaviest, and willed a taxi to come around the corner. Nothing! She wished she hadn't left her car at home. She was going to be late. Very late. The knot of tension in her chest tightened another notch. Cursing under her breath, she started to walk.

'Ah, we thought you'd got lost,' Eric called to her when she finally arrived at the restaurant, forty minutes late.

'Sorry.' She came round the large circular table to kiss his cheek. 'There must be a taxi strike that I don't know of – didn't see one the whole way in. I'm glad you didn't wait to order.'

Patsy stood up to give her a hug. 'God, girl, you're skin and bones.' She looked down at Sarah's high-heeled shoes. 'Not exactly walking shoes, are they?'

Sarah grimaced, her feet aching. 'Tell me about it.'

Laura, who was busy trying to coax spoonfuls of food past two-year-old Jessica's pursed lips, said hello, as did Mark, who was dabbing up something that looked liked spilt juice. Jessica stretched her lips to smile at Sarah but was crafty enough not to leave enough space for her mother to get the spoon through.

Laura and Mark's second child, a tiny four-week-old baby girl called Lucy, was asleep in her pram. Sarah peeked in and allowed the baby's fingers to curl around hers. She always felt a little sad around Laura and Mark's babies. It had been the same when Nuala's kids were young, but they were five and three now, no longer babies, and Sarah found it easier.

'Sit down,' instructed Eric and patted the seat next to him. 'Have a glass of wine. I'll ask the waiter to bring out some starters for you.'

Would my baby have been this tiny? Would it have had this much hair? Would it have been a girl or a boy?

Sarah extracted her finger from the baby's clasp. 'I'll just wait for the main course – won't say no to the wine, though.'

She sat next to Eric and slipped off her shoes. The carpet felt lush under the burning soles of her feet.

'You look tired,' he said accusingly as he poured the wine.

'Well, you should know better than anyone how busy I am,' she replied.

'Being tired and uptight are not necessarily part and parcel of being busy,' he retorted.

It sounded like the birthday boy had a bee in his bonnet.

'Excuse me!' She regarded him with mock outrage. 'I am *not* uptight.'

'Yes, you are,' Patsy chimed in. 'You look like the slightest thing would push you over the edge.'

Sarah looked from wife to husband bemusedly. 'What's this? Some kind of *flog Sarah* convention? And I thought I was coming to a birthday party!'

Her quip didn't get as much as a smile from either of them.

'You need to find a way to wind down, Sarah,' Eric told her in a deadly serious voice. 'I used to relax by playing a few rounds of golf. You need to do something too – yoga, pilates, whatever's necessary – otherwise the stress will kill you.'

Sarah glanced across the table to see that Laura and Mark, even Jessica, were listening intently.

'Oh, stop ganging up on me, would you?' she said crossly and took a gulp of wine.

Later, when it was time to go home, it became apparent that it wasn't her day for taxis. Having no luck outside the restaurant, Sarah set off down the street. A car slowed and beeped. Mark's head stuck out the passenger window.

'Are you sure you'll be okay?'

The sedan was full to capacity, Eric and Patsy squashed in the back with the two children.

'Yeah,' Sarah waved him on, 'I'm grand. Goodnight.'

She walked on to a taxi rank that had a formidable queue. She sighed at the thought of a long wait. She'd be lucky to get home before midnight at this rate. If only it wasn't such a busy day tomorrow.

Feeling herself growing panicky at the thought of not having enough sleep, she started to do her breathing exercises. One, two, three, in. Hold. One, two, three, out.

Her turn came round quite quickly in the end.

The taxi driver was one of the ones who liked the sound of his own voice.

'Had a good night out, luv?'

'Work early tomorrow?'

'And what do you do to earn a bob?'

Sarah mumbled something about working in a bank. He seemed satisfied and began to talk about himself.

'I do this taxi driving at night only. I work as a mechanic during the day. I don't do it for the money, you know. I like meeting people, talking to them – beats having your head stuck under a car all day.'

He was very approving as he drove through her neighbourhood.

'Nice area, this.'

She asked him to pull in outside her house. She saw his lips blow a soundless whistle as he sized it up.

'Renting?'

'No,' she replied abruptly and handed him a ten pound note.

She got out of the taxi before he had the gall to ask how much she'd paid for it. What if she told him she owned six such houses in Dublin? That whenever she felt unsettled or unfulfilled, she would go out and buy another? Some she renovated and sold on, others she retained for investment purposes. She could live quite comfortably off the rental income if she so desired. She laughed to herself at what the nosey taxi driver might make of all that.

Swinging the wrought-iron gate inwards, she walked up the short path to the house. It had a pretty little garden that she never took time to appreciate. A man came round every fortnight to cut the grass and weed the flowerbeds. She left his money under the mat. When she came home from work, the money was gone, trimmed edges and the sweet smell of fresh grass in its place.

She turned the key in the lock and pushed the heavy door inwards. In the darkness of the hallway she saw the red flashing from her answering machine. She flicked on the lights and walked over to play her messages.

Hi, Sarah. Nuala's chirpy voice filled the silent hallway. *I'll be in Dublin on Friday. Just wondering if you're free for lunch. I have some news to tell you. Give me a ring as soon as you get this.*

Sarah's ears perked up. What news? Surely Nuala wasn't pregnant again. Pity it was too late to phone her back.

The machine went on to a second message.

Hi. It's me, Emma. Just wanted a chat. Jason's away on business. Maybe you could pop over? That's if you get the message, of course.

Jason, Emma's boyfriend, travelled a lot and she hated being alone in the house. Sarah often slept over in her spare room. She made a mental note to call Emma in the morning to arrange something.

Sarah went into the kitchen to get a drink of water. She drank it back and filled the glass again. Then she trawled up the stairs, yawning on the way. In the bathroom, she removed her make-up with a soft cotton pad and brushed her teeth. The mirror above the basin was harsh. It showed one or two grey hairs along her parting and tension lines around her eyes. Patsy's words of warning rang in her head.

'*You look like the slightest thing would push you over the edge . . .*'

Slowly, thoughtfully, Sarah moved away from the telltale mirror. She undressed and slipped into her most comfortable cotton pyjamas.

The sheets of her bed felt cold and unwelcoming. She began her breathing exercises. One, two, three . . .

Ten minutes passed, then twenty. Her body had all the physical signs of tiredness: compulsive yawns, aching feet and leaden arms. But her mind was despairingly alert.

Is there anywhere close by that does yoga classes?

I wonder what Nuala's news is about!

How do I feel about Tim coming back to live in Ireland?

The new year was rung in, winter gave way to spring, and then spring to early summer. Sarah's sleeping worsened. She was too cold, too hot, too anxious, or simply too sad to sleep. She was always tired, though. Bone tired. So tired that she could barely get out of bed in the mornings.

'You need a holiday,' Eric urged.

Fine for him to offer advice in that fatherly tone of his, but how? When? Who with? The logistics of organising time off were overwhelming. So Sarah continued on. She worked hard. She ran hard. She tried to control her thoughts. But her mind and her body did not respond; her coping strategies were simply not working.

One day, when Tim had been back in Ireland for five months and Sarah was at an all-time low, he phoned and offered a lifeline.

'You don't sound yourself,' he commented when he heard her voice.

'I'm not feeling very well,' she admitted. 'I'm tired. Everyone tells me I need a holiday.'

She didn't tell him that the blackness, which she had kept at bay for so long, had crept back into her life. Sapping her energy, gnawing at her confidence, making happiness seem like a privilege only others could enjoy – like Nuala, who was expect-ing another baby, and Emma, who had got engaged to Jason.

'Come down to the farm,' Tim suggested. 'I haven't seen you since I got back.'

'It's not that easy.'

'Come on! It would do you the world of good. The fresh air, the smell of shite –' He laughed. 'The ridiculous sight of me in overalls and wellies . . .'

It wasn't easy but it made sense. A lot of sense.

The next day Sarah announced that she was taking a week off. She handed over the reins to one of the managing directors. His name was Leo Carmichael. He was experienced, reliable and terribly ambitious.

'Where are you going on your break?' he asked.

'To a farm down in Cork.'

'Oh.'

He was perplexed. Why Cork when you had the means to go to Tahiti or Mauritius or somewhere else similarly exotic?

Sarah didn't try to explain it; she simply focused on telling him what he needed to do to hold the fort while she was away.

She set off straight from work on Friday. It was a slow run out of Dublin. There seemed to be no accident or any other good reason for the hold-up, just too many cars on the road.

Sarah changed the channel on her radio. She knew some of the words of the song, 'Don't Speak', but didn't know the name of the singer.

You're so out of touch, she sneered at herself.

She was ridiculously nervous about seeing Tim. It was one thing catching up in New York, with both of them dressed in business attire and using work talk to gloss over any awkward moments. This was an entirely different prospect: jeans and baggy jumpers, real conversation, in fact very like their college years.

Tim will never equate you to the girl he knew in college.

Sarah wound down the window and a warm breeze floated through the car. People were saying that it was shaping up to be a good summer; she had been indoors so much that she hadn't noticed until now.

Finally, she got through the set of lights that were causing all the trouble and she was able to make some progress. As the speed of the car picked up, so did her spirits.

Stop expecting the worst of Tim – of everything. Think positive!

Three hours later, as night was closing in, she passed the sign that read, *Welcome to Cork*. Just another couple of small towns to pass through and she'd be there. She was looking forward to getting out of the car. She hadn't stopped along the way and now her lower back was aching from sitting in the one spot for too long.

Tim's family farm was in a country area a short drive from the end of the motorway. Sarah had been there a few times before, many years ago. She drove along the spindly road and kept her eyes peeled for the white-walled entrance to the property. She reached an unfamiliar T-junction.

Damn! I must have gone too far.

She turned around and drove slowly back along the road. Perhaps the outside wall had been painted. She re-examined every entrance. None of them, even accounting for the possibility of a different shade of paint, looked vaguely familiar.

She gave herself a stern lecture on staying calm.

It can't be far. No need to panic.

Easier said than done! Panic seemed only a hair's breadth away these days.

She pulled into the gateway of a field to give herself time to think.

I wish I'd brought my mobile phone with me . . . But if I had, I wouldn't be able to get away from work . . . I guess I can knock on someone's door and ask to use the phone . . . Embarrassing – but not the end of the world – no need to panic!

She was preparing to pull back out of the gateway when a tractor trundled round the corner. Its headlights shone straight through her car before it passed by. It came to a stop a few metres down the road. The driver switched on the hazard lights and his shadowy figure hopped down from the cabin.

The face that appeared at her window was weather-beaten and concerned.

'Are ya all right there?' he shouted through the glass, spittle on his cracked lips.

Sarah wound down the window. 'Just a little lost,' she said meekly.

'Where are ya going?'

'The Brennans' place.'

The farmer straightened. She noticed a length of twine tied around his waist like a belt.

'Ah, sure, you're on the wrong road altogether.'

'Oh.'

'You should have turned right off the Old Glanmire Road.'

'Oh.'

He scratched his head as he pondered the problem. 'Sure, I'm in no rush. Drive along behind me and I'll show you the way.'

'Thanks.'

Sheepishly, she put the car into gear and swung it around so it was tailing the tractor. Off they set, going no more than twenty kilometres an hour.

At this rate, Tim will have a search party out for me.

A number of kilometres and turn-offs later, the tractor slowed and flashed his hazard lights to indicate they'd reached their destination. Sarah would have never found it on her own and, to thank the farmer, she flashed her hazards in return.

Her wheels crunched along the gravel of the driveway. She felt her heart begin to hammer. God, she was so nervous! And still panicky after getting lost. Not a good combination.

The front door of the house opened as she pulled up outside. Tim's silhouette appeared, an arm raised in welcome. Sarah turned off the ignition, took a deep breath to steady her nerves, and opened the car door.

'I thought you'd got lost,' was his greeting.

'I did,' she replied.

There was a pause as they looked at each other to assess how they'd changed since they'd last met. Tim looked well. He wore a bulky grey sweater and denims. Dark stubble covered his lower face. The rugged look suited him. It reminded Sarah of their college days, long before EquiBank and designer suits.

She feared, though, that she wouldn't come off as well in his assessment. That he'd see the lines in the corners of her hazel eyes, the few stubborn greys in her hair, and the sadness she carried inside.

Tim stepped forward, the gravel grating underfoot, and Sarah found herself embraced in a warm hug. It lasted long enough for her to know that he was very happy to see her, regardless of how she looked. Then he dropped his arms away, exposed her to the suddenly cool night air, and got down to the business of moving her in.

'Pop the boot open and I'll get your bags.'

'I've put you upstairs at the back of the house.'

'The bathroom is across the way.'

'I have some dinner ready downstairs. Hope you're hungry.'

The house, despite its stark stone exterior, was newly reno-vated on the inside. The kitchen had modern appliances and a top-of-the-range benchtop. New furnishings and fresh paint had transformed the bedrooms upstairs.

'You've made a really good job of it,' Sarah commented as he showed her around.

The renovations had not only modernised the house but had also capitalised on its character. The kitchen's hanging saucepans and oversized fireplace testified that it was still a farmhouse at heart.

'Don't you miss the penthouse?' she asked when they sat down to dinner.

'A little,' he replied with a shrug. 'But Manhattan never felt like home. This does.'

His words struck a chord with Sarah. She owned six houses but not one of them felt like home.

'You're lucky to have had all this waiting for you while you were away seeking your fortune,' she said with a smile.

He smiled too. Then he raised his glass. 'Cheers. To old friends – and new beginnings.'

'Cheers,' she echoed.

Their glasses clinked. Their eyes locked.

He spoke in a voice soft with innuendo, 'Right now I'm very glad that I made the decision to come back.'

Sarah held his gaze for a few excruciating moments before breaking away. Although food was about the furthest thing from her mind, she began to cut the meat on her plate. It was surprisingly tender and came away easily onto her fork. She looked closer at the contents of her plate: thin slices of beef and char-grilled vegetables, surrounded by a red wine sauce.

'Well,' she declared, having chewed her first mouthful, 'since when did you learn how to cook like this? I seem to remember that pasta was the extent of your capabilities when I lived with you in New York.'

His eyes stared through her, not fooled by her avoidance tactics.

But still he answered, 'I dated a master chef a while back. She taught me some basics.'

'Oh.'

Jealousy bittered the taste in her mouth. Obviously Tim had dated many girls over the years, just as she'd dated countless faceless men. Had this master chef been someone special to him? Had they spent hours cuddling and laughing in the kitchen as she'd taught him elementary cooking?

'No, Sarah. She wasn't special.'

Sarah felt her face blush with colour.

She began to worry that this was all a very bad idea: alone with Tim on this isolated farm; nowhere to run to hide her feelings, whatever they were; on tenterhooks that he would break down her defences. So much for rest and relaxation!

Sarah drank her first glass of wine rather quickly and the alcohol helped ease her edginess. And the food went some way to filling the emptiness she felt inside. The conversation, after the rocky start, veered to safer topics: what mutual friends were doing; Tim's impressions of Ireland after being away for such a long time; Sarah's career, as Tim didn't have one to speak of these days.

'I love my job,' she told him. 'Being chief dealer means that I have to keep an eye on all the markets: foreign exchange, bonds, metals, equities – I love the diversity. I told the bank that I would only accept the job if I could continue to trade. I never want to be in a job where I'm so swamped with paperwork and bureaucracy that I've lost the art of knowing a good deal . . . That would be my hell.'

Tim swirled the wine in his glass. He looked thoughtful. Sarah wondered if a small part of him regretted walking out on his career.

'So where have you set your sights?' he asked after a longish silence. 'How far up that corporate ladder do you want to go?'

She laughed. 'To the very top, of course.'

He smiled but didn't laugh. 'What spurs you on? Power or money?'

'Power,' she responded with a shrug. 'I like to be in charge of where I'm going. I can't drift, like some people do. I need to have goals, deadlines, pressure – otherwise I don't know what to do, or who I am – sad, isn't it?'

'Not necessarily,' he replied.

Sarah took a sip of wine. 'Some people think so. It doesn't matter how successful you are in business, all that counts to them is marriage and kids. If you haven't achieved in those particular areas, well, you're a loser, aren't you?'

Tim grimaced. 'That makes us both losers, then.'

'Easier for a man. No clock ticking away in the background.' She tilted her head from side to side. 'Tick-tock. Tick-tock.'

'You sound like a bomb waiting to go off.'

'That's closer to the truth than you think,' she said darkly, her mood taking a turn for the worse.

She felt the weight of his gaze again. She was suddenly very aware that he knew there was something wrong and he was giving her the green light to confide in him.

I have to get out of here before I blurt everything out.

She got to her feet. Her knees felt unsteady.

338

'Thanks for the dinner. It was great. But I'm wrecked. Got to go to bed.' As she passed, she leaned down to peck his cheek with the friendly kiss she thought appropriate for the circumstances. Suddenly she was up close to his rough stubble and fathomless eyes. Another bad idea!

'Goodnight,' she croaked and fled the room.

The drapes in the bedroom were heavy and maintained a darkness that induced the deepest of sleeps. When Sarah finally opened her eyes she was astounded to see that it was midmorning. She could not remember the last time she'd slept so soundly. Her body was the perfect temperature, not too cold or too hot, and she had no urge whatsoever to push the covers back.

She stretched her toes. Dozily, she told herself that she really should get up. Tim would be wondering whether she'd died in her sleep.

A soft knock sounded on her door.

'Sarah?'

'Yes.' She sat up and ran a quick hand through her hair to smooth it down.

A fresh earthy smell came into the room with Tim. He was in his stockinged feet, his boots most probably left at the back door. His work jeans and T-shirt were soiled with dirt, oil and a variety of other farm stains. Last night's stubble shaved away, she could see the paleness of his skin underneath and the lines of his squarish jaw. His vitality jolted her senses and aroused all sorts of dormant feelings.

'I was worried about you.' He had a sheepish look on his face. 'I remember you as being an early riser, and when I didn't see you make an appearance, well I thought . . .'

'That I'd done a runner?'

'Well, yes.'

He sat on the side of the bed. He looked embarrassed. 'I'm sorry about last night.'

'Why?'

'Because I think I may have overstepped the mark.'

Sarah could have pretended not to know what he meant. But this was Tim. Her old friend. With whom she'd been half in love for most of their friendship. If she was honest with herself.

She swallowed a lump in her throat and forced herself to be brave. To face up to whatever was between them.

'You said that you were glad you'd made the decision to come home,' she said in a hushed voice. 'And if *I* was any part of that decision, then that's okay with me.'

His eyes filled with disappointment. 'Only okay?'

'No.' She reached for his hand. The farm work hadn't yet taken its toll and his skin was still banker smooth. 'It's more than okay. It makes me very happy. And that's not an easy thing to do these days.'

His face was close, his lips just a kiss away. She did it. Kissed him. His mouth moved gently against hers; he knew she was fragile. He pulled her close, and she felt safe with his arms around her, so safe that tears of relief started to flow down her face.

He stopped the kiss, but his lips stayed close to hers. 'Why are you so sad, Sarah?'

His eyes beckoned her to take the leap, to admit the truth.

'I think I have depression,' she whispered. 'It runs in my family – my mother had it too. I can't seem to pull out of it this time, Tim. I need help.'

Sarah was in the psychologist's office for over an hour. He was a man of about her age, with a nondescript face and voice. He spent most of the time asking questions which Sarah answered honestly. She told him everything, her life history. But not about the abortion: that was locked too deep within.

'From what you've said, it seems that the depression you suffered in the past was because of major life events – your boyfriend going away to study, your grandmother dying. This time the cause of your depression appears to be stress.'

'But I love my job,' Sarah protested. 'It's always been something that has made me feel good, not bad.'

The psychologist nodded, as if in agreement. 'Normal work stress can invoke excitement and challenge. It can charge you up. But if you overstep the mark and have prolonged periods of high stress, then you will feel flat afterwards.'

Sarah listened to what he was saying. She was prepared to do whatever it took to get better. 'How can I manage the stress?'

'Balance,' he replied plainly. 'Balance across work, leisure, family and other interests. And I'd like to discuss medication options with you, that you can follow up with your GP.' The psychologist paused to look her in the eye. 'You're overworking because you're still trying to prove yourself. Stop trying to prove yourself, Sarah. You are a smart and successful young woman: a proven entity.'

Sarah was about to challenge him, to say that she did have friends and other interests, but then she got it. He was saying that her friends and other interests weren't a big enough part of her life. He was right. But Tim was waiting outside. Tim who had made the appointment, who had driven her to the city, who had told her he loved her. Tim would even up the balance.

Chapter 29

Six weeks later

Sarah stood up to address the crowd gathered in the banquet room of the hotel. She smoothed down her figure-hugging dress with its flattering V neckline. Accustomed as she was to public speaking, she didn't need to consult notes.

'Good afternoon, everybody.' They clapped benevolently at her greeting. 'There are many people I need to thank for making today possible. First on the list is my bridesmaid, Nuala, who looks so gorgeous today that I think she may be trying to upstage me.'

The guests laughed and Nuala, eight months pregnant, threw her eyes to heaven as if the bride was telling an outrageous lie. She simply couldn't be persuaded that the gold-coloured dress complimented her baby bump and her glowing skin.

'Thank you, Nuala, for all your help with the organising. I wouldn't have known where to start . . .'

Sarah and Tim had both liked the idea of a summer wedding.

Friends and family had warned that they were mad to think they could pull the whole thing off with less than six weeks' notice. Nuala, though, had risen to the challenge and dragged Sarah around to venues, florists, printers and dressmakers until everything was organised.

'And a big thank you to Eric and Patsy MacDonald, who have been like a father and mother to me . . .'

Eric and Patsy sat at the top table, Eric perfectly content with a glass of good red wine, and Patsy with an enormous hat that was as over-the-top as her personality.

'Finally . . .' Sarah turned to face Tim. His dark suit and gold-embroidered waistcoat looked so good on him that he could have been a model groom out of a wedding magazine. For the rest of her life she'd wake up next to this man. Every day she'd see his dark hair, pale skin and the strong bones of his face. 'I'd like to tell my husband that I feel incredibly proud to be his wife. Most of you will know that Tim and I go back a long way. I'm not sure what excuses or reasons we had not to get together before now, but I feel very lucky that we finally saw what was right before our eyes . . . Tim, I love you more than anything in the world . . . and this is the happiest day of my life.'

Sarah sat down to an enthusiastic round of applause, with a few wolf whistles thrown in for good measure. Feeling quite emotional, she leaned forward to take a steadying drink of water. When she put the glass back down, Tim's hand reached for hers. He smiled. A private smile, just for her. He looked emotional too and Sarah could tell that her words had touched him deeply.

Everything she'd said had been straight from the heart. She'd wanted the sixty-odd guests, who were undoubtedly perplexed at the speed of their nuptials, to understand why they couldn't wait another minute to be married, to understand how happy they were. Sarah knew that her happiness came from deep within and wasn't due to the box of antidepressants she had in her medicine cabinet.

The best man, Tim's older brother, who had flown from his home in Germany to do the honours, began to make his speech. As he recounted funny incidents from Tim's childhood, Sarah glanced at the faces around the room. Most of the guests were from Tim's side: aunts, uncles and cousins. She didn't have names for all the faces yet but they were such a friendly lot that she knew it wouldn't be long before she was in the thick of the family dynamics.

The guests on Sarah's side were split between friends and colleagues. Emma, with a big rock on her finger, sat with Jason's arm around her waist as she listened intently to Tim's brother. Her wedding was planned for eighteen months' time and she in particular was astounded at how quickly Sarah and Tim had got to this point.

Colin sat at the same table. His face had become smugger and his outlook on life gloomier with each passing year. But he was a good husband and father. His children verified that.

'Daddy plays lots of games with us.'

'Daddy kisses Mummy and us before going out to catch the baddies.'

'Mummy says that Daddy is the bravest and most handsomest garda in all of Ireland!'

Nuala and Colin weren't the romance of the century, but they were solid, rock solid. They'd created three children and a loving home, and their marriage was far from the mistake Sarah had feared it would be.

Laura and Mark sat one table over. Laura wore a pretty pink wrap-over dress that matched the colour of her flushed face.

After two pregnancies relatively quick in succession, the wine was possibly going to her head. Or maybe her heightened colour was brought about by the sheer excitement at having a day out without the kids. Tim's brother announced that it was time to cut the cake. Sarah saw Laura exchange a smile with Mark. It was obvious that they were remembering their own wedding day.

Sarah walked to the cake stand, hand in hand with Tim. Cameras flashed in their faces.

'I feel like a rock star,' he whispered in her ear.

She laughed.

Another flash went off.

That photograph, when she saw the wedding album a few weeks later, was instantly her favourite. Unlike all the other photographs, it wasn't posed. Tim's head was close to hers, his bow tie a little askew. A few curls had come loose from Sarah's French knot. They looked completely relaxed with each other, and very, very happy.

Jodi: Old Crush

Chapter 30

Singapore, 1998

A firm hand cupped Jodi's chin and adjusted its position. 'Now, tilt your head deez way – yes, good – now, a smile, pleeze.'

The photographer ran back behind his camera and a flash went off as he took the shot.

'A smaller smile, pleeze,' was his next request. 'Perhaps you could look a little thoughtful?'

Jodi obliged, although a grin was itching to escape. The shots were being taken for the bank's annual report. All of the new directors were to have a photograph and brief biography included. Hers was to read:

Jodi Tyler was promoted to director in March 1998 and is responsible for client service for a number of key institutional accounts in the Asia-Pacific region. Jodi joined CorpBank's London office in 1994 and moved to Singapore in 1996. She has extensive sales experience in bonds, equities and currencies. Prior to CorpBank,

Jodi worked for Invesco, where she designed and sold pension funds.

The photographer darted out from behind his camera to adjust the light reflector screen. He stared hard at Jodi, moved the screen another millimetre, and looked satisfied with the result. After a half-dozen rapid-fire shots, he was finished.

'Thank you, Mizz Tyler. You are very photogenic!'

Jodi smiled and stood up, straightening her clothes. A quick check of her watch confirmed that there was plenty of time to get to the airport for her overnight flight to Sydney. She just had to collect her bag from the office and ask her assistant to confirm that one of the corporate cars would be ready.

Half an hour later Jodi was in the back of the car and heading for the airport at a steady pace. Speed limits were strictly enforced and adhered to in Singapore. On one particular occasion, when she hadn't lived in the city for long, Jodi had missed a flight because the driver refused to go a smidgeon over the limit. That particular experience had been a lesson well learned and she'd never again cut tight the travel time to the airport.

Today, the driver had the airconditioning turned up to the max and it was deliciously cool in the car. Jodi gazed out the window. The landscape was familiar: she did this journey to the airport at least a few times a month. Usually her trips were to visit clients in other capital cities in the region. A few times a year, like this time, she was on her way home, to Sydney.

The car passed by a line of towering palm trees, planted along the divide in the road. The leaves formed rich green fans under the swollen grey sky. The heavens would open soon, making the surface steamy and dangerous for the dated cars. In this city, only the richest of the rich could afford to keep a vehicle. Jodi's hand ran along the smooth leather of the backseat. This luxury was a rarity. A privilege.

The car pulled up outside the terminal and Jodi got out. The heat hit her face and stole her breath away. The driver lifted her bag onto the pavement.

'Thank you.'

'You're welcome. Have a good flight.'

The same exchange could have happened in Sydney, London or New York.

Little had Jodi known that she'd end up living in the heart of Asia when she'd moved to CorpBank in 1994. At the time London was suffering from a shortfall of experienced professionals and Jodi was getting a few calls a week from head-hunters. Her career with Invesco had gone as far as it could and she was looking for a change. Something about the CorpBank role caught her attention. It was nothing like what she was doing at Invesco, but the idea of selling bonds was exciting; she guessed it would be more immediate and dynamic than selling pension funds. She cashed in her Invesco shares, which had quadrupled in value, and sent the entire proceeds to Shirley for her place by the sea. Then she handed Brian Hughes her letter of resignation.

Jodi learned the ropes quickly and became very good at selling bonds. Good enough for CorpBank to accommodate her when she said she wanted to switch to selling equities. And good enough to transfer to the Singapore office where there were grand plans of expansion into Asia.

Jodi checked in at business class where the queues were significantly shorter than the other desks. She made her way to the Qantas Club lounge and whiled away some time with a strong coffee and a crossword. Every now and then, she unconsciously smiled at the thought of spending a quiet week in Sydney with her family and friends. Her last trip, over the Christmas holidays, had been far too busy. There had been no time to engage in one of Grandma's meandering chats. Or to help around the house. Or to plunge into the waves at Dee Why beach. This holiday was going to be different.

The boarding call was announced over the intercom. The flight was en route from London, Singapore a stopover on the way. The transfer passengers were already seated when Jodi got on board. Their faces were grey and weary, and some of them looked enviously at the influx of new passengers who had to endure only half the journey.

Jodi pulled her bag along as she scanned the seat numbers overhead. While she should have been focused on finding her seat, her eyes were inexplicably drawn to a man in the left-hand aisle. There was something familiar about him. The way he bent his head as he read his book. The dark wavy hair. Her heart missed a beat. Was it him?

He looked up, as if he sensed her gaze. Their eyes met. It was him: the professor. Recognition flooded his face and his lips parted with astonishment.

'May I see your boarding pass, please?'

It was a helpful hostess, who assumed that Jodi had stalled because she was having trouble finding her seat. Jodi distractedly showed her the boarding pass. The hostess ushered her further down the aisle and, checking with Jodi that she didn't need anything from her cabin bag, hoisted it into the overhead locker. Jodi sat down. Her face was flushed and her heart was beating erratically in her chest.

Am I ever going to outgrow that stupid crush on him?

The plane sat on the tarmac for another twenty minutes. The crew gave no explanation for the delay. Jodi stared at the back of the seat in front. The fabric had an intricate pattern but it wasn't what she was seeing. She saw a young girl in a terrible mess; she saw a compassionate man who had pulled out all the stops to help; she saw him sitting at the back of the courtroom, in his dark office crammed with textbooks, and in his car the time he'd dropped her home.

Finally, just as the passengers were beginning to grow fidgety, the plane started to edge backwards. They were on their way. What would happen after take-off? Should she go over to him? Or wait for him to find her. It was eight years since that silly argument on the phone. What, if anything, had changed for him in those years? Where did he live? Sydney? London? Some other city? She wished she had thought to look in the seat next to him to see if he was travelling with someone.

The plane levelled out in the sky and the seatbelt sign switched off. Jodi stayed seated, staring fixedly ahead.

'Jodi?'

Slowly, she turned her head. His grey eyes were quizzical. He wore a few extra lines around his mouth and some strands of grey in his dark hair, but he was even more handsome than she remembered.

'Hello, Professor Phelps.' She was pleased to hear how composed she sounded. Her voice gave no indication of her pounding heart and sweaty palms.

'This is an astonishing coincidence,' he exclaimed. 'We run into each other like this after so long . . .' He indicated to the vacant seat on the opposite side of the aisle. 'Is that free?'

Jodi hadn't seen anyone sit there during take-off. 'I think so.'

He sat down and swung around to face her. The aisle offered little buffer from his powerful gaze.

'What are you doing these days?' he asked. 'Where do you work?'

Jodi's nervousness propelled her into giving a blow-by-blow account of her career. 'I'm working for CorpBank in Singapore. I'm a director there. I manage the key accounts in the region – there's a lot of travel involved . . .'

She told him about her first job at ComBank and all the roles she'd had at Invesco. His gaze never wavered.

'I always knew you'd do well,' he said, looking pleased.

'Did you?'

A smile played on his lips. 'I remember the first day I saw you in my office. So young and determined. I knew that you had it in you to succeed.'

Jodi felt flattered that he, who'd seen so many students over his illustrious career, should recall their first meeting.

'Aren't you forgetting that I was there because I drank too much and passed out?'

His smile widened. 'How could I forget that? But what I remember best was your parting shot: "The next time you hear of me, it will be because I've got the best marks."'

Jodi remembered.

'What about you, Professor?' she asked, finding the courage to meet his eyes. 'Where are you working now?'

'Call me James, please. I'm a management consultant in London. I left the academic world some years ago.'

Jodi was stunned. She couldn't imagine him working in commerce, or anywhere outside the university.

'That must have been a big change.'

He shrugged. 'My wife had divorced me, my career had stalled – it seemed like the right time to find a new direction.'

Jodi's eyes, with a will of their own, dropped to his hands. No wedding band.

'Champagne?' enquired the hostess as she appeared from the galley with a flute-laden tray.

'Yes,' they replied in unison.

They sipped from the glasses without clinking them together. This chance meeting was too disconcerting to sum up in a toast. They couldn't say 'to old friends' because their relationship had not been one of friendship. Neither would a toast to the future be appropriate.

Silence descended for a few moments. With their careers already spoken about, Jodi wondered what they would discuss next.

'Are you married? Have any children?'

It seemed they were on to the personal stuff already.

'No. You?'

His face screwed up in a grimace. 'No major relationships since my divorce. My children, Carla and Jack, are adults now. Luckily they don't seem to have been impacted too much by their warring parents . . .'

A debate began to rage inside Jodi's head. Should she tell him about Andrew? What could be gained from dredging up the painful memories? Yet, wasn't she belittling Andrew's memory if she omitted to mention him? It was seven years since his death. She'd had a few relationships since, but nothing that lasted more than a few months, and nothing that evoked a fraction of what she'd felt for Andrew.

'I did have a major relationship,' she said quietly. 'He was the reason I moved to London. He died. He was hit by a car. It took me a very long time to get over it . . .'

*

Grandma's house was different. Brighter. Jodi noticed it the moment she walked in.

'You've had it painted.'

'Yes.' Grandma looked pleased with herself. 'I let the painter choose the colours. He was a lovely young man . . .'

The hallway and kitchen were now soft beige, complemented by the white trimmings and rosewood floorboards.

'It's great, Grandma,' said Jodi enthusiastically. 'It makes the place look really modern.'

The old lady filled the kettle with water and took two of her good cups from the top shelf of the cupboard. Jodi knew it would be of no use to offer to help. This was Grandma's territory. She made the tea.

'You look tired, child. Didn't you get any shut-eye on the plane?'

Jodi smiled to herself. Grandma still thought of her as a child, and could tell when she'd been up all night.

'I ran into someone I knew on the flight,' Jodi explained. 'We chatted for most of the journey.'

They had connected. Not as teacher and student. Or father-figure and child. As adults. Equals.

James, Jodi said now in her head. *James*.

The journey had flown by. They'd talked into the night, in lowered voices so as not to disturb the other passengers who were trying to sleep. They discussed the big issues, like poverty and social justice and the little trivialities of their everyday lives. Jodi felt that she was really getting to know James, what made him laugh, what made him tick, when the head stewardess announced that the plane was beginning its descent into Sydney.

'I'd better go back to my seat and get my belongings,' said James. 'I'll see you when we land.'

He was waiting when Jodi disembarked. They walked to the luggage carousel together. He asked which suitcase was hers and then lifted it clear of the moving black belt.

'You go first,' he said at the taxi rank.

She paused. It was against all her instincts to leave him.

Ask to see him again, her inner voice urged.

'Are you coming or not?' the taxi driver enquired impatiently through the half-open window.

'Take care of yourself, Jodi,' said James.

'You too.'

She got into the cab.

Now Jodi had an ache inside. A fear that it would be another eight years before she saw him again. Or maybe never.

'Your mother is working today,' said Grandma, setting the steaming cups down on the heavy oak table. 'She wants you to call in to the deli at four when she finishes.'

Sarah knew her mother would suggest a coffee at one of the trendy new cafés on Dee Why's beachfront. Stirring her frothy cappuccino, Shirley would enquire about Jodi's job. Then she would tentatively ask if there was anyone special in her daughter's life.

What would she say if I told her how I feel about James? Jodi wondered.

Shirley had been steadfastly single since Bob's death. Still an attractive woman, she dressed well and kept fit. She made the effort for herself, and certainly not with the aim of attracting men.

'I don't need a man to be happy,' she declared whenever Jodi broached the subject.

Now, Grandma sliced some fruitcake to have with the tea.

'Shirley's taken up yoga,' she said conversationally. 'She does a lot of meditation these days. And Marlene's got into all this feng shooey business. Only last week, she was trying to convince me to move my furniture around . . .'

Jodi laughed at her grandmother's mispronunciation of feng shui. Grandma cackled too, the mispronunciation obviously quite deliberate. The phone shrilled through their laughter and Grandma picked it up from the mount on the wall.

'Yes?'

Grandma never said hello when she answered the phone. She didn't like to encourage prolonged phone conversations.

'It's for you.'

Jodi took the phone from her outstretched hand, thinking it was perhaps her mother, or Alison.

'Jodi, it's James.' She shivered at the sound of his voice. 'I should have asked you earlier – I don't know why I didn't – but would you have dinner with me? I know you must be busy – after all, you're only home for a week – and I'll understand if you can't fit it in –'

'Yes,' Jodi cut in, a smile lighting up her face. 'Yes, I'd love to have dinner with you.'

When she hung up she noticed that Grandma had an odd look on her face.

'That was the friend I met on the plane,' she explained and took a calming sip of her tea. Her heart kept missing beats. It was alarming. Exciting.

I'm having dinner with James. Tomorrow night.

'I recognised the voice.' Grandma's tone was solemn and all signs of her earlier mirth had disappeared. 'Quite distinctive. He phoned this house many years ago. The professor . . .'

'Yes.'

'You're treading on dangerous ground, child.'

'I'm a big girl now,' Jodi smiled. 'You keep forgetting that.'

*

The restaurant was one of the city's best. Their table looked out over the rippled black water of the Harbour, the food and service superb. Unfortunately, James didn't seem to be very hungry or talkative. He spent a lot of time staring out the window, lost in his thoughts.

'I'm not sure what's happening here,' he said eventually. 'But whatever it is, I feel that it's wrong . . .' He paused, his face troubled. 'You and me, we're wrong, we shouldn't be together – I shouldn't have invited you here . . .'

Jodi covered his hand with hers. 'What's so wrong about us?' she asked gently.

'You were one of my students –'

'Eight years ago.'

'I'm twenty years your senior –'

'What difference does that make?'

'I know everything, yet nothing, about you –'

She looked at him steadily. 'The fact that I don't have to explain my past is a blessing. Andrew was the only man I told about it, my other relationships didn't progress far enough to survive such a bombshell. As for the things you don't know about me, I'm sure our relationship will evolve, just like any other.'

He wasn't convinced but Jodi was. She knew that she could no longer pretend that this was just some childish crush and she knew she would lose him if she didn't lay her cards on the table.

'This is right, James. I know it in my heart. And I'm not about to let it go just because of your silly hang-ups.'

'I don't want to take advantage of you –'

'I'm thirty years old, for God's sake! A consenting adult!'

He seemed to have no answer for that.

'Come on, let's get the bill,' said Jodi and motioned to the waiter.

Outside, she linked his arm and they strolled along the water's edge to his hotel. They didn't talk much. Their pace was leisurely, but it seemed all too soon before they were standing at the hotel's grand entrance.

She took the initiative. 'Should we have a nightcap?'

His face was a picture of reticence.

'If you don't find me attractive, then I'm happy to turn around and make my way home . . .'

'Of course I find you attractive,' he replied tersely.

'Then show me,' her voice was as soft as the breeze, '*show me*.'

He drew her to him. She waited, half afraid that the chemistry wouldn't be there. It was an angry kiss; after all, she had bullied him into it. His arms tightened around her, moulding her body to his, and the anger melted into passion. His kiss deepened. It reached her soul.

'Take it inside,' someone yelled from a passing car.

'I think that's a good suggestion,' Jodi whispered.

James acquiesced and, hand in hand, they walked into the hotel.

His room was very elegant, dominated by a large bed with a luxurious chintz cover and tasselled cushions. Jodi sat on the two-seater sofa while James assessed the contents of the bar fridge.

'White wine, red wine, Bailey's Irish Cream, or beer . . .'

'Baileys, please.'

He poured two tumblers and added some cubes of ice. Jodi gulped hers back, seduced by the scent of the liqueur and the decadent taste.

'Would you like another?'

'Yes, please.'

While he refilled their glasses, Jodi dimmed the lights until shadows mellowed the room. She smiled when he handed back her glass with a double measure. He moved his lips in return, but it was more like a grimace than a smile.

'Don't change your mind, James,' she said.

'It's wrong –'

'No, it's right.'

Nothing more was said.

They drank their drinks until right and wrong became blurred. Then he kissed her. His lips had the same taste as her drink: vanilla, cream and whiskey. He drank her in, and she him.

At some hazy point, they transitioned from the sofa to the bed, the chintz cover silky beneath their bare skin. As their bodies joined, Jodi thought it was right, so right, for them to be together.

'James is the best thing that's happened to me since Andrew,' Jodi told Shirley on the last day of her holiday.

They were sitting at one the beachfront cafés her mother liked so much. They sat upstairs, on the balcony. The sea breeze billowed their hair and tried to snatch their napkins until Shirley anchored them beneath the salt and pepper canisters.

'How do you know it's not just a crush you've held onto over the years?' she fretted. 'You were very vulnerable when you were at university. The professor was someone you looked up to, idolised . . .'

Jodi shrugged. 'I know there's more to it than that, Mum.'

Shirley was drinking herbal tea; her yoga teacher had recommended that she lay off the cappuccinos. Privately, Jodi thought that a good dose of caffeine would have taken the edge off her mother's worries.

'I'm very *concerned* about this *relationship* of yours,' Shirley stated. 'And so is Grandma.'

'Don't worry,' Jodi shrugged again. 'I'm a big girl. I know what I'm doing.'

'But do you?' Shirley enquired heatedly, and some of the other patrons glanced their way. 'Do you *really* know what you're doing? Have you discussed what you want from life with the professor –'

'James,' Jodi corrected.

'*James*,' Shirley repeated. 'He's almost the same age as me, darling. He's had his family. He won't want to do it all again.'

'Hold your horses, Mum,' Jodi laughed. 'You're getting ahead of yourself with all this family talk . . .'

'You need to discuss these things now,' Shirley persisted. 'Otherwise, it can become a big issue later on.'

Jodi drained her cup of coffee. 'Mum, if James and I ever get to that point, then I'm sure we'll work it out. Now, I want to pop over to the surf club to see if Sue is around. Are you coming?'

Shirley, still clearly unhappy, slid her sunglasses down from the top of her head and over her eyes. 'I just don't want you to make bad choices like I did . . . Still, it's your life . . .'

They got up from the table. They made a striking pair, with their blonde flyaway hair and svelte figures. On closer inspection, their faces had the same round shape and their eyes were the softest brown, although Shirley's were now hidden behind her sunglasses. One of the diners, who had overheard their conversation, idly wondered whether the young woman was fated to make the same mistakes as her mother.

Chapter 31

Three months later

Jodi's copy of the bank's annual report came in the mail. It was a high-quality production, with vibrant pictures to relieve the thick glossy print. Jodi's photograph was on page six. She looked thoughtful, as the photographer had suggested, and every inch the successful businesswoman, but there was a hint of forlornness beneath her poise. Needless to say, the photograph had been taken before James came back into her life.

Jodi read the report from cover to cover. There was nothing in there that she didn't already know, but she thought it worthwhile to refresh her memory. Key clients across the region would also receive a copy of the report. They would have questions, particularly when they saw the profit and bonus figures. They would feel that the bank could comfortably afford to reduce its commission and handling fees. It was Jodi's job to convince them otherwise.

When Jodi finished with the report, she poured herself a glass of iced water and went out to the balcony. She stood at the railing and looked down. Little black dots, people, moved industriously along the pavement, like a line of busy ants. Jodi's apartment was thirty-two floors above ground level. She looked back up, a sense of vertigo wobbling her insides. At eye level, she was surrounded by other apartment towers, tall and narrow, mostly white in colour. Singapore was famously short on accommodation space. It was also short on air. Jodi could only ever stay out on the balcony for short periods of time. After a while, the mugginess made her feel as though she couldn't breathe. She couldn't say why, but she was a lot more forgiving of Singapore's shortcomings than she ever had been of London's.

As Jodi sipped her drink, she heard the phone start to ring: James.

She ran back inside and was breathless when she picked it up.

'Good morning from chilly London.'

'Good afternoon from sunny Singapore.'

They delivered their greetings in their most formal tones: the weather man and woman; their own little act.

'How are you?' asked James in his normal voice, which was still rather formal.

'Good. Enjoying the weekend.'

'Have you been anywhere today?'

'No. I've been reading the annual report. Riveting stuff. Especially my photograph on page six.'

'You're in the annual report? Really?'

'Yes.'

'Can you send me a copy?'

'Why?'

'So I can see you. Be proud of you.'

'Okay.' Jodi's smile was a little bashful, but he couldn't see. 'What's happening with you?'

'Well, I just woke up. You were my first thought. So I rang.'

Jodi could see him in bed: his hair ruffled and eyes sleepy; his torso bare and sprinkled with dark hair. How she'd love to be lying next to him. To have his hands run over her body. To feel his lips follow in the path of his hands.

'Jodi? Are you there?'

'Yes, still here,' she murmured. 'Just thinking of you in bed.'

'Good night from muggy Singapore.'

'Good afternoon from soggy London.'

'What are you doing?'

'Actually, I'm running late for an important meeting . . .'

Jodi's face fell. But he couldn't see, of course. 'Oh.'

'Sorry,' he sighed. 'I didn't mean to be so abrupt. What are you doing?'

'Just getting ready to turn in.'

'I'll call you later, okay?'

Later meant early the next morning when she was rushing for work. Later meant his midnight, when he wanted the day to be over.

'Bye, James. Good luck with the meeting.'

Jodi hung up the phone and, instead of getting into bed, sat on the side, thinking. Sometimes their phone calls worked brilliantly, a connection of minds and moods defying the thousands of kilometres between them. On those occasions it didn't matter as much that they couldn't touch, because the closeness was there in other ways. But sometimes it didn't work so well and then it was never more obvious how far apart they were: different hemispheres, different time zones, different stages of life. That was when touch became so vital: it could bridge the bad mood, the hard day, whatever it was that was preventing the connection. She could briefly stroke his face, peck his lips, or give him a loving look as she said, 'Good luck with the meeting'. Instead, she was left with her hands tied, helplessly distant, and frustratingly unable to carry out the small action that was needed to end the conversation on the right note.

With a discontented sigh, Jodi flicked the light switch and slid between the light cotton covers of the bed. The next few months were going to be extremely busy. She had a lot of travel, some new clients and a significant product launch on her agenda. Still, she mentally tried to find a crack in her diary so she could get over to London to see James. Maybe October, two months away. Would they last until then? Without a single touch? Without a bridge?

'Goodnight from rainy London.'

Jodi blinked at the digital clock next to her bed: 4 am.

'Good middle-of-the-night from too-dark-to-tell-the-weather-yet Singapore.'

'Sorry. I just needed to hear your voice, to talk to you.'

Jodi sat up in the bed and rubbed the grogginess from her eyes with no inkling of the bombshell that was coming her way.

'This isn't working, is it, Jodi?'

She stopped mid-yawn, suddenly wide awake. What was he saying? That it was all too hard?

With a giveaway waver in her voice, she rushed in before he could say anything further. 'I think I can get some time off in October. Maybe four or five days . . .'

Her big plan was met with silence. Tears pricked her eyes. For the first time she was glad he couldn't see.

'I don't think four or five days will solve the problem, Jodi.'

So it was over. They hadn't made the distance. Their love wasn't so special or enduring after all. She let the tears fall, too devastated to keep them back.

'Don't cry', she heard him say from far away. 'I'm obviously not being very clear about what I want – I want us to be together.' She wiped the wetness from her face and tried to listen to what he was saying. 'Will you come to live in London, Jodi? Will you live with me?'

In a matter of seconds, she swung from utter despair to extraordinary joy. It wasn't over between them. She'd assumed the worst instead of trusting her instincts: she and James were right together, they were meant to be.

But it was the second time in her life that a man had asked her to go to London. The first time hadn't ended happily. Would the odds be improved a second time round? Could she return with a new love and a new optimism and forget the past?

'I can't answer straight away, James. I need to think about it carefully. My heart says yes, though.'

Two Paths Crossing

Chapter 32

The Naos Road was more like a parking lot than a main road. Again. A helicopter hovered overhead. Sarah wished that she was in it. How long would a chopper take to fly down to Cork? An hour? Less? How much would it cost? Maybe she should charter one!

She was sick and tired of this commuting, of pretending that she lived on the farm in Cork when in fact she spent most of the week in Dublin. Husband in Cork. Job in Dublin. Never the twain shall meet.

Her fingers drummed the steering wheel. Anxiety bubbled in her stomach. It was making its presence felt a lot more often these days. She was denying it, though. She'd been off the antidepressants for two years. She couldn't go back on them. No way. The drugs would not help the baby-making business one little bit.

Three years they'd been trying for a baby. Right from the word go, really. How many pregnancy tests had she used up? At the

371

start Tim would wait anxiously outside the bathroom. Now she didn't even tell him when she did the tests. Blue line? Chuck it in the bin. Another month gone down the drain.

Tim was talking about IVF now. He had been casual at first.

'Don't worry, Sarah. If it comes to it we can go down the IVF route.'

In his mind, it must have 'come to it' because he was talking about it a lot more often now.

Sarah resisted the idea.

Too invasive. Too contrived. If it can't happen naturally . . .

But he had counterarguments.

Why not try? We can handle a few blood tests and a short stay in hospital, can't we? Look at the success rate, Sarah!

Sarah understood where he was coming from. But there was one big problem: Tim didn't know the full facts. He didn't know about the abortion. He didn't know that she'd suffered bad cramping afterwards. Or that she hadn't gone back for her six-week check-up after the operation.

Sarah didn't want to go through with IVF for two reasons. First of all, she'd be obliged to tell the consulting doctor about the abortion and it was inevitable that Tim would find out too. He would be awfully, and justifiably, hurt and angry. He hated deceit of any form. Secondly, Tim aside, Sarah knew in her heart of hearts that IVF wouldn't work. She was sterile. She knew this fact instinctively and didn't need it confirmed by any doctor. Three years of trying to fall pregnant was proof enough. It was her punishment for aborting the baby. God didn't allow people to pick and chose when it was convenient to have children. She'd had her time. It wouldn't come again.

Sarah saw the lights change up ahead and edged her car

forward until she was just a whisker away from the bumper of the car in front.

Come on. Move! Move!

But the lights changed back to red without a single car getting through.

Damn! Damn! Damn!

She was trapped in this dreadful traffic. And trapped by a decision she'd made when she was too young and scared to understand how far-reaching its consequences would be.

In the end, the journey to Cork took close to four and a half hours. Sarah exited the main road and negotiated the narrow country roads before turning into the gravelled driveway of the farm. The sensor lights switched on and illuminated the way.

Tim came out the front door as she got out of the car. He wore a khaki T-shirt and shorts. His feet were bare and his face stubbled. She noted, in a tired way, that he looked good: trim, healthy and relaxed, but for the concerned expression on his face. Gently, he kissed her forehead and hugged her to him. Her anxiety abated with the familiar earthy smell of him and the cocoon provided by his arms.

'The traffic was horrendous,' she told him.

'I guessed as much.'

He kissed her forehead again before breaking away. Then he took her bag from the boot of the car. He always carried her bag in. Just as he always had a light supper ready on the table. Once she'd eaten, he would massage her tired shoulders while she lay face down on the lounge. Then he'd make love to her. It was Sarah's favourite part of the week: her homecoming.

Life on the farm started early, even on weekends. The first sounds were that of birds hopping along the roof tiles. Their feet ran lightly along, not too disturbing at all, until they emitted an ear-piercing squawk on take-off.

Sarah cursed them and squeezed her eyes shut, not wanting to wake up just yet. She lay curled into Tim's naked body. One of his hands loosely cupped her breast. She suspected he wasn't fully asleep either and soon that hand would start stroking her nipple. Or his lips would brush against the back of her neck. Or he'd do any one of the number of things he did to initiate their lovemaking. She felt anticipation stir within her, awakening her even more.

The commuting aside, her weekends with Tim were wonderful, a precious two days and three nights. Tim never complained that it wasn't enough. He understood how she felt about her job. With his support, her career had gone from strength to strength and she was now in charge of the entire Irish subsidiary. As general manager the breadth of her role ranged from internal finances to marketing strategies, and from staff initiatives to liaison with the New York head office. Denise, her old mentor, was now the CEO of the bank and in charge of worldwide operations. Sarah couldn't have asked for a better boss. The bank was growing aggressively and it was a thrill to be at the helm alongside Denise.

The only downside was that the day-to-day trading was no longer her direct responsibility. Sarah missed it and was often lured away from her office to the buzz of the trading floor. She'd nose out whatever big deals or calamities were going down and become directly involved for long enough to give her the adrenalin fix she needed, then she would return to her office and work with renewed vigour.

On the whole, she loved her job. And she loved her husband, whose hand had slipped from her breast and was provocatively edging its way between her legs. Sarah was very sure that her anxiety would go away of its own accord if she could solve the two problems that were marring her happiness: finding a faster means of getting up and down to Cork, and conceiving a baby.

Sarah eventually went downstairs at nine. She opened the fridge. It was well stocked with dairy produce, fresh vegetables and meat. A local woman, Joanne, came two days a week to clean, do the laundry and buy groceries. With her help, Sarah was free to spend the entire weekend with Tim. She much preferred to be outside helping him with the animals or crops, than inside catching up on a week's worth of household chores.

Sarah drew out a carton of eggs from the fridge. She cracked four into a jug and whisked until they were smooth. She chopped up some spinach and leg ham and threw them into the mix. Tim loved her omelettes.

Breakfast was ready by the time he came downstairs.

'Mmm,' he smacked his lips as he peered into the pan, 'you spoil me.'

His dark hair glistened from the shower and his jaw was freshly shaved.

She kissed the lips that had kissed her all over only a little while before. 'Don't think this would happen every day if I lived here full-time.'

He rummaged through the cutlery drawer and laid out the forks and knives on the table. Meanwhile, she took up the omelette and cut it in two, putting the larger piece on his plate. Once he'd poured chilled orange juice into two tall glasses, they were ready to eat.

'Compliments to the chef,' he declared as he tasted the fluffy egg.

'Thank you,' she smiled. 'What's on the agenda today?'

She expected his response to entail a litany of chores: collecting eggs from the chicken pen, feeding the goats, administering medicine the vet had left for the cows, moving bales of hay from here to there.

An ominous pause preceded his reply. 'Actually, I thought we might take the morning off and go into Cork . . .'

Sarah looked up in surprise, her fork midair. His face was difficult to read. 'Why?'

'Because we'll need a referral from our GP before seeing the IVF specialist.'

Sarah became aware that her hand, still holding a forkful of omelette for which she had totally lost appetite, had begun to tremble. She tightened her grip on the fork, steadied herself.

'I haven't agreed to IVF, Tim,' she pointed out in a tone that was more forceful than she'd intended.

She saw his shoulders tense.

'Are you saying a definitive no to it?' he asked, his own voice dangerously controlled.

'No,' she assured him quickly. 'I'm just not convinced it's the right way forward for us . . .'

He drew a ragged breath. 'Can't you at least see the people at the clinic and discuss whatever concerns you have?'

He made it sound so reasonable. So simple. But then it was to him.

Frantically she tried to formulate a response in her head. Something that would sound just as reasonable.

'Why are you resisting IVF so much?' He stared straight at her. 'Why don't you want to try it? Is there something you're not telling me?'

There was no way she could avoid the issue. He knew she was holding something back. This was it: the time of reckoning. Yet, the truth was choking in her throat. The abortion was something she'd held inside for fifteen years. It wasn't something she could just blurt out when put on the spot.

Tim saw her struggle and came to his own conclusion.

'You don't really want a baby at all, do you?'

'Of course I do.'

'Oh, for God's sake, Sarah. It's as plain as day. A baby would mess up your career . . .'

'That's not true!'

'It *is* true.'

Tim pushed his plate away. He stood up, his face dark with rage. Normally he was even-tempered to a fault. Twice, maybe three times, she'd seen him lose his cool. Once at a careless poacher who had accidentally shot one of the farm dogs. Another time, when the tractor wouldn't start, he jumped off and kicked the wheel several times in frustration before laughing at himself.

But he had never so much as raised his voice to her. Many a Friday night she'd come home cranky from the terrible traffic and spoiling for a fight. He'd never rise to the bait. He'd absorb her biting remarks without retaliation. Eventually his calmness would calm her. He was a very peaceful man, much more suited to this life in the elements than the cutthroat banking world.

'Please, Tim,' she beseeched him. 'Please, sit down.'

He ignored her. His expression thunderous, he walked to the door where he pulled on his boots.

'I can't believe you've been lying to me all along. I can't bear to look at you right now, I really can't . . .'

The slam of the door behind him was the last word of the conversation.

*

Sarah methodically signed the pile of outgoing letters on her desk while Linda, her secretary, looked on. Over the years her signature had condensed to a brief scrawl. It was required on all manner of documents in any one day. Her eyes were alert as she skimmed through the content of each letter. She spotted an error and put the document in question to one side.

'You'll have to redo that one,' she said to Linda. 'You forgot to put a full stop at the end of the second sentence.'

Sarah firmly believed that the bank's clients deserved the very best of service, right down to the absence of grammatical errors in written communications.

Finally, all the letters were signed and Linda departed. Sarah emitted an involuntary yawn. She was exhausted. She'd slept very badly last night. And the night before. And all the other nights since the fight with Tim.

Damn him.

They'd hardly spoken for the remainder of the weekend. Tim had slept in one of the spare rooms: it seemed he was telling the truth when he'd said he couldn't bear to look at her. Sarah had returned to Dublin on the Sunday afternoon, seeing no point in staying another night if they weren't talking.

At the start, she'd felt terribly guilty about the bitter argument and thought the fault was all hers. But once she was away from Tim and back to her office, she saw things differently.

I have a right to say no to IVF. How dare he bully me into having a baby!

It seemed that there was a side to Tim she hadn't seen before now.

Go to the doctor and get a referral.

Have IVF, get pregnant.

Deliver my baby.

Who did he think he was dealing with? A little wife who would do exactly as commanded?

Sarah's mouth tightened stubbornly and her shoulders straightened with resolve as she sat behind her desk.

I won't allow you to bully me, Tim Brennan. I haven't got to this level in my career without some backbone. A lot of backbone!

It was this defiant train of thought that made her decide to stay in Dublin the following weekend.

Time slowed without the rush to start the drive down to Cork. Sarah glanced at the miniature Waterford Crystal clock on her desk countless times: 10 am; 11.30 am; 12.05 pm. The day was crawling; an unfamiliar sensation for her.

Yet, despite the slow pace of the day, she dilly-dallied in the office until 10 pm. She even stopped to chat to the security guard on the way out.

'Miserable evening, miss.'

'I'm glad I have the car downstairs,' she smiled.

'Not heading off to Cork at this hour, are you?'

Her mouth tightened. 'No. Not this weekend. Goodnight, Frank.'

Frank was right: it was indeed a miserable evening. Rain streamed down the windscreen, making futile the wipers' attempts to flick it away. Traffic was heavy for the late hour but Sarah didn't feel the anxiousness she usually did when hindered by slow traffic. In fact, she hadn't felt anxious all week. Just increasingly angry.

She drove along the slick roads towards her apartment in Blackrock. The apartment was a recent addition to her ever-growing property portfolio. In a rundown condition when she'd first acquired it, the renovations had cost a small fortune and caused a lot of frustration. Now, to see the restored fireplace, the smooth walls, the elegant velour sofa and armchair, Sarah was of the opinion that the costly builder and interior designer's fees had been worth every penny.

The rain didn't relent as she drove along the broad sweep of Dublin Bay. If anything, it intensified. She turned past the stately grounds of Blackrock College and, a short while later, she was home. The only downside of the apartment was that it didn't have off-street parking. Sarah turned off the ignition and reached across to the passenger seat for her black leather brief-case. Then she swung the car door open and ran as quickly as possible, her head bowed against the driving rain.

The phone was ringing as she unlocked the door of the ground-floor apartment. She shook the rain from her hair, ignoring the phone. It wouldn't be Emma or Nuala: they'd expect her to be at the farm. It would be Tim, wondering where she was. She wasn't ready to talk to him just yet. She'd call him back later on.

Sarah made herself a salad sandwich in the compact kitchen with its heavy white doors and polished wooden counter. The interior designer had thought it appropriate to restore the entire apartment, even the kitchen, in line with the period in which the property had been built. The result was a luxurious yet unique kitchen area. All the mod cons, like the fridge with its ice-making functions and the pull-out pantry, were hidden behind the old-style white doors. Everything was spotlessly clean. Just like Joanne down in Cork, a local woman came in here to clean and stock the apartment. With the salary and bonuses Sarah now earned, she could afford all kinds of hired help to make her life easier. However, tonight she wished that everything wasn't so perfect and she could busy herself with wiping down the counter, or washing the dishes, or doing some other mundane chore that might help take her mind off Tim.

Sarah took the sandwich to the living area and switched on Sky News. A British reporter stood outside the Irish Central Bank, and discussed the imminent demise of the Irish pound.

> *The Irish pound ceased to be an independent currency at the start of 1999 with an irrevocably fixed exchange rate to the Euro, then a virtual currency, and all the other currencies of the participating member states. However, the general public are only now coming to terms with the fact that the notes and coins will no longer be accepted as legal tender from 1 January 2002 and the Euro will become real. The extent of the change covers the conversions of all bank balances, ATM machines, and ensuring that the retailers at the frontline of the conversion are properly equipped . . .*

Sarah listened carefully. Disappointingly, the reporter merely glanced over the issue and didn't address some of the more significant impacts. He made no mention of the monetary policy instruments that had to be brought into line with the other member states, or that inflation was going to be extremely hard to control. Sarah was very well read on the matter. She had to be. As general manager, she was fully responsible for the Irish profits of EquiBank and any impacts the currency conversion would have on those profits.

The phone rang again. Sarah bit into her sandwich. Chewed. Swallowed. Then finally got up to answer.

'I've been worried sick about you . . .'

Sarah felt a twinge of guilt when she heard the concern in Tim's voice.

'The weather is too bad for driving down to Cork,' she said. 'The rain is torrential here.'

'Why didn't you call to say so?' he asked tersely. 'I've spent the last two hours imagining the worst.'

'I got caught up in the office,' she replied lamely.

An awkward pause followed. Sarah suddenly wished that he wasn't at the end of the phone. That he was here, or she was there. That they could touch as they talked over their differences.

'Look,' she heard him sigh, 'I'm sorry I got so angry last weekend . . .'

She resisted the urge to rush in with an apology of her own.

Hold tight, she cautioned herself. *You have the upper hand now.*

Marriages were fundamentally the same as business, she realised. Two people negotiating to get the best deal. If you showed too much softness, you lost power and respect.

'But I felt you had been deliberately dishonest with me,' he went on, 'that you've just been humouring me, that you're not really committed to the idea of having a baby.'

Sarah held her tongue. But it was hard. Every fibre of her being wanted to break down, apologise, tell him her terrible secret and seek his forgiveness.

No. You don't have to tell him everything. You're allowed secrets. He has no right to bully you into this . . .

'This conversation is feeling rather one-sided,' he commented.

'What do you want me to say?'

'That you're sorry too?' he suggested with a hint of sarcasm.

'No, Tim,' she said in her firmest tone. 'I'm not of the opinion that this is my fault. You're the one who flew into a temper last weekend. You're the one who tried to force me to go to the GP –'

'I did not try to force you,' he protested. 'I was –'

She cut in over him. 'I won't allow you to push me around like that.'

Once again there was silence. And once again Tim was the first to break that silence.

'It makes me sad to hear that you think I push you around . . .'

There was something in his tone that chilled Sarah's heart. She felt his withdrawal and the balance of power tilt in his favour.

'Look, Tim, I've had a long day. I'm tired. I just want to go to bed now.'

His response was resigned. 'Goodnight, Sarah.'

Sarah put the phone down. She kept her hand on the receiver, as if she might pick it back up at any minute. She had a horrible feeling she'd crossed a line with Tim. Gone too far.

Despite her misgivings, Sarah didn't pick the phone back up. The dismal weather lingered on for the rest of the weekend. She slouched around the apartment and tried, in vain, to unravel her mixed-up feelings. About Tim. About having a baby.

She tried to visualise herself as a mother: nursing, feeding, changing nappies, singing nursery rhymes, pushing a pram around the local shopping centre. Which brought about the question of which shopping centre she'd be pushing the pram around. Would it be in Cork or Dublin? How could a baby fit into their current lifestyle? They lived separately for the greater part of the week. Who would the baby live with? Mum in Dublin, or Dad in Cork?

By Sunday night Sarah had reached only one conclusion: she'd spent the last three years trying for something she wasn't fully sure she wanted. Yes, she'd been all clucky with Nuala's and Laura's babies. But in hindsight that seemed like a flimsy basis on which to proceed. Emma and Jason were at the other end of the spectrum. They had gone against popular trend and decided not to have children. They liked their lifestyle just as it was; no need for any complicated additions. Maybe she was more like them.

Finally, when she was ready for bed and exhausted from all the self-analysis, Sarah phoned Tim.

'Hello,' she said warily.

'Hi.'

She smoothed down an imaginary crease in her pyjama pants.

'Tim, I'm not really sure what I want any more . . .'

He didn't comment, evidently waiting for her to continue.

'Maybe you're right.' Her voice was hoarse. 'Maybe I don't want a baby . . . I need time out . . . to think through what I really want.'

'Okay,' was all he said.

That was the end of the discussion. And possibly the end of their marriage.

Chapter 33

Jodi, London, 2001

'Yes, the price does sound good.' Jodi tapped her pen on her desk, impatient for the call to end. 'But let's give the company a closer look before jumping in . . .'

'It's a guaranteed winner,' claimed the caller, Steve Sanchez, a hotshot trader who had come across from CorpBank's New York office a few months ago. 'I'd only have to hold the bonds for a couple of weeks . . .'

Jodi's response was measured. 'There are no *guarantees* in this business, Steve. You know that as well as I.'

'Those bonds will be snapped up by someone else.' Frustration loudened Steve's voice. 'Goddamn it, this is no time to sit on our ass . . .'

Jodi didn't as much as flinch. Sadly, she was used to it. Verbal abuse was part of the culture, all the way from the trainees to the executives, and Jodi had been well aware of this fact when she had been appointed as head of the capital investment division eight months ago. She was quietly convinced that a positive, respectful, team-orientated environment would boost the profitability not only of her division but of the entire organisation, and had implemented some changes straight away to encourage that kind of behaviour. However, she was realistic enough to realise that it would take more than eight months to achieve such a fundamental change in attitude.

'Let me check with valuations.' Her voice was cool. 'I'll be back to you when I've established if the bonds are worth their money.'

'When will I hear from you?' he demanded. With Wall Street under his belt, he was clearly very anxious to prove himself on the other side of the Atlantic. 'Tonight? Tomorrow? *Next month?*'

'Shortly,' she replied and hung up the phone.

She sat still for some time after the call, lost in thought. Steve was only one of the two-hundred-odd staff under her management. He spoke with a different accent to the rest, but other than that he was, disturbingly, just the same as his colleagues: impatient, conceited, disrespectful and too used to getting his own way. Somewhere along the line someone had told Steve, and all the others, that a bad attitude was good. Now Jodi had an uphill battle on her hands to get them to change.

She sighed deeply and rubbed the stirrings of a headache from her forehead. Most days she didn't doubt her capability. But doubt was weighing her down today. Did she have the right to be sitting here in this ultramodern office? Was she correct in her assumption that the lack of teamwork and general respect was detrimental to the overall profitability? Was she tough enough to pull off such a mammoth change to the culture?

Yes, she told herself as she straightened. *I can do it. I'm just feeling a little deflated after last night.*

Across the Thames, James would be in his office too. Was he, like her, not giving it his all today? Was he replaying their argument? Regretting what he'd said? Or, more worryingly, had he put it right out of his head, regarding the subject as closed?

Ten out of ten to Shirley, who had predicted this would happen. What words had she used? 'He's had his family. He won't want to do it all again.'

James most definitely didn't want to do it all again; he'd been explicitly clear about that last night. Jodi had come home especially early to make beef bourguignon, his favourite dish. She'd uncorked a soft-bodied merlot and decanted it, allowing the wine to breathe amongst the mood-setting candles that flickered at the centre of the table.

James was surprised and pleased when he came in from work.

'She's home before me!' he exclaimed, looking upwards, as if to thank the gods for their benevolence. 'And cooking dinner!' He planted a kiss on her lips. 'What's the special occasion? Another promotion?'

'No. I still have my hands full with the last one.' She smiled and threw him the oven mitts. 'Just make yourself useful by getting the casserole dish from the oven.'

During the meal he told her about his day and she told him about hers. The beef was tender and the sauce rich. Jodi resolved that she would do this more often: come home early and cook. James usually made dinner. In fact, he did most of the domestic chores around their chic two-bedroom apartment. His job was less demanding than hers.

'My career is in decline as yours is on the rise,' he would often joke. 'But it's nice to know that you'll have the means to keep me in style in my old age.'

He always made disparaging remarks about his age. He didn't listen when she said he looked much younger than his years. His hair was still mostly black and his face relatively unlined. He was far more attractive than any of the younger men Jodi worked with.

Now, his plate scraped clean, he looked relaxed and open to wherever the conversation might take them. Still the academic at heart, he was very well informed about current affairs and their dinnertime conversations often became hearty debates. He had no idea that world news was far from Jodi's mind this evening.

'James, what do you think about us having a baby?'

A frown instantly descended on his face. 'Are you saying you're pregnant?'

'No,' she laughed uneasily. 'I'm just thinking about it, that's all.'

'I'm fifty-four years old, Jodi.' His tone was as austere as his expression. He looked every bit the professor he used to be, and she felt like the wayward student. 'Too old for bawling babies and tantrummy toddlers.'

Jodi set down her cutlery and reached across the table to rest her hand on his. 'But I'm only thirty-three, James . . .'

His frown only deepened. 'I already have two children. My age aside, I have no desire to be a father again.'

'Please, James,' she beseeched him in a tone that would usually have him acquiesce to whatever it was she wanted. 'Can't you just consider it? Is that too much to ask?'

He shook his head with unnecessary vehemence. 'I'm quite clear on this and it wouldn't be fair to pretend otherwise. I'm sorry, Jodi. I really am.'

He rose and began to clear the table. Jodi stayed sitting,

swirling the wine in her glass, unsure for the first time in their three-year relationship, and trying not to think of Shirley saying, 'I told you so.'

Later on in bed, James's hand circled her waist and pulled her close. His other hand began to stroke the line of her breast. She pushed him away.

'How can you?'

'Because I love you. But if you're not in the mood, then that's okay.'

'You bet I'm not in the mood!' she retorted. 'Don't you realise how much you've hurt me? How little you must think of me to say you won't even consider what I want! *What any woman of my age would want!*'

His voice, unemotional, cold, sliced through the darkness. 'If a baby is what you truly want, Jodi, then maybe you should find a man of your own age to father it.'

'You're a prick,' she spat. 'Do you know that? A hard-hearted prick.'

He rolled over on his side, obviously not thinking her worthy of a response. Seething with fury, she faced her back to his, forming a chasm through the centre of the bed.

James was still asleep, or pretending to be, when Jodi got up for work. She disguised her puffy eyes with concealer and left without saying goodbye. She slammed the door of the apartment, and immediately felt immature and childish, the last way she wanted to feel given the issues at stake.

The day passed with the usual stream of meetings and phone calls.

Jodi called Steve Sanchez back to her office at four.

'Sit down.' She nodded towards a seat.

He did as she requested. They were eye to eye.

'You picked well,' she said in a level voice. 'Those bonds are undervalued.'

'I knew it!' He sprang up and punched a victorious arm into the air. 'How much can I buy?'

'Let's leave the buying aside for a minute.' She nodded again to the seat he had just vacated in his excitement. 'Sit down.'

He remained standing, ignoring her request. 'The markets will be closing soon. I need to get on the phone –'

'Sit!' She commanded and, reluctantly, he did as she asked. 'Now, let's have a talk. I have certain ideas about how things should be done around here. Some basic rules . . .'

'Like what?' he asked, and pointedly looked at his watch.

'Rule number one: we work as a team. Valuations, market research, and all the other departments, are there to be consulted. The more you consult, the less likely you'll make a multimillion dollar mistake –'

'But I *knew* those bonds were undervalued,' he interrupted.

She cut in just as quickly. 'As far as I'm concerned, you know *nothing* until you've consulted with the right people . . . Rule number two: we act and speak like professionals.'

'I am professional!'

'Raising your voice is *not* professional.'

'Everybody yells and carries on,' he claimed. 'It's what investment banking is all about.'

'Maybe other banks,' Jodi tightened her mouth, 'but not Corp-Bank and *certainly* not my division.'

He shrugged with thinly veiled impatience. 'If you say no yelling, then no yelling. You're the boss.'

His words lacked any kind of sincerity.

'Which brings me to rule number three.' Jodi stared him in

the eye. '*I am indeed your boss*. And I expect respect. Don't forget that again. Understood?'

Finally, the penny dropped and he realised that his job was on the line. Suddenly, he looked rather vulnerable.

'Understood.'

Jodi spent the next few hours on administrative tasks that she could have easily delegated to her assistant. She was procrastinating, avoiding going home. Her office had every comfort: a fridge with an ice dispenser, a flat-screen TV, and a luxurious two-seater lounge, making it all too easy to stay longer than she should.

She switched on the TV to catch the news.

'The Irish pound ceased to be an independent currency at the start of 1999 with an irrevocably fixed exchange rate to the Euro, then a virtual currency, and all the other currencies of the participating member states. However, the general public are only now coming to terms with the fact that the notes and coins will no longer be accepted as legal tender from 1 January 2002 and the Euro will become real. The extent of the change covers the conversions of all bank balances, ATM machines, and ensuring that the retailers at the frontline of the conversion are properly equipped . . .'

Jodi listened attentively to the Sky News broadcast. The change didn't stop at Ireland. France, Germany, Italy, Spain and Netherlands were in it too, a marriage of countries, for better or worse. Jodi believed that the United Kingdom was making a massive mistake by staying out. The benefits of a single currency were widely documented in terms of trade, transparency of costs, macroeconomic stability and currency stability. Sterling would be the odd one out in the playground – it had already hit a fifteen-year low against the dollar. When would everyone put their sentimentality to one side and see that the Euro was in the best economic interests of the country?

Shortly before seven, Jodi's mobile began to ring. She knew it was James, wondering where she was.

'Yes?'

'Your mother just phoned.'

He sounded uptight. Good! Last night's argument had chinked his armour.

'I'll give her a call from here.'

Jodi looked at her clock and worked out the time difference: 10 am in Sydney, an unusual time for Shirley to phone.

'She's not at home,' said James. 'She's at the hospital. It's your grandmother . . .'

Fear seized Jodi's heart. 'What? What's happened to Grandma?'

'She's had a stroke, Jodi.' James's voice was heavy with sympathy. 'Shirley's not sure if she'll make it . . .'

'Of course she'll make it,' Jodi insisted frantically. 'Of course she will. I'll go there, to the hospital, to Sydney . . .'

Already she was logging out of her computer.

'I'll see if there's a flight available tonight,' James offered.

A few minutes later, jacket and bag in hand, Jodi ran out on the street and waved madly at an approaching taxi. He pulled over and she climbed in the back.

'Chiswick first,' she told him breathlessly. 'You'll need to wait while I pick up my bag, then it's on to Heathrow – and please hurry.'

James had managed to find an available seat on a British Airways flight, and had packed some of Jodi's clothes in a travel bag.

'Do you want me to come with you?' he asked as she rushed around the apartment. 'There's another free seat that I could reserve . . .'

'No. It's okay.'

She didn't want him there. Shirley would see straight away that things were strained between them and Grandma had always disapproved.

James didn't argue. He picked up her bag and walked her to the waiting taxi.

'Call me when you get there,' he leaned to kiss her cheek, 'and we'll talk about things when you get back . . .'

What things? she thought irritably as the taxi sped off. *Hadn't he said all that he wanted to say? Why reiterate his position? Was he afraid that she was still harbouring some hope?*

Business class was booked out and James had got her a seat in economy. Unfortunately, it wasn't an aisle or a window seat. She was stuck in the middle, a man on either side, one with unpleasant body odour and the other bulging out of his seat. She closed her eyes, feigning sleep. Memories replayed behind her lids: Grandma sitting in the middle of family gatherings with her stick between her legs, chastising a grandchild here and there for some perceived misdemeanour, moments later defending the same child against an irate parent; Grandma standing in the witness box, shoulders back, squaring up to the judge and, later on, talking strategy with Prue as if she'd been dealing with criminal lawyers all her life; Grandma trying to impress Andrew with the afternoon tea charade, pretending to be lady of the manor rather than the tough old broad that she was.

Please, Grandma, please be okay. Please don't give in.

Guilt dulled the vividness of Jodi's memories. Two years had passed since she'd last seen Grandma. London was too far away, too inconvenient for nipping back to Sydney. They'd spoken on the phone often enough, but that was little consolation now.

Damn James for asking me to move to London. I should have stayed in Singapore. Close by.

The cab in Sydney was white to London's black. Jodi asked the driver to take her straight to Mona Vale Hospital. He smiled, happy with the big fare he was about to earn. Jodi sat in the back seat and willed every red light to turn green. She didn't dare ring ahead to Shirley to let her know she was on her way. She was afraid that her mother would say it was too late.

Jodi enquired at the hospital's reception where to go. She followed the directions up a creaking lift and along a drab corridor. She remembered that there had been talk of knocking down the hospital when she was last home. It didn't inspire a great deal of confidence to think of Grandma's life being dependent on doctors and nurses who didn't know what their future might hold.

Jodi pushed open the wide door to Grandma's room. Shirley sat on the far side, bleary-eyed, but signature red lipstick perfectly applied. She came around the bed and held Jodi tight.

'Alone?' she asked.

'Too much short notice for James to get on the flight,' Jodi lied.

She kissed Grandma's wrinkled cheek. It felt cool under her lips. The old woman was lying in a sea of white: the bed linen, her nightgown and the shock of hair around her head. Her skin was translucent, her eyes closed and her mouth slightly ajar.

'She's asleep most of the time,' Shirley explained. 'Too weak to be awake.'

Jodi pulled up a seat, made of hard blue plastic, and sat on Grandma's other side. She and Shirley talked across the bed in whispers.

'I'm so glad you got here . . .'

'I was lucky. Another time of the day and I would have had to wait a lot longer for a flight.'

'She collapsed at home. Marlene found her.'

'Was she there long?'

'No, thank goodness.'

'Has she been able to talk?'

'A little. She's been asking about you.' Shirley stifled a yawn. 'It's been a long twenty-four hours. We've kept a vigil the entire time . . .'

'Why don't you go downstairs and get yourself a coffee,' Jodi suggested.

'Yes. I think I will. Can I bring anything back for you?'

'No, thanks.'

Shirley closed the door softly on her way out.

'Just you and me, Grandma,' Jodi said to the old lady. 'Gosh, you should see the view from here.'

The window gave a panoramic view of Mona Vale beach. In the distance, children played on the orange sand and surfers rode inside the curl of towering waves. Closer, a golf buggy bumped across the rolling course, the green separated from the beach by a thick layer of low-lying bush. It was a spectacular view, worth millions and millions of dollars. Was that the real reason they wanted to knock down the hospital?

Grandma's eyes flickered open.

'You're here,' she said faintly.

'Yes.'

'I was hanging on for you . . .'

'Don't say things like that.'

'I know my time's up, child.'

'Don't be silly – you have years left in you yet.'

Grandma shook her head very slightly in disagreement. 'The house . . . the house is yours, child, I'm leaving it to you . . .'

Jodi felt tears well in her eyes. 'I don't need it, Grandma. I have plenty. Give it to one of the other grandchildren.'

'It's yours.' Her voice, though weak, was insistent. 'No matter what big city you live in, you'll always have a home to come back to.'

Tears slipped down Jodi's face. 'Thank you, Grandma. I'm sorry I haven't been back to see you recently . . .'

'No regrets, now. I know that you love me – you're here, aren't you?'

She drifted away, back to sleep. Shirley returned shortly after. Then Marlene and her children came in, followed by Jodi's uncles. They sat around the bedside, three generations of family, ensconcing Grandma in a circle of love until she passed peacefully away.

Chapter 34

The ultimate job

Sarah missed Tim, but not as much as she thought she would. He phoned every few days. She told him she still didn't know what she wanted. That wasn't entirely true.

She could hardly tell him that she felt as though a dead weight had been lifted from her shoulders now that she had no immediate need to think about babies. She could hardly admit that life was much simpler without the stressful commutes up and down to Cork. Yes, she was lonely. But loneliness was like an old friend who had been around long before Tim. Maybe it was her destiny to be alone. Maybe Tim had been nothing but a temporary aberration from the way things were meant to be.

The phone on her bedside unit rang and rang until she opened her eyes.

'Hello,' she muttered into the receiver, her voice thick with sleep.

'Sarah! It's Denise.'

Sarah rubbed her eyes and sat up in bed. She and Denise spoke regularly, but it was usually prearranged, and not at one in the morning. Something big must be afoot.

'I know it's late at night over there,' said Denise, her voice urgent. 'But I need to tell you something that can't wait.'

'What?' Sarah asked, all sorts of thoughts rushing through her head.

'A position has come up, honey. The most *perfect* position for you.'

Sarah's heart began to beat a little faster. 'What position?'

'My job: CEO of EquiBank.'

'*You're leaving?*'

'Yes.'

'To do what?'

'To kick back and enjoy all the money I've earned.'

Sarah was stunned into silence. She couldn't imagine the bank without Denise. She couldn't imagine Denise without the bank.

'Your grassroots trading background makes you ideal for this job, Sarah. You started out at exactly the same place as me – the board will like the similarities between us – they'll know what they're getting . . .'

Sarah's brow creased in concentration. 'Am I the only candidate being considered?'

'You know the go, Sarah. The board likes to have a choice when it comes to a top-level position like this. A specialist headhunting firm has already been engaged to find other suitable candidates. But that doesn't change the fact that you're on the inside track . . .'

Denise's voice became hurried and Sarah could tell she had something pressing she needed to attend to.

'Thanks for calling me, Denise,' she said, her mind already

preoccupied as it began to weigh up this unexpected turn of events. 'I would appreciate if you could ask your assistant to send me through the details of the interview process.'

'Of course,' Denise responded. 'I have to go. But we'll talk again soon.'

Sarah didn't sleep a wink for the rest of the night. Being CEO of EquiBank was the ultimate achievement and she was immensely flattered that Denise believed she was ready for it.

Could I handle such a massive promotion? Could I successfully leapfrog from the Irish subsidiary to worldwide operations? Yes, I think I could. This is what I'm good at – banking, business – it's the personal stuff I suck at, like being a wife.

In her head, Sarah nailed out her terms of acceptance: the salary, the bonus and the relocation package. Carried away by the adrenalin of her ambition, she didn't pay much heed to her conscience.

What about Tim?

He has no desire to live in New York again.

And even if he did, a baby would be out of the question with such a demanding job.

Jodi returned to London five days after Grandma's funeral. James met her at the airport. They held each other for a long time, but a distance had formed in her absence and Jodi wasn't sure it could ever be bridged.

'I'm going to sleep in the spare room,' she said as soon as they got back to the apartment.

His face paled and, for the first time since she'd known him, he looked his full age. 'Please, Jodi, there's no need to take that step. You're still grieving, not thinking straight . . .'

She corrected him. 'I'm thinking very clearly, James. The

bottom line is that we want different things. You've been perfectly honest about your position, which I appreciate. I just need some space to think about *my* position.'

He put his hand on her arm. 'This isn't you . . .'

She shrugged free of his touch. 'How do you know, James? How do you know what's me when I don't know myself? All my life I haven't known who I am: an innocent child or a teenage seductress; a hapless victim or a cold-blooded killer; a woman destined to have her own family or a woman alone.'

'You have me. I love you. You're not alone.'

She couldn't afford to listen to him, to weaken. This was hard enough as it was.

'I'm shattered after the journey. I think I'll go straight to bed now.'

She was tired. So tired she could cry. She climbed into the spare bedroom's single bed. The room was too small, the pillow too plump and the sheets too starchy. It didn't feel as though she was in the same apartment at all. Little over a week ago she'd made that special dinner for James. Now she was sleeping in the spare room and contemplating a future without him. Sitting at Grandma's deathbed had crystallised the importance of family, of new generations carrying on the torch of the old. It had made Jodi more certain that she wanted a baby, which made an even bigger problem of the fact that James didn't.

Should I accept his position and just get on with our lives together?

It didn't feel right to simply accept it. Their relationship would never again have the same integrity, the same give and take.

Have I come this far, gone through everything I've gone through, only to make such a massive compromise?

Dawn seeped through the crack in the bedroom's curtains.

Jodi swung her legs out of bed, showered, and left to catch the tube. Outside the air was warm with the promise of a sunny day. But that didn't change the underlying coldness of the city.

There was an announcement at the tube station: there would be significant delays; a fatality had occurred; someone had jumped; apologies for the inconvenience.

It was well after nine by the time she reached the office. Steve Sanchez knocked on her door no sooner than she'd shut it behind her. He told her he was resigning, going somewhere else, somewhere he could yell and carry on to his heart's content. She wished him good luck and asked him to clear his desk straight away.

Her assistant was hot on Steve's heels. She had various documents that needed to be signed and stacks of phone messages to pass on. Everything was urgent, as always.

Jodi put her head down. Got on with her work. But at the back of her mind she continued to mull over her personal situation.

Should I stay with James and make the best of what we have? Or should I hold out for a man with whom I don't have to compromise? Does such a man exist and, by the time I meet him, will I be too old to have a baby anyway?

If she left James, she'd have to find somewhere else to live. She tried to visualise herself calling real estate agents, telling them what size apartment she wanted, what price, what suburb. The thought left her cold. Not only because she would be on her own, without James, but because London had never been her choice. It had been Andrew's, and James's. Never hers.

Can I live in this city for a moment longer if I'm not with James?

At 4 pm Jodi received an unexpected phone call. It was a headhunter, one of the most prestigious in the city. He spoke of a job in New York and Jodi listened carefully to what he had to say. She hung up some time later believing that fate had dealt its hand. The CEO of EquiBank: the opportunity of a lifetime: her ticket out of London.

Chapter 35

The EquiBank building soared into the blue sky, an imposing column of glass and stone, a force to be reckoned with. Sarah stood outside, looking up. Thirty-five floors of employees. Thousands of computers and telephones. Billions of dollars of investment funds. She took an indulgent moment to imagine herself in charge of it all.

When she stepped into the building, the time for daydreaming was over and a mask of professionalism settled over her face. Her first interview of the day was with Denise. A formality, but still too much at stake to be taken for granted. She called the lift and soon she was being whizzed up to the top floor of the building.

'Sarah Ryan to see Denise Martin,' she said to the impeccably groomed receptionist.

'I'll call her assistant and let her know you're here.'

A few moments later the assistant appeared and escorted Sarah to Denise's office.

'Sarah!' Denise rose from her desk and came forward to engage in a warm embrace. 'I'm so happy to see you here.'

Sarah smiled. 'And I'm very happy to be here.'

It was the truth. She was happy to have a reprieve from Ireland, Tim and the awful baby guilt. And she felt a deep fulfilment that her hard work over the last eleven years had culminated in this amazing opportunity.

'Sit down. Would you like a drink?'

'No, thanks.'

Denise nodded at her hovering assistant and the woman departed, closing the door quietly behind her.

'Well!' Denise slid into her seat. She wore her trademark tailored white shirt and her hair was as short and chic as ever; she had always kept her femininity to an absolute minimum. Her face had acquired some lines since Sarah had last seen her. She carried them well, though. 'I know this is meant to be an interview, but that seems like a waste of time, considering our history. I was there when you started as a filing clerk in the settlements department and since then I've watched every stage of your career. Sometimes it was from afar, but I was always watching, Sarah.'

'Yes, I know,' Sarah acknowledged. 'And regardless of whether I get this job or not, I want to thank you for being a wonderful mentor over the years.'

'It was a pleasure, Sarah. I see myself in you, I always have. We have the same determination and commitment. We have the gut instinct, the *flair*.' Denise stopped to smile briefly. 'So, as there's nothing further I need to know about your capability for this job, I thought I'd spend this interview time telling you about it, telling you what it's *really* like to sit in this seat.'

Sarah nodded. 'I'm listening.'

'I've lived and breathed this role for the last three years.' Denise clasped her hands and rested them on the desk. 'I consumed it and it consumed me. My phone was never turned off, it rang around the clock. My mealtimes weren't my own – breakfast, lunch and dinner were allocated to clients, visiting executives, politicians. But the status, the respect, and the glow of being so revered buoyed me from the physical exhaustion. I felt god-like – I'd open my mouth and my wishes would be carried out. I'd make a decision, see immediate consequences. The last three years have undoubtedly been the best of my life.' Denise paused, her expression suddenly becoming very grave. 'But they've also been the worst. This job, wonderful as it is, has a hefty personal cost. It would be very remiss of me, as your mentor and friend, not to point that out.'

Her words, an unmistakeable warning, hung between them. Sarah was about to speak, to reassure Denise that she understood the extreme level of commitment that came with the job, but Denise cut in ahead of her.

'I know that you and Tim have a strong marriage, Sarah. I'm glad of that, because it will take a great deal of sacrifice and resilience to survive the demands of this job. To be brutally frank, Larry and I have struggled. We're still together, but we have a lot of repair work to do.'

Larry was Denise's third husband. He adored Denise and she adored him back.

'This one's for keeps,' she'd said when she married him. 'The other two were just practice runs.'

Sarah, shocked at Denise's revelations about the state of her marriage, almost blurted out that her own marriage was far from strong right now. But she stopped herself. This was an interview, not a tell-all. She couldn't afford to lose sight of that fact.

'Thanks, Denise,' she said quietly. 'I feel immensely privileged that you've been so honest with me.'

Jodi had never been to New York before. It instantly bowled her over. It was brash yet stylish, gritty yet colourful, rude yet engaging. It was everything she didn't like, yet she loved it. She couldn't quite explain why.

The EquiBank building was in the middle of the financial district, side by side with all the other big banks, not as tall as some, but holding its place with dignity. Jodi paused for the briefest moment before going inside.

'Jodi!' Bradley Simons, the vice-president of human resources, had a firm handshake and an unnerving stare. His eyes were warm, though, and Jodi felt instantly at ease. 'I hope you had a nice trip over from London.'

Jodi smiled. 'Yes, I did, thank you.'

'And how are you finding your hotel, the Renaissance?'

'It's charming – it would be only too easy to forget that I'm here on business.'

'You've been to New York before?'

'No. Most of my travel has been around Europe and Asia.'

'This role involves a lot of travel,' said Bradley. 'Denise, the current incumbent, is away about fifty per cent of the time. Do you see that as a possible issue for you?'

'I had to travel extensively when I was head of client services in Asia Pacific,' she replied. 'I enjoyed being out there, living and breathing the business, rather than being locked away in some ivory tower.'

Bradley looked down at a document that Jodi assumed was her résumé. 'You were based in Singapore, is that right?'

'Yes.'

'Why did you move back to London?'

She smiled disarmingly. 'I met a man. The love of my life, or so I thought.'

Bradley had been interviewing people for most of his professional life. He was somewhat disillusioned with the process, prospective employees pretending to be something they were not, employers likewise. Relationships and personal aspirations were rarely discussed, yet they were underlying factors that influenced everything. Bradley got a strong sense that Jodi Tyler wasn't afraid of the truth, be it matters personal or business.

Bradley consulted his interview notes before asking his next question. 'Who has been your most difficult customer?'

Jodi didn't have to think twice. 'A Korean businessman who detested women and didn't speak English. Initially he refused to deal with me directly – he corresponded through a more junior male colleague. I was patient, didn't force the issue, and I eventually won his respect.' She fingered the white-gold rope chain around her neck. 'He gave me this when I left for London.'

Bradley's eyes were drawn to the chain. It looked solid, unbreakable. Was that how the Korean businessman saw Jodi Tyler?

He cleared his throat. 'Tell me about London. What challenges did that present?'

Jodi talked through her first job in CorpBank London and all the subsequent promotions. Her account was clear and concise. She didn't oversell herself. She didn't need to. Her extensive experience spoke for itself.

Bradley listened to her every word. If she got the job, Jodi Tyler would be his boss. He decided he would be very happy to work for her.

*

At the end of the day, Bradley, armed with his shortlist, left his office to ascend to the thirty-fifth floor for the specially convened board meeting.

'Ladies and gentlemen of the board,' he began, a microphone carrying his voice to the board members at the far end of the table, 'I'm pleased to announce that our search for a chief executive officer has been narrowed down to two outstanding candidates . . .'

Bradley felt like a duck out of water in the vast boardroom. For a start it was quiet, so quiet that you would think all the board members were asleep on the job. The heart of the business was not up here, it was down on the lower floors, where the hubbub of traders buying, selling and furiously tapping their keyboards created an excitingly distinct atmosphere. Never quiet.

Then there was the uninterrupted view of the Manhattan skyline. It was almost impossible to take your eyes off it. How could any cold, hard business be done against a backdrop of such breathtaking beauty?

'The first candidate I am going to present is Sarah Ryan. Some of you will already know her name. Sarah has run our operation in Dublin for the last three years – the subsidiary has achieved record profits under her leadership – she's very well regarded both here in New York, as well as in the wider banking community . . .'

Sarah walked out of the Renaissance Hotel and paused to allow her eyes to adjust to the garish oversized billboards. Seventh Avenue was bumper to bumper with cars, a good proportion of which were the quintessential yellow cabs. The drivers hooted at each other for no other reason than impatience. Steam hissed from a nearby manhole. The whole scene was as noisy as it was colourful.

Sarah wore shorts and runners, suitable attire for a jog through Central Park, but for some inexplicable reason she found herself going in the opposite direction. The pavement was busy and she had to be content with a brisk stride. Her mind was heavily pre-occupied as she walked.

Tomorrow morning she had to present herself to the board of directors: a daunting prospect. The directors would have Harvard educations and embody all the snobbery that comes with old money. They would be able to tell straight away that she wasn't one of them, that her background was far from privileged. Was her experience and long history with the bank enough to compensate? Would they offer her the job? Did she really, really want it? Was it worth the hefty personal cost Denise warned of?

As she walked, Sarah glanced intermittently at the shops and eateries that lined the walkway. In the eleven years since she'd first come to New York, most had changed hands, name and frontage a number of times, desperate to keep up with the latest trends, desperate to be the hottest new place. In this city, only a select few got away with age.

Sarah reached the theatre district. Dusk was beginning to fall; she should turn back. Her mouth was dry; she should at least stop for a drink. But something was pushing her on. She didn't understand what until she reached 57th Street.

There was his name. Across the street, all lit up and impossible to miss.

JOHN DELANEY

She stared and stared, oblivious that she was standing smack in the middle of the pavement, a cardinal sin in New York City.

'Move out of the way, lady,' advised a middle-aged man who bumped against her shoulder.

She hardly heard him. She was back in John's front room, his slender fingers racing up and down the keys, his head bent, the plush red curtains in the background. It felt like yesterday, not fifteen years ago. The boy was now a man. The front room had become Carnegie Hall, one of the most prestigious stages in the world. The audience was no longer the girl-next-door; it was hundreds of discerning classical music fans.

Sarah crossed the road in a trance.

'What time is the concert?' she asked the lady at the box office.

'Eight o'clock,' the woman replied. 'It's almost fully booked but I do have a seat in the dress circle, if you're prepared to pay that much . . .'

Without enquiring how much was 'that much', Sarah took her credit card from her purse.

'I'll take a program too, please.'

The woman rang up the sale and handed Sarah her ticket and the program. Suddenly John's photo was staring her in the face. He looked young, impossibly so, his fair hair a little longer than it used to be, his smile so familiar that it brought an instant ache to her heart. She shoved the booklet into her shoulder bag.

With an hour to kill before the recital, she ordered a glass of water from the café outside the auditorium. The water quenched her thirst but did nothing to steady her nerves. She was shaking all over. She ordered a cocktail, a cosmopolitan. She sipped it slowly whilst the program, and John's photo, burned a hole in her bag.

Finally the bell sounded and people began to move inside. A black grand piano stood centre stage, dramatic against the largely white backdrop. Conversation hummed until the lights dimmed and anticipation commanded quiet. John appeared from back-stage. He was the same boy that Sarah once knew, and she felt a lump in her throat. He raised his arm to greet the audience and acknowledge their applause. He angled himself to the left, then the right, so that each person in the auditorium could see his face. When he sat at the piano his shoulders and head were perfectly straight. Someone along the line had taught him not to hunch over.

John struck the opening chords, strong and rich and noble. Then his right hand raced away, scaling through octave leaps, the melody quite playful.

Sarah finally took the program from her bag.

Franz Schubert: Sonata No. 20 in A Major, D. 959
This sonata was composed in 1828. Schubert, knowing he was fatally ill, wrote the work in a frantic race against time. He died aged thirty-one, but his wondrous lyricism and rich harmonic vocabulary live on and continue to engage audiences today.

John's biography was on the next page. Sarah lifted it closer so she could read in the dim light.

Pianist John Delaney is currently on a world tour and comes to New York after performances in London, Paris, Rome and Vienna. John began his studies with the late Cécile Marcel in Paris and continued them with Philip Brown in Toronto. He has made a number of recordings with Naïve Classique Records and often performs with his wife, the acclaimed violinist, Sophie Devant.

He was married! To a violinist! Before Sarah knew it, or could control it, fifteen years of pent-up emotions exploded in a rush of tears. She cried for the young love that she and John had shared. She cried for the fact he knew nothing about the abortion and what she had gone through afterwards. And she cried because he was married to a violinist, someone so clearly in his own league.

Eventually she became aware of the odd looks she was getting from the people on either side. She fumbled in her bag for a tissue and dabbed her eyes. There was a pause in the music; the first movement was over.

The second movement, the Andantino, started slowly and sadly. It carried Sarah back in time: their first kiss, the heavy red wine and freshly cut grass; the night of their Leaving Certificate results, seeing him at the doorway of the hall, dancing to 'Crazy for You', making love in his dad's car. She started to cry again. The tissue was sodden.

The third movement was crisp and sprightly. The fourth started melodically but ended authoritatively, and she knew what she had to do.

During the intermission, Sarah went to the rest rooms and splashed cold water on her face.

'You need to do it,' she told her reflection. 'You *must* do it.'

Outside the bathroom, she approached one of the ushers.

'Is it possible to get a message to John Delaney?'

He nodded and took a pen and a small notepad from his pocket.

'Write your message down and I'll pass it to Mr Delaney's attendant.'

Sarah thought for a moment. Then she wrote, *Sarah Ryan in tonight's audience and wondering if she can see you after the show.*

She handed over the note just as the bell sounded for the end of the intermission.

In the second half John played six piano pieces that were known as 'Moments Musicaux'. The pieces were songlike and of varying lengths. The music was probing and touching, and Sarah felt as though he were talking to her. But the fifth piece, angry and argumentative, shattered their rapport. The final piece expressed an array of emotions, from tenderness to outrage, sadness to resignation. Just as when she and John had formalised the end of their relationship. But it hadn't ended that day in the park, which was precisely the problem. John Delaney had stayed in her heart. Him and his baby.

The show ended after two encores. Sarah stood with the rest of the audience and clapped till her hands were stinging. The crowd spilled out to the foyer and her eyes sought out the usher she'd given the message to.

'Well?'

'Mr Delaney will see you. Follow me.'

For some reason she hadn't thought it would be that easy. She faltered while the usher strode ahead and unlocked a door that led to a flight of stairs.

'The maestro's suite is at the top.'

Sarah forced herself forward to face her past. She ascended the stairs and knocked on the door of the dressing-room. John opened the door.

'Sarah!' He caught her up in a hug. Then, hands on her shoulders, stepped back to look her up and down. 'I can't believe it's you. Here in New York!'

'I know,' she smiled waveringly. 'I was passing by . . .' She looked down at her running clothes. 'Actually, I was going for a run . . . Then I saw your name . . .'

'What are you doing here? Do you live here?'

'No, I live in Dublin. I'm here with work.'

John dropped his hands and she had the opportunity to study him. He looked well, very well. His face was youthful, his body trim. But then appearances were important in his profession, almost as important as talent.

'You're married?' he asked, his eyes glancing to her wedding ring.

'Yes. To Tim.'

'The boy from college?'

'Yes. And you?'

'I'm married to Sophie.' His whole face smiled as he said her name.

Sarah swallowed. 'Do you have children?'

'No. This life – the constant touring and antisocial hours – isn't suitable for little ones.'

Sarah took time to absorb that. Children weren't part of his life. They didn't fit. Their baby wouldn't have fitted.

'How about you?'

'Sorry?'

'Kids. Do you have any?'

'No. Not yet.'

Silence filled the room, creeping along the red carpet and up the beige walls. A sad, sad silence.

'Do you ever go back?' he asked quietly.

'To Carrickmore? No, no, I don't.'

'My mother and father are still there, running the pub. Sophie thinks it's quaint. Mother loves her, of course.'

Yes, his mother would be happy with the violinist. In her eyes, Sarah had never been good enough.

'Listen, do you want to go for a drink?' he asked suddenly. 'I have to shower first, but I'd be ready in ten minutes.'

'I can't,' she replied in a rush. 'I'm here for business – I've a big day tomorrow.'

They stared at each other.

414

'I'm glad you called by, Sarah . . . I often think about you . . .'

'And me you.' She stepped forward and kissed his cheek. 'Good luck with the rest of the tour.'

She needed air. Quickly. She hurried out of the dressing-room, down the stairs, past the auditorium and down more stairs, until she was finally out on the street. She bent over, hands on her knees, and inhaled big deep gulps of New York's air.

'Goodbye, John,' she whispered, looking up at his neon-lit name.

She could breathe again. In fact, she could breathe easier than she'd been able to for years.

She threw the program into a nearby rubbish bin and began to run, back towards the hotel. Her legs were fluid, her body buoyant and her lungs full of delicious air. She was free of John Delaney.

Bradley Simons paused for a moment before briefing the board on the second shortlisted candidate.

'Jodi Tyler originally comes from Sydney but she has worked extensively in London and Singapore. Her background is largely in sales and her strength lies in client relationships. Jodi has been with her current employer, CorpBank, for seven years, testament to both her loyalty and capability. Her most recent role is head of the UK capital investment division. In her interviews, Jodi presented as very professional, and evidently demands the same standards from those around her . . .'

Only the most discerning ear could detect that Bradley favoured the second candidate. In truth, he thought very highly of both women. Sarah Ryan was a trader. She had a sharp mind, faultless instincts, and she was good with people. But in Bradley's considered opinion, Jodi Tyler was the better woman for the job. She had considerable international experience and knew how to sell across markets and countries. She would revolutionise EquiBank's culture and values, and lead the bank to new levels of growth and success.

Bradley looked around the board table at the directors with their predominantly grey hair and solemn expressions. It was anyone's guess which candidate they would favour tomorrow. And Sarah Ryan did have a formidable ally on her side: the current CEO, Denise Martin.

Jodi knew that she should stay in her room and prepare for the panel interview in the morning, but New York was like a candy jar she couldn't keep her fingers out of. She changed into a knee-length denim skirt and a white singlet top, and took the lift down to the hotel's foyer. Outside dusk was giving way to night and all the billboards were lit up, brazenly competing to catch the eye. The traffic behaved in a similar fashion, revving and hooting, wanting to be noticed.

Jodi walked at a leisurely pace past the shops, restaurants and bars. She drank in the atmosphere. It had much the same effect as alcohol: it made her head spin and her blood pump with excitement and a feeling of invincibility.

On impulse, she went into one of the bars and ordered a Bloody Mary. She had no sooner sat down than her mobile phone began to ring.

'Hello.'

'Jodi! It's me.'

It was James. He'd been shell-shocked when she'd told him she was going to New York in pursuit of a new job. There'd been too little time to fully talk it through.

'Hi. Is everything okay?'

'Yes . . .' He paused awkwardly. 'Well, actually, everything isn't okay. *I'm* not okay. I miss you. I love you.'

Her heart squeezed. 'I love you too, James. But –'

'Please, Jodi, don't leave me.'

'Oh, James . . .'

'I'll have a baby with you.'

'No, James. You don't want a baby, you just want me.'

'And I'll live in New York, if that's where you want to be . . .'

His voice was raw and desperate. She didn't feel any sense of victory. Only sadness. Because it was too late. She'd already distanced herself from him. He was part of her past, like Andrew and, in a more unpleasant way, Bob.

She sipped the Bloody Mary and winced at the bitter taste.

'I'm sorry, James. It was you who said at the start that we shouldn't be together, and I know now that you were right.'

She was in a new place, a new city, where she could make another clean start. There was no going back. To London. Or to James.

Sarah was out of breath when she arrived back at the hotel. She hurried through the foyer, ignoring the curious looks that were being cast her way. When she reached her room, she pounced on the telephone. She called Denise first.

'I'm pulling out,' she said in a rush. 'I should never have come here. I don't know what I was trying to prove –' She stopped and corrected herself. 'Actually, I do know what I was trying to prove, but that's a long story. I'm sorry, Denise. I hope I haven't put you in an awkward predicament with the board . . . and I hope my existing job isn't impacted in any way . . .'

Denise's reaction was calm. 'Of course your job won't be

affected. Are you sure you're doing the right thing? That you want to stay in Dublin?'

Sarah was very sure. 'Yes, I am.'

'Well, don't worry about the board. They'll understand.'

Sarah put down the phone, took a few deep breaths, and then picked it up again. The phone at the farm rang through to the answering machine.

'Tim! I'm ringing to let you know that I'm coming home in the morning, and to tell you how sorry I am for being such an idiot, and for not being honest with you . . . You see, there's something you don't know about me, something that happened when I was eighteen, and it might explain why I am the way I am. Why I feel I don't deserve to have a baby. Why I'm always pushing to get to the top, to be the best. I know I'm talking to a machine . . . but I just needed you to know that I'm sorry . . . and that I'm coming home . . . I hope you can forgive me . . . I love you . . .'

She didn't say on the message that she was willing to try IVF. Nor that she'd been to a classical music concert and had finally let go of her first love. She would explain all that when she saw Tim face to face. She would explain the self-hatred after the abortion and how it had nurtured the notion that she didn't deserve another baby. She would explain how the need to prove herself had compelled her to fly to New York in pursuit of a job she didn't really want or need. Only now could she see the past few weeks for what they were: her old demons disguised as self-righteous anger rather than their usual manifestation of depression and anxiety.

Tim would forgive her, Sarah was sure of it. He'd already shown her in a thousand ways how much he loved her. He would gently tell her that she shouldn't hate herself or feel unworthy.

'You're more than good enough as you are, Sarah,' he would say. 'There's no need to be better.'

The following morning dawned with heavy cloud and drizzling rain. The traffic on Seventh Avenue was even more aggressive in the wet, but the double-glazed windows of the Renaissance muted the squealing tyres and honking horns.

Jodi looked critically at her reflection in the mirror. The suit she wore was grey, the skirt falling to her knees and the jacket nipping in at her waist. Her pastel green shirt softened the grey, as did her hair, golden and loose. Her make-up was subtle, her lips glossed. She looked both feminine and professional.

Who is Jodi Tyler? She's smart. She's loyal. She works hard. Family is important to her. She likes the smell of the sea and the feeling of sand between her toes. She doesn't compromise. She's a survivor.

Jodi checked her compendium to ensure that she had everything she needed: a few spare copies of her résumé, a notepad and a pen. She felt quietly confident. She'd always been good at interviews, possibly because she was good at sales, and what were interviews, after all, but a sales pitch?

She could do this job and she was quite certain that she would be able to convince the board of this fact. She would share her enthusiasm with them, let them see how much she wanted to live and work in this city, to breathe in its vibrancy. In a few years' time, when she'd tired of the glitz, she would return to Sydney, to live in Grandma's house, her inheritance, her home. But that was not for her interviewers to know and it didn't in any way diminish what she could achieve for EquiBank in the interim.

With her compendium under her arm, and her matching Oroton bag on her shoulder, she closed the door to her room and headed towards the lift. It came without delay and she stepped inside. Just as the doors were closing, she saw a woman rushing down the corridor, pulling along a travel case.

'Can you hold it, please?'

Jodi had lived in London long enough to be able to pick an Irish accent. She pressed the button to hold the lift open and the woman smiled her thanks as she got in. With a slight jerk, the lift started downwards. The woman smoothed her chestnut hair, which had fallen out of place in the rush. Her skin was pale and clear, typically Celtic.

'Going home?' Jodi enquired politely.

'Yes,' she nodded. 'A last-minute change of plans.'

They said nothing for the rest of the journey down. When they alighted at the foyer, the woman headed for the desk to check out and Jodi went outside to get a cab.

'There's not many around this morning, miss,' the bellboy told her. 'It's the wet weather.'

Jodi had plenty of time to get to her interview, so there was no need to worry. After a few minutes, the Irish woman hurried outside and her expression became panicked when she saw that Jodi was still waiting.

'I hope I don't miss my flight!'

She seemed to be in a very big rush to get back to Ireland.

Jodi smiled reassuringly. 'I'm sure there'll be other flights this morning.'

The woman still looked anxious. 'My husband is meeting me off the plane. I don't want him to have to wait, he's been patient enough.'

Her face brightened as not one but two taxis pulled up outside the hotel.

'Thank goodness for that.'

Jodi smiled. 'Have a good trip home.'

Moments later, the yellow cabs rejoined the heavy traffic, one behind the other. Shortly after, the second one changed lanes and the cabs were abreast. They stayed like this until the next inter-section, and there they went their separate ways.

extracts reading groups
competitions books new
discounts extracts events
competitions extracts discounts reading groups
books new extracts
events books
new extracts reading groups
new interviews
reading groups books events extracts discounts new
events extracts events books
discounts events interviews
new books events
events new

www.panmacmillan.com

discounts extracts discounts books
extracts events reading groups
competitions books extracts new